Three Cats Publishing

First Edition
(May, 2020)

ISBN: 9798642525098

Publisher:
Three Cats Publishing

Printed in the United Kingdom by Book Printing UK

Available in paperback from Amazon
Also available as an eBook at Amazon Kindle

Nick Robson can be contacted by email at:
nickrobson7@gmail.com
www.nickrobsonbooks.com

Cover design by Nick Robson
Interior design by Nick Robson
Lucy's Cats by Lucy Robson
Interior art by Jodi Whitby

Author Photo by Victoria Lugton, Arundel, England
Mustang Photo courtesy of Niall McAtasney
at www.drivewildhorses.com &
Self Drive Classic Mustang Hire - +44 (0)7802 930740

MALIBU
HOBO

A NOVEL

NICK ROBSON

For Lucy

xoxo

Look around, what do you see?

Hold my hand, you'll understand

What this means

To be here with you

I'll take care of everything

Secret, secret...

Simi Valley
Moor Park
Agoua Hills
Thousand Oaks
Highway 101
Woodland Hills
Van Nuys
North Hollywood
Calabasas
Griffith Observatory
Bel Air
Topanga State Park
Beverly Hills
Riviera G.C.
Hope's Grotto Dude Ranch
Pepperdine University
Pacific Palisades
Surfrider Hotel
Pacific Coast Highway
Zuma Beach
Malibu
Santa Monica
Sunset Restaurant
Los Angeles Airport
Pacific Ocean
Three Miles

Chapter 1

Part One

Tuesday, November 5ᵗʰ, 2017

It was the strangely distant but gentle rumbling of the undercarriage that first began to wake her from her sleep. She tried valiantly to stay submerged in her dream, but realized it was just that, only a dream. It was too comfortable to be able to feel at ease with everything and to banish all thoughts of the sad events she'd had to face recently. But as she woke from her reverie, she felt the gentle touch of a hand on her shoulder and reluctantly, she forced herself to open her eyes.

"Tess, I'm so sorry but we'll be landing soon so I need to put your bed back in the upright seated position."

Tess looked up and realized it was one of the cabin crew she'd been chatting to during the flight. They were around the same age and had clicked instantly and had already exchanged numbers and email addresses for the future. Becky was a kindred spirit, a gentle soul, although clearly more worldly than Tess at twenty-six years of age.

"Sorry, Becky, I was in such a deep sleep and I didn't want it to end. But really, you're serious? We're almost there?"

Becky laughed, "Yes, we're about fifteen minutes out from LAX, you've been asleep for almost six hours. Here, drink some orange juice, sweetie, it'll make you feel better."

Tess gratefully took the glass and greedily drank it down, aware that she was still only half awake. Her mouth tasted like something had died in there. But at least she wouldn't feel too tired once she arrived in Los Angeles. She was still naïvely amazed that you could leave London at 11am, fly for eleven hours and that when you landed in Los Angeles, it was only 2 o'clock in the afternoon.

She clambered out of her seat to use the bathroom while Becky restored the seat, grabbing her toothbrush and toothpaste from the toiletry bag that British Airways gave to its First Class passengers. It still didn't feel right that she should have one of these goodie bags of toiletries, let alone be traveling in this ridiculously sky-priced cabin. But she was grateful that she hadn't had to pay for the ticket. She'd never before 'turned left' when boarding a plane, assuming that it was strictly the domain of the privileged few. Hell, she hadn't even flown that many times before.

Eleven hours ago, once they had departed Heathrow and the pilot had extinguished the seatbelt sign, Tess had got up from her seat and begun to explore the cabin. It had what they called 'mood lighting' a very calming ultra-violet color that seemed to make the First Class cabin feel like a club lounge. At the beginning of the cabin, there was even a circular bar and six barstools so that people could grab a cocktail and chat with fellow passengers as they flew across the Atlantic.

She had peeped through the dividing curtain at the economy section behind her and felt sorry for the poor things wedged into very small spaces. It must be horrendous for tall people to sit in that position for eleven hours, she'd thought.

Tess hadn't planned to sleep during the flight, astonished that nearly everyone else in her cabin had immediately converted their seats to beds within thirty minutes of taking off from London, a chorus of snoring and farting following soon after. She had no idea how much a ticket in this section would cost, but once she had taken her seat at the beginning of the journey, Tess had intended savoring every moment of it whilst still wide awake. She had compiled a list of the latest movies she would watch and looked forward to the silver service meals and copious offerings of chardonnay. But the past few weeks had caught up with her quickly and she'd succumbed to sleep soon after eating lunch, having watched just one single movie. Well, almost.

Now nearing the end of the journey, and taking the opportunity to stand in the galley for a few moments to stretch her legs, Tess looked beyond to the twenty-seat cabin, feeling vaguely refreshed and almost human after her trip to the bathroom. She saw that Becky and her male colleagues had rousted everyone from their slumbers and were busily handing out refreshments for landing. Tess wondered how the cabin crew managed to stay awake, let alone look as fresh as daisies after a transatlantic flight with an eight hour time difference.

"I have to hand it to you," Tess said when Becky eventually returned to the galley, "You hardly look like you've just put in a twelve hour work day, how on earth do you do it?"

"You just get used to it, I guess, and you go to the loo frequently to spritz and re-apply make-up!" Becky replied, "But listen, Tess, I'm only here in the city for one night and I know you've got a lot going on in Los Angeles but once you get through it all, and if you then plan to stay for any length of time, give me a call or text me. Although I'm based in London, I'm often in L.A. so I'd love to meet up again."

Tess hugged her and said, "You may be my only friend here so I'm going to hold you to that."

The familiar sound of the 'fasten seat belts' sign prompted Tess to get ready for landing. She dutifully returned to her seat, buckled up and for the very first time during the flight, her stomach began to churn. She looked out of the window, the endless rows of enormous planes waiting on the tarmac becoming bigger and bigger as her own plane descended into LAX. And then she felt it, as the gigantic airplane's tires hit the ground and the engines roared into reverse thrust, that strange feeling of stepping into the unknown alone, a veritable stranger in a very strange land.

~

Having followed the other passengers from her cabin as they disembarked from the plane, Tess found herself in the Immigration Hall of the Los Angeles airport terminal. Once again, her stomach began to roil as she found herself surrounded by people dashing to her right and left and pushing ahead of her. Everyone seemed to know where they were going, except her. She held on tightly to the handle of her cabin bag, feeling that everything could slip away from her at any moment, as a bout of claustrophobia began to hit her.

Get a grip, Tess, look around you, work it out...

She spotted a sign that pointed to the queues for non-American passport holders and made her way toward it. It seemed like she might be waiting hours to get through Passport Control and she was desperate to use the bathroom. But thankfully, there appeared to be upwards of thirty desks manned by immigration officers and the line seemed to be moving along pretty quickly.

Oh God, I so need the loo...

In only a few minutes, Tess found herself being beckoned forward by a particularly stern-faced official seated behind one of the Plexiglas counters. She glanced at the engraved name on his badge, 'Carlos T. Fuentes'.

"Good afternoon, Miss, passport and landing card please," he said, his expression remaining stoically unchanged and neutral.

She handed over both documents, attempting a smile which failed miserably, quickly turning into a cockeyed grin. She was nervous, more than.

"What is the purpose of your visit, Miss...? Valentine?" Carlos asked, still not looking up from her passport, casually flicking through the bare and unstamped pages.

"There's been a family death," she replied, not knowing what else to say.

"So, not for pleasure, I assume?"

"No, sir."

"How long will you be staying?"

"I... I don't... I don't know. A week? Maybe two? I'm not sure yet, I'm sorry," Tess responded weakly.

"You didn't enter the information on your landing card that states where you'll be staying during your visit to Los Angeles," he added, looking up at her for the first time.

"I... I don't actually know yet. I'm really sorry... I guess I'll find a hotel. I'm being collected from the airport, that's all I know at the moment," she stumbled, an impending fear quickly consuming her as a trickle of perspiration trickled down the inside of her arm. She was grateful that she was wearing a loose fitting shirt that wouldn't show anything.

"Do you know anyone in Los Angeles?" he asked.

"Oh crumbs, just the attorney. And I haven't even met him so I don't really *know* him, I suppose," she replied, now deeply worried that she would be dragged off to an interrogation room and body searched.

Oh God, please not me!

She'd seen it in films and on US television shows, the dreaded latex gloves used for internal searches. She'd even seen Trump's ICE agents dragging immigrants out of buses, off the streets and dumped into vans before deporting them.

"It's okay, Miss Valentine, do not concern yourself at this time," he said, now with the faintest hint of a smile. "Please look into the camera and then place your right hand on the scanner in front of you."

She did as instructed and waited while the agent typed some additional information into his computer.

He stamped her passport, handed it back to her and finally smiled, revealing brilliantly white and perfect teeth

"Welcome to the United States, Miss Valentine, I hope everything works out for you during your stay. Have a nice day."

She returned his smile, thanked him, and quickly walked away to find a restroom before heading off toward the Baggage Claim carousels.

~

She'd spent twenty minutes or so in the restroom, just trying to put herself back together after the terror of standing in front of Carlos's cubicle. She'd pee'd for what seemed like forever and she'd already been before she left the plane.

How is it that men can go for hours without the need to use a bathroom? Do they actually have bigger bladders?

Tess wasn't a girl to wear too much make-up, just some eyeliner, minimal mascara and a light lip gloss. She didn't really need it all, she was naturally blessed with a face that didn't require many additional enhancements. But she did apply a small amount anyway; it was what her mother had taught her when she had first discovered make-up.

Feeling a lot calmer, now that she'd washed her face and her bladder was empty, she took her beloved Mason Pearson hairbrush from her cabin bag and brushed her hair.

Tess Valentine had inherited exceptional genes. Some people are lucky, others not so much. Life isn't fair in that regard. Standing at an athletic and toned 5'8", her naturally attractive, sophisticated and sculpted face was further enhanced by a mane of long and very slightly wavy, shiny chestnut hair. She never worked out; in fact, she had never even seen the inside of a gym and didn't watch what she ate but somehow she maintained a model figure. Go figure.

And in an age where almost every girl, armed with an iPhone and instant picture-editing tools, desperately strives to be the prettiest girl on the block, Tess was really quite different, an oddity almost. Her charm and beauty were rare attributes in most girls of her age, in that she really wasn't aware of the effect she had on men, or even on women. She was almost blind to male attention which only made her more attractive. In fact, as she looked at herself in the mirror, she didn't see a beautiful English Rose, she just saw a regular East London girl, someone who was really nothing special at all.

She looked around the restroom, noting how spotlessly clean it was and was suddenly aware of the gentle music emanating from somewhere within its walls. A muzak version of Elton John's "Candle In The Wind" was playing.

So this is Los Angeles. Where Marilyn finally met her maker...

Tess always dressed casually. Formal attire wasn't really in her vocabulary. She'd never been able to afford expensive clothes

7

anyway, but she always managed to make the least expensive things look tailored just for her. Again, just good genes. You see it in airports everywhere, girls and guys who just carry themselves exquisitely, an air of confidence and sophistication that has no connection with arrogance. A shirt stylishly untucked, jeans a little ragged and travel bags appropriately shabby chic, nothing planned, just the way they live and breathe. They just have it all going on, naturally and effortlessly.

Tess had put on faded blue jeans for the trip, that she wore beltless at the hip and which ended around six inches above her ankles. They were very worn and partially torn, not by design but through age. She'd had them for over a decade and they still fit the same as when she was sixteen. She completed the look by discarding her travel shirt and donning her beloved but simple, silver cashmere cardigan, a gift from her father that she had always cherished since it arrived in the mail seven years ago.

She glanced down at her tanned legs and feet, the lightest of pink nail polish highlighting her toes as she stood in a simple pair of tan flip-flop style sandals. She wasn't admiring herself but just painfully aware that she wanted to look okay, didn't want to embarrass herself in any way. But she was grateful for the fabulous and long English summer they had experienced back home, so that she hadn't arrived in the City of Angels looking like a complete tourist.

"Long flight?" asked a voice from the next wash basin.

Tess turned to look at the lady next to her.

"Yes, eleven and a bit hours, I just arrived from London," she replied.

"I love London, one of my favorite places in the whole world. They say that if you ever tire of New York, you're tired of life itself but I think it applies more to London than any other city I've ever visited," said the lady, "I'd live there in a heartbeat if I could."

"I was born there so I don't know much different," Tess replied, "But I still love it, I guess it will always be home for me."

"First time here?"

"First time anywhere, I suppose," said Tess, "I'm not what you would call a seasoned traveler."

"Well, be careful out there. L.A. is a unique town full of unique people, not all of them nice either. This place can bite you in the butt when you're not looking so don't believe for a minute that you won't be a target for some of the assholes here," said the woman.

"Thanks... I'll remember that," Tess replied.

"Oh, and welcome to LaLa Land," she said, but this time with a smile as she turned to dry her hands under the electric dryer.

Chapter 2

The only airports Tess had experienced up until today, were those in Luton and Malaga. Luton Airport in Bedfordshire, England was best forgotten; a shrine to football fans and holidaymakers who wanted cheap flights to Spain for thirty quid, and Malaga Airport in Spain was like a throwback to the 1960s. You'd barely have got off the plane before young Spanish men were trying to chat you up, pawing at you, urging you to give them your hotel name and phone number. It also made traveling less than glamorous when you then hailed a taxi, having escaped the oily Lotharios, and then subsequently had to put up with the stench in the car while the driver cheerily puffed away on filterless Camel cigarettes.

But this morning at London Heathrow had been a revelation. It was like being transported into the future, a vast glass and metal building that ensured a seamless and easy path through check-in and security, and then on to the airport shops, restaurants and departure gates. Los Angeles Airport was not as modern as Heathrow but it still had a sophisticated air about it and it didn't feel uncomfortable in any way. It was also pretty easy to navigate, for which Tess was grateful.

She followed the signs to Baggage Claim and realized that she must have spent quite some time in the bathroom because the carousel for her flight was almost empty of suitcases, the passengers from her flight having mostly reclaimed their luggage. She quickly identified her own suitcase. It was gray like most cases but her mother had instructed her to tie a pink ribbon to the handle so that she'd easily recognize it. And she was right. There it was, still circling lonely on the carousel.

She hauled the case off the conveyer belt and was thankful that it had wheels because she didn't want to pay five dollars for a luggage cart. A sickening feeling hit her when she suddenly realized that from this point on, from this very moment, she was reliant on someone being on the other side of the glass doors to meet her in the public waiting area of the airport.

What if there's no one there? What the heck am I going to do then?

She had around five hundred dollars in her purse but she knew it probably wouldn't last long in this city. Hoisting her cabin bag over her shoulder and pulling her suitcase behind her, she set off toward the exit. Once through, and out onto the main thoroughfare, she scoured the countless faces of people waiting for their loved ones, but of course, Tess recognized no one at all. Why would she? She didn't know anyone here.

She looked around at the various home-made signs with names written on them, held aloft by people searching for their wives, husbands, sons and daughters, and initially, she couldn't spot her own name. But thankfully, after only a few seconds, she spied a small, but fit and wiry-looking Asian man, maybe Chinese, or Korean? He was holding up a piece of cardboard with the name VALENTINE printed on it in marker pen.

Phew!

She waved at him, smiling with relief that she had found her ride.

"Miss Valentine?" he called out above the din from the hundreds of people milling around amongst them.

"Yes, that's me," she replied loudly, as they walked toward each other, the man's outstretched hand extended toward hers.

"I'm Sammy, Sammy Chan, I've come to collect you and take you to your hotel," he said, a smile brimming from ear to ear.

"Sammy, you're a sight for sore eyes!" she said, shaking his hand, relieved that she'd made the connection with him so quickly, her heart-rate now rapidly reducing.

"Follow me, Miss Valentine, let's get you out of here, my car isn't too far away."

~

Frank Buchanan watched from his car as the Asian man and the girl exited the elevator and entered the third floor of the parking garage, briskly making their way along Zone F. From his vantage point two rows back, he looked through his binoculars as they finally arrived at a gleaming black Buick Riviera Boattail, which he assumed to be a recent frame-off renovation.

Well, the little fella has taste…

Buchanan shifted his magnified vision to the girl. He was taken aback; she was much more attractive than he'd been told. But then again, Bobby V was not an unattractive fucker, was he? No, this girl was the real deal. A raw and unpolished, but completely unflawed diamond.

Be a shame to kill her…

They stopped to inspect the car as the girl was clearly taken with this re-born piece of 1970s Americana. He remembered of course, that she'd never been to the US before. Actually, from memory, she didn't have many passport stamps at all. And the little slant-eyed fella, well, he was obviously pretty proud of his shiny, black baby.

Better not get too attached…

13

Once the pair had circumnavigated the car and discussed it in some detail, Buchanan continued to watch as the Asian man, having loaded her suitcase and cabin bag into the trunk, began to carefully reverse out of the parking space.

You take care of that baby for me, Gook, I'll look forward to putting her in my garage with the others…

Buchanan let the Buick turn the corner toward the exit lane before he backed out and followed in his Toyota Camry. Can't go wrong with a Camry, he thought, no one notices them because everyone's got one or knows someone with one. A completely forgettable turd of a car but perfect for the job he did. Especially in beige. And so stupidly reliable.

Fucking Japs…

No one knew him as Buchanan, except those who needed to know. Occupationally, he was known as The Watcher. He was paid to watch people, see where they went, what they were up to. Occasionally, it was necessary to kill them too. That didn't bother him much though, it was part of the job description, and the world was overpopulated anyway.

Pretty girl though, would be a terrible waste…

But although he'd often killed, always ruthlessly, he wasn't overjoyed about another nickname he'd acquired, The Killer, much preferring The Watcher. Had more mystery to it, he felt like he could be a character in a novel, a thriller maybe.

The Watcher, man of mystery…

And then he recalled the old television series, *Cannon*, that was on the box in the 1970s.

That could be me, Frank Buchanan, Private Eye…

He had guessed that the girl would be staying in the city, but from the route the Buick was taking, it seemed they were heading

14

toward the coast, probably Santa Monica. The traffic was strangely light on the 405 heading north and it was easy to hang back a half dozen cars and still keep a track of them. He followed them off the ramp and closed the gap as they joined I-10 going west toward the ocean.

But oddly, they didn't stop in Santa Monica, which surprised him. He'd assumed one of the many hip hotels that engulfed the place would be a perfect fit for the girl, but instead, the Buick continued north on PCH, headed toward Malibu. Whatever. It was a nice drive this time of the day and heck, he was being paid plenty. But what is it with the cars in this town?

Range Rover, Bentley, Ferrari, Range Rover, Lambo, Tesla, Tesla, Range Rover... so lacking in originality. Not a fucking Camry in sight...

Twenty minutes later, the Buick turned into a hotel driveway on the east side of the PCH, and Buchanan pulled the Camry to a stop in the emergency lane just a few feet short of the hotel's entrance so he could still keep eyes on the girl.

"The Surfrider Hotel, huh? Good to know where you are, lovely Tess Valentine. I'll be seeing you soon, sweetheart," he whispered to himself as he pulled out into the now heavy northbound traffic on the Pacific Coast Highway.

Chapter 3

Sammy retrieved Tess's suitcase and cabin bag from the trunk of the Buick and passed them to the porter waiting at the hotel's entrance.

"I'll let you check in and make yourself comfortable, Tess. I'm sure you're exhausted after your travel day and you probably need to get some rest. Mr. Delaney will call you later this evening or in the morning, and update you on everything. And don't worry about the hotel costs, everything has been prepaid so just relax and enjoy!" said Sammy as Tess looked around, examining her new surroundings.

It seemed so paradisiacal here, palm trees gently swaying, the noise of the waves intermingling with the sound of the traffic, and the sky remained infinitely blue, not a cloud to be seen. And as she breathed in the coastal air, she began to feel a new sense of calm, something she hadn't felt for the last few weeks back home in England.

The hotel itself looked like it belonged in a California era back in the 1950s and although Sammy's car appeared to be period correct, she felt as though some huge red and white convertible with those enormous tail fins would be more appropriate here. It was pure retro Americana in every sense, so much so that she planned on doing some drawings of it once she'd settled in. Any time she could snatch a couple of hours to sketch or paint was pure decadence for Tess.

"Thank you so much, Sammy... will I see you again?"

This was the moment she wondered whether she should tip the man. She already knew that America was the tipping capital of the world. But no, he wasn't just a driver, this man was a little more than that. Right?

"Oh I'm sure, Tess, don't worry, we'll meet again shortly. Meanwhile, go and relax and by the way, welcome to Malibu. I hope you enjoy it," he said, climbing back into the Buick, firing up its big grumbling V8 engine and gently edging the huge vehicle out into the early traffic.

It hadn't escaped Tess's attention when they'd pulled up in front of the hotel that all of the Pacific-view rooms at the front of the building, had hammocks installed on their balconies. She'd never seen that before but secretly and guiltily hoped her room might be one of them.

After briefly checking in at Reception, she hurried up the stairs to her room, hauling her bags with her, and after unlocking her door, was overjoyed that hers was indeed one of those rare rooms with a hammock.

The room was perfect, no not just perfect, but very hip, super cool and quite fabulous. She gazed around the space, trying to take it all in. She'd never before stayed in a hotel room like this; actually, she'd barely ever stayed in a hotel room at all, except for a couple of vacations in Benidorm.

It was so... sophisticated, she thought, and it was big! The wood flooring was either reclaimed or original but not perfectly refinished, the walls half-clad in plank, painted matte white. The bed was a four poster but not an old-fashioned one, this was light wood, beech maybe, and it was minimalist in its simplicity. Just an identical set of three-by-threes dovetailed together by a skilled carpenter's perfect mortise and tenon joints. Simple lighting and a modern wood and chrome ceiling fan completed the effect.

18

The light cotton drapes hung floor to ceiling in muted tones, the linens and pillows a calming collage of taupes and creams and grays. A cashmere-colored sofa sat before a beech coffee table, a fireplace beyond, pre-prepared with wood that she wouldn't dare dream of lighting. Books on furniture, design, elemental architecture and Vegan cooking, lay patiently awaiting her inspection.

It was a far cry from where Tess was from originally. She wondered what her colleagues would be doing right now as she opened the French doors and devoured the sights from the beach beyond the Pacific Coast Highway. But then she remembered the time difference and realized that they'd probably all be home by now, and most of them would be sleeping. She was grateful that the advertising agency where she'd been working for less than a year as a junior creative, had allowed her to come away on compassionate leave. She really hoped she still had a job when she returned to London. Because she really needed it.

Tess collapsed on the bed, immediately aware of the unique and fragrant scent of freshly laundered cottons, and she felt instantly consumed by a mattress that simply begged her to sleep. But she mustn't, not yet anyway; it was still only late afternoon in Los Angeles. She decided that she should unpack, hang up her limited suitcase of clothes and then go and explore the hotel.

But when she opened the suitcase, it wasn't how she remembered packing it. She'd been oh-so-careful in making sure she folded and packed everything perfectly to avoid wrinkles, but it was as though the case had been opened and the clothes tossed around. But then she remembered that she'd read something about air travel to the USA and that sometimes the TSA opened and randomly inspected suitcases during transit. But she also remembered that out of respect to the owner, they would normally leave an official TSA note in the case telling the passenger that the case had been opened and inspected. And she couldn't find one in hers.

Maybe they forgot…

She put any weird thoughts out of her mind and spent the next fifteen minutes hanging her clothes in the closet. She laughed at the fact that she only had four pairs of shoes to her name and that she was wearing one of those pairs. But she was also pinching herself that she was here in a swish little hotel in Malibu and the sun was bathing her terrace with a warm and late afternoon golden glow. The hammock would have to wait for the moment but it wouldn't wait long.

Oh, God! The bellboy! I said I could manage my suitcase myself but that's his job! What was I thinking?

She pushed the case inside the closet and ran out of the room, her long legs double-stepping the two flights of stairs as she rushed down to Reception.

"Excuse me!" she said, already out of breath, "I'm so sorry!"

The bellboy, Nathan, turned to face her, "Is there a problem, ma'am?"

"No Nathan, that's just it, there's no problem at all but I just realized I'd taken your job! Thank you so much for letting me stay here," she gushed, pressing a twenty dollar bill into his hand.

"Wow, thank you, ma'am! But it's not necessary, really it's not, and anyway, you carried your own bags upstairs."

"Yes it is necessary because I need a pot of tea and you need to eat," Tess replied, "And it's Tess, not ma'am!"

"Give me five minutes and I'll bring a tray to your room with some snacks too. It would be my pleasure," he replied.

She ran back up the stairs, again two at a time as Nathan looked on.

Sweet girl, beautiful too…

20

Chapter 4

After Nathan had brought a tray of tea and cookies and other nibbles to the room, Tess took it outside and put it on the table next to the hammock. She climbed in, precariously holding the teacup as she did so, and lay back to take in and absorb this place they called The 'Bu.

Across the PCH, she noticed seven or eight women and young girls, leisurely strolling along the beach, occasionally bending down to pick up shells or other gems that the ocean had deposited. They were like birds picking at the sand as the waves delivered new treasures. Tess enjoyed spending time doing just that back in England on the south coast, but it suddenly dawned on her that this was something that perhaps only the female race did.

She realized that she'd never seen any men or boys on the beach back home doing the same thing, wistfully hoping to find something beautiful in the sand. She'd seen them with metal detectors looking for buried treasure, but never just searching for something of natural beauty, something they could pass to their kids or grandchildren, or even something they could secret forever for themselves.

Must be a girl thing, I suppose…

The tea was outstanding, Nathan had used Twining's English Breakfast Tea and it was pretty much what she'd have back in the U.K. And Nathan was kind of cute too, although, since Simon, she'd chosen to stay away from boys for the time being. They could be such twats and Simon was a perfect example. But Simon was hopefully now just a bad mistake in her past and best forgotten.

Palming her iPhone, she retrieved the email she'd received from the attorney a couple of weeks before, and began to re-read it, a solemn reminder as to why she was here…

Dear Tess,

It was heartbreaking to make the call to you yesterday; it's not something I ever look forward to doing. Your father was not only a charming man but he was my friend too, although recently more distant. I'm so sorry for your loss and although I realize that you have had little contact with him since you were born, I can assure you that you were the only thing that ever mattered in his life.

He was a good person, always trying to help others and the only sadness for him is that he was edged out of your life so early on. But he never stopped talking about you, never stopped showing us photographs of you as you grew into a young woman. He was probably the proudest father I've ever known and he loved you more than life. He really did.

He didn't die a penniless man but he didn't appear to be a wealthy one either. He should have been but I'll explain that when we meet. But he did leave a small sum of cash with explicit instructions to me as his executor, that it to be used to enable you to come and enjoy and understand where he lived, and why he chose this place as his home. And also to hopefully give you the vacation he'd never given you before.

With your permission, I'd like to make arrangements for you to come to California and to spend some leisure time here and at the same time we can finalize his estate, or what there is of it. I'll arrange an open-ended return ticket from London Heathrow to Los Angeles International and I'll ensure your stay is comfortable while you're here.

I hope also that my family can meet the girl her father talked so much of and that you'll enjoy spending time with them too. I very much look forward to meeting you, and once again, Tess, I'm so sorry that your dad has left this world; he was a dear friend and a very kind and sweet man.

Kind regards.

Yours faithfully,

Jake Delaney

Jake Delaney

Attorney-at-Law

Law Offices of Delaney & Camarillo

24252 Mulholland Hwy,

Calabasas, CA 91302

Tess could feel the tears once again blurring her vision, escaping in trickles down her cheeks, reminding her that she could never get back that chance. The chance to have met her father again, to have known him and loved him as she knew he loved her. And so Tess sobbed once more, over and over and over again…

Chapter 5

Tess could hear a phone ringing but she knew it couldn't be hers. She knew the sound of her iPhone and it definitely wasn't that. And then she realized as she opened her eyes fully, that she wasn't at home in a leafy village in England, but that she was actually here in Southern California. She almost had to pinch herself but then remembered that the room-phone was still ringing.

"Hello?" she said, wishing for some odd reason that she had at least brushed her teeth first.

Ugh!

"Good morning, Tess," said the calming voice of a man in the receiver, "It's Jake Delaney here. Did you sleep well?"

"Oh hi Mr. Delaney, yes... gosh... I've just seen the time," she replied, looking at her iPhone, "I must have slept for fourteen hours!"

"You probably needed it; whenever I do a transatlantic flight which thankfully is rare, I always seem to need sleep more than usual. And please, call me Jake, everyone else does."

"I will, I'm sorry Jake, I'm just feeling a little groggy still."

"I completely understand," he continued, "But I was wondering if we could meet today and talk about your father's estate, or is it still perhaps a little early?"

"Sure, well, it's eleven now, I could be ready in forty-five minutes?" she said, already sweeping aside the bed sheets.

"Perfect, I'll get Sammy to come and pick you up at noon and bring you to my offices in Calabasas. It's about a thirty-minute drive from The Surfrider, so I'll see you at around 12.30'ish?"

"Great, perfect, I'll see you then."

Having said goodbye to the lawyer, Tess stumbled to the bathroom and brushed her teeth as she waited for the shower to warm up. She knew she didn't have time to wash her hair and then dry it too, so it would have to do for now.

After showering and toweling herself dry, she examined her reflection in the mirror. Her tanned athletic body would fit right in with the Malibu surfer crowd.

"Not bad," she thought, "You'll do."

She turned around, looking back at the mirror, checking herself from behind, happy with what she saw, long slim legs ending at a still pert bottom. Turning back to check herself, once again facing the mirror, she secretly admired her fairly small breasts that still pointed north, never requiring a bra, and her tummy which although flat, still retained a delicate feminine curve.

Tess chose to keep her pubic area trimmed short, with the use of a No.1 trim guard on a men's hair trimmer that she'd 'borrowed' from Simon. She just liked it to be neat, that was all, nothing sexual. But not shaved like Simon was always asking her to do.

What is it about men who want their girlfriends and wives to shave down there? Jeez...

She didn't swear often, and when she did, it was mostly in her head, but when she thought of all the wasted time spent with Simon, it made her curse inwardly.

As she brushed her hair, she thought back over the last two years. She'd been engaged to Simon until the beginning of the summer at which point she decided that she'd had enough of him and of his juvenile friends. He had a good job, sure, a nice family and excellent breeding, but she realized *he* wasn't someone she wanted to breed *with*. And, of course, because he just couldn't bear to be without a trophy girlfriend on his arm, he had already moved on to someone else before the summer had finished… Camilla Huntley-Farnsworth. Well, Camilla Fucksworth was welcome to the little weasel.

She slipped on a turquoise thong, a simple but ultimately comfortable piece of underwear with a small lace edge that she'd bought in a bargain-bin sale at a store on London's Regent St.

Fifty quid down to five, my kind of sale…

She picked out one of three casual summer dresses that she'd brought with her; again, end of season bargains, this time from Oxford St. in London. Elegantly and loosely fitted and minimally floral on a white background, she looked the very essence of a sophisticated English girl. She took a jade and topaz necklace from her handbag, fastened it around her neck and finished the look with a pair of chic silver sandals.

Good to go…

She was a little early but decided to pop downstairs and wait on the hotel bench outside so that she wouldn't keep Sammy waiting. She might even bump into Nathan…

Chapter 6

Sammy was already waiting outside by the time she arrived, which to be honest, she half expected. Here was a man who was not only courteous and a complete gentleman, but any lack of punctuality was probably an unforgiveable sin in his eyes. He had an unusual look, in that his face wasn't typically Asian. It was quite chiseled and sophisticated and the man had extraordinarily attractive eyes. He had an almost James Bond villain-with-a-heart look to him. On this second meeting, Tess realized that he was really quite handsome, quite sexy in fact and faintly Eurasian in appearance and style.

If he was six inches taller, I'd fall for him…

After exchanging pleasantries and climbing into Sammy's car, they headed north on PCH, the morning traffic now light after the end of the morning commute rush hour.

Rush hour in Malibu… now there's an oxymoron…

Sammy drove the Buick at a calm and respectable speed, pointing out landmarks along the way that he thought she may have heard of in the past… The Getty Villa, Malibu Pier, Pepperdine University…

Nope, no clue…

They headed east at the university and followed the winding mountain road up through the canyons, an image that oddly reminded her more of Europe than America, until they came to Malibu Creek State Park.

Sammy slowed down at this point, pointing to what seemed like an endless area of hills, hikes, trails and lakes.

"This is the famous park where they shot the opening title sequence for *M.A.S.H.*" said Sammy, "It's amazing because I always thought it really was filmed in Korea. How stupid am I?"

"Really?" she replied, smiling as she did so, but having no clue as to what or who *M.A.S.H.* was. Was she so uneducated on all things American, or was this thing called *M.A.S.H.* just before her time?

He started singing now, turning and smiling at her,

"Su... icide is painless... It brings on many changes... And I can take or leave it, if I please..."

She still didn't get it but kept smiling and laughing with him anyway. She realized that she really was a stranger in a strange land.

A few miles further on, they joined the 101 freeway heading south toward Calabasas, before exiting after maybe only three miles and arriving in what seemed to Tess, a quaint old American town that might have once been some kind of cowboy trading-post back in the day.

"Cute town," she said.

"Ah, this is Old Town Calabasas, has lots of history. But then they messed it up by building freeways, malls and country clubs," laughed Sammy.

During the ride, Tess had learned that Sammy was anything but a taxi driver. The man was apparently a private investigator, or P.I. as he'd said, and from what she could glean from the conversation, he was very much in demand in these parts, although he did say that he tried to work mainly on Jake Delaney's cases.

A few minutes after leaving the Old Town, they arrived at a single story, white stucco building with terracotta-colored barrel tiles on the roof. It reminded Tess of some of the Spanish buildings she'd seen in Benidorm.

"Okay, here we are, this is Jake's office. Go on through that entrance and you'll meet my wife, Teresita, she works here too," said Sammy.

"You're not coming in?' Tess asked.

"Nope, I've got a couple of subjects I need to keep an eye on this afternoon," said Sammy, "But don't worry, Mr. Jake don't bite!"

She got out of the car, said goodbye to Sammy and made her way toward the building's arched entrance.

As soon as she was inside, immediately grateful for the refreshing burst of air conditioning, she was greeted by the receptionist, a dark-haired and sweetly attractive Hispanic lady whom she guessed to be Sammy's wife.

"Hola, you must be Tess, I'm Teresita, Sammy's wife, so nice to meet you finally - ¡Bienvenidos!" she said, a lady who was charm and happiness personified.

"That's me!" Tess replied, "I guess you know I'm here to see Mr. Delaney?"

"Ee's no Señor Delaney, everybody call him Jake!" she bubbled, "I let 'im know you are 'ere."

Tess looked around at the immaculately but simply furnished offices, wondering how she would ever be able to pay for the lawyer's time today. As she took in her surroundings, a petite, stylishly dressed and sharply attractive woman emerged from the office at the front of the building, smiled briefly at Tess and said "hi" as she passed her. Tess looked back at the nameplate on the door that announced, 'Edie Camarillo – Attorney'.

Seems friendly…

Teresita dialed an internal number and spoke to her boss and then looked up at Tess after replacing the handset.

"Please go through, Tess, last door at end of corridor, I bring you some refreshments, momentito."

Everything still felt so surreal to Tess as she walked down the corridor of the law office building. One moment she was working long hours in London, barely making a living and now she was eight thousand miles away in the land of Hollywood, being treated like royalty.

Someone wake me up…

She knocked on the door and it was immediately opened by a tall and strikingly handsome older man.

"And you must be the lovely Tess," he said, taking her hand and steering her into the office, "It really is wonderful to finally meet Robert's daughter, please take a seat and I'll get Teresita to bring some cold drinks in."

"I think she's already on the case, Mr. Delaney, she's way ahead of you," Tess replied, as Teresita followed them into the office carrying a tray with a selection of beverages and pastries.

The lawyer's office was fairly informal, more of a home office setup than the overkill lair of a successful attorney. Instead of taking a seat behind his desk, Jake led Tess to a large and ridiculously comfortable, but aging Chesterfield sofa, and they both sat down. She also spotted a dartboard in one corner of the room which seemed oddly out of place but it was pretty sweet and unusual.

"Thanks, Teresita, I've got everything I need now so why don't you go and take a nice long lunch for a change?"

"Gracias, Jake, nice to meet you, Tess, see you again soon," said Teresita, closing the door behind her.

Chapter 7

The attorney was not what Tess had expected. Sure, he was super polite on the phone and the email he had sent her was really sweet and caring but damn, this man was a silver fox! He had a full head of wavy salt and pepper hair, looked pretty damned fit, and at first glance, she would put his age at around forty, maybe forty-five at most. But she guessed that if he was a friend of her father's, he had to be mid-fifties, maybe older.

But he was a good looking fella, nonetheless. Kind of reminded her a little of that doctor that used to be on *Grey's Anatomy*... McDreamy, or something like that, but much taller and less Irish looking.

What's up with you, Tess? Are you on heat or something?

"Well, you've met Teresita and Sammy now, so you're gradually getting to know us all," said Jake, "Believe it or not, they're actually married to one another, and blissfully so, I should add."

"Yes, Sammy told me in the car. I also bumped into another lady who I think works here... Edie?"

"Ah yes, Edie. They broke the mold when they made Edie. She's actually my partner in the firm and she's been my rock ever since I moved out here from New York. She helped me as a friend and business partner when I was in a very dark place once upon a time. I honestly couldn't have survived without her, and her husband Alan is a super nice guy too."

"I didn't know you were from New York, I thought you were California born and bred? Although your accent does seem a little different to the ones I've heard so far since I've been here. What happened to make you relocate from New York to sunny California? Seems a pretty radical step."

"Just a number of unforeseen events that meant I had to make the move to California, that's all," Jake replied.

"C'mon! Share the details, Jake, I love a good story!" said Tess, immediately realizing that she was possibly being too personal.

"Oh Tess, my life story would bore you rigid, you don't want to hear it. Too much tragedy too, although life has worked out really well for me in the end. I'm very grateful for everything I have, and to be honest, I haven't had to work as hard as most people, so I count my lucky stars."

"Well, maybe one day you can tell me," said Tess, toning down her effervescence, "I think it's a story I'd love to hear someday."

They made small talk, just getting to know one another and helped themselves to what Jake called, *Arnold Palmers,* which seemed to be a particularly delicious and cooling sweet tea cocktail of sorts.

Jake explained to Tess that there were some formalities to go over and that she would need to sign a number of documents, witnessed by him and then he would explain to her what was left of her father's estate, which he said that sadly, there wasn't very much.

"But your father was no fool, Tess. He was a gifted entrepreneur in his day so the fact that there appears to be little to nothing left from his travails is a bit of a mystery to me."

"I'll be honest, Jake, I really didn't know him at all. I knew what he looked like from photographs but the real truth is that I only ever remember meeting him on two occasions. Once when I was around four or five years old and then once again when I was thirteen, maybe fourteen even, both times back in England when he came to visit me. But my early memories from those times are pretty blurry."

"I'm assuming your mother didn't want him in your life?"

"I don't think it was really that, but she had moved on after Dad. She told me that just before I was conceived, which was accidental by the way, Dad had big ideas about moving out to the States. He thought he could make his fortune here but Mum didn't want to go because she loved London so much and all her family was there."

"I didn't know that, Tess, it wasn't something he shared with me," said Jake.

"So… Dad realized that Mum wasn't on board and that they really didn't have much in common if she didn't share his sense of adventure. So he went. Just like that. And this was before 9/11 when moving to America for the Brits was a relatively painless process."

"I know, that single awful event changed the world forever as we knew it," said Jake, sadly remembering his own memories of living in New York, "By the way, you say mum or mom?"

"Mum," Tess replied.

"Got it."

"Anyway, Dad had been gone for almost seven years when my mum finally revealed to him that he had a daughter, me."

"Wow! This really is all news to me, Tess, I had no idea at all."

"We were living in East London at the time when I first met my father. It's where I was born and where I grew up until I became a teenager."

"Which is when you next saw your father again?" asked Jake, "When you were thirteen or fourteen?"

"Exactly," said Tess, "Although by this time we had moved to the countryside which was a huge change and a major teenage upheaval for me. My mum had married ten years earlier, a nice Italian man called Franco, and we went from living in a tiny terraced house in a narrow East London Street to a much larger eighteenth-century cottage in Chiddingfold in Surrey. It was like chalk and cheese."

"Chalk and cheese?

"It's just an expression, it means wildly different."

"Whereabouts is… Suuurry?"

"Surrey," she corrected.

Suri…"

"Don't worry, it's a tricky word. Same for us with Massawotsit… Anyway, Surrey is one of the many counties that surround Greater London but it's in the south of England and the village of Chiddingfold is one of those quaint places that I suppose many Americans might imagine England to be like. It's like a perfect picture postcard that you'd send home from your vacation."

"Sounds wonderful," said Jake.

"And the truth is, that's exactly what it was for me, quite wonderful. After I'd managed to get over the culture shock of leaving London, I began to love where we lived, where I still live, in fact. It was village life personified and I'm glad Mum and Franco moved there, although I still work in central London, in Soho."

"I used to live in Soho but not your one, mine was in New York," said Jake, "I loved it while I was there but I always knew it was a temporary chapter in my life."

"Oh, do tell!" said Tess.

"It's another long story, so let's keep it for another time, but please carry on, tell me what happened next."

40

"Dad wrote to me often, he sent photos of where he lived over here and I still have them," Tess continued, "And on many occasions, he told me that if ever I wanted to come and live in America, I had a home with him."

"That was definitely Robert," said Jake, "A gentleman and a dad who loved you from afar."

"And part of me really *wanted* to go, just spend time with him and get to know the father I had only ever met briefly years earlier."

"I completely understand, Tess," said Jake, "It's perfectly natural to want to reconnect."

"And then, as I said previously, he came to visit when I was thirteen or fourteen, and by that time I was enjoying school in Surrey and Mum wanted me to go to university in England. Dad begged her to let me spend just six months or so with him in California, even just a summer, but she wouldn't allow it. And in retrospect, she was right. I was at an important point in my education and she just didn't want it to be disrupted. But looking back, I think she was also scared that if I came out here, I might never go back."

"I get that, please, go on…"

"So when Dad came over to England, he stayed for two weeks in a hotel near to where we lived in Surrey and I spent as many days as possible with him, just doing dad-and-daughter stuff, touristy things I suppose. The thing is, Jake, I remember that particular time with him quite vividly, as though it was yesterday. It's like I've put a film inside a little memory box that I can play over and over again. And he never tried to secretly coax me into going back with him, because he realized it would be a battle with Mum that he knew he couldn't win. And I knew that all he wanted was for me to be happy, even if he couldn't see me."

"This is terribly sad, Tess. For everyone involved."

41

"I know, really sad. And then the last time I saw him was when we drove him to the airport to catch his flight back to Los Angeles. And I knew… I just knew that when he wrapped his arms around me, kissed me on the cheek and held my face in his hands, he realized he might never see me again. He cried and cried and was inconsolable as my mum stood there, unable or unwilling to offer any support. It was like seeing someone die in front of you. And that was the last time I ever saw my father."

"Oh Tess, that is one of the saddest stories I've ever heard, I'm so sorry," said Jake.

"It's okay, I wish I'd had more time with him but my life has been pretty good, and Franco has been a fantastic stepdad. It's just that he'll never be my real dad. Poor Franco."

"Well, while you're here in California, I hope to spend some time with you, and perhaps I can give you more of an insight as to what your father was like as a man and as a friend. I'm glad you have photos that he sent you, and I think I have quite a few of him during our younger years. There is a lot to discover about Robert Valentine and honestly, I don't know if I ever knew everything about him myself."

"So… was he your best friend out here? How did you meet him?" Tess asked, desperate to find out more about the man they called Bobby V.

"I'll tell you everything I know, Tess, but unfortunately we've let two hours slide by us today and sadly I have to meet with my next client. However, I have an idea. Why don't you come to our home on Saturday and have dinner with us, meet the rest of my family?" suggested Jake, "They're all desperate to meet you."

"I'd love that but I don't want to intrude or be an imposition, Jake, you've already done enough for me."

"It would be my… our pleasure, Tess, it really would."

"Okay, deal!" said Tess.

"In the interim, I'd like to spend the best part of a day with you tomorrow or Friday to show you what's left of your dad's possessions. It will involve a little bit of driving but we can have lunch out and make a day of it for you, if you like? And fortunately, my schedule is pretty light for the rest of the week."

"I'd love that and I'm really looking forward to meeting your family at the weekend."

"One last thing, do you have a cell phone?" asked Jake.

"I do, but my phone-plan doesn't allow me to make calls to U.S. numbers."

"Don't worry, here's a phone you can use while you're here, it's a spare one we keep in the office," he said, handing her what appeared to be a brand new iPhone.

"Wow!" said Tess.

"And lastly, you need to eat. The hotel where you're staying does great food, particularly at breakfast time, but you're going to want to venture out and try all the many restaurants around you so here's some walking-around money, as they say, to spend as you wish," he said, handing her an envelope of cash.

"But where did this come from, Jake? I can't accept gifts like this."

"It's not a gift, Tess, it's what your father planned in his will so it's my duty to follow his requests as his executor. There's a couple of thousand bucks in there but there is a little more if you run out. As I say, don't worry about a thing as this is what Robert wanted."

"But two thousand in cash?"

"Your father didn't trust banks, Tess, what can I say?"

The Watcher sat in his Camry, a couple of hundred yards from the law firm's building. He stared at the entrance through his military field-glasses, waiting to see where the girl would go next.

He'd been sitting in his car sweltering in the heat for almost three hours now and he was getting antsy. And hungry.

"Jake fucking Delaney. I'd kill that cunt just for fun."

Chapter 8

When Tess finally arrived back at The Surfrider, Nathan was on duty at the door.

As she stepped out of the Uber cab, he rushed down to meet her, almost in a hurry to see her.

"Hi Tess, a man stopped by a couple or three hours ago who said he was your father and asked if he could leave some flowers in your room. I hope that's okay with you?"

"My father?" Tess asked.

"Oh don't worry, he had ID with him and it all checked out, so no problem. He left the flowers in your room, as promised."

"My father's dead," she replied.

"Oh no, I'm so sorry. Did I just make a huge mistake?"

"I don't think so, Nathan, but I don't know anyone in this town except my attorney, so I've no idea who it could be."

"A secret admirer, maybe?"

"One, I haven't been here long enough to have secret admirers and two, I've never had a secret admirer in my life," she replied, laughing.

"Let's go up and check then, make sure he wasn't a bad guy," grinned Nathan.

They went up to the room and everything seemed to be in its place and nothing was missing that she could see at first glance. And there, sure enough, was a vase of flowers, twenty-six almost black roses with a pink peony in the center.

"What the fuck?" she said, not knowing what to make of the arrangement, "Oops, sorry Nathan, that was a bit coarse."

"Don't worry! But it's a bit of an odd choice of flowers," Nathan replied, "I'm not sure it would be my first choice to send to a beautiful girl."

Tess turned to face Nathan and saw from his reddening cheeks that he'd suddenly realized what his words meant.

"Why thank you, Nathan, I'll take that as a compliment," she said, in a vaguely Southern Belle accent, smiling now at his increasing embarrassment.

"Call me Nate, Tess, everybody calls me Nate…" he stuttered.

"I'll stick to Nathan, if you don't mind, it has a nice ring about it. Sounds like a particularly nice young man," she continued in the same lilting accent.

"Can I get you some tea?" he asked, desperate to change the subject, aware that he was perspiring a little.

"Tea would be lovely," she replied, "But putting the strange flowers aside for now, I'm at a bit of a loss at the moment. I've arrived here in another world and I don't know anyone who could show me around. Forgive me if this is a little forward, but if you have some spare time when you're not working or not with your girlfriend, I'd love to have a guided tour of the area, see what's where and what to avoid?"

"Sadly, no significant other in my life but I'd be more than happy to show you around, not a date, of course, nothing like that, more as your tour guide. How would that work?" he said, astonished that this English beauty would want to spend time with a bellboy.

"I'd like that very much," Tess replied, "How about tonight? Are you working? And don't tell me girls don't flock around you, I know you're not short of broken hearts," she giggled, thinking that maybe she was overdoing the teasing, but enjoying being playful anyway.

The blush returned immediately to his face but he had an idea.

"Can I take you somewhere unique tonight? There's something that most people miss when they come to L.A. and it's one of my favorite places… The Observatory in Griffith Park up on Mount Hollywood. The views are spectacular and the best of it is that it's free."

"In that case, Nathan, my sweet American tour-guide, I'll be ready at seven."

"Wonderful, I'll get that tea for you, ma'am."

Once Nathan had left, Tess examined the flower arrangement, and saw that buried deep inside amongst the stems, there was a small envelope with her name on it.

"I guess that means they were definitely for me," she said aloud.

Opening the envelope, she pulled out a card that read,

Dear Tess,

I very much look forward to making your acquaintance.

A Secret Admirer.

She thought it was weird, disturbing actually, but anyone who would go to the extent of seeking out and purchasing black roses, must be keen.

Chapter 9

Tess had never seen anything like it before in her life. The views weren't just staggering, they were jaw-dropping. And the building itself was a thing of beauty too. The Observatory was a magnificent triple-domed art deco structure that sat majestically in Griffith Park overlooking the whole of the Los Angeles basin.

"The land was donated to the City of Los Angeles by Griffith J. Griffith back in the late 1800s," said Nathan, proudly.

"His parents weren't big on coming up with original names then?" asked Tess.

Nathan laughed, he hadn't ever given the donor's name that much thought before.

"But in his will," he continued, "He left enough funds for the construction and also a set of detailed plans on exactly what he envisioned being built on the land after his death. He was extremely particular in his grand plan for the park."

"Oh to be that philanthropically wealthy," Tess replied.

Nathan was slowly getting used to her English humor.

"Don't people worry about earthquakes sending this place tumbling down the canyon?" she asked.

"It's always an issue," Nathan replied, "But, in fact, the biggest threat to the Observatory has been brush fires, one of which years ago, got real close to destroying the building before the blaze was mercifully extinguished."

"Crumbs! I'd never have even thought about that."

"Crumbs?" asked Nathan.

"Sorry! English expression."

"Gotcha. But anyway, we haven't seen half of it yet; the biggest part of the Observatory is the Planetarium which is housed in the large center dome," he continued, "It's pretty epic."

"We've got a Planetarium back in London but nothing the size of this place," said Tess, "Is everything just bigger and better in the States?"

"Well, sometimes bigger, but not always better," he replied, "If you look over there to the southwest, that's where your hotel is on the Pacific, far to the right of the Santa Monica Pier. And then if you look over here to the southeast, that's downtown L.A. where all the tall buildings are. But if you look up behind you at top of the Hollywood Hills, you can see in the distance, the famous Hollywood Sign."

"Wow, I never thought I'd get to see that in person," said Tess, "Do you think we can get closer to it, it seems kind of small from here?"

"It's a bit of a trek to get there and all the rich people living in the Hills have tried everything to stop tourists going up there," Nathan replied.

"How do you mean?" she asked.

"Well, it's actually a public right of way, but the residents do things like putting up fake street signs telling people that it's a private road, or that there's no access, or that the road's closed, things like that."

"That's a bit mean!"

"It is, but you know what people are like once they get too much money, they act like Donald Trump and think they rule the world," said Nathan.

"So, can we go up there afterwards?"

"Sure, I'm a native of L.A. so I know the quickest way up there and even now, I still think it's pretty cool. And it does sit in protected parkland so we wouldn't be breaking any laws."

"Why is the sign there, is it just a thing that indicates where L.A.'s film industry is?"

"Well, yes and no. That is, it didn't start out that way. I'll give you the short story," he said.

They continued walking through the Observatory, Tess marveling at the attractions that it housed, still bemused that there was no admission fee. Eventually, they arrived at the Café at the End of the Universe and Nathan suggested they stop for a sandwich and cold drinks.

They found an available table next to the window of the café, and once Nathan had returned from the counter with sandwiches and iced teas, he told Tess the story of the sign.

"The sign actually began life as a real estate advertisement. A property developer was building a new residential development for wealthy whites only, believe it or not," grimaced Nathan, "And the subdivision was named Hollywoodland. This was back in around 1920, I think."

"I'm learning all the time, go on," said Tess.

"So, as with all entrepreneurs or politicians or gypsies, they never bother to clean up their mess after them so once the property company went bankrupt, the sign fell into disrepair over the years. Until finally, the City of Los Angeles adopted it and removed the last four letters, so Hollywoodland became simply, Hollywood. They then set about restoring and dedicating it to mark where the emerging L.A. film industry happened to be situated."

"So the ad that was temporary, finally became permanent?" asked Tess.

"Almost. Eventually, they realized that the sign couldn't last because its original temporary construction just wasn't strong enough, so with the help from generous local donors, including Alice Cooper I believe, the original thirty-foot-high sign was torn down and replaced with a brand new forty-five-foot version made from steel and permanently cemented in a concrete foundation. In a way though, it's become a national monument."

"Wow, you're right, everyone knows it these days. Come on then, Nathan the tour-guide, let's go see it, up close and personal!"

Chapter 10

She was beginning to piss him off. She didn't seem to stay put in one place for very long and she always seemed to have someone with her. And now it looked like they were about to trek all the way up to the Hollywood fucking Sign.

Hollywood, really? Who the fuck cares?

Buchanan followed them in his Camry at a safe distance from the kid's Volkswagen. But then when they arrived at the top of Doranda Drive, he hung back just in case they surprised him by turning around and heading back. He knew the road didn't go any further; he'd off'd someone in a property four houses down, about three years ago so he knew the lay of the land.

But then, to piss him off even more, they both got out of the truck and headed toward the Hiking Trail on Mount Lee, the one that tourists took to get really close to the sign. But he knew that was a long, tough and exhausting climb.

What am I, a fucking mountain goat?

There was no way he was following them, his bad knee wouldn't get there anyway and his heart had recently been giving him some issues.

"Fuck it, fuck it…

He took the thermos from his night bag and unwrapped a pastrami sandwich that was still warm.

Gotta stop fucking cursing…

Two hours later, he was tired and getting hungry again, and realized he was wasting his time. He needed a drink too, something a bit harder than monkeyshit coffee. The two lovebirds were probably fucking each other's brains out, up there on the 'H' of the sign. Nothing new there, been there done it.

He stowed the remains of his snack inside his bag, put the Camry in gear and began his journey back to the city, another wasted day.

~

"It's incredible!" shrilled Tess, "I can't believe we're here!"

They were sitting on the gravel path now, looking down on the entire city of Los Angeles, and just a few feet below them, sat the Hollywood sign itself, almost within touching distance.

"Yep, it never gets old," said Nathan, proud to have shown Tess part of where he grew up.

"Do you know, I've had two of the worst weeks I've ever had, losing my father and everything, but the last couple of days have really helped. And you've been wonderful, Nathan, thank you so much."

She had spent the last three hours with this handsome young Californian and maybe it was the thin air up here that made her feel light-headed but she couldn't help herself. She leaned in to kiss him as a 'thank you' but was surprised when he gently withdrew.

"Oh God, I'm sorry Nathan. You *do* have a girlfriend and I'm just making assumptions, aren't I."

"No, Tess, not that at all. I think you're adorable, really sensational, just an incredibly beautiful, and perfectly gorgeous girl and if you were a boy, well, I guess it really would be perfect."

Chapter 11

"Jeez, what was I thinking? Two days in L.A. and I'm gushing over the first man I meet."

Actually, correction; every man I meet…

But Nathan was a breath of fresh air, and so damned nice too.

She looked at herself in the mirror.

Nice job, Tess, when it comes to men, you don't know your ass from your friggin' elbow…

But she had had a brilliant time with Nathan, probably one of the best evenings of her life. He was a perfect gentleman and just really great fun to be with. He made you feel like you were the only person in the world and that his sole purpose in life was to make you happy.

And he's so damned pretty…

It had been a cathartic experience to spend time with Nathan, gay or not, and compare it to her relationship with Simon. It wasn't that Simon was a complete asshole but he did a lot of asinine things. Particularly if he was trying to impress his friends or if he'd had too much to drink, which was a common occurrence.

And Simon ain't that pretty…

Tess realized she hadn't been born with a silver spoon in her mouth, she knew that she would have to fight for everything in life and she was happy to do so. It's just how it was. But what she abhorred most about Simon, was his general lack of manners toward her, just because she didn't come from the same social class. It was almost as though her origins were a green light for him to act atrociously in the worst of caveman ways. She hated the way he would just fart in front of her, thinking it was both acceptable and funny. It made her feel sick.

I bet the dickhead doesn't fart in front of Camilla Fucksworth...

She had found that working at the agency had been a little on the 'laddish' side to begin with, but none of the guys she worked with were ever bad-mannered or discourteous. They acted like schoolboys sometimes, but they were never sexist. Although to be fair, most of them came from her side of the tracks, so they knew what it was like to come up the hard way.

Yeah, they ribbed her for being a girl and they could be a bit mucky but if you bit back at them, they could take it as good as they gave, and in good humor. The ad business was still mainly a male domain and would likely never change. It wasn't quite John Hamm in the 1950s *Mad Men* series but it still had its roots there.

And John Hamm, well...

Most of Tess and Simon's problems lay in the fact that they didn't talk much either. At least not about anything that was important or even mutually funny. If it was about football or rugby or cricket or pubs, he could talk all night but if it was about anything vaguely emotional, he immediately put up a roadblock. He seemed unable to have any kind of serious or interesting conversation without it ending with him getting pissed at her. If an idea wasn't his, then it wasn't worth discussing.

But if he suggested going to see a movie, which was rare, she could guarantee it would be fucking *Star Wars* or *The Walking Dead* or some other piece of garbage, but never a Nicholas Sparks film or something set in another period altogether. And then he'd want his mates to go too. That had happened on one too many cinema trips, almost like it had been pre-arranged.

"Oh come on, Tessy, (*she hated that*) they want to see it too," he'd say, "Don't spoil it for everyone else."

Right...

And Simon would think that taking her home to his apartment, stinking of the pub, and then fumbling with her bra while he burped alcoholic sweet-fucking-nothings in her ear, was meant to be sexy. And then, when he'd finally managed to get himself undressed, his penis invariably failed to launch, a victim of over-fueling from alcohol. But oddly, when that happened, she was actually relieved that she wouldn't have to go through an act and pretend that she was enjoying it. Thankfully, on those occasions, she could simply turn over and go to sleep.

The truth was, they just weren't suited to each other but maybe she wasn't suited to any man, maybe they were all like this, if what you really wanted was a heterosexual man that communicated with you?

And maybe a relationship with a gay man would be far nicer? Apart from no sex...which to be truthful, wasn't a deal breaker...

Simon had been her first serious boyfriend and since splitting with him, she had made her mind up that she wasn't ever going to get involved with anyone else in the short term. Too much aggravation.

She brushed her teeth, rinsed her face and slipped off her jeans and camisole top and collapsed into the bed. The thousand-thread-count, Egyptian cotton sheets felt like silk against her nakedness and her head floated in the goose down pillows as her eyelids grew heavy and she slipped into the deepest of sleeps, Simon now a very distant and best-forgotten memory.

Chapter 12

Stepping outside the hotel at ten the next day, as the cool morning sunshine swept over her, she was more than surprised to see the car that Jake had arrived in.

"An E-Type!" she gushed.

"And a very good morning to you, Tess!" said Jake, standing next to the immaculate and pristine 1960s English sports car.

"I guess this wasn't something I expected to see you in. Doesn't everybody have Teslas here?" she asked.

"Well, you're not wrong there but I'm not a fan; too bland and anonymous for me," he replied, "Anyway, I'm a New Yorker, not a Californian, we're different."

"So what do you do with it, just get it out on special occasions?" she asked.

"No, far from it, this is my daily driver. I know on the surface it looks like a genuine vintage Jaguar but underneath, the running gear is all modern. Come on, get in and I'll show you."

The baby blue painted, tan interior Jaguar cruised along the PCH, its roof down as Tess's hair blew in the mid-morning Californian sunshine. They headed north, this time past Pepperdine University, driving up toward the Ventura County line.

"It really is quite stunning, Jake, you must adore this car," said Tess, "I'm not really a car girl but this is beautiful."

"I pinch myself every time I drive it," Jake replied, "But it's not something I ever thought I'd own, more to do with a good friend of mine steering me toward it. But I'm glad he did."

When they'd got as far as La Piedra State Beach, Jake took a turning on the right onto Encinal Canyon Road.

"It's not far now, just a few more minutes," he yelled, through the whipping noise of the wind.

"By the way, Jake, you didn't happen to send me flowers, did you?" she asked.

"No, why do you ask?"

"Oh, no reason…" she said, grateful that the wind noise precluded further conversation.

Finally, Jake took another right turn onto a road that Tess identified as Old Broad Beach Ranch Road.

Try saying that to the taxi driver when you've had a few drinks…

"And, we're here," said Jake.

Really? Seriously?

They had arrived at what Tess could only assume was a trailer park. The name at the entrance proudly announcing, 'Hope's Grotto Dude Community'.

Hmmm…

"Don't be put off by what you see, Tess, it's actually a pretty cool place."

"If you say so…"

They pulled up outside a manufactured home.

Blimey, it's a trailer! Double wide, but still a trailer…

"This is your father's home, has been for the last twenty years or more," said Jake, getting out of the car and beckoning Tess to follow.

There was a padlock on the front entrance door and Jake pulled out a set of keys from his pocket, selected one and quickly removed it from the key ring.

"Welcome! This is all yours now," Jake announced, having finally removed the padlock and opened the door to her father's home.

"Really?"

"Don't worry, you don't have to live here, Tess, you can sell it but you might want to spend some time going through your dad's things and get to understand him a little more. I can tell you that he was the most immaculate and house-proud man I've ever met."

Tess looked around at the surrounding trailers, and she had to admit that there was a certain coziness to the place. Yes, they were manufactured and movable homes but it didn't feel like any of the residents planned on moving out anytime soon. All of them had a feeling of intimate love and care about them. The plant pots, trailing bougainvillea and colorful signs with silly messages that hung on the exterior walls, lent a warmth to the trailer park and were clearly reminders of permanence.

Fishing rods leaned against the homes, old but lovingly restored pickup trucks were kept protected under awnings, and makeshift fire-pits with deckchairs surrounding them, could be seen outside most of the trailers. She wondered what it might be like in the evenings to sit and chat to the neighbors, just cooking some burgers or sausages on the fire with a couple of beers, and she began to understand what had attracted her father to this place.

They entered the trailer and Jake was right. The place was absolutely beautiful inside. Her father had been fastidious about cleanliness and his style was very cool, with some almost museum-quality art deco pieces of furniture. It even smelled good too.

"Well, you got me, Jake. From the outside, this was absolutely not what I expected to see inside."

"Told you," Jake said with a grin, "Your father was a special man."

"I'm learning more about him every day, it seems."

"There's a laptop on the desk over there. I have no idea what the password is because Robert didn't leave it in his instructions. He said you would know what it was."

"Me?" said Tess, "How would I know what his password would be?"

"That's down to you, I can't help there," replied Jake, "But listen, Tess, your father was very careful about everything and everyone outside of his circle. He was fairly secretive and my own feeling is that anything he wanted to say to you, anything for your ears only, would not have been included in his instructions to me."

"But how would I know what he wanted to say if he hadn't written it down somewhere?" she asked.

"All I know is that during his final months, the only person who mattered to him was you. The curious thing is that Robert ought not to have died a poor man, he had had numerous successes over the years, in various types of businesses, so if he had hidden anything, it would be down to you to find it. So I can't really help there," explained Jake.

"So you're saying he may have left some kind of paper chase for me?" asked Tess, "But why would he do that?"

"He didn't trust many people, that's all I know, Tess."

"Well, I suppose I could take his laptop back to the hotel and see if there's anything in what you're saying, but honestly, it all sounds a bit too cloak and dagger to me."

They continued to walk through the home, Tess taking in some of the many things her father had bought during his life in California. There were no knickknacks, just very carefully selected items that were purchased for either a reason of value and investment or, as seemed more likely now, they just pleased him artistically and emotionally.

She spotted a mint condition, and what looked to be an original Barcelona Chair, designed by the renowned German artist, Ludwig Mies van der Rohe from the late 1920s. She could picture her father sitting there of an evening, the doors and windows of the trailer open wide as he sat enjoying a glass of brandy or something, just savoring the moment sitting in that iconic chair.

She was learning so much about Robert Valentine in such a short space of time and she felt sad that she'd never spent any real time with him, just learning from him and loving him as a dad.

He shouldn't have died...

"The home is paid for, by the way, but the ground it sits on requires a monthly rent," said Jake, "Although I should say that it's been paid for two years in advance by your father."

"Good to know, I guess," said Tess, "But what the heck would I use it for?"

"Well, I do know that some people in the community rent their places out to tourists here, so it may provide a nice income, and pay for itself too," offered Jake, "Might even turn a healthy profit."

"Who's going to rent this place?" asked Tess, "We're in the middle of nowhere!"

"If I said that you could get six, maybe eight grand a month from it, would that make you feel any better?" asked Jake, knowing how Tess would react, "Dollars though, not pounds."

"Are you serious??" Tess blurted, "Six thousand a month for this place? Who would pay that?"

"You'd be surprised, plenty of people actually. You're in Malibu, lots of state parks, walking and hiking trails, bird watching, naturalists... this place would appeal to many different types of people. And it's in immaculate condition too, just look at it," said Jake.

"I hadn't thought about it that way, but I suppose I don't really know the area that well either," Tess admitted, quite amazed that her father had left her a fairly sizable annual income if she wanted it.

"There's something else," said Jake, "Come on outside for a moment."

Tess followed the attorney outside and watched as he untied the strings of a tarpaulin covering something sitting under a makeshift carport.

"Tada!" said Jake, whipping the tarp away to reveal its secret.

"What is it?" she asked.

"Well, I'd say it was a car but correct me if I'm wrong," he laughed.

"Dad gave it a girl's name too?" she said as she walked around the ancient car, spotting a white calligraphic decal on the side, "Shelly?"

Jake laughed at her clear lack of knowledge on American cars. "Not Shelly, Tess... Shelby! This, is a 1968 Ford Mustang Shelby GT!" he announced, barely able to hide his glee, "Carroll Shelby was a legend in the automotive world."

"So it was *designed* by a woman?"

"No, Carroll was a he, not a she!" said Jake.

"Umm... still not getting it, Jake, I think you're going to need to clue me in. All I see is an old car."

"I apologize, Tess. You see, I didn't realize what this was until I sent some photos of it to an old friend of mine who works in the historic car business. He's up in San Luis Obispo, a fella by the name of Preston Pryor. Anyway, when he called me back, he said that this was like the Holy Grail of Ford Mustangs."

"So is it worth anything?" asked Tess.

"I think that might be an understatement," said Jake, realizing that she had no clue as to the car's value, "Preston's conservative estimate of the car's current value, given that it is in extremely good condition for a fifty-year-old vehicle, is probably in excess of $80,000, and it may be valued at a lot more depending on matching serial numbers and original parts and add-ons."

"Jeepers!" exclaimed Tess, "Sorry, Jake, but why was Dad living in a trailer with an eighty grand car sitting outside?"

"There's no simple explanation Tess, but as you can see from looking inside his home, your father liked fine examples of art. And to him, this car was the epitome of the greatest period of American muscle cars, which I guess is why he bought it."

"So what do I do with it now?" asked Tess, clearly overwhelmed at the secrets she was discovering about her father.

"Either sell it..." suggested Jake, "Or, you could drive it."

"Are you serious?"

"Can you drive?" he asked.

"Yes, of course, Franco gave me lessons when I was seventeen. I used to drive him crazy by doing 20mph every time we went out, but he was really patient."

"So why not? I know it's left-hand-drive and we drive on the right here, but Malibu is pretty much the nicest place in the country to drive for fun, although the problem is it's a stick…"

"A stick? Oh, you mean it's a manual transmission. That's not a problem, I grew up driving manual cars," she said.

"My kids wouldn't have a clue how to drive one, they've all grown up driving automatics," Jake replied.

"Oh! How many kids do you have?"

"Three, one of each!" he laughed.

"You're so funny, Jake, but crikey, you were busy, right? And you're still young so I guess you started early in the kids' department?"

"I'm only joking, Tess, actually I have a son and two daughters and also a stepson I adopted when Summer and I married. They're all amazing young people, I'm very lucky," said Jake, "And you're very sweet, but I'm not so young now. In baseball terms, I'm at the bottom of the sixth and in cricket terms, I guess I'm looking down the order in the second innings."

"Yeah, right!" she replied, wondering what this good looking silver fox's son would look like, "But I can't wait to meet them all, I'm really looking forward to it."

She walked around the dark green car that sported a horse badge on its grille, noting what appeared to be an immaculate black leather interior with a wood-rimmed steering wheel.

"So, what do you think? You want to try it out?"

"I'm not sure, Jake. Anyway, what about insurance? I don't have any."

"That's fine too, you have a UK license, right?"

"Yes, since I was seventeen."

"Then you're covered on your father's policy which runs until next April."

"I don't know, Jake, this is all a bit too much to take in right now. Can I think about it?"

"Of course, come on, let's go get some lunch, there's a great place not far from here that's fun if you like down and dirty!"

The Camry was parked in a side lane just opposite the trailer park. Buchanan lazily watched the pair through his hunting rifle scope, drawing a bead from one to the other, his finger playing on the trigger.

It was so much hotter inland from the coast and he was sweating now, itching to get out of this shithole. He continued to watch them through the gun's scope, desperate to test its accuracy.

"Come on sweetheart, give him a blow job… see if I can kill two birds with one stone."

Chapter 13

It wasn't the type of restaurant that Tess had imagined Jake frequenting. Neptune's Net was further north, almost at the Ventura County line and it was a first-come, first-served kind of place. Well, not exactly served, more like you grabbed an available table inside or outside, placed an order at the desk and then waited for your number to be called out. But the location was outstanding even if the noise level from the diners was deafening.

"So, what do you think?" asked Jake after he'd retrieved their food order from the bar and they'd begun to hungrily dig into the fried seafood and French fries.

"Love it!" Tess replied, "The place looked a bit of a dive when we parked up but this seafood is beyond scrumptious."

"Scrumptious?" said Jake, "I'll note that down in my 'quaint English expressions' notebook."

She punched him playfully on the shoulder, "Stop mocking me, it's where I'm from!"

"Just teasing Tess, but I'm glad you like it here, it's one of my favorite places to drive up to for lunch, and look, the ocean's right there, it doesn't get any better."

"I was thinking when we were driving here that maybe it's not such a daft idea after all, you know, me driving Dad's car?" she said, tucking into a giant fried shrimp, "At least I'd have transport while I'm here which would save on Ubers."

"I'm glad you think so but why the sudden change of heart?" Jake asked.

"I just think that if my father bought that car for a reason, then I think he would want me to drive it too and to understand why he chose it, that's all," she said, "I'm even beginning to understand why he chose Hope's Grotto as his home. It's actually a pretty cool place."

"I agree, but we need to make sure the Mustang is roadworthy for you, Robert would want that," replied Jake, "I'll tell you what, I'll get the guy who looks after my E-Type for me up in Calabasas to come and collect it, give it the all-clear and have it dropped off at your hotel. If there's anything that needs to be done, I'll know that it's been done properly. How does that sound?"

"Sounds perfect, Jake, and thank you, thank you again for everything you're doing for me. I'd be lost without you," Tess said, finishing off a large serving of French fries and quietly sneaking a couple more from Jake's plate.

Jake smiled as he looked at his late friend's daughter. He couldn't help but draw comparisons with Tess to his own girls who were of a similar age. There's nothing a father wouldn't do for his daughter and by extension, there was nothing he wouldn't do for Tess.

Chapter 14

After Jake had dropped her off at The Surfrider, Tess retrieved her key from Reception and found Nathan walking the corridors.

"My favorite man," she said, hugging him like a long lost brother, "It's been too long!"

Nathan laughed, "My favorite girl," he said, "I'm off tonight, would you like some company for the evening?"

"I'd like that," said Tess, "Where are you thinking of going and I promise not to embarrass myself again."

"You didn't embarrass yourself, Tess, I promise you, but I was thinking that maybe we could just run up to Malibu Village and grab a coffee or something?"

"Sounds cute, meet you at five?"

"See you then," he said, squeezing her hand and continuing his daily rounds of the hotel.

She changed out of her dress and pulled on a pair of cut-off jeans shorts and a t-shirt, and took her father's laptop outside to the balcony. Fortunately, it had been left on charge so she settled back into the hammock and began to try and discover what the password might be.

She began with birthdays and then name combinations and then tried various words like Hope and Grotto and Malibu and Surfrider. She even tried her own name with her date of birth attached,

Tess2807 but then realized that in the US, the month came first so she tried Tess0728 but that didn't work either. Even when she tried transposing the letters and numbers, nothing seemed to be working.

"Arrgghh! So frustrating, Dad!" she said out loud, "I just don't know you well enough."

She slipped back into the room and found a bottle of Evian water in the mini-fridge and took it back out to the balcony.

Gazing at nothing in particular, she wondered where everyone was heading as she took in the light early afternoon traffic on the PCH below her. The gentle din of road noise coupled with the waves from the ocean could send her to sleep right now. Paradise found. She wondered if they all must have interesting and fun-filled days in this unique and extraordinary part of the world.

But I guess you need to be rich to live here...

And then something quite amazing happened. A pair of tiny hummingbirds were hovering in mid-air just a few feet from her. They couldn't have been much bigger than her thumbs and they seemed to be staring at her as their wings flapped at what felt like a thousand times a second. They appeared to be as intrigued with her as she was with them. Tess had never seen anything quite so small and so incredibly beautiful. She carefully put out her hand to invite them to meet her but as quickly as they had arrived, they were gone, almost in the blink of an eye.

She waited almost twenty minutes, hoping that her new-found friends would return but soon realized that the chance meeting was over and that she still had work to do.

"If only I could get into the computer, I could find out more about you and then I'd know the password," she muttered, realizing the frustration of her Catch-22 situation.

She tried her mother's name and birth date too and then wondered if it could be connected to any of the businesses he'd been involved in, but realized yet again that she had no clue what they were.

It would be too obvious to use her own details as a password because a good hacker could pretty much work it out by a process of elimination after not too many attempts.

But what else did he love?

And then something dawned on her.

She began to type... 6...8...s...h...e...l...b...y...

And as if by magic, the screen came to life.

Maybe I do know you better than I thought, Dad...

And there it was, an impeccably neat desktop with precious few icons and a single shortcut to Documents in the top right-hand corner.

Chapter 15

It wasn't far to go, maybe a mile north on PCH, but Tess really enjoyed riding in Nathan's vintage triple-white VW Beetle. It had white bodywork with white leather interior and a white soft top and it was obviously Nathan's pride and joy.

"Did you restore it yourself?" she asked, having to shout above the noise of the engine.

"Believe it or not, I did," said Nathan, "Some gay men actually like to get their hands dirty!" he laughed.

She looked at him, enjoying having found a new friend and hopefully maybe, a friend for life. Simon would love him. Not.

After only a few minutes, they arrived at Malibu Village which was not exactly what Tess had expected. She looked around as Nathan tried to find a parking spot and realized it was more of an upscale plaza than a cozy little canyon village.

As the pair began to wander along the sidewalk, occasionally stopping to gaze into the windows of the high-priced boutiques and galleries that lined the square, Nathan began to sense a feeling of sadness from Tess.

"You okay?" he asked, "You're very quiet. Is it not what you were expecting?"

"No, I'm fine, really," she replied, "It's just that when you said it was a village, I had imagined something else entirely. But it's lovely, honestly."

"Ah, I see, well in truth it's the locals that call it Malibu Village although its actual name is Malibu Country Mart. But I'd guess that your idea of a village is something quite different back home?"

"It is, but that doesn't mean I don't like this place," she replied, "Villages back in England have their own idiosyncrasies."

"Pray, tell?"

"Well, a neighbor of ours at home in Chiddingfold, does some strange things sometimes. She's eighty years old and likes to garden naked."

"Oh. My. Lord!" exclaimed Nathan, a look of mock horror spreading across his face.

"And this lady knows that the eighty-three-year-old man next door, likes to watch from his upstairs window. So every two weeks or so, she gets a bikini wax. When I asked her why she bothered, she said that if he enjoyed the view so much then it was only polite to make an effort."

"That is so hilarious," said Nathan, "You'd be arrested if you did that here!"

"I know, right?"

"Ooooh, I'd love to spend some time with that lady, maybe get a waxing with her. We could trim each other's bushes in the garden!"

Tess laughed with Nathan but she couldn't help but notice that he had become much more openly gay in his voice and expressions and actions since she had embarrassed herself the other evening. Or maybe she just hadn't noticed and he'd been like it since she'd met him. It didn't matter though, she had begun to adore him, as a man and as a friend.

They continued to navigate the village and came upon a small park area where parents could sit and watch their children as they played in the sandpit or on the swings and slides. There was a small café called The Coffee Bean & Tea Leaf and Nathan suggested they stop to have a Frappuccino and Tess was parched so they bought two to go, along with some banana cake.

As they sat at a bench table, watching and listening to the kids shrieking with delight in the park area, Nathan asked Tess the question he'd been wanting to ask.

"Can I ask you what happened to your dad, Tess? Was it cancer?"

"No," she said, "Suicide."

Chapter 16

"I'm so sorry… how did he die?"

"A single shot to the head. They found a handgun next to his body. They say that he wouldn't have felt any pain, it was an instant death," said Tess, "But I can still feel his pain, even now."

"I'm so, so sorry," Nathan replied, "I had no idea. Me and my big mouth."

"It's fine, Nathan, honestly. When I first found out from my attorney, I was as shocked as you are now, but I'm coming to terms with it. But I guess I still don't understand why?"

"So you had no idea at all?"

"I barely knew the man."

"But you communicated with each other?"

"Not very often, maybe once a year, a call or an email, Christmas and birthday cards, just an update on what had happened in previous year."

"That's so sad. I don't know how I would cope without my parents. They are everything to me," he said.

"I mean, I do have a mum and dad, well, stepdad anyway, so I don't feel deprived in any way, but I think I'm just beginning to find out things about my real dad, things that I think he wanted to share with me," Tess replied.

"How do you mean?"

"I went to his home today with my attorney, his attorney actually. We found his laptop and I was able to work out the password. Dad *knew* that I would work it out!"

"An unbreakable connection, a survivor of time and distance fueled by a unique love," Nathan replied.

"Exactly. I'm going to spend time going through his computer to find out as much as I can about him. I think I have so much still to learn, and I think that laptop is the key."

~

The Watcher sat listening three tables away in the park.

Guy's a fucking faggot... no straight dick comes out with shit like that...

Buchanan had been through her room when she'd left and he had found the laptop, but decided to leave it where it was for the time being. And he'd secured a tracking device under the rear fender of the kid's car. He sensed that they might spend time together and it saved having to follow her all the time.

But the laptop was password-protected and there was no point in taking it when he could eventually get her to tell him what the password was.

Who knows, I might even have a little fun with you too, Tess Valentine...

Chapter 17

Saturday arrived and Tess was suddenly nervous about meeting Jake's family that evening. She hadn't thought too much about it until right now when she was getting ready to leave.

Do I go for casual chic or elegantly formal?

In the end, she compromised and having showered, washed and blow-dried her hair, she slipped on a pair of white jeans and a tangerine silk and cotton pullover, along with her pale blue casual loafers. No jewelry tonight, save for a small starfish necklace on a fine silver chain. And just a quick spray to her neck of Jo Malone's *Lime, Basil & Mandarin*, her favorite scent.

She was still early so she unplugged the laptop from the wall charger and sat on the bed and signed in.

68shelby... you're so funny, Dad, never had you down as a car nut...

She opened the Documents folder and began to scroll through the files.

Accounts, Banking, Car Stuff, Furniture Suppliers, Music, Photos...

Until she came to a file, boldly marked 'TESS'. When she double clicked on the file, she was astonished to see literally hundreds of photos of her, from way back in 1992 when she was just a baby, right up until earlier this year.

How did you get all of these, Dad?

But she realized quickly that photos of everyone were available all over the internet on various social media sites so he must have downloaded them.

And right at the bottom of the file, she saw a single Word document, labeled *Dearest Tess*. She double clicked on it and waited while Word opened it…

My Dearest Tess,

If you're reading this, then it means that I am no longer around. If you've opened the TESS file, you know that I have been charting your progress from when you were just a baby, a baby I originally knew nothing about.

I cannot begin to tell you, that of all the mistakes I made in my life, the biggest by far was that I couldn't be with you as you grew, to watch as you matured from a skinny and lovely, cute little girl into the breathtakingly beautiful young woman you have become. If I could rewind time, I would do so in a heartbeat.

And you're smart too. Look how easily you found out the password to access this computer, no one else could have done that, only you. The people you work with have an amazing addition to the creative team at the agency, and I know they must be proud to have you working there.

Your mum is an amazing mother and I take my hat off to Franco too, for all the love and time he's given you over the years, he really is a good man. Of course, I would have loved to have been with you as you grew but your mum and I just didn't get along and she was in love with another. But she was really good at sending me photos and updating me on everything you were achieving in life, so I'm grateful to her for that.

There is a lot you don't know about me but I'm sure that eventually you will discover who I am and what I've been doing during the last twenty-five years or so. Most people who knew me, also knew that I lived a fairly careful and inextravagant existence but I was a saver too. I have put enough by so that you can enjoy an extended vacation out here, really for as long as you like, in fact. If you need money, talk to Jake, he's also one of the good guys and he has control of my finances.

Also, I hope you will use the Mustang. I loved that car so much and I hope when you eventually drive it, that you will understand why. But it's fast, Tess, so I want you to be super careful! But also, I don't want you to think you need to keep it just because it was mine although that would be lovely. But it is quite valuable to collectors and I know you don't earn a lot yet in your job. Although in a few short years, I know you will!

My home doesn't look like much from the outside but you have to trust me, Tess, it has much greater value than you could possibly imagine. Please don't sell it, not immediately anyway. I wouldn't expect you to live there because it's too far out in the boonies for you. You need to enjoy everything that Los Angeles and Malibu have to offer while you're here.

But finally, Tess, I want you to be careful. I've made some enemies over the years, not because I'm a bad person but because there are people in this town who think they should have more than is due to them. So don't take risks while you're here, and if you're concerned about anything at all, just call Jake. He'll be there in a hurry if he knows you're in danger.

I love you Tess, I love you more than I've ever been able to tell you. I'm the proudest man that ever walked the planet and I have the most beautiful, talented and incredibly lovely daughter of all. Take life and everything it has to offer you and feel as strong as the wind and as free as the birds. Don't settle for anything and never believe you can't reach for the very top of the skies. No dream is impossible, Tess, as I found out the day you were born. But ironically, I can give you more in death than I could ever give you in life. You'll see, trust me.

Always watching over you, always admiring and rooting for you, and always loving you from here to eternity.

Dad xxxxx

Tess was all cried out but once again, her tears and wracked emotions flooded back to her, and when the sobbing finally stopped, so it began again.

Chapter 18

Tess stepped into the Uber and hoped that she'd managed to perform enough make-up repairs, so that they wouldn't see that she'd been crying when she arrived at the Delaney home. Her eyes had turned red from the tears she'd shed after reading her father's letter, so she had put some 'White Eyes' eye drops in to try and relieve them.

But she still felt so emotional after reading her father's words, wondering why she had never really had the opportunity to spend more time with him before he'd gone. And she blamed herself in part because she could easily have got on a plane and come out here any time in the last seven or eight years. But then again, she had no real idea how much she clearly meant to him.

Why didn't you tell me, Dad, why?

The address that Jake had given her for his home in Malibu was around twenty minutes north of her hotel so she used that time wisely and relaxed in the back of the car, using breathing exercises to calm herself down. If she'd had a meditation app on her phone, she'd probably use it right now, but instead she chose to take in the sights on the journey to the Delaneys.

She had quickly come to realize that there were two very different Malibus. The one further south toward Santa Monica where her hotel was situated, was far busier than the northern area of Malibu. The homes that lined the sand in south Malibu formed a real hodgepodge of designs and architectural periods. There would be the brand new and extraordinary cubism-style, glass, metal and stone obelisks with opaque green glass garage and entry doors, standing just a couple of feet away from an original home from the 1950s, in dire need of repair or demolition.

It was easy to see that those older and dilapidated homes had been bought by the original Californian bohemians who had discovered Malibu when it wasn't quite so expensive. And the brand new futuristic homes were built by the new money moving in as they attempted to elbow out the neighboring 'paupers'. But all of the residents were there for one reason, and one reason only; the beach. Location rules, OK?

She marveled at the expensive cars, some of them costing almost half a million dollars or more, left parked out on the highway because garage space was too valuable and could be converted to use as a room on this exalted playground.

Oh, to have that problem…

As Tess watched the miles drift by as they headed north, her mind returned once again to the letter from her father that she had found earlier. He had left some clues in it and she would need to read it over and over to find out what he meant. What she had learned so far since arriving in California, was that her father had many layers to him. She had begun to understand more about him in the last few days than she had in the last twenty-six years.

"It's just a little further up on the left," said the Uber driver, it's on an unmarked road I think."

Tess awoke from her reverie and saw where he was pointing to, a hidden turn-off that could be missed if you weren't looking for it.

"The address he gave me is 33598 Pacific Coast Highway, is that what you have on your screen?" she asked.

"Yes, yes, is okay, I find," replied the driver, in faltering English.

The address they arrived at was not what Tess was expecting. She couldn't actually see a house, just a very pretty eight-foot-high hedgerow with an English style arched gate set into the center of it. If she ignored everything else around her, she could literally feel as though she was back home.

She depressed the thumb latch on the iron handle of the gate and was surprised to find it unlocked. When she opened it, what she saw before her, took her breath away.

"So pretty," she murmured.

The house itself was quite old, a wide single story cottage-style home with a pretty English front garden. But what really made her gasp was the abundance of color in an explosion of flowers and shrubs that framed the picturesque home. She counted three shades of bougainvillea draped across the building and countless plants and flowers that lined the borders of the lawn… poppies, lilacs, lavender, azaleas and sunset trumpets. A weeping willow took up an entire corner of the garden providing perfect shade for afternoon tea, and the scent of magnolia trees, camellias and jasmine was intoxicating.

"Are you going to stand out there all night?"

Tess turned to where she had heard the voice come from, as Jake ambled down the wooden steps of the house, greeting her with his inimitable grin.

"I couldn't help it Jake, this garden is so beautiful!" she said, "It's just so unexpected."

"We call it a yard here, but garden works too," said Jake, "But come on in and have something cool to drink and meet my wife," he continued, hooking his hand under her arm and leading her up the steps onto the sun-faded plank porch.

Chapter 19

As she entered the house, Tess couldn't have been more delighted with what she saw before her; the Delaneys' style was like something she'd seen in American property shows on television back in England. If she was correct in her thinking, this was more akin to a New England style of décor, lots of white painted wood, natural oak beams and half-paneled walls in matte white beadboard. The furniture too was organic in style and comfortable looking, big sofas and armchairs that looked like they weren't on show, more aimed toward comfort than style. The artwork that graced the chalk white walls was stylish too, unframed canvasses of oceanscapes and abstracts of dazzling colors and flamboyant designs.

"Tess, let me introduce you to my better half, this is Summer, my long-suffering wife," Jake announced.

The woman who now stood in front of Tess, was according to her calculations, just shy of fifty years old. But the tanned and obviously natural blonde Mrs. Delaney, looked like a thirty year old who'd just stepped off the beach. This was the original Beach Boys California Girl.

She's a babe...

"Mrs. Delaney, it really is so nice to meet you, Jake has told me so much about you," said Tess, "And your home is just... well, it's just gorgeous!"

"You're so sweet, Tess, thank you, but you must call me Summer," said the petite and strikingly pretty woman, "Now, what can I get you? Would you like something alcoholic or just a refreshing iced tea or maybe a pink lemonade?"

"I brought some wine," said Tess, handing Summer a bottle that she'd snagged from Nathan at the hotel's bar, "I hope that's okay?"

"Cakebread! My favorite!" exclaimed Summer, "Jake buys this for me on special occasions, let me put it in the cooler to chill. Would you like a nice cheap glass of local Chardonnay while you wait?" she laughed.

"Thank you, yes please," replied Tess, grateful that Nathan's choice of wine had been appropriate.

"Come on through to the lounge, Tess," said Jake, "The view is pretty nice from there."

Tess was astounded when she first caught sight of the floor to ceiling view of the Pacific as she entered the lounge, stepping down two steps into a magnificent great room. A large circular fireplace with a round extractor hood that looked like an inverted stainless steel funnel, occupied the center of the room, a nest of mismatched lazy armchairs surrounding it.

"Wow, this must be worth a fortune!" she said, "How does anyone afford a place like this?"

"More through luck than judgment in my case, Tess, but it's probably not as expensive as you think."

"Could have fooled me," Tess replied, "This is like something out of a film."

"Well, if this home was near where you're staying, you'd be looking at around fifteen mil because down there, it's so much closer to the city and therefore commutable. But up here, I guess it's probably worth around three million, give or take, maybe four."

"That's still a lot of money though."

"But we didn't pay that much. We used to live up in Avila Beach which is around two hundred miles north of here and we decided to sell that house once Summer and I got married because our kids were living in L.A. And we just wanted to be closer to them, and really I suppose, just start again with a fresh page. From memory, we paid just under a million five, around six or seven years ago."

"It was a bargain!" she said, "Would you ever move again?"

"Not if I can help it," said Jake, "They can bury me here when I'm gone!"

"You're not going anywhere, Jake Delaney," said Summer, as she came into the room carrying a tray with three wine glasses and a bottle of white wine, "Don't even think about it. Mind you, Tess, I told Jake this morning that if I ever get Alzheimer's, I'd want him to put me in a home."

"That's the fifth time you've said that today, Sum!" Jake replied, his wife immediately squealing in fits of laughter at his joke.

Crikey, it's like Fifty First Dates with these two…

Tess laughed, easily consumed by the passion and love that still existed between the pair, reminding her of her own mother and stepdad.

"Please, Tess, sit down and make yourself at home," Summer urged, as she opened the glass doors of the lounge, bringing in a welcome breath of cooling ocean air.

"I'm so sorry to hear about your father, it must have come as an enormous shock to you," Summer continued, "I lost my own parents in a tragic auto accident so I feel your pain."

"Thank you, and I'm so sorry to hear that. It must have been awful?" said Tess.

"It was, but it was a very long time ago now and everything eventually heals, given time."

"I suppose that even though I barely knew Dad, it's been difficult trying to come to terms with everything. I'm only just beginning to find out how much I meant to him and how he had followed my growth throughout my entire life."

"I was chatting to Sammy yesterday too," said Jake, "He sends his deepest apologies because he was singing that *M.A.S.H.* theme song the other day when you drove past Malibu Creek State Park, you know, the "Suicide Is Painless" song and he now understands how inappropriate it was. He also realized you didn't have a clue what he was talking about during the journey!"

"He wasn't to know, Jake, and he's such a lovely guy. It really didn't bother me one bit," Tess replied, "Anyway, what is M.A.S.H.? I still don't know!"

"It's a US television show that aired long before you were born, so don't even concern yourself," replied Jake.

"Well, let's drink to your being here in California, Tess, and once again, I am so pleased to finally meet you after all I've heard in the past from chatting with your dad," said Summer, "And from his description of his beautiful daughter, he didn't do you justice. You remind me in many ways of my own girls."

~

Summer had prepared a simple but delicious meal for them, and they sat down at an unusual table that seemed to have been made as a personal and loving homage to redwood. She also noticed that the table was set for six, but there was only the three of them sitting down, with Summer at the head of the table, Jake and Tess flanking her on either side.

"Stunning table," said Tess, "Where did you find it?"

"This is Jake's one and only attempt at carpentry," said Summer, "And hopefully, probably his last."

Jake added, "We were up in Napa a couple of years back and we stumbled on a wood yard, mostly turning out redwood logs for furniture manufacturers. Anyway, I was deeply enamored with the look and the smell of the wood so I bought three or four pretty large pieces because I suddenly had a yearning to build a table. We rented a pickup truck and drove them back, and I spent the next nine months on weekends, sawing, planing and sanding until I finally had what I wanted."

Chick magnet, wood connoisseur…

"I'm impressed, lawyer by day, carpenter by night!" said Tess, "But it is beautiful."

"You see?" said Jake, turning to Summer, "Someone appreciates my talents."

"You know I appreciate all your talents, Jake, but let's be honest, if you were a carpenter, we'd die of hunger!"

The trio laughed at this and Tess felt more and more comfortable in their company.

"So tell me how you met," said Tess, "Is it one of those great love stories?"

"How long have you got?" asked Jake.

"Oh really?" said Tess, "I'm all ears!"

"How about the short version, Sum?" Jake asked his wife, "We might bore her senseless if we give the unabridged version."

Summer laughed, her love for her husband clear for anyone to see, and the feeling was obviously mutual from Jake toward his wife.

"Well," Summer began, "I first met Jake when I was sixteen in Florida. The problem was that he was almost twenty-four."

So not a Californian girl, after all…

"Blimey!" said Tess, "Sorry! English expression. It means… Good Lord, or something like that anyway."

Summer giggled at Tess's explanation, "But the truth is, I fell in love with him the moment I saw him."

Who wouldn't?

"And I with her, I might add," said Jake.

Ditto…

"But this was in the early 80s and the age difference was non-negotiable at that time, so we waited."

Didn't bother Woody Allen or Elvis Presley…

"And then you got married when you were eighteen?" asked Tess.

"Err… no, if only it had been that simple," added Jake.

"When I turned eighteen in the summer of '86, Jake and I finally became an item," Summer continued, "We spent two glorious and memorable months together in New York and Florida, barely apart except for when Jake had to work."

"Wow, this is like a Nicholas Sparks novel," said Tess.

"Kind of, but then it all came crashing down," said Summer, "We both knew that we would spend so much time apart in the future as I was due to go off to college at the end of the summer, and Jake was pursuing a career as a lawyer, but we tried to spend as much of our time together as we could."

"But a couple of months before that," added Jake, "I made a mistake or rather, I think I was date raped."

What??

Tess laughed but suddenly realized that Jake was being serious, "What happened?" she asked.

"I had had an on and off relationship with a girl I'd met in Florida. Her name was Tara, and she came from one of the wealthiest families in the country, the Fitzgeralds. She was a beautiful girl and a lovely person, but she just wasn't for me. You can't fall in love with someone just because they're beautiful," he said.

I haven't had that opportunity yet, but go on…

"I took her out on what I hoped was our final date together, at the end of which I had planned on telling her that we had no future as a couple and that I was in love with Summer. The evening went well, but I have no recollection of what happened once we arrived back at her hotel until I woke up the following morning."

"If this wasn't sad it would be funny," Summer added.

"And then one day, a few months later, Tara called me, by which time Summer was already in college. Tara was pregnant, with our child," said Jake.

"Jeez!" exclaimed Tess, "This really is Nick Sparks!"

"So, Jake did the right thing," said Summer, "As they say over here, he put a ring on it."

"Yep, I offered to marry Tara, be the father to our child and pretty much immediately after we'd tied the knot, her father shipped us out to California so that we wouldn't embarrass the family."

"But," said Summer, "During the summer that Jake and I had spent together, I had become pregnant myself."

"I can't believe this, are you making this up?!!"

"Seriously, Tess, you couldn't write this if you wanted to," Jake replied.

"My parents were furious," said Summer, "They wouldn't even utter Jake's name because of what they thought he'd done. You know, knocked up an eighteen year old and then gone off and married someone else in California."

"But the truth was, I had no idea that Sum was pregnant," said Jake, "And I was still in love with her. Never fell out of love," he said, smiling at his wife.

"So what happened?" asked Tess.

"It's difficult keeping the story short but I'll try," said Jake.

Summer began dishing up grilled shrimp and lobster on a bed of couscous and diced tomatoes to each of their plates as Jake continued with the story.

"While I disappeared off to California, a new wife and an unborn baby in tow, and then opened a fledgling law office in San Luis Obispo, Summer began college, knowing that at some point she would be unable to continue once she was close to giving birth. In fact, as soon as Summer left for college, she went radio-silent on me and I became depressed thinking that she must have met someone else in school. Our daughter, Poppy was born in the spring of 1987, although sadly, I knew nothing about it. My daughter Lily was born to Tara a couple of months later in California."

"You have to understand, Tess, that this was quite some time ago when unwed mothers were frowned upon," added Summer, "So as far as my parents were concerned, they would help me raise Poppy at the beginning, but they expected me to be married at some point."

"So what happened next?" asked Tess, now eager to hear how the story turned out, "This is delicious by the way, Summer, really yummy."

"Awww, you're so sweet!" said Summer, feeling inexplicably drawn to this girl who'd popped up in their life.

"Summer met a guy at college, a couple or three years older than her, graduating that year," said Jake.

"He seemed like a good guy too," said Summer, "And he was ambitious, wanted to be a dentist, have his own practice and everything."

"So did you fall in love all over again?" Tess asked.

"No. No, I didn't," Summer replied, "I only ever fell in love with one man, but James Larsen seemed like a pretty stable guy and he fell in love with me, knowing I was pregnant. What could I do?"

"What a situation to find yourself in," said Tess, "In love with someone else who had no idea you were pregnant with their child, and then marrying someone you were never in love with? How did you cope? Did you tell Jake anything?"

"I didn't. My parents forbade me. They said that they would support me but I was to have nothing to do with Jake ever again. I was heartbroken. I didn't even know where Jake was; remember that this was all before the internet was born. Even emails and texting didn't exist back then."

"I was heartbroken too," added Jake, "I'd spent one glorious summer with the only girl I'd ever loved and then she just vanished out of my life forever."

"What happened to Tara, your first wife?" asked Tess.

"And that's where it really gets sad," Jake replied, "A couple of years after Lily was born, Tara gave birth to our son, Tom. But Tom never met his mom. Tara died during childbirth. It was such a terrible time."

If this was a movie, I'd have to leave right now and sob my eyes out...

"Oh my God, Jake, I can't believe this, look at me, I'm crying!" said Tess, dabbing at her eyes with her napkin.

103

"Have some more wine, sweetie," said Summer, "It always makes things seem much better," she added, pouring Tess and herself a couple of healthy refills before passing the bottle to Jake to replace.

As Jake went off to the kitchen in search of more wine, Summer continued the story.

"After he had completed dental school, James and I moved from Florida to Tennessee where he found a position as a partner with a local orthodontist. We made a home, James learned his craft and we added to our family with the birth of our son, Casey."

"But you were never in love with him," said Tess.

"No, I wasn't. In fact, over the years, I realized what a sexist and misogynistic man he was. And he had a terrible temper."

"So Jake is in California, raising two children on his own, running a small law firm, while you're in Tennessee, in an unhappy marriage, raising two children, one of which is Jake's?"

"I told you it was complicated," laughed Summer.

So Jake never met or married anyone else. If he'd never found Summer again, he would literally have died of a broken heart... Oh. My. God...

"But I don't understand how you would find each other again when you were two thousand miles away in Tennessee?"

"The power of the internet and social media," explained Summer, "Jake found me online and we slowly rediscovered and rekindled our love for each other."

"Caramba!" said Tess, "You're right, you couldn't make this up!"

"My own marriage had become increasingly violent and in the end, with Jake's support, I escaped it with my kids."

"I'm so sorry, Summer, it must have been awful," said Tess.

"It was, but I don't regret anything, I finally got my man, we got married, we were blessed with four children between us and we were finally both so happy," said Summer.

"And I got the girl of my dreams," added Jake, returning to the table and uncorking the Cakebread, "And a wonderful stepson in the process, not to mention another lovely daughter."

"Oh Lord!" said a voice from the front of the house, "I must have heard this story a thousand times."

"And you'll hear it a thousand times more, Tom!" said Summer, as a tall and ruggedly handsome Jake-lookalike came ambling into the dining area.

"This young man, Tess, is my wonderful inherited son, Tom," Summer announced, as the young man lifted her off the floor and cuddled her.

"How are you Mom, miss me?"

"Always, sweetheart, you know that," she replied.

Tom was easily 6'2" in height, he was muscular and lean with a thick shock of dark and wavy hair, much like his father would have had at that age. His eyes, which were almost a green gold color, made his face uniquely striking and compelling.

"Hey Pops," he said to Jake, "Who's this you're boring rigid?"

"Hi Tom," Jake replied, his love of his son so easy to see, "This is Tess, Robert Valentine's daughter. I've told you about her before, remember?"

Tess was unable to take her eyes off the man, she felt giddy and embarrassed all at the same time.

"Sorry Tess, I do know who you are, of course, I'm really sorry to hear about your dad," said Tom, taking her hand and gently squeezing it, "He was a wonderful friend to our family and we miss him."

"It's okay, Tom, I'm getting through the worst of it now but it's so nice to meet you and put a face to the name," she said, squeezing his hand in return as she spoke.

"Well, I hope you won't be a stranger, would be nice to get to know Bobby's daughter, he talked of you often over the years."

Chapter 20

After dinner, they adjourned to the great room where Summer had prepared some petits-fours along with a tray of Amaretto and cappuccinos. The sun had almost set over the horizon but Tess could still see and hear the ocean's waves lapping up on the beach just yards from the house.

The group had increased in size now with the arrival of Lily and Poppy, the Delaneys' two daughters. From the conversation over dinner, Tess deduced that the two girls must be of similar age, perhaps twenty-nine, almost thirty years old. But they didn't seem that much older, more like Tess's own age, so she felt comfortable chatting to them.

Poppy was the image of her mother, a mini-me if you like, although somewhat taller. Tess guessed she was her own height, around 5'8". She had the same hair as Summer, an almost white blonde mane that cascaded down her back. But her eyes were what really held your gaze, the deepest liquid brown, almost the color of hot chocolate, just like Jake's.

Lily, on the other hand was similar in looks to Poppy, but must have shared more of her genes from her mother, Tara. Long, thick, straight hair, appearing as if it had been spun from gold. Her green catlike eyes were uniquely attractive as was her slim and athletic form.

Jeez, is everyone this beautiful in California?

"Don't you have another son too? Tess asked Jake, I noticed six place settings at the table."

"We do, his name's Casey but sadly for all of us, he's over on the east coast getting his coaching badges so we don't get to see a lot of him at the moment, Jake replied, "But I'm hoping that's just temporary."

"Coaching badges?"

"Yes, believe it or not, he wants to be a soccer coach!" Jake replied, "Which I'm more than happy about, because although Casey wouldn't have ever known about it until after he'd got hooked on the game at college, it's what I played at high school and college. I love it! And Tom played soccer at college too so we're a bit of a soccer family."

"Oh, football… right."

"I'm up every Saturday morning at seven to watch one of the live games from the English Premiership, I wouldn't miss it for the world. I'm a Manchester United fan!"

"That's a shame," Tess replied, "Never mind."

Jake laughed when he realized that Tess was messing with him, really enjoying this entrancing English girl's wit.

"I didn't ask you, Summer, if you had found time for a career, what with raising children and everything. I know what Jake does for a living but I couldn't imagine you'd ever want to leave this house and go to a job each day," said Tess.

"Oh, nothing like a career, Tess. But I've been making my own jewelry designs since my early twenties and I still really enjoy it," she replied, "Although nowadays I have a small store down at Malibu Village."

"Isn't that expensive real estate?" asked Tess.

"It is, but I was fortunate. When we moved down here at the end of 2011, California was still suffering enormously from the recession caused by the sub-prime mortgage fiasco of 2008. And Jake was able to secure a long-term lease on a store for next to nothing so we really got lucky."

I need some of this luck...

"You should come by one day, it's only a stone's throw from your hotel," Summer continued. "It's called The Sea Glass."

"Cute name," Tess replied, "I'd like that, and I promise I will. Thank you."

"How long do you think you'll be staying?" asked Lily, "Do you have to get back to London for work?"

"I do. The timing couldn't have been worse. I've only been with my company a fairly short time but they've said I can stay here as long as I need to. I just don't think that extends beyond a couple of weeks, or maybe less," Tess replied, feeling a little under the microscope as the group sat around the fire-pit, mainly focused on her.

"You could always come back," offered Tom, "I'm sure Mom and Dad would love to have you stay here."

"It might be a full house with one more!" Tess said.

"Oh, none of us live here anymore," Poppy added, "We just like to come back for free food every now and then."

"Anyway," said Lily, "It's impossible to live with these two now, they're like honeymooners on Groundhog Day. It's soooooo annoying."

Everyone laughed at this but their children were right about Jake and Summer, they really did seem like teenagers in love.

"Well, I know you have to go back at some point," said Jake, "But knowing that you wouldn't want to stay at your dad's place, I think I may have an idea for where you might like to stay through the winter."

"If she comes back, Dad!" said Tom, "She might not want to."

"Talking of going back, I think it's time I went back to the hotel, I'm in danger of overstaying my welcome here!" said Tess, realizing that it had suddenly become quite late in the evening.

"You can stay for as long as you like," said Summer, "But you're probably tired now anyway. I'll get Tom to drop you off."

"No, please, I wouldn't dream of putting him out, I can get a taxi," said Tess, "I'm sure he doesn't want to go back out this late at night."

"That's me, Uber Tom! Come on Tess, it's fine and I'm driving past your hotel on the way home anyway, it would be my pleasure."

Chapter 21

The drive back south to The Surfrider was more than pleasant. Tom owned a restored Ford Bronco. It was pale green with white faux-leather interior, and it had neither roof nor doors but thankfully, it had been fitted with safety belts and a roll cage. It was perfect for the journey as it was such a wonderfully warm evening.

Tess was surprised that Tom had chosen this car, but once they were strapped in, she saw that it really suited his character. In fact, the car really seemed to suit him in so many ways. It wasn't ostentatious, or a muscle car, or flashy like a Porsche. The old Ford was just nicely understated and a lot of fun. Much like Tom, she guessed.

"What made you buy a car like this, Tom?" she asked, "Are you a 'surfer dude'? giggling as she said it.

"No! Not at all! I can barely swim!" he replied, laughing, "It's just that my Mom had one, actually it was the first car she ever had. Given to her by her parents on her seventeenth birthday, I think."

"Oh, right, so sentimental value, then?"

"Not really. She had a terrible accident once when she was running from her husband, and the cops said that it was only the fact that the Bronco was so strong and sturdy that she hadn't died in the wreck," he replied, "And I figured if it was that safe then it would do for me so I bought one just like it. But I did the restoration myself over a period of two years."

Tess enjoyed the fact that he referred to Summer as his mother, it made him appear even more attractive in her eyes, if he wasn't already attractive enough.

"I'm glad she came through it okay, Tom, your mum is really lovely. Your dad too."

"Yeah, I'm a really lucky guy, I lucked out with those two."

Twenty minutes later, when Tom pulled the Bronco into the hotel's driveway, he jumped out and ran around to the passenger side to help Tess out of the truck.

"You're such a gentleman, Tom, I'm so not used to this!" she said, taking his proffered hand as she climbed out of the vehicle.

"Maybe it's something you *should* get used to," he replied, "And I hope I see you again before you leave, so I can prove that us Americans can be just as well-mannered as your boys back home."

Tess momentarily flashed back to occasions when she'd been out with Simon, realizing that she couldn't recall him ever opening a door for her or helping her out of a car.

"They're not all gentlemen, Tom, believe me," she replied, "But I hope we'll meet again."

~

The Camry had followed Tom's Bronco at a respectable distance as soon as they had left Jake's house. Buchanan was nothing if not patient. He watched from the safety of the grass verge outside the hotel entrance as the two said goodnight to each other.

New boyfriend, Tess? Well you get around don't you, pretty lady? Gonna run out of tracking devices if you keep this fucking game up...

Chapter 22

Frank Buchanan lived a double life. Well, what else would The Watcher do? He could hardly brag about his occupation to Ted and Phyllis next door. His wife had no idea what he did for a job in reality. She thought he worked in insurance, which in Buchanan's mind, wasn't too far from the truth. Well, kinda. The irony of it was that he actually used to work in insurance, a proper nine to five job but he soon tired of it. Too fucking boring for Frank Buchanan, man of action.

Buchanan had wanted to be a Navy SEAL when he left college but he couldn't swim. He'd failed to take that into consideration on his application. And he was too short and not particularly seal-like in his physique. He opted instead for the Navy's Marine Corps but realized fairly quickly, that any aspiration he had of rising through the ranks was ultimately limited by the fact that he'd never graduated with a degree from college. In their eyes, he'd always be a common little grunt who'd probably never even get his sergeant's stripes. But he proved them wrong.

He became a specialist marksman, discovering a natural ability and affinity with practically every type of firearm he came across, vaulting to the rank of gunnery-sergeant in just a few years. But he realized that even with the extra money he was making from selling ammo and gun parts he'd stolen from the ASP, the Ammunition Supply Point on the base, there was no real future for him, no big pensioned retirement at the end of his career.

And then he'd met his new boss, a loan shark out of east L.A., an old-fashioned gangland shyster, who went by the name of Mickey Carlisle. Carlisle had become aware of Buchanan's weapons mastery and offered him a job working for him. Better money, more excitement, Frank couldn't turn it down. Carlisle set the policy premiums, Buchanan collected the monthly nut. Sometimes Buchanan ended the policies too, which had turned out to be occasionally beneficial to him personally. Sometimes he was forced to foreclose but not in the traditional sense of the word. Better dead than… well, better dead.

At first, his wife, Maisie, had begun asking why he often brought home a different car. She knew the Camry was his work car although she hated the thing. It was the first of five Camrys that her husband had bought during their marriage. All in that shitty beige color. Made it look to the neighbors as though they couldn't afford a decent car. And it always stank of fast food and other strange smells.

A couple of years back, Buchanan had built a car barn at the rear of the property, such was his growing collection of vintage automobiles that needed housing or hiding away. He'd told Maisie that the cars were 'repos', repossessed from owners who hadn't made their monthly payments, and he had a personal 'in' with the guys at the insurance companies. For some unknown reason, she believed him, but she still hated that fucking Camry. Sometimes on a Sunday, they would take out one of Frank's repos for a drive through the countryside and she enjoyed that, so she gave the Camry a pass.

Frank and Maisie had never had kids, weren't able to, although Buchanan thought it was a blessing in disguise. He would have hated having a couple of little monsters running around the place, getting into everything. And he needed his peace and quiet when he got home. More so than ever now.

But the odd thing about Frank Buchanan was that he loved his wife. She was about the only person he did love. She never pried

116

into his life, was always in the kitchen making something delicious for them, made sure his shirts were ironed and kept the house looking nice. She worked too, downtown in Ojai at a travel agent. Icing on the cake.

But when they first began to try for kids, something Buchanan reluctantly agreed to, just to placate Maisie, it hadn't worked so they'd gone to see the doctor. The doc sent them to a clinic and they had tests and were told to wait for the results which would take a month or so. When the test results finally arrived in the mail, it turned out that Buchanan was firing blanks but there was nothing wrong with Maisie.

Instead of sharing the report with Maisie, he tossed it on the fire and told his wife that he'd received a phone call from the clinic and that sadly, she was barren. Kids were never gonna happen. Fortunately for him, she always took his word on everything and never followed up with the clinic. Buchanan then called the clinic without telling Maisie and said that they had decided against other routes like IVF or surrogacy or adoption, but thanked them for their time and effort.

Dodged a fucking bullet there…

The Buchanan house was nothing extraordinary, just a plain three bed, two bath ranch home on around an acre of land. Buchanan didn't dislike where they lived in sleepy, rural Ojai. In fact, he really quite enjoyed it, although the constant treks driving out to the Los Angeles coastal region was beginning to piss him off. It was fine when he first began working for Mickey Carlisle almost thirty years ago but recently the whole thing had gotten a bit old.

And what Mickey had gotten away with decades ago, was no longer really happening in today's world. When people wanted to borrow money to start a business now, they went to their local Wells Fargo or Chase bank and took out low interest loans. Robert Valentine had been an easy mark back in the day, like so many of

117

the fucking hippies that wanted to start up new business ventures in California but those days were long gone.

And Valentine was a stupid fucking English prick, and he was even more naïve than the rest of them so he was an even easier target. Collecting on his two hundred and forty percent interest loan had been like taking candy from a baby. Until it wasn't.

But Mickey's client list of people who would take his cash for twenty percent a month interest was growing shorter each year and Buchanan knew it, even before Mickey had finally cottoned on. The easy pickings, quick money, loan shark days seemed to be coming to an abrupt end after all these years and Buchanan was growing restless.

Might be time to get out of this business and try insurance again...

Chapter 23

Tess had expected the phone call. She'd been out in California for almost a week now and she knew she couldn't push her luck. Her company had called and asked when she might be returning to work. No pressure, they'd said but she knew it meant the opposite.

She'd called Jake that morning and asked if he could book a return flight for Saturday, knowing that at least she'd have most of Sunday, the following day after she got back to England, to recover from the jet lag before she caught the train into London and got back to the grind.

God it's going to be pretty much winter when I get back, my timing sucks…

Jake seemed sad when she told him she had to return but he promised to organize the ticket for her. Actually, Tess was more than sad that she was going home, much as she loved it in England; it was just that she had begun to enjoy her time here. She'd met so many nice people in such a short space of time, and she wasn't quite ready to leave yet. And there was Tom too. Although she guessed that he probably already had a girlfriend. No, strike that, lots of girlfriends. It reminded her of a silly joke she had once heard, and in the privacy of her own mind, she made it into a joke of her own.

"I've come for the job of being Tom Delaney's girlfriend"

"You'll need to go to Vancouver for that."

"But Vancouver's in Canada and Tom lives in California!"

"Yeah, that's where the queue ends..."

The knock at her door shook Tess from her thoughts.

"Thought you'd like some tea, love," said Nathan as she opened the door to see her new best friend standing purposefully with a tray balanced on one hand.

"You must have read my mind!" she replied, "Hope you've got two cups."

"I took that liberty, ma'am," he said, placing the tray on the coffee table and setting out the cups and saucers.

Tess was still kicking herself. How could she have not known Nathan was gay? Had he become more overtly gay over the few days she'd known him or had she just not seen it because she was still getting over Simon, and any true kindness shown by a good looking man was a welcome breath of fresh air?

"I brought scones and jam too," said Nathan, "I know you English love those things!"

If only you liked girls!

They sat back on the sofa, with Tess bringing him up to speed on what she'd been doing over the weekend. She told him about her dinner invitation to the Delaneys and the almost unbelievable story of how Jake and Summer had found and then rediscovered each other.

"Sounds like a real-life love story," said Nathan," and by the way, I know her store down in the village, you know, The Sea Glass?"

"What's it like, I bet it's super expensive, too rich for this girl's taste?" asked Tess, her mouth full of scone.

"Well, definitely too rich for *this* girl's taste," Nathan replied, "But it's a cool store, kind of unusual, bohemian really. Like a twenty-first-century hippy place but I like it. I met her once when I was there with my then boyfriend. And Summer, she's super sweet."

"I need to pop in and say hi," said Tess, "I liked her very much too and I might be able to find something to take home with me as a memento of this trip."

"I'll come with you, if you like," he said, "Oh and by the way, you had a delivery this morning, it's downstairs."

"Really, what is it? A package or something?"

"No, love, it's a car."

~

Tess was overwhelmed by the sight of the classic antique automobile sitting in a parking spot in front of the hotel. Her father's Mustang shone brilliantly like a polished emerald.

Jake had been a man of his word and had had his friend collect it, check it over and had then had it valeted and polished before delivering it to her.

"What did the guy say about it when he dropped it off?" she asked Nathan, who had already opened it up and sat gazing lovingly at the interior from the driver's seat.

"He said there was nothing much that needed doing. He changed the oil, fluids and filters, checked the brakes and lights were all working okay and put some air in the tires. It was pretty much good to go already."

Learning so much about you, Dad…

"I've never driven in the US," said Tess, "I'm more than a little apprehensive."

"There's nothing to it!" said Nathan, "The steering wheel is on the other side, we drive on the right and when you come to a roundabout, make sure you go counter-clockwise instead of clockwise. That's all there is to it."

"Hmm... if you say so... listen, are you down for coming out for a drive with me? It'd be nice to have someone with me who's experienced at driving on the right-hand side before I venture out on my own."

"I can't right now but I get off at three, would that work?" Nathan replied.

"I can wait, besides there are two more scones to be eaten..."

Chapter 24

Tess and Nathan had spent that afternoon driving north on the PCH, stopping at a couple of the beaches along the way, and taking an early dinner at a restaurant he knew whose menu was inexpensive, but delicious.

For Tess, her initial apprehension at driving in the US was fairly quickly forgotten as she drove her father's pride and joy with ease, enjoying the instant power when she changed down on the stick shift. Slowly, bit by bit, she was beginning to really understand him, to actually know him and discover what made him tick, because the same things were having an identical effect on her.

She was experiencing a crazy mixture of emotions. On one hand, she was angry that she hadn't really known her father in life, and had only finally discovered him in death, and on the other hand, she was excited about every new thing she found out about the man. She felt anger at her mother that she had somehow deprived Tess of her real father, but on the other hand, she felt grateful for the love her mother had heaped on her, and of course, from Franco too.

And finally, she was so happy to be experiencing life here in Malibu where her father had made his home, but incredibly sad that in just a few days she would be leaving to go back to England. It wasn't that she didn't enjoy her job, she did. And it wasn't that she didn't love England, she had a wonderful life there. She just felt there was so much yet to discover and the clock was ticking faster.

I just wish I had a little more time, Dad...

Chapter 25

Having returned to The Surfrider after her road trip with Nathan, Tess had once again laid down on her bed in the hotel room and rummaged through the endless files on her father's laptop. There was little of interest, save for the photos he'd kept in a file marked, *Photos for Tess*, which she'd downloaded to her iPhone.

These photos were almost like a timeline, a pictorial story of his time in California. She noticed a number of them showed him standing next to another man, a surfboard planted in the sand between the two. She had assumed that her father must have taken up the sport soon after he'd arrived here, although her mom had told her that he was afraid of the water which seemed odd.

The man that stood to the other side of the surfboard in the photos, and there were many similar photos with just the two men and the same board on different beaches, was quite a bit taller than her father. She guessed that he was maybe six-five compared to her father who was maybe six-one, and the man was lean and tanned with white blond hair. And he looked like a real surfer whereas, really and truly, her father didn't. It suddenly dawned on her that there were no photos of her father with women, just lots of shots with this other guy. She began to wonder if he might have been gay. It would certainly explain the many photos of him with the mystery man.

The only file inside the folder that was a little obscure, contained just one document; a square of letters that meant nothing to her at the moment, almost like some kind of ancient cryptogram.

```
AAZHBOYMCEXIDSWWEHVEFRUE
GTTHHESHIERAJRQTKIPSLAONM
DNDNEMEOPLBPEKLQOJWRWIHS
EHRTEGTUHFEVREAWTDTXLCEY
SBNZAAKAEZSBRYOCAXMDHWIE
DVEFSUAGGTIHFSTITRHJAQTKIP
GLIOVMENTNOMYOOLUPIKLQOJ
VREIYSOHUTTGEUSFSVDEAWDD
```

She stared at it like one of those puzzles where you have to spot the hidden word. Facebook was full of them these days, clickbait to grab your personal information. But the square of letters really made no sense to her whatsoever. She was completely baffled. The best she could come up with was, 'boy' 'kips' 'hut' and 'my' but that didn't mean anything. There had to be much more to it than finding a few obscure words. There had to be some sort of secret message.

She opened up an internet page and did a search for 'code breaking' but there were so many sites that it became even more confusing. She tried copying and pasting the text into four or five of the programs, but still nothing made sense to her. She looked up 'cryptograms' and was so inundated with thousands of websites, that she didn't know where to start.

And truthfully, this could just be some bit of fun her dad was playing, entirely for his own amusement, that had no importance at all to anything or anyone else. Maybe he was into crosswords and codes and things and was experimenting by making up one of his own. She'd seen a couple of Dan Brown novels on his bookshelf which coincidentally, she'd also read. They were full of secret codes and ancient cryptograms that were far too difficult for the layman to solve.

But even as she downloaded the cryptogram square to her phone for safekeeping, she knew in her heart that it had to be something important. The one thing she was learning about Robert Valentine was that he never seemed to do anything without a reason. There had to be purpose and meaning. And she was pretty sure the puzzle was for her eyes only. Even the font he'd used looked vaguely familiar, although she didn't know its name. But she needed a clear head to find out what was in the cryptic message and she probably needed help too.

Could take weeks, months, years even...

Abandoning it for now, she decided to have an early night with plans to set off the following morning, Tuesday, to make a return visit to Malibu Village and hopefully meet up with Summer at her store.

The Sea Glass, interesting name...

Chapter 26

He watched as the Highland Green Shelby Mustang entered the village and parked away from the other cars on the northeast side. The car was unmistakable, Robert Valentine's love of the Steve McQueen movie, *Bullitt*, was well known amongst the Malibu locals, as was the movie's unique car. And *The Great Escape*, often considered one of McQueen's best films, was a firm favorite of Robert Valentine's. Hell, he was a Steve McQueen nut, never used to stop yakking about him.

He sat on the small terrace outside Starbucks and watched the girl make her way from the kiddie park area toward the main square. She was in no hurry, and he sensed that as she walked, she took in everything around her, colors, smells, snatches of conversation and people's actions and reactions. She looked strikingly pretty and blended in perfectly with the locals, saying hi to people as she passed them.

Must be an English thing...

She walked right past him, so close he could almost have touched her but he could smell her eau de cologne as she wafted past. He had assumed that she wouldn't even notice him sitting there, an old man with a weather-beaten face in grubby clothes, sporting a silvery and white, shaggy seaman's beard and long silver-gray hair under a corduroy cap. But she did notice him. Just a casual glance and the hint of a smile as she ambled past.

How about that?

He continued to watch as she headed toward the southwest corner of the plaza, realizing that the girl was methodical in what she did. She wanted to appraise each store and not miss any of them, starting at the beginning and ticking them off as she continued her circuit in a precise order.

A creature of habit...

She stopped briefly at the Marmalade Café and appeared to be looking at the menu pasted on the window, probably wondering how far her vacation budget would take her. She even took a photograph of it on her phone, perhaps to study later.

As she walked further around the plaza square, he temporarily lost sight of her, so he quickly walked around to the front of Starbucks and padded along the decking until he arrived at Malibu Kitchen & Gourmet which was an organic style café with some pleasant outdoor tables. But more importantly, the café's location gave him a clear and uninterrupted view of the girl's progress.

She stopped at a store called lululemon and he took the opportunity to dash inside the café to purchase a coffee in order to secure a table outside. He may be old, but he knew that any young girls who went into that store would be inside for at least twenty minutes, if not longer. And he could hardly just sit at a café table without having purchased anything. They arrest you for that in Malibu.

But even now, after all these years, it always amused him whenever he entered any of the 'chichi' stores in the village, the looks of horror on the faces of the new servers or store assistants. The ones who had been working there for a few years or more, recognized him and greeted him with respect and humility but the newbies, well, they looked like they wanted to run a mile. He understood though, his general appearance was not very Malibu. Actually, his general appearance was just not particularly social, almost anti-social.

Sipping his coffee at one of the patio tables, the latest cup already his third caffeine fix of the morning, he once again watched the entrance of the lululemon store to see where Tess would go next. But it wasn't as if he had anywhere he needed to be, right? Heaven was still waiting.

Oddly, he had to wait a full forty-five minutes before she finally emerged, laden with three shopping bags. Either she had just fallen into some money, or her credit cards were taking a pounding. But he had to hand it to her, the girl could shop, and she was time efficient into the bargain.

As he followed her progress, he noticed other young girls, and also older women, who had adopted this new style of twenty-first-century dress. He had read about the clothing style and remembered it was called 'athleisure' or something like that. In his own mind, he thought it was just a bit too revealing and made all the ladies look the same. A bit like the women in the Stepford Wives movie. But who was he to talk? He was hardly Malibu's Most Eligible Bachelor.

Again, he continued to watch her progress as she circumnavigated the square, but this time she walked without hesitation, into a store called The Sea Glass. He knew who owned it, of course, and was unsurprised that the girl had made her way there. He would have been much more surprised if she hadn't.

Chapter 27

"Hi, can I help you with anything or are you happy just to browse?"

"Actually, I was wondering if Summer was in today?" Tess replied, dropping her bags of recent purchases onto the tiled floor, "I think I have the right place?"

"She's out back in the design studio, let me go and find her for you," replied the girl, "Can I say who's asking for her?"

"Tess," she replied, "Tess Valentine."

The store assistant left Tess waiting at the counter as she went off to find Summer out back.

"Hello you!" said Summer a few seconds later as she emerged from the rear of the store, "You found us!"

"I did, and I was a little naughty on the way," Tess replied, pointing to her shopping bags, "But I couldn't resist."

"I love that store, I'm in there way too often, or so Jake keeps on telling me," replied Summer, "But I dress in that style more and more these days, as does everyone else around here!" laughing as she suddenly realized that she and her assistant were dressed almost identically in black lululemon apparel.

"Me too, but it's so much cheaper here than in London," Tess replied.

She gazed around the place, noting the enormous crystal rocks and precious stones, set on tall pedestals that were clearly designed to be centerpieces in the homes of Malibu's rich and famous, and definitely not for the likes of Tess Valentine.

"I love your store, by the way," said Tess, "I was having a look around while I was waiting. I have a little cash that my Dad left me; do you think you have something in my price range, maybe some earrings or a pendant?"

"Actually I do, and we have a very special discount for our friends," Summer replied, "Come over here and see what you think of this."

Tess noticed that nothing in the store was locked away inside a display case, which in itself surprised her. There were clearly many valuable pieces here but everything was displayed artistically so that customers could see and touch and feel the jewelry and crystals, without needing to request that a display case be opened for them. She asked Summer why she opted for these open displays.

"It's simple really, it takes the pressure off the customer. Whenever I've been to a similar store before, which honestly is rare, if I have to ask for something to be unlocked from a glass case, I feel as though I'm almost obliged to buy it, it's way too pressurized," she explained, "And my stock is not terribly valuable so I would prefer that the customers have a more organic experience for themselves, find out if something is really meant for them. Silly, I suppose, but it's just my way of thinking."

"Actually, it makes a lot of sense. I can't tell you how pressurized I often feel in shops back in England, so I get it, I really do," Tess replied, as Summer took a piece from a mannequin.

"Now… this is what I had in mind for you from the first moment I laid eyes on you on Saturday evening," said Summer, her smile as infectious as her laugh.

"It's beautiful, really, really lovely," Tess said as Summer fastened the green sea glass necklace around her neck, "But even with a discount, I doubt this is in my price bracket."

"I've been making jewelry for almost thirty years, Tess, and I can let you into a little secret that the cost of making this isn't close to the retail price. And you remember I told you about that special discount for friends?" leaning in as she whispered in Tess's ear, "Well this is my gift to you."

"I... I... I couldn't accept it, Summer, I've only just met you!"

"But your father was almost family, Tess, and by extension as Jake always says, you're family now," she laughed, "Whether you like it or not!"

"I can't believe how kind you and Jake have been, thank you, thank you so much. I don't think I'll ever take it off!"

"You're so welcome. Now... are you hungry? I'm famished!"

~

After fifteen minutes or so, and having purchased his fourth coffee of the day so far, this time a macchiato, he watched as Tess emerged with the store's owner, and retraced her steps back toward where Tess had begun her shopping spree. It was almost lunchtime and his stomach was rumbling as he realized that he'd already over-caffeinated and he needed something to eat.

Should have brought some Pepto-Bismol with me...

But he didn't want to let the pair out of his sight until he saw where they were headed. After seeing them stop at the Marmalade Café and take a table outside, he realized they were having lunch together so he took the opportunity to quickly run inside the Kitchen

& Gourmet again to order their exceptional blackened Ahi tacos. Which he'd only ordered around a hundred times previously…

Chapter 28

Summer said that they should walk back toward the Marmalade Café because the lunch salads there were delicious. Having taken a seat at a table outside the restaurant, they sat and chatted, stopping for bites in between conversation, looking like two old friends or mom and daughter catching up, a clear frisson of mutual enjoyment building between the pair.

He thought to himself, having now seen the two women together for the first time, that they looked more like sisters than friends, although Summer was easily old enough to be Tess's mom. She just didn't look it.

Florida girl...

After maybe forty minutes had elapsed, Summer got up from the table and hugged and kissed Tess, clearly signaling that she was on a short lunch break and had to get back to the store. He immediately got up from his table and walked briskly across the square, but slowed his pace as he approached the restaurant. The Marmalade Café only had room for four tables on its limited-space patio, and he took the table furthest away from where Tess was sitting, where she was casually tapping out something on the screen of her iPhone.

A waiter pushed through the door and looked at the unkempt and apparently homeless man sitting at the only other occupied table.

"Can I get you anything, sir?" he asked, praying that the man would just get up and wander away.

"You can, son, I'd like my regular please, but I think you're new here so maybe you want to write this down," he replied, "It's a triple java cappuccino with a pinch of turmeric, three pinches of black pepper, a teaspoon of cinnamon and a half-teaspoon of ginger. Have you got that?"

"Yes sir, triple java, turmeric, ginger, cinnamon, no problem"

"Don't forget the black pepper. Oh, and one of those little biscotti biscuits on the side, if you don't mind?"

"Be right out," said the waiter, dashing back into the café, thinking that he'd give him the drink for free, if only he'd get the hell off the patio.

The man watched as the waiter scampered off back to the safety of the restaurant within. It was clear that the boy couldn't get away fast enough.

Another newbie... needs training...

He watched Tess from the corner of his eye as she rummaged for something in her bag. She glanced over at him, having retrieved a cologne bottle, applying one quick spray to her neck before stowing it back in the depths of the purse. His eyes were still eagle sharp, from spending many years on the ocean. He could read the label on the bottle from twelve feet away, *Jo Malone of London*.

Tess realized that he was casually glancing in her direction. She had seen the man before, quite recently. She remembered faces with an almost eidetic memory. It was as though as soon as she had seen someone, their image was instantly and photographically imprinted in her mind forever.

Starbucks, he was sitting outside of Starbucks...

The waiter returned, carrying a tray with a tall glass of dark and creamy cappuccino, a biscotti sitting to one side of the glass's saucer. He disappeared back inside the restaurant almost as quickly as he'd arrived.

138

He took a sip.

"Mmmm…"

"Looks good," said Tess, making polite conversation with the man. She hadn't liked how the waiter had looked at him, as though he had no right to be sitting at the table. She felt sorry for the old man. In her mind, no one had the right to pre-judge and dismiss people based solely on their appearance. She realized she was maybe a little naïve and that she was in an ever-decreasing group of people who enjoyed old-fashioned manners and courtesy. But it annoyed her how instantly-judgmental society had recently become, when a book was judged solely by its cover.

"It's unbeatable," he replied, "I have this every time I come to this place. A good friend of mine from back in the day, a really lovely girl, shared the recipe with me and I'll always be grateful to her for enlightening my caffeine addiction. That waiter's new; otherwise he'd have known what I always have. But he'll learn in time."

Tess laughed. It seemed the man didn't need her to defend him; he was clearly smarter than he appeared to most people he encountered.

"Well, I should be going," said Tess, "I'll remember that drink next time I'm here."

"You won't be disappointed," he replied, "That's a promise."

"Well, it's nice to meet you," she said, "My name's Tess, what's yours? I might bump into you here again, one day," she added, as she continued to get up from her seat.

"People who know me, call me Hippy Bill. And people who've known me longest… they call me the Malibu Hobo."

Chapter 29

Of course, Buchanan knew who the man was. Well, he didn't know his name but he just recognized him, mostly because he was so tall, and for a homeless dude, he looked pretty fit. He'd seen him walking around Malibu many times in the past. Mostly he walked barefoot too, probably because he couldn't afford a pair of shoes. There were plenty of these old geezers here, all living in cardboard boxes, never getting cold because of the climate, urinating on the sidewalks after they woke up, and then scaring the tourists for the rest of the day.

Fucker should be dead by now. I should put the cunt out of his misery...

He could almost hear Maisie chiding him for his bad language. "Frank! Do you have to use that word?"

Hey ho...

Buchanan had watched the man approach the Marmalade Café, almost stealthily, like he was on some kind of mission. Hadn't noticed him at first or where he came from, just that he'd casually selected a table close to where Tess was sitting.

The blonde had attracted Buchanan's attention too, she guessed it was Delaney's wife although he couldn't be sure.

So many girls, so little time...

He'd get to her later. Afterward.

But as he continued to watch the scene unfold, he was surprised by what he saw. The old fuck had ordered something from the waiter, a young kid who looked distressed about the hobo that was now sitting at one of his tables. Buchanan could only assume that the man had been panhandling somewhere in the village, and had begged enough dollar bills from the rich yuppies in the area to buy himself a cup of coffee.

But once the waiter had delivered some tall kind of coffee concoction to the man, Buchanan was astonished when the old bastard began to talk to Tess.

What the fuck could he have to talk about with her?

Chapter 30

Malibu Hobo?

Tess sat down again.

"And... it's nice to finally meet you too," the man added, getting up from his own chair and offering his hand to her.

Finally?

Tess noticed as he stretched to his full height that he was tall, 6'5' or more, and broad. As his coat opened, she realized that he probably carried no fat either; underneath his t-shirt, he looked muscular, lean.

She took his hand, noticing how gnarled and weather-beaten it was but also how immaculate his fingernails were, the white lunulae extending from neatly manicured cuticles. His grip was strong, but gentle too. As she felt his hand dwarf her own, she was aware of how hard and dark the skin was, as though he'd spent years in the sun. But the man had a lived-in face, one that could tell many stories and his smile was disarmingly sweet and tender.

"Pretty necklace."

"Pardon?" said Tess.

"Your necklace, it's a sea glass, no value, but very pretty."

"Thank you, it was just given to me as a gift by a friend."

"Summer's good at what she makes, she's got a very creative mind."

"Wait, you know her… you know Summer?"

"Have done for years, nice girl. Came out here from Tennessee a few years back. Bad marriage. Originally a Florida girl."

"I'm just visiting, a kind of vacation I suppose," Tess replied, amazed that the man knew Summer, "My father used to live around here. His name was Robert Valentine."

"I know. You're the spitting image of him."

"Wait… Wh… What?!! How do you know that? Did you know my father?"

"Finest man I ever knew."

"Wow! Such a small world. How did you meet him?" she asked, astonished that she was chatting to one of her father's old friends.

"Well, believe it or not, and I know my appearance might indicate otherwise, I used to be in business with your dad. That was before they started calling me Hippy Bill, and way before they called me the Malibu Hobo.

"Malibu Hobo… That seems a bit unfair."

"It's not really, Tess, more a term of endearment. You see, your father and I were business partners back in the day. He used to come down to the beach at Zuma and watch me and the other surfers riding the waves, although he wasn't a surfer himself. Claimed he was scared of the ocean. And, of course, he had this English accent which kinda stuck out from the crowd."

So he never lost his London accent…

"But your dad knew who I was. I'd won a number of state and national surfing championships and he admired my board, said that it gave me an edge," Bill explained, "He told me that I was the most gifted surfer out there, but I also had the best board. In fact, the truth was that I didn't have the cash to buy one of the super expensive boards the other guys had, so I made it myself but your dad saw something special in it."

"I had no idea my father was interested in surfing," said Tess, "What was his interest in your board?"

"Well, that's the thing, your dad was scared witless by the ocean, couldn't surf if his life depended on it. But he had a good eye, knew a good thing when he saw it, thought my board was a work of art.

"Yes, I'm just beginning to understand his appreciation of fine art and true quality," Tess replied, "He seems like he was an intelligent man."

"He was, really intelligent. More than. So he said he'd like to copy my board, build them and sell them as a business; you know, we should become business partners," Bill continued, "He said it was the hottest board in California, so that's exactly what we did."

"You sold surfboards together?"

"Precisely. I was broke and had nothing to lose anyway so he borrowed some money, set up shop, copied the exact design, had a bunch of them manufactured by some old-time board makers who'd been laid off, and we began the business."

"Wow!" exclaimed Tess, suddenly realizing that Bill was the man in the photos with her dad that she'd found on his laptop.

So, definitely not gay...

"And it was your dad's idea to call the company, *Malibu Hot Boards*, or *Malibu HoBos* for short. And consequently, when I started to win more and more events with the new and improved version of my original design, *The HoBo*, I became known as the Malibu Hobo. That's how my nickname came about and to be honest, I'm really okay with it."

145

"That's amazing! So what happened to the business, did it go under?" she asked, desperate to find out any nuggets of new information about her father.

"No way," he replied, "That business was a brilliant idea, all your dad's idea really, and it's still going strong."

"So, you still run it?" she asked, "You still make surfboards?"

"I don't, no, but the business is stronger than ever, the Malibu Hot Board, or HoBo, is still regarded as the best board out there, although it's been improved even more since we sold the company."

"Oh, you sold it?"

"We sold it back in the early nineties; we were the original dirt poor California kids who got rich, doing what they did for fun. And the London kid, of course, your dad, he got rich too."

"My father was rich? I never knew that. He just died recently, suicide."

"I know, Tess, but he died a very wealthy man and I don't for one minute believe he killed himself."

Chapter 31

Tom Delaney was a private man. He knew that he apparently exuded some kind of reputation as a guy that girls were attracted to, but the real truth was that he wasn't like that at all. They may have been attracted to him but he was quite insular, and he chose his friends carefully and his girlfriends even more so. And girlfriends for Tom, were rare as hens' teeth. The reputation was therefore pretty much unfounded. He had always preferred female company but rarely found himself in bed with anyone. He didn't know if the reason for his preference of female company was because he grew up never knowing his mother, or if it was something he had inherited from his dad.

But on Saturday evening, he had been instantly struck by the English girl that his parents had recently brought into their lives. Tess Valentine was truly different from anyone he'd ever met before. She wasn't a typical SoCal girl, which was the type of girl he was used to, and she didn't talk about shallow things, as many of the girls around him did. She'd come up the hard way and she was smart. And so damned gorgeous, too.

Of course, he hadn't met too many English girls in the past and he wondered if they were all like this. The question he kept running around his mind this morning, was whether she had felt a reciprocal feeling toward him which right now, he sorely doubted.

"You're deep in thought this morning, Tommy boy," said a voice, awakening him from his thoughts.

"Sorry, Matt, just trying to get my head around something," Tom replied, "What's up?"

"The client's screaming about final approval on the drawings, that's all. You know how Mrs. DiMarco can be," said Matt Fenton, Tom's business partner.

"She with the resting bitch face, yeah, how can I forget?"

Tom and Matt had tentatively begun a fledgling architecture and design business two years previously and although they were doing reasonably well as a new start-up, they also realized that they would have to put up with the whims, changes of mind and the endless attention required by newly-moneyed newlyweds.

"It makes me laugh, she's twenty-six, has never owned her own home before and just because her brand new nerd husband made eight figures from selling a pointless app in Silicon Valley, suddenly she's the friggin' queen of California," said Tom, exasperated by the woman's constant neediness.

"Yeah, but the difference between you and me, Tom, is that I want to slap the bitch and you just let her roll over you like you're Teflon. How the hell do you do that?" asked Matt.

"Someone's gotta do it, otherwise Fenton Delaney isn't going to last. It'll die before it's even born," said Tom, "And anyway, she's actually not so bad. Wait a few years when she's on her fifth husband, then you'll know what a real bitch is."

"Well, whatever's got your mind in a daze right now, it'll have to wait. She's out front in Reception and she needs Thomas Delaney, and she needs him now, so go do that thing you do," Matt chuckled, wandering back to his own office.

Chapter 32

As Tess drove south toward Santa Monica, she couldn't get the conversation out of her head that she'd just had over lunch. She had instantly warmed to the man they called Hippy Bill. He was an extraordinarily charismatic man and he had a sense of authority and kindness about him, even though he dressed down to his 'Hobo' nickname. She'd seen it in the waiter's reaction when he ordered his fancy coffee, the man oozed charm and knowledge.

She also realized that everything he had relayed to her today was probably true, he just had a certain vibe that told her he'd been there, seen it, done it. And when she thought back to the photos she'd found on her father's laptop, it was very clear that the two men were partners, and friends too, and Bill was really just an older and silver-haired version of the surfer standing next to her dad on the beach. He hadn't changed much. Although he could benefit from a shopping trip for some new threads.

"But murder?" she said aloud to herself, "Who the hell would murder my father?"

She realized that perhaps Jake could throw some light on the subject. Bill had said that it was something to do with a loan that Robert had taken out when they began the surfboard business, but also that her father had kept a fairly tight lid on all things financial as far as Bill was concerned. Which, Bill had said, was fine with him because he was clueless when it came to money back then. Her dad had always made sure that Bill had money in his pocket, which for

Bill had been pretty novel, having never had a pocket full of greenbacks in his life before he'd met Robert.

The drive south was slow this afternoon but Tess was enjoying driving the Mustang. She thought about all the boys at work. If they could see her now, they'd be so jealous. She was truly *livin' the dream*, as they say.

As she drifted lethargically along the PCH, accelerating and braking every few seconds, she could hear her phone chirping from deep within her handbag on the seat next to her. She tried valiantly to blindly locate it whilst trying not to bump the car in front as she rode the Mustang's violent clutch.

When she finally retrieved her phone, she didn't recognize the number displayed, but then again, she didn't know many people here…

"Hello? This is Tess," she said, holding the phone between her shoulder and her ear as she double-clutched and changed rhythmically from third to second gear.

As the traffic suddenly sped up, the phone dropped into her lap as she whipped the car back into third…

"Tess… it's Tom, Tom Delaney…"

The phone slipped onto the floor.

"From Saturday night… I dropped you home from my parents?" said Tom into dead air.

Tess felt around under the seat as the lurch of the car's enormous horsepower threw the iPhone backward from between her feet.

"Hello? This is Tess," she said, finally retrieving the device and putting it to her ear with a now available hand.

But the caller had gone.

Chapter 33

The evening was another perfect yellow and orange sunset on the Malibu coastline. The Delaney home enjoyed one of the prettiest and most enviable secluded positions in God's playground and that fact wasn't ever lost on the Delaneys. They pinched themselves most days when they woke up and invariably once again when they went to sleep.

"I had lunch with Tess today," said Summer, as she made a pair of evening martinis for her and her husband "Love that girl."

"She's something special, right?" said Jake, coming up behind her and wrapping his arms around her waist, "Kinda reminds me of you at that age."

"You didn't even know me at that age! I was history by then and you were thousands of miles away!" said Summer, turning around in Jake's embrace and putting a martini glass to his lips.

"Yeah, well, you know what I mean," Jake replied, squeezing his wife to him, "She's a lovely girl."

"So did you notice anything on Saturday?"

"How do you mean?" asked Jake, "I'm not with you, did I miss something?"

"It was pretty obvious! Tom was smitten. Didn't you see it in his face? He could barely take his eyes off Tess."

"I hadn't noticed, but now that you mention it, yeah, maybe there was something going on between the two of them."

"Wouldn't be a bad thing," said Summer, "She seemed to fit right in with this family. Shame she's going home though…"

"She doesn't have much choice, Sum, she's new in her job in London and she doesn't want to lose it," replied Jake, "But who knows, she might come back some day?"

"I know, but the thing about Tom, once he finds something that grabs hold of him, he would wait forever for it to return to him, you know what he's like," she replied.

"I do, he's his father's son."

Chapter 34

Santa Monica was a disappointment. Maybe she had seen too many glossy shots of it on television and in movies, but for Tess, the 'in the flesh' version was not something to write home about. Too many people, too much traffic, nowhere to park and concrete everywhere. She tried to imagine what it must have been like in the old days, back when her father and Bill were first starting to sell their Malibu Hobo surfboards.

They paved paradise, then they put up a parking lot…

When she finally made it back to her hotel, the evening traffic now heavy, hot and impatient, she found Nathan leaving for the night in his regular clothes, his bellhop uniform cast aside after another day at The Surfrider.

"Hello stranger!" he said, when he saw the green Mustang pull into the driveway, "How's my English Rose?"

She pulled up next to him as he leaned down to her open window.

"I've been exploring, I had lunch with Summer, met someone who knew my father, and then decided to see what Santa Monica was all about. I'm being the quintessential English tourist."

"I could have told you not to waste your time," said Nathan, "But you're here, so at least you've done it now. Fun or disappointing?"

"The latter. Anyway, where are you off to, all spruced up?"

157

"A date," he replied, "First date too, so don't hold your breath!"

"Is he nice?"

"I'll let you know in the morning," he said, winking at her.

"Okay, I want a full report though, all the juicy bits!" said Tess as he walked toward his Beetle.

"Oh, I forgot to tell you," he said, turning back toward Tess's car, "You got more flowers today, I put them in your room myself this time."

"Wow, really? Who are they from?"

"I've no idea but the delivery boy was to die for," Nathan said, "Gotta run, hun!"

The flowers were stunning. There was no way that they could have come from the same person. Whoever sent these blooms had taste. The vase was a startling myriad of colors, purple freesias, pink and white roses, yellow lisianthus, cerise oriental lilies, orange Carthamus and amber chrysanthemums tied together with gypsophila, aspidistra leaves and eucalyptus. The scent in the room was intoxicating, like a spa on speed.

This time, Tess immediately searched for a note amongst the display and found a pink envelope with her name once again written by hand. She opened it and withdrew the pretty card and read the message.

Dear Tess,

My dad told me that you're returning to England in a few days and I was wondering if I could show you downtown Los Angeles one evening if you have time? Although I know you've probably planned the rest of your trip already, but if you'd like to see the sights, it would be my honor.

My cell is 818 878 2221

Best wishes and hope to see you soon,

Tom Delaney.

"Really?" Tess said aloud, "You're asking *me*?"

She looked at the number on the card and seemed to recognize it. When she compared it to the number that last called her iPhone, she realized that it was Tom who'd called earlier.

And to think I might have missed out on a date with you... Jeez Louise!

Chapter 35

Buchanan had guessed that at some point Tom Delaney was going to ask the girl on a date. It wasn't rocket science. He'd congratulated himself on having the foresight to plant another tracking device on the boy's Bronco while Tom was at work. But he was getting tired of the job now and he couldn't be bothered to follow everyone everywhere when he could simply look at the dots on his tracker screen.

He'd spent the evening following the bellboy, Nathan or whatever his friggin' name was. Pretty quickly, he realized he was barking up the wrong tree if he thought there was some kind of love connection between him and Tess. When he saw him making out in his Beetle with a boy he'd just been out to dinner with, it all became pretty clear.

Fucking fruits…

And after he'd watched the Delaney boy stop by the hotel and pick up Tess tonight, there was no way he was gonna follow those two on another fucking loved-up date night. He couldn't even be bothered checking the tracker because there was no likelihood of catching her alone tonight. No, tonight he was taking the evening off and heading back for a large dose of Maisie's home cooking; he was fed up with fast food eaten in a car that now stunk like a hybrid takeout.

But he also realized, mainly due to Mickey Carlisle's recent intel, that the lovely Tess was flying back to jolly old fucking

England this very weekend so he only had a few days left to get the job done.

Enjoy your evening, Tessie girl, time's almost up…

Chapter 36

"Nobu," said Tess, "What's that?"

"It's the place to see and be seen at!" Tom replied, already excited about the evening ahead.

"It's a restaurant?"

"It's *the* restaurant in L.A.," he replied.

Tess had been impressed with Tom's appearance when he'd arrived to pick her up from the hotel. He wore a simple navy suit with a white shirt, collar opened and plain black loafers. He looked simply gorgeous. Tess had chosen a lime green crêpe dress, shredded and ragged at the knee à la Tinker Bell in Peter Pan. And her silver sandals had gotten another wearing too.

"You look so beautiful," he'd said, "You're like the fairy on a Christmas tree."

And he says all the right things too…

Tess had marveled at the glass skyscrapers that intermingled seamlessly with the older Spanish architecture as they drove into the city itself. Before she'd made the trip to Los Angeles, she had become interested in the history of the city. The high-rise monoliths were fairly recent additions and she wished she had been able to see the original genteel city of the early twentieth century, back then a mix of adobe Spanish renaissance and tenement architecture.

The intoxicating feel of a warm fall evening, an open-roof drive with the breeze in her hair and a very handsome fella as her date for the night, brought a smile to Tess's face as she looked over at Tom. She glanced down at his hand as he effortlessly changed gears through the non-synchronous gearbox, wondering what it would be like to have her own hand wrapped in his.

Although she had partially seen downtown from a distance when Sammy had collected her from the airport, the city seemed to change so much at night. She'd seen the epicenter with Nathan at the Observatory, the compressed collection of tall buildings in the middle of the Los Angeles basin. But once she was within the city itself, the place just lit up with color and electricity and she felt dazzled by it, like a fledgling movie starlet on her first trip out in the City of Angels.

"So what's so special about Nobu?" she asked, the wind now whipping her hair in a chestnut cascade over her head.

"All the famous people go there, it's like a who's who of the entertainment industry. We were lucky to get a table but Dad has some contacts at the restaurant," Tom replied, thrilled at his good fortune to be taking Tess to dinner.

"How far is it? Where are we now?" Tess asked, suddenly aware that she sounded like the kid in the back of a car, asking, "Are we there yet?"

Tom wasn't taking a direct route to the restaurant tonight, instead deciding to criss-cross the L.A. streets and boulevards so that Tess could get a better sense of the changing character of the city.

"Right now, we're on Sunset Boulevard, heading up the canyon through Pacific Palisades and then up past the famous golf course at Riviera Country Club," he replied, smiling at Tess's starstruck expression.

Tess gazed out at the stunningly beautiful mansions that lined the road, wondering who lived in them, what they would be doing right now. And did this incredible wealth make them happy?

Probably...

The architecture of each enormous house was so individual, palaces that lit up the night sky, in styles merging together in ways she'd never before seen in England. Dozens and dozens of French Chateau, English Country, Spanish, Colonial and Gothic homes the size of small hotels, lined the way; a million light bulbs showing the world where the truly wealthy really lived.

Would hate to see their electric bill...

"Okay, now we're going to catch Barrington and take it all the way down to Santa Monica Boulevard..."

"When the sun comes up over Santa Monica Boulevard!' sang Tess, suddenly reminded of the classic "All I Wanna Do" song by Sheryl Crow.

"You like that song?" asked Tom, "It's one of my favorites of all time, just makes me smile!"

"Love it!" said Tess, "It's one of those songs that came straight out of God's top pocket! Let's stay up all night and watch the sun come up," she laughed, singing more of the song that they both loved.

"All I wanna do, is have some fun, I've got a feeling, I'm not the *only* one..."

Tom laughed and sang along, loving the idea of staying up all night with Tess, and blissfully aware that he was quickly falling in love with the English Rose seated next to him.

165

Fifteen minutes later, Tom pulled the Bronco to the curb in front of Nobu. Tess looked around, and if she was honest, the street looked a little rundown, almost shabby, and the Nobu building itself looked kind of out of place, like a Japanese bamboo and glass single-story structure that had landed in L.A. like a spaceship directly from Tokyo. But, there was a huge line of people outside waiting to get in, so the food must be good, she thought.

Before Tom could jump out to help Tess from the car, a parking valet had already done so and was taking her hand guiding her to the sidewalk.

"Now I do feel like a movie star," she said, "I could seriously get used to this!"

"Oh, this is so normal in Los Angeles, Tess," joked Tom, "Didn't you realize that every day is like this? It's how we live over here all the time!"

He handed his keys to the valet, thanked him as he took a ticket from the young man, and guided Tess toward the entrance of the restaurant, casually slipping a hand very lightly around her slender waist.

Chapter 37

"I love sushi," said Tess, "I can't get enough of it. We have it for lunch often in London when I'm at work. There's a place called *Yo! Sushi* in Soho and it's been there forever I think, but I love it."

"Me too, although I rarely take a lunch break," said Tom, "Goes with the territory of new business start-ups, I guess."

After the couple had arrived at the restaurant, they had been seated fairly quickly but Tess had gulped when she looked at the menu. Not at the exotic and beautifully prepared sushi variations on offer, but more at the prices which were as astronomical as the skyscrapers that littered the city of Los Angeles.

Forty dollars for four pieces of sashimi!

"So you're a workaholic?" she asked.

"Not really," Tom replied, "But it's only my partner and me at the moment, you know, just trying to keep costs down while we develop the business. We don't even have anyone to answer the phones for us so it's pretty much hands-on for the time being."

"The company I work for started very much in the same way," said Tess, "Just three guys with an idea that they could change the world of advertising. And they did, and now it's the coolest place for clients to sign up and there are over two hundred employees there now."

"Do you miss being at work?" he asked, almost hoping she didn't.

"I miss some of the people and I do enjoy what I do, but sitting here with you right now feels like a million miles away from London."

"I'm sorry you're having to go back to England so soon, it feels as though you've only just arrived," said Tom, realizing that his time with Tess would be short-lived.

"I haven't gone yet!" Tess replied, not wanting to think about flying home at this moment, "Shall we order?"

They ordered individually rather than for the table, Tom surprised at how little Tess had wanted and equally bemused that she had asked for regular water. No cocktail, no wine, not even San Pellegrino.

Cheap date…

As they waited for their drinks to arrive, Tess looked around the restaurant, a little surprised at what Tom had told her about the waiting-list to get a table here. She guessed that the food must be simply outstanding because the décor looked like it had survived the 1980s.

"So tell me about California," Tess said, unconsciously pushing her hair behind one ear, "This being the Golden State and everything, home of Hollywood, movie stars and Tom Delaney," grinning mischievously as she said it.

"How long have you got?" said Tom, "This state is so big and so different north to south and everywhere in between."

"Weren't you born here though? You must know more than most?"

"I guess so, what do you want to know?"

"For starters, all I see everywhere I go, are huge beautiful houses and crazy expensive cars. Is everyone in California rich and glamorous, or am I missing something?"

"No, not everyone's like that, of course not, there are tons of normal working-class people living here. My parents both still work for a living," said Tom.

"Tom, I love your parents but come on, they're rich!" she said, "Anyway, if I ever got to be rich, which isn't ever going to happen, the first thing I'd do is employ a full-time back-scratcher, I love my back being scratched."

"They're not rich and they haven't always had money," Tom replied, now a little defensively, but also amused at Tess's idea of what money could provide.

I'd scratch your back until the sun went down and keep on scratching 'til it rose again...

"Where I come from," she continued, "Your parents would be classed as beyond wealthy, and I'm so sorry, Tom, I'm not attacking them, they're fantastic and so generous, but really, where do the other ninety percent of Californians live?"

"Okay, okay, I get what you're saying. So, if you look around you, even in this super-exclusive restaurant, you'll see a degree of sadness, a sense that we're among a group of people and couples who don't know where the gold is at the end of the rainbow," said Tom, "Yeah, the ladies have the big rings, they both have the nice exotic cars, and they live in houses that most people can only ever dream about. But look at them, Tess, tell me if you see true happiness here."

She looked around at other diners in the restaurant, and Tom was right, no one, except maybe a couple of tables with seven or eight diners, looked like they'd discovered the yellow brick road.

"When you look closer, the smile is replaced by a frown. They worry about the cars that they lease but don't actually own, and whether they'll always make the monthly payment on them. They worry about the ninety-eight percent mortgages they have on their

169

huge homes, scared that one day they'll be taken from them because they might lose their jobs and the banks foreclose. And even if they manage to keep up those payments, throw in the school fees, the country club fees, gym memberships, healthcare and the true California cost of living and eating, you can see the real stress of living in paradise."

"I've never thought about it that way, I suppose. You just see all this wealth and assume that everyone can easily afford it, everything's bought and paid for," said Tess, now understanding the reality. Financially and psychologically.

"And God forbid, apart from the thought of losing it all, that the wives and in some cases the husbands, can't afford to have the constant plastic surgery to keep them looking young," laughed Tom, sipping at his glass of water.

"Jeepers, you'd need to rob a bank to pay all those annual costs," said Tess, "And I guess it will never change? Once you enter the lifestyle, the cycle just continues?"

"I think where you're staying at the moment at The Surfrider, might be misleading you on how you perceive the whole of the state", said Tom, "The thing about Malibu, as is the case for all of California, the real attraction is always going to be the beach."

"You're right, the first thing I noticed when I walked into your parents' house was that it was right on the ocean, paradise truly found."

"I know, they're very fortunate. But if you go inland, and I don't mean very far from the coast," Tom continued, "Just a few miles in, people lead very different lives in arid, greenless and humid towns, where the populace looks bored to death and not particularly happy."

"I haven't managed to explore that far yet, apart from where my father lived, but even his place is only just off the PCH so it's not exactly Povertyville."

Tom took a sip of water and paused as the food order began to arrive. He waited while the server set it out on the table before them and after the man had bowed and left, Tom continued to talk about his home state.

"Traveling in the cities is also mind-numbing here, and stressful all at the same time. I guess if you have a home overlooking the ocean in Malibu and you're filthy rich, it's probably pretty good but people here, even in those golden places, seem bored, almost like they're waiting for something."

"I suppose it will always be that way, so don't beat yourself up over it, Tom, there's not much you can do about it. It happens all over the world."

"I guess, but a man can have pipe dreams, right?" said Tom, lifting a piece of bluefin tuna sashimi to his lips.

"What's your dream, do you have one, apart from designing big McMansions for the new money you were telling me about?" Tess asked, savoring the salmon that had literally just melted on her tongue.

Wow! Now that's sashimi…

"It's only a dream at the moment but what I'd love to do, what would make me really happy, is to design affordable housing in green villages further inland where all the homes aren't cookie-cutter," said Tom, a sense of excitement suddenly enveloping him.

"Cookie-cutter?" said Tess.

"Oh right, yeah, sorry, an American expression. You know, it means where all the homes are identical in rows or circles, like they've been stamped out of pastry with those metal shape-cutting things people use in the kitchen."

"Got it. Quaint expression though, but I would assume it makes for fairly boring and soul-less houses?"

171

"Exactly!" said Tom, now more excited than ever, "I want to build real villages, in an old fashioned way, where every home is different and unique and in a community that delivers the joy that's been missing for so many decades here. You know, the real old-fashioned American apple pie and picket fence kind of ideal, I want to see people truly living the American Dream."

"Never give up on your dreams, Tom. I didn't even have one, and look at me, I'm actually living a dream, even if it's only temporary," she laughed, finishing the salmon and octopus on her plate.

"Tess?" he asked.

"Tom?" she replied.

"You've hardly eaten anything."

"I know, but look at the prices here, Tom, they're ridiculous."

"But it's my treat, and I can afford it. Well, just about, anyway!"

"See? You don't need to impress me, Tom, I have terribly simple tastes."

"But you must be starving?"

"I am, I could murder fish and chips right now!" Tess replied, salivating at the thought of an English fish and chip shop.

"I'm not sure I can find you what you're used to in England, but how about the best damned cheeseburger and fries in town?"

"C'mon, Tom Delaney, let's get out of here!"

Chapter 38

When Tess got back to her hotel room, she felt a buzz inside her, feelings never felt before, something that she had truly never experienced in her life. Tom was more than nice. He was almost too good to be true. She had really enjoyed his sense of giving back, realizing that he was born into money but wanting to somehow make the dream available to others who couldn't afford it. And as soon as he became aware that she was uncomfortable in restaurants with crazy prices, the evening had gotten much better once they'd found the special food truck that he always went to when he was in the city.

After he had dropped her back at the hotel, she had pecked him on the cheek and hugged him when he'd said goodbye, and there was no feeling that he somehow wanted more. There was no pressure like there had been before with Simon. Although she would have snogged Tom's face off, given half a chance. She still felt silly that she had said she would employ a full-time back-scratcher if she got rich, but something told her that Tom understood exactly what she meant.

And if you have a partner who can scratch that itch, well you don't need to pay anyone, do you?

After she had changed into a silk nightshirt and brushed her teeth, she removed the sea glass necklace that Summer had given her, and laid it down next to her on the bedside table. She brushed her hair, remembering how her mother had always done for her each

175

night before she went to sleep when she was a little girl. And as much as she missed her mom and Franco, she was beginning to realize that she didn't want to leave.

How is it that just when you begin to dream, reality kicks in and knocks you flat on your back?

Chapter 39

The following morning, Tess was once again looking through her father's computer, pausing to revisit the photo file that contained the shots of Bill and her father, the two of them standing together on the beach, a surfboard planted in the sand between them. He was an interesting man, the aging hippy known as the Malibu Hobo. Almost as soon as she had left the café that day in the village, she wished that she had spent more time talking to him. There was something about him, something that told her that he had a lot to tell, but he wasn't going to overload her with new information just yet. But she had to see him again before she left for London, she thought as she dialed Jake Delaney's number.

Once she was connected with Jake, they exchanged all of the usual pleasantries, and Tess briefly told him what she had been doing since he'd last seen her.

And as she lay back on the hammock outside, tasting the air and the gentle busy-ness outside, she told Jake what a gentleman his son had been the previous evening. She fell short, however, of saying that he was probably the man of her dreams...

As she continued chatting with Jake, she noticed the bougainvillea that enveloped the balcony, its rich red color seemingly lit up by electricity.

Mum would love that. I wonder if I took a cutting home, whether it would take in the English weather...

"But I just wanted to ask you about someone I met, whether you know him or not?" she said, suddenly aware that she was taking up Jake's valuable time this morning.

"Oh, don't tell Tom you've met someone else, he'll be heartbroken!" Jake laughed, clearly enjoying a little teasing at his son's expense.

Jesus! Am I blushing on the end of this phone line?

"No, no, I met someone down in the village and wondered if you knew him."

"Does he have a name?"

"Kind of... although I don't know his last name. He goes locally by the nickname of the Malibu Hobo," she replied, not knowing if Jake would have any clue.

"Oh you mean Hippy Bill!" said Jake, "Everyone knows Bill, he's a legend in these parts, although his full name is Bill McLaren."

"So he's not a crazy man?"

"Far from it, but how did you meet him?"

Tess explained what had happened that day and how they had struck up a conversation, but she omitted the part where Bill had said that her father's death was no suicide, and that he thought Robert had actually been murdered. She didn't want to discuss it until she had spoken more with Bill.

"I just met him after I had had lunch with Summer but as you seem to know him, well... is he safe? I know that sounds bad but he knew my father and I wanted to ask him a few more questions."

"Bill McLaren? He's safe as houses, as I think you say in England. I don't personally know him that well, but I do know that he and your father were once business partners."

"I know, and I liked him. He seemed a really genuine and caring chap. It's so sad that he's fallen on hard times," Tess replied.

"Oh, I think you've got the wrong end of the stick there, Tess…"

He's throwing in Englishisms like they're going out of fashion!

"How do you mean?"

"Bill's rich!" he continued, "He just doesn't look it most of the time."

"He's rich? Are you serious?" said Tess, completely floored by what Jake had just said, "He looks like a tramp, dresses like one too!"

"I'm serious as a heart attack. It's all a big illusion with Bill, he likes to promote the idea that he doesn't have a dime in his pocket, but the man has a friggin' house in Malibu and not in the area I live, he has prime real estate down in the expensive part," Jake explained, laughing at the fact that Bill was obviously still continuing to ply the Malibu Hobo legend.

"Wow!" she said, "Who'd have known?"

"That's the idea, Tess, he doesn't want anyone to know the reality. He just likes it that way."

"So, do you have a number for him," she asked, "I'd really like to chat with him before I go back to London."

"Bill doesn't really use phones, so no, you're out of luck there. He kind of lives by the idea of the Malibu bush telegraph."

"So how can I find him?" she asked, now sad that she may never see him again.

"You won't, Tess, but he'll find you."

Chapter 40

Tess was on her third latte by the time she spotted the loping 'homeless man' ambling along the sidewalk in the direction of the Marmalade Café.

As he approached her table, his teeth sparkled white as snow when he grinned at her, proving that he could definitely afford premium dental care. She wondered why she hadn't spotted that on first meeting.

But that's what we do, isn't it? We're always judging books by their bloody covers…

"Thought you'd be back," he said, "Mind if I sit with you this time?"

She pushed her latte to one side as she got up to shake the hand that he was offering her. It was hard, calloused and deeply tanned like his face. She also noticed a simple gold wedding band on his left hand.

"I was hoping I'd see you again but I didn't know you'd be back today," she said.

"I guess we have some type of metaphysical connection going on," he replied, "Must be the coffee."

"Not sure about that," said Tess, "But I tried one of your special cappuccinos and if I drank four of those, I'd be awake for the next three weeks!"

He laughed, again showing a radiant smile that belied his gruff exterior.

"I get the feeling you want to ask me some questions," he said, "That's why I figured you'd be back."

"I do, Bill, I can't stop thinking about what you said about my dad," she said, noticing that the same waiter from the previous meeting was eyeing their table with concern, "Do you truly think he was murdered? That it really wasn't suicide?"

"Well, no one's about to listen to what my thoughts are on it, but I think it's a certainty. You see, although Robert was a great entrepreneur, he wasn't too careful about who he borrowed money from. He was way too trusting and even though he paid back our loans in full to the scumbags who lent us the start-up cash, those assholes never stop coming back for more. And they saw your father as the proverbial golden goose."

"So how do we go about proving it?" Tess asked, "I wouldn't know where to begin."

"We don't," he said, "It's not our job and as you told me, you go back to England on Saturday so you don't have the time, even if you had the resources."

Tess felt immediately saddened by what Bill was saying but she also knew he was right. There was no way she could find out anything more. But while she was somehow relieved to know that her father hadn't killed himself, she felt anger that someone had gotten away with killing him, and she knew that anger would never ease.

"Can I show you something?" she said, pulling a photo from her purse and offering it to him.

He took it from her and as soon as McLaren saw the image of him and Robert standing with a surfboard between them, she could sense a feeling of sadness from him, a melancholy that grew immediately from his features.

"Sunset Beach," he murmured, "Salad days…"

"Do you think you could tell me where the photograph was taken," she asked, "I'd like to see what my father saw, feel what he felt."

"I can do better than that, Tess, I'll take you there myself."

Chapter 41

He'd asked her to wait by the Jack In The Box a few yards up from her hotel and told her he'd pick her up at five thirty. She wondered why he didn't want to simply come by the hotel, but she was beginning to learn that Bill had his own reasons for everything, and he had his own unique methods.

As she stood outside the burger joint, feeling a little uncomfortable to be standing at the side of the road on her own, at exactly five-thirty she heard before she saw, what she assumed to be a Harley Davidson motorcycle approaching her and slowing. The noise was deafening and she stepped back from the sidewalk as the powerful-looking bike came to a halt beside her. She realized it was Bill and suddenly understood why he didn't want to pull up at the hotel, given the thunderous noise it was making.

"Want a ride?" said Bill, as he removed his crash helmet, not one of the full-face modern ones but instead an old-style retro, matte black 'skid lid'.

Tess had never been on a motorbike before and just the noise made her feel nervous.

"Is it safe?" she asked, I've never been on a Harley."

"It's not a Harley, this is an Indian, they were making these way before Billy Harley ever met the Davidson brothers," he said, grinning at Tess's trepidation, "Come on, we need to make sunset."

The ride north on PCH was exhilarating for Tess. Her early fears quickly replaced by a feeling of joy, a sense of total freedom, like she was living the 60s dream that everyone talked about. Even the helmet that Bill had given her, identical to his own, felt right and it fitted perfectly.

She held on tight, her hands gripping Bill's leather jacket as he cranked the engine and they ripped along the coast, the setting sun glinting in the chrome-work that covered the magnificent machine.

Twenty minutes later, they arrived at a beach, eventually finding it by navigating a winding set of side roads. You couldn't see the beach from the PCH so you would need to know how to get there. Bill found a space to park the bike and cut the engine as his foot released the kickstand.

Sunset at Sunset Beach doesn't get much better than this, Tess," he beamed, "And it's free."

"It's really beautiful," she replied, "Thanks so much for bringing me."

When Bill climbed off the Indian and removed his leather jacket, Tess was pleasantly shocked at his appearance. No longer resembling a homeless man, he was dressed in clean and faded jeans, brown suede Chelsea boots and a white shirt, untucked and opened casually, a large bronze 'S' on a string of leather nestling in his silver-haired chest.

And once he had removed his crash lid, she saw that his wavy silver hair was shiny and swept back into a ponytail and his beard had recently been trimmed. The fact that he was obviously still very fit and lean, and that he carried himself in a confident way, belied his true age.

He reminded her in many ways of an actor she liked called Sam Elliot. One of Franco's favorite films was The Big Lebowski and Elliot was in the movie. Even Bill's voice was similar to Elliot's, so deep and resonant, it was uncanny. But there was no doubting that when he emerged from his hobo character, Bill was the epitome of a sexy older man. She noticed that he smelled good too, when she'd been sitting behind him on the bike.

God knows what he must have been like forty years ago…

"You look…"

"Yeah, I know, I scrub up okay."

"I didn't mean that…"

"It's okay, Tess, you won't be the first to look shocked!"

"No, I mean you look really nice, you look different."

"I'll take that as a compliment, but come on, we're running out of time, sun'll be down soon."

They found a spot at the north end of the beach, where other nature lovers and sun worshippers had had similar ideas, to watch the sun going down on what was a completely clear evening sky. Bill had brought a blanket with him that he'd retrieved from one of the Indian's side panniers and he spread it out on a flat area of sand, gesturing for Tess to sit down.

"Should be a beauty tonight," he said, "Couldn'a picked a better evening."

Tess noticed to her right and behind her, an enormous gathering of birds. There must have been hundreds and hundreds of them, so many different varieties but all of them sitting calmly together like a blanket of shimmering and quivering feathers facing the sun, seemingly hypnotized as the golden orb continued its descent toward the ocean. There wasn't even a sound, just a muted communion that felt strangely church-like in the silence amongst them. Like nature's disciples.

Bill didn't utter a word either, he just sat on the blanket waiting in silence, smiling inwardly as the sun began to set, its fiery shroud becoming a deep orange glow as it sank lower and lower and then with a final blip of last light, disappeared over the horizon.

And as soon as it had gone, so too did the birds, taking flight in one enormous mass, softly flapping wings eager to find their resting place for the night, another day over and a new one yet to begin.

Chapter 42

"Sunset Beach, that's such a perfect name for this place," said Tess, soaking up the silence and the beauty of the ocean.

"I should say it's not actually called Sunset Beach, it's real name is Zuma Beach, or legally, Westward Beach," Bill replied, "But the locals call it Sunset, have done for as long as I've been coming here."

"That, I can definitely understand," Tess replied, "It's simply sensational!"

"But there's more than one good reason to come to Sunset Beach than just to watch the sun go down," said Bill, as he gathered up the blanket and folded it into a neat square,

"That was good enough for me," Tess replied, "I'm starting to understand my father's love of this place more and more every day."

"Well, the evening ain't over just yet, c'mon, let's go eat," he said, gently taking her arm and leading her across the sand and back toward the bike.

After replacing the blanket back inside the pannier, Bill draped his jacket across Tess's shoulders, noticing that she had begun to shiver, now that the sun had gone. Taking the two crash helmets in one hand, he led her along the road to a small restaurant, now lit up in the quickly darkening evening, a sign above it announcing its name, *The Sunset, Malibu.*

They didn't have a reservation but it wasn't long before they were taken to an elevator in the far corner, which Tess hadn't noticed while they'd been sitting waiting for a table. After they stepped out onto the upper floor of the restaurant, they were escorted to a corner table. This particular table was surrounded by windows, all of them ajar, allowing the evening breeze and the sound of the ocean to permeate through. The other tables were already occupied and it seemed odd to Tess that this one, probably the best table, was available.

"What a wonderful setting, thank you," Tess said to the young waitress, who had taken them upstairs. Tess noticed a couple of interesting tattoos on her shoulders and arms and was enchanted by the smile from this slim, pretty, redheaded and super-friendly girl.

"We always give Bill this table," she replied, "It's his favorite and he's been coming here since before I was born!"

Tess could see that Bill was feeling suddenly conspicuous as the waitress offered them menus, promising to return with some San Pellegrino sparkling water for the table.

"I'm finding out more about you every minute, Bill, seems like you're a celebrity in these parts."

"Not really. The real truth is that this table was the exclusive domain of the late Johnny Carson, he of *The Tonight Show* fame. Apparently, this was his favorite restaurant and this was his table every time he came here. And I think he came here often!"

"I've no idea who that is," she replied, "But I guess it's Malibu Bill's table now. What's good to eat here?"

The moon was high up in the midnight blue sky now, its torch-like beams lighting up the ocean like a giant spotlight. As Tess stared at its intensity, she realized that it must be what they called a Harvest Moon because she'd never seen it so big, so brilliant and so magnificent.

They ordered a dozen oysters to share, with Bill opting for the lobster rolls as an entrée and Tess, the fish and chips. Bill asked for a tomato juice with lots of Worcestershire sauce and Tess ordered a glass of Sauvignon Blanc. She'd put her phone on silent/vibrate but she noticed that Tom had been calling her. She decided to ignore the calls for the moment, knowing she could talk to him later after dinner.

"Do you ever drink?" she asked.

"Not now. Used to drink like a fish but it almost killed me so I stick to water and juice now," Bill replied, "Anyway, I've got to get you home safely and the bike won't ride itself."

"I noticed your ring," Tess said, pointing to the wedding band on his left hand, "Are you married?"

"I used to be, many moons ago. Still am, I guess…"

"How do you mean?"

"My wife, Sandy… she died."

"I'm so sorry," Tess said, "What happened? When did she die?"

"Oh, it was years ago, Tess, and she was a surfer like me. She was pretty awesome too, had no fear at all and she was beyond talented. We were out in Barbados, on the south of the island which is totally different from the north that you see in vacation brochures. It's wild, windy and dangerous but it's a surfing Mecca," he said.

"I think I'd prefer the sun loungers and the cocktails on the beach," Tess replied.

"Oh, believe me, I like that too," said Bill, "But surfing's in my veins and it was Sandy's lifeblood. Anyway, it was during a competition, all the top guys and girls were there back in eighty-six. In a way, the event should have been canceled, it was too dangerous, even for pro surfers like us, but Sandy wasn't ever going to back off from a challenge. It's what I loved about her."

"A stretch-the-limits kind of girl?" asked Tess.

"Exactly. She didn't just push the envelope; she ripped the damned thing apart. Anyway, most of us were skipping the second day and just hanging back, hoping it would be a little better on day three but Sandy wouldn't listen. She caught a monster wave, and if she'd have ridden it, it was a competition winner, hands down, a no-brainer, but it just swallowed her like she never existed. Took her onto the rocks and it broke my baby up. She died before we dragged her body out of the water."

"Oh God, Bill, that's so awful, I'm really sorry!"

"It's okay, it happened many years ago, although I still think about her every day. But the thing is, I wouldn't change anything because she was her own woman and she died doing what she loved best."

"And you never met anyone else, never remarried?"

"You don't, Tess. Once you find the one, I mean really, the *one*, there can never be another."

"I'm sorry, Bill, it's just such a terrible tragedy."

"Don't be, I'm okay with it. I had eight years with the girl of my dreams and I wouldn't trade it for anything in the world. And I'm not a religious man but I know we'll be together again, one day soon in another life," he replied, "Anyway, how's your fish and chips? Is it anything like back home?"

"It's good, it's really good," Tess replied, "It's different, but I love it anyway!"

They talked for two hours while they ate, Tess asking every question she could think of about her father, with Bill doing his best to answer. She enjoyed his company; he was a gentleman and a gentle man. He was interesting too, he'd had an extraordinary life and he'd watched Los Angeles and Malibu grow, although he didn't like the recent changes. He hankered for the life there in the 50s, 60s and 70s but knew that he couldn't stop growth.

As they ate, Tess looked at Bill and was still amazed at how he had metamorphosed from the down-and-out man she'd met in the village to this extremely manicured older man with the manners of a saint. It was as though he enjoyed playing a daily act to everyone who saw him dragging through the streets in his tattered clothes, willing them to deride him, knowing that he scared them. And then without fanfare, he would transform back to his real life, when no one was watching. There was no doubt that he was a unique, highly original, and totally engaging individual.

You're a conundrum, Mr. Hobo, no doubt about it...

After realizing that their stomachs could take no more, they decided to ask for the check and enjoy a slow ride back south on the Indian to Tess's hotel. Bill paid in cash, leaving a huge tip for the waitress, Tess realized, as he put down five twenties for her.

Tess said goodbye and thanked her for a lovely evening and Bill gave her a brief hug, whispering something to her as he left and she pecked him on the cheek. After taking the elevator down to the ground floor they enjoyed a slow moonlit walk back to Bill's Indian, which was parked a couple of hundred yards away, both enjoying breathing in the salty air in the coolness of the night.

"The waitress likes you," said Tess, impishly, "Does she have a thing for older men?"

"No! She's just a sweetheart of a girl who was born on the wrong side of town and she gets a lot of harsh treatment from some of the idiots around here," Bill replied, "And so I try to look after her every now and then. If she was my daughter, I'd be a very proud dad but sadly, her dad is an asshole."

"That's so lovely, Bill, and she seems really sweet too," said Tess.

193

"Damn! I left the skid lids under the table. Wait here, Tess, I'll be right back," said Bill, trotting back toward the restaurant.

"Don't worry, I'm in no hurry," said Tess, pulling her phone from her purse to check her messages. She knew Bill would be gone a couple of minutes finding his way back to their table, so at least she wouldn't appear rude checking her phone in front of him.

As she scrolled down the list of unread messages, she saw that Tom had called three times and sent four texts. She began to read them, knowing she didn't have time to call him but she could do that later once she got back to the hotel… and then suddenly, Tess's world went black as something covered her face and tightened around her throat. She tried to scream but a hand was already clamping around her mouth, and she felt the wind knocked out of her as a fist ripped into her solar plexus.

Fear overcame her as her silent screams went unheard, the noose tightening around her neck, and the smell of chloroform coming through the material of what she thought was a hood on her head. She felt woozy and weak, the world spinning as another blow to her stomach made her legs buckle. She wanted to choke but her throat was being constricted by the noose, and she felt herself being dragged away down the sandy path.

She realized that there must be two of them because she could feel four hands on her as they tried to drag her away and she was utterly helpless to their combined strength. She tried to dig her heels into the ground but they slipped uselessly through the sand, so she tried to fall down into it to stop them but they were too strong for her.

"Hey! Hey!! Get the fuck away from her!" she heard Bill's distant voice yell, as he came running down the path toward her. But it was too late, she was beginning to lose consciousness now, the chloroform beginning to make her head light, and the pain in her stomach making her want to throw up. Bile seeped up into her mouth as a third blow tore into her stomach.

"¡Sostén los brazos de la perra!"

"¡No puedo abrazarla, es demasiado fuerte!"

"¡Joder joder joder, el cloroformo ya debería haber funcionado!"

But as she began to black out, she heard the crunching sound of cartilage and bone cracking as Bill raced to her aid, pummeling her attackers with his skid lids, his wild yells splitting the night air in an untamed violence as he unleashed havoc and fury on the men.

Punch after punch rained down on them as she heard and felt the aging surfer beat their faces and bodies to pulp, the men yelling something over and over again in Spanish.

"No están pagando lo suficiente por esto, ¡Vamos, vamos!"

"El hombre es loco!"

She felt so sleepy now; even in the clutches of the two assailants, she was losing all feeling in her body, no longer hurting from the pain deep within her stomach.

"A la mierda este viejo coño, este hombre es un maldito asesino, ¡Vamos!"

"Si, ahora... ¡Vamos!"

And then finally, Tess fell to the ground, the hands no longer dragging her, the panicking footsteps running away as Bill undid the rope around her neck and pulled off the hood, his breathing harsh and frenzied. She couldn't even remember exactly where she was but the pain from her stomach was disappearing quickly with the onset of unconsciousness.

She looked up at Bill's grave and stricken face, trickles of blood seeping from fresh wounds, as he whispered to her.

"Tess, Tess! I'm so sorry, can you hear me, Tess? Please say something, anything!" said Bill, "I should never have left you on your own!"

She gasped momentarily for air, her eyes glazing over as she glimpsed Bill's frantic face, and then finally succumbing to sleep as he took her in his arms and held her tight.

Chapter 43

When Tess awoke, she didn't remember much of the previous evening, in fact, she didn't even know where she was now. She lifted her head from the pillow, aware that she was in a bedroom, a huge one at that. It was a simple room, painted white, sparse except for the bed and a pair of side tables. Even the floors were painted white wood. A large painting, maybe eight feet by six occupied the wall on the other side of the room, Tess recognizing it as a well-known Jackson Pollock. And it looked original, it definitely wasn't a print.

The patio doors to the room were wide open, the white linen drapes billowing in from the ocean breeze, as Tess sunk back down again into the soft pillow, her stomach muscles aching for some reason. She realized that she had gone to sleep fully clothed, and fragments of the previous night's encounter slowly and haphazardly began to form in her mind, but she couldn't quite get the picture focused.

Where the hell am I?

Minutes later, she heard a very soft knock at the oak door to the room, and a whisper calling out her name.

"Tess, are you awake?"

She recognized the voice.

"Bill?"

"Are you decent?" he said from outside the room.

"Yes, yes, of course, but where am I?" she asked as the door slowly began to open, revealing a saddened looking Bill stepping quietly into the room.

He was dressed almost for the beach, a pair of casual white knee-length shorts showing deeply tanned calves, a navy blue t-shirt slashed at the neck showing his silver chest hair, and tan flip-flops revealing that he enjoyed a pedicure occasionally. And he seemed to be carrying a fresh set of women's clothing over his arm.

"You're at my house, Tess, I didn't want to risk leaving you on your own at the hotel after what happened last night."

"What *did* happen? I don't remember much. I feel like someone slipped me a *roofie*," she replied, the evening's events still beginning to haphazardly form in her head, like a partially finished jigsaw puzzle.

"No roofie, just chloroform," said Bill, "And you were attacked by a couple of Mexicans from what I could make out. When I came back from the restaurant, it looked like they were trying to kidnap you."

"*Kidnap* me? Why? What do I have that anyone would want?"

"I think it has to do with your father," Bill replied, sitting down on the far corner of the bed, "I think he left something for you that they want."

"But I don't have anything, Bill, all Dad left me was a few thousand dollars, his trailer and a car! Surely that's not worth kidnapping someone for, is it?"

His face was knit with worry and Tess could tell that he hadn't had much sleep, if any at all. Something about the attack last night was bothering him, more than a one-off attempted mugging should have done. There was deep concern written all over his face and it was beginning to scare her.

"Tess, look around you. Look at the bedroom you're in, look at where my home is. I'm not poor."

"I don't understand, Bill, what has that got to do with my father?"

"Think about it, Tess, your father was a good businessman. I was never good with money, I was just a dumb surfer who built a board."

"I still don't get it, tell me what you mean," she replied, "Because I'm not seeing it. Surely, I mean... looking around this place, shouldn't it have been you they were after and not me?"

"Look, if someone as uneducated as me can end up in a house like this and believe me, I don't have any money worries in my future... then how the heck would someone like Robert end up with next to nothing? That's what makes no sense at all," he said, sitting down on the bed beside her, handing her the clothes that he'd brought with him.

"You're saying... you're trying to tell me..."

"That your father was rich, Tess, rich beyond most people's wildest dreams, he just didn't flaunt it."

"So where would he have put all this money?"

"That's the big question, Tess, but I don't think it's safe for you to be in Los Angeles right now."

Chapter 44

After Tess had showered and changed into the clothes he'd left for her, Bill gave her a brisk tour of his home. She could see now that it was completely white with occasional splashes of color from very carefully selected paintings, a minimalist approach to life in Malibu. There was nothing in the house that wasn't there for a reason, no trinkets, no photos, nothing much at all. But strangely, it still felt like a home.

Kinda like Dad's…

They sat outside on the patio, where Bill had prepared a breakfast spread for them, croissants, pastries, a selection of fruit and jugs of orange and cranberry juices. The morning was still fresh, even though it was edging closer to noon.

God, I could get used to this…

"Would you like some coffee?" he asked, "I've got one of those new Gaggia espresso machines from Italy. It's pretty good."

"I'd kill for one," Tess replied, delicately touching her stomach that she had seen was bruised from the night before, when she'd showered minutes earlier.

"Still painful?" he asked.

"Yes, a little, what the hell happened? I feel like I've been beaten up. My stomach is red and black from what looks like having been used as a punching bag."

"You *were* beaten, could have been a lot worse too. It's all my fault, I should never have left you on your own," Bill replied.

"Don't fret, Bill, honestly, it wasn't your fault. I'm from London, they breed us tough over there! And in any case, if it hadn't happened last night, it seems to me like it would've happened at some point anyway, after what you've already told me about Dad. I'm just glad you were there."

Bill loved this girl. She was definitely her father's daughter. Nothing seemed to get to her and she seemed to be able to find the positive in the most negative of situations.

He set two cappuccinos down on the table and took a seat, offering a plate of Danish pastries and cinnamon doughnuts to her. She took a Danish and bit hungrily into it. Bill drank a big gulp of coffee, still exhausted from spending the whole night watching over her.

"I didn't realize how famished I was," she said, "And this cappuccino is to die for... actually, strike that, I don't relish experiencing last night all over again."

Bill said nothing, angst once again writ large on his features, the reminder of the attack front and center in his mind.

"So, do you have any ideas about who was responsible," Tess asked, waking him from his thoughts.

"I do," he said, "And I'm going to personally deal with it if my hunch is right."

"Are you going to tell me, or do I have to work it out like one of Dad's cryptograms?"

"Well... I'm not a hundred percent certain but I think it has to do with the money we needed for the business back in the day. We borrowed... your father borrowed money on our behalf from loan sharks."

"I get it. Dad never paid them back, right?"

"No, that's not it; he paid back every cent including around two hundred percent in interest. That's how it was back then, but your father never owed anything to anyone, he always repaid our debts even if it was gouging us at the time."

"So the loan sharks are out of the picture then? It's not like they're owed anything," said Tess.

"No, they're not owed anything, but I don't think they're all out of the picture at all. I think one of them wants whatever your father left for you. When a man gets desperate, he gets greedy too and as far as those guys are concerned, you're an easy target, Tess. You're nothing to them that they couldn't just erase once they've gotten you to tell them where Robert stashed his money."

"But I don't know anything about any money, Bill!" Tess replied in exasperation, "This is all news to me!"

"That doesn't stop them. They won't give up until they've got what they want, even if it doesn't belong to them. These are desperate times for the old-time thugs. They'll feed in a frenzy on someone like you and whatever they think you're hiding."

"I wish I knew whatever secret my father left for me, but right now, I don't have a clue."

They ate in silence, both deeply contemplative, thinking similar thoughts. Robert Valentine had secrets. But it seemed to Tess that he wouldn't have died without leaving clues. She mentioned to Bill that she'd found a cryptogram on his computer, but that it didn't seem to mean anything to her. She wasn't even sure it was meant to mean anything.

"Do you still have that cryptogram?" Bill asked.

"Yes, I saved it on my phone."

"Show me, let's see if we can figure it out together."

Chapter 45

After Bill had dropped Tess back to her hotel, she texted Tom to give him the bare bones of what had happened the previous evening, and apologized for not having called or texted him sooner. His replies were clearly frantic, and it wasn't long before her phone was ringing insistently.

"It's okay, Tom, I'm fine, really, I was in good hands."

"Oh God, Tess, I've been worried sick! Why were you on your own down there at night?"

"I wasn't on my own, we'd gone to Zuma Beach to watch the sun go down and we had dinner there at The Sunset restaurant, but when we came back to Bill's bike, he realized he'd left the crash helmets under the table, and ran back to get them. But he wasn't gone more than two minutes."

"But Tess, don't you see, two minutes is long enough to get killed in L.A., you have to be more careful, even out there in the 'Bu."

"I know, and I've learned my lesson now, and apart from some bruised ribs, I'm fine, so please don't worry!"

"Well, I *am* worried, this is awful to have happened to you and I feel so useless that I can't do anything about it. I want to kill those guys."

"Seriously, Tom, you have to calm down, I'm really okay and the bruises will disappear. Trust me, it's fine," she said, hoping that she'd assuaged Tom's inner fears.

"If you say so," Tom replied, "But I'm still worried."

"I do say so, so please don't be concerned, Tom, I'm fine."

"Anyway, dinner with Hippy Bill? How did that go? Don't tell me you have a thing about older men, I'll be crushed," said Tom.

Tess sensed a tiny inkling of jealousy from Tom, but if only he knew the truth.

"No! Of course not, he's pushing seventy! But I'm learning so much from him about my father. Do you know Bill?"

"Everyone knows Bill, the man is a legend around here. He's also a really great guy, smart too, although he doesn't let on, just loves to keep pushing the hobo image to everyone who doesn't know him. He's a bit of an actor, I think he missed his vocation."

"You're right, he's definitely unique and I like him a lot but not in that way, if you know what I mean," Tess replied, teasingly.

There was a moment of silence at the other end of the line.

"Well, can I see you again before you go back to England?"

"Of course! I'd love that, Tom, but I think I'm going to take tonight off, relax in a hot bath with Epsom salts and soak my bones if that's okay, but I'm free tomorrow?"

"Well... I could take a day off and we could have some fun if you like? Do you play golf?"

"Golf? No, I've never even thought about it. Who was it that said, "golf is a good walk spoiled"? Your Mark Twain, wasn't it?"

"That's funny! But I think he had already died by the time it became a phrase. The original theory is that it was a quote from an unknown golfer who said that, "to play golf is to spoil an otherwise enjoyable walk." But anyway, it's not true, it's a great sport, fun too," said Tom.

"So you're good? Wouldn't I be an embarrassment?"

"Not at all, you'd have fun. I only ever started playing because Dad is pretty good at it. I thought it was an old man's game but once you get hooked, there's no going back. And even if you don't feel up to playing, it's a nice ride in the golf buggy with pretty scenery."

"Alright, Mr. Delaney, you're on but you'll need to teach me."

"I would welcome the opportunity in a heartbeat, so shall I pick you up at around nine in the morning?" Tom replied, knowing that his partner, Matt, wasn't going to be overjoyed about Tom missing a day's work when they had so much to get through.

"Deal!" said Tess, "But what the hell do I wear?"

"Don't worry about that, we'll get you some things in the pro-shop at the club. They've always got a great sale rail there."

"Fantastic! Well, I'd better let you go, Tom, night night, have a lovely evening."

"You too, Tess, and don't go out on your own, okay?"

Tess ended the call and once again she felt butterflies in her tummy. Tom was not just stupidly handsome; he seemed to be a genuinely lovely man too. He was witty, he was kind and he had impeccable manners. And that smile? If she could wake up to that smile every morning, she'd never want to go to sleep.

Was that really possible in a man? Can you actually find someone who has it all? It certainly hadn't been that way with Simon and if she was honest with herself, she couldn't remember dating anyone who was even close to the kind of man that Tom seemed to be.

But golf? Really?

Chapter 46

The street was calm, lit solely by the occasional still-functioning bulb in the sporadic and haphazard streetlights that lined the sidewalk. It was like any other working-class street in Los Angeles, smaller single-story homes, built fairly close together, almost to the lot-lines, and half the driveways had pickup trucks parked on them. Others had twenty or thirty-year-old Nissans or Chryslers parked outside, their paint dulled from the incessant L.A. sun and the owners' lack of time to polish them. Making the monthly mortgage payment was priority. Pride of home ownership was still the focus.

Front yards showed patchy brown areas in the turf that relied on infrequent doses of rainfall to stay green but were inevitably losing the battle. Basketball hoops bolted above garage doors, footballs lying in parched flower beds and rusted bikes discarded for the evening, waiting for the morning to come. The kids here didn't see themselves as poor or working-class, all they saw was their own little adventure playground that lay right outside their doors, and they couldn't wait to get back to it when they woke up again, when morning came.

It was after eleven now, and the children would be tucked up in bed and the husbands and wives would be relaxing with a beer or a glass of wine or two, watching some cable television before they themselves turned in to be ready for another day in the City of Angels.

But Buchanan was alert, this was the time he loved most, when everyone was in their bunkers and The Watcher was ready and waiting, hanging in the shadows. The sound of the 405 buffered any noise from the now quiet suburban street, but he still chose to creep stealthily through the withered palms and brush, that failed dismally at muting the interstate's continued rumble and hum. He'd walked a little over a mile, having already dropped the Camry at a parking garage before eating a steak dinner at a Longhorns restaurant. He'd remembered at the last moment when he dumped the Toyota, to snatch a pair of license plates from the many he kept in its trunk, so he could swap them out on his target vehicle.

Arriving at the address he'd noted down, he saw that the house was already in darkness, but decided to wait for another twenty minutes or so before he made his move. He hunkered down behind a nest of palms and unscrewed the lid from his thermos. He poured some of the now tepid coffee into the plastic cup and greedily unwrapped a pastrami on rye sandwich, biting into it as though he hadn't eaten in a week, even though he'd just finished a steak dinner a couple of hours ago.

Fucking Jews and their food, gotta love 'em...

Buchanan thought that he could probably survive on deli food for the rest of his life although he wasn't sure about gefilte fish.

What was that all about?

And it wasn't that he disliked the Jews as a whole, he didn't really discriminate; he pretty much disliked and despised everyone. In his mind, he wasn't selectively racist, he was a global hater. All creeds, all colors, all religions. Pretty well balanced, as far as he was concerned. Chips on both shoulders. And he'd never been with a black girl, or a brown one or even an Asian for that matter. But he did love a Jewish deli. He liked Jewish women too, they'd always give it up.

He checked his watch, it was past midnight now, time to move. This would be a nice little payback on all Delaney's goons who seemed to be spending their lives protecting the girl. There was no chance of snatching the Indian from the hobo, particularly after the abortive fuck-up by his Mexican clowns at Zuma Beach last night, but the Buick would be a much nicer prize anyway. It pissed him off mightily to see a Chinese fence-jumper driving a piece of American history.

Time to take back America and make it great again...

He emerged from the brush and padded across the road and up the driveway, reaching inside his coat for his cherished tool. He checked the door handle on the off-chance that the car had been left unlocked, but seeing that it wasn't, he slid the metal 'slim jim' carefully down between the window and the rubber seal, and gently moved it around until he found purchase. He pulled the tool slightly upwards until he heard the click he was waiting for.

Opening the now unlocked driver's side door, he slid into the leather seat, put the car in neutral and released the handbrake, grateful that the driveway was on a sharp incline down toward the street. With his foot hovering above the brake pedal, he let the car slide silently in reverse out of the driveway and onto the road, turning the wheel sharply to his left as he allowed the slope of the road to take the car further away from the house, its own camber an added bonus in Buchanan's muted theft.

Once he had covered enough distance and the road had begun to level out, he applied the brake and put the car in park. On cars of this age, the idea of hotwiring was irrelevant. There was a much simpler solution. Taking a thin flathead screwdriver and a hammer from his coat, he slid the tip of the screwdriver into the ignition lock and banged hard on the top of its grip with the hammer. Once the head had torn through the lock pins and was about an inch and a half in, he simply turned the screwdriver clockwise and the Buick's throaty

V8 immediately burbled into life. Shifting the car into drive, Buchanan let the engine's idle speed slowly take him back past the Asian man's home until he was clear, and then gunned it out of the suburb.

So long, Chinaman, and thank you, I'll be taking care of this little beauty for you. Fucking gooks…

Chapter 47

The following morning, Tess was up at six to take the opportunity to call her mother, who was eight hours ahead of her because of the time zone difference. She gave her mom an update on most of what had happened during her time away but was careful to exclude the events of the previous two days. She realized that her mother would be worried sick if she knew that Tess had been attacked, and would try to 'ban' her from traveling again, so it was easier to avoid the issue.

By a quarter to nine, she had eaten breakfast and was outside the hotel entrance, waiting for Tom to arrive. She breathed in the morning air, it was clean and fresh and she realized that in a couple of days, she was really going to miss it. Her time in Malibu had passed far too quickly and she suddenly wondered if she would ever see the place again. And it made her sad. In such a short space of time, she had met so many nice people and made friends easily, so it was going to be hard to walk away from it.

Just as Tess was sinking into a minor gloom about her upcoming trip back to England, the sound of Tom's Bronco was unmistakable as he made his entrance into the hotel's small semi-circular driveway. She saw his brimming smile immediately, but also spied two sets of clubs in the back of the truck and wondered where he had found a second set.

Maybe an ex-girlfriend?

He jumped out of the driver's side and gave Tess a huge hug and a kiss on her cheek, as he helped her into the vehicle.

Such a gentleman…

"Are you ready?" he asked, "Ready to have a good walk spoiled?"

"I'm not sure I'll ever be ready for this but I've never been the type of girl who won't give anything a try," Tess replied, buckling her seatbelt.

"Well there won't be much walking, I guess, we'll be taking a buggy out so it's going to be a completely relaxing and awesome day," said Tom, "Come on, let's have at it!"

~

"That was a clusterfuck last night."

"It wasn't meant to be, the guys I used have always been good, never had an issue."

"You pay peanuts, Frank, you get fucking monkeys!"

Buchanan and Carlisle were sitting in Mickey's Los Angeles apartment in Koreatown. Frank had been there numerous times before, and it was a long way from the sprawling acreage Mickey used to own years ago in Bel Air. Even Frank's house out in Ojai had to be worth more than Mickey's place.

How the mighty have fallen…

Buchanan knew he was going to feel the wrath of Mickey Carlisle's temper but the whole 'you work for me and you do as I tell you' shtick was wearing a bit thin. It further reinforced his intention to get out of Mickey's grasp, once this job was done and dusted.

214

"I've used 'em before, Mickey, it's never been a problem, okay?" Buchanan replied, "Just stay out of my face, will ya?"

"Yeah, those clowns are so fucking good, they got beaten off by a chick and a septuagenarian fucking hobo!" Mickey replied, "Sometimes I think you've lost your edge, Frank, maybe it's time for you to quit."

"I don't think he's even sixty, Mickey, and you didn't see him, he's built like a fucking bull, strong as a frickin' ox!"

Mickey knew that he was maybe pushing Buchanan's buttons more than he should, even as soon as the words had left his mouth. Frank was the only muscle who still worked for him, if you could call Frank 'muscle'. He also knew that his fading empire, such as it used to be, was on thin ice now. The schmucks he used to skim from, were no longer around. And he was getting old as well, at seventy-eight he was probably way too old for this game, but he also hadn't been smart at putting money away and he needed one last big payday.

"Anyway, there's no way I'll have another chance at the kid this week because she leaves Saturday, so we're shit out of luck for the moment," said Buchanan.

"She's leaving? Is she coming back?"

"How the fuck do I know, what am I, her fucking babysitter? Jesus, Mickey, just leave it with me, I'll know something soon."

Tess was dumbstruck when Tom guided the Bronco through the gates at the Riviera Club. She'd never been to a golf club before, let alone one in Pacific Palisades which seemed to literally drip with money. The grounds were better manicured than her nails and the cars in the car park, as Tom searched for a spot amongst them, were like something out of a Saudi prince's garage.

"There are so many people here, Tom, I'm going to look silly on the course, having never played before," said Tess, now suddenly nervous, butterflies performing somersaults in her stomach.

"Don't worry. Firstly, most of the members here couldn't shoot under a hundred if you paid them. Secondly, the majority of them come here to meet their buddies and get away from their wives," Tom replied, "Some of them come here just to take a nap!"

"Under a hundred?"

"Yeah, sorry. I should explain. If you're a really decent golfer, you should go round in par or better, so that would be seventy-two shots or less over eighteen holes. Except that here, par is seventy-one."

I knew that…

"So how good are you?' she asked.

"I'm around scratch, maybe one or two more," he replied.

Ditto…

"I think I'm going to live to regret this," she said, "My mother told me never to listen to handsome men."

"Don't be silly, you're going to love it… and can I take that as a compliment?" Tom replied, almost blushing.

"You can. But do we get to practice first?" asked Tess, as Tom hauled the two bags out of the back of the truck and they began to make their way toward the pro-shop, "I just think I ought to find out if I'm going to be a complete disaster before I inflict myself on others."

"Of course, but don't worry, they have a driving range here so we can spend an hour or so there, just getting you acclimatized," he said, handing the golf bags to one of the guys in charge of the buggies and thanking him, "But first, as you Brits say, let's get you suited and booted!"

Chapter 48

Bill hadn't expected to experience the kind of feelings he already felt for Tess. If he was forced to admit it, even if only to himself, he already knew that she would be the daughter he always wanted, but never had. Damn, she was a breath of fresh air! Sandy would have been a great mom, a free, wild, crazy kind of hippy mom but the best a daughter could ask for. And he still missed Sandy after all these years. No one could ever replace her.

And he was only just now beginning to understand what Robert must have suffered, having this incredible daughter thousands of miles away but never being able to see her, love her, take care of her. It made him want to cry just thinking about it.

Yet in all those years, even when Sandy was still alive, Robert had never really talked to him about Tess, and right now Bill was thinking how Robert had never even shown how much he was obviously suffering, and how hard it must have been for so long. But at least Robert had had the benefit of knowing he'd brought something wonderful into this world. It was too late for Bill. And it was much too late for Sandy. But Bill could still be the best friend a man could have. Even after Robert's death.

He leaned out over the patio as the early morning waves crashed down on the sand below, the sun already an orange glow in the Malibu skyline and said a silent prayer to his great friend and business partner. Without him, he would never have the life he'd had. Robert was to him what Bernie was to Elton, two peas in a pod from two entirely different plants, but for whatever reason, they were made for one another.

I'll look after her, Bobby, I'll keep her safe…

But even as he thought this, he knew it was going to be difficult while Tess was still in L.A. and all the wrong people had all the wrong ideas about her. And although he cherished the idea of Tess being a part of his life, he also wanted her out of the country as soon as possible. It was a terrible dichotomy, but he had things to deal with before she would ever be safe again.

Chapter 49

When Tess had first begun studying English Literature at school, she was assigned three novels by the American author, John Steinbeck. At the time, she had never previously heard of him but understood that he was an esteemed novelist in the United States. When she'd finally finished reading the books, she realized that they weren't exactly vacation brochures for America. They were grim, dark, painful and depressing. Particularly *Grapes of Wrath*, which was hard to read and comprehend, as the Joad family made its long and treacherous journey across America from Oklahoma to California, in search of a new beginning and a new life. So at twelve years old, Tess had already decided that America wasn't on her bucket list and likely never would be.

Should have read F. Scott Fitzgerald...

But as she gazed around at the extraordinary Spanish architecture that graced the golf course at The Riviera, she realized how reading someone else's words could affect you in completely the wrong way. It seemed that every literal image in Steinbeck's novels was in black and white, everything drained of color, but here in Los Angeles, the Riviera clubhouse sat majestically on a hill, almost like a monastery, in a sea of Technicolor.

Its simple architecture of white stucco walls, towering arches, cloisters and wooden-shuttered windows, crowned with vivid and barreled terracotta roof tiles, was something that only a Spanish architect could have designed. It was only further enhanced by the rolling verdant slopes and valleys that surrounded it, so green they might have been painted.

Inside, the magnificence continued and became even more opulent in a Hispanic-Italianate meeting of design minds. Carved wood architraves, lacquered oak floors and intricate ceilings were the antitheses of its simple exterior. Majestic stairways, sumptuous décor, and furniture to literally die for, lay beyond in every grand room she encountered.

"Tess? Tess, anyone home?" asked Tom.

"Sorry, I was just taking all this in. I don't think I've ever been anywhere so sumptuous," she replied.

"Come on, we need to get you kitted out," Tom replied, Let's see what we can find."

They spent twenty minutes trawling through the sale rail and Tess was pleasantly surprised how cool and cute some of the ladies apparel was; she'd always assumed that any woman who played golf had to be over sixty and not really into fashion. More akin to needlework, bridge and book clubs. But she was so wrong, she'd already encountered a number of young women and girls in the clubhouse, and some of them looked like models as well as athletes.

I guess golf has come a long way...

She'd opted for a pair of figure-hugging white pants because she thought her butt looked good in them, and paired them with a pale blue sleeveless top. And she absolutely couldn't resist the belt she'd spotted on the end of the rail, a pink mock-crocodile thing with a bright silver buckle in the shape of a turtle. And while Tess had taken an armful of items into the changing room before deciding on her outfit, Tom had been on his knees in the corner of the pro-shop, rummaging through the sale shoes. After opening more than fifty shoe boxes, he finally and jubilantly exclaimed,

"Eureka!" as he held aloft a matching pair of pink mock-croc golf shoes, "And in a size seven!"

"I can't believe you found those! I hope they fit," Tess replied, rushing over to where Tom sat so that she could try them on.

"Well, let's find out," he said, slipping one of the shoes onto Tess's right foot.

"It's perfect," she said, "I guess I am going to the ball after all!"

Chapter 50

The day was a thousand times better than Tess could ever have imagined. They didn't bother keeping score but Tom told her that she had a natural ability and that she should keep it up when she returned to England. But even Tess had to believe that he wasn't just buttering her up like most men would, because she had felt pretty confident once she'd had some coaching from him and had spent time on the range. And Tom was the kind of guy who would tell you the truth, he'd pretty much say it how it was. She had to admit, he was pretty special. And she loved his accent…

After Tom had taken her back to the hotel, she asked if he would have dinner with her the following evening and he hadn't had to think about it, immediately agreeing and asking what time he should collect her. She said that maybe she should come to collect him this time and Tom had loved the way she'd turned it around so that he was the one being taken out.

"I don't think I've ever had a girl take me out before," he'd said.

"It's 2017, Tom, not 1720!" she'd replied.

"Oh, don't get me wrong, I'm totally down with that, I love a dominant woman! Tom had replied, excitedly, "Your wish, my command and all that good stuff."

A man in touch with his feminine side…

For the first time since she'd been in California, Tess was feeling torn. The only reason she had come over in the first place, was to deal with what she thought were just administrative issues after her father's apparent suicide. She thought it would be done and dusted in a matter of days and she'd be hightailing it back to England, to her family and to her career.

But since she'd arrived, it had been like a fabulous vacation. Only after having finally experienced California, did she realize what had originally attracted her father. And then the surprise discovery that her father had left her things that he obviously wanted her to have and to use for her own benefit. When she stopped to think about the value of her inheritance, the mobile home, the car and cash, it was probably close to a quarter of a million dollars, maybe even more. If she sold it all, she could probably put a deposit on a pretty nice cottage back in England.

But it wasn't really about the money. She really liked this part of California, and the people she had met so far had been fantastic, apart from the two Mexican muggers. Nathan, Bill, Tom, Sammy, Jake, Summer and their daughters, they had all embraced Tess like she was part of their own family and she was enjoying it. If she was truthful to herself, she didn't really want to leave but she couldn't afford to stay, and also, she didn't have a job. Added to that, she didn't even have a Green Card so there was not much chance of her ever making California her home.

Just as she was thinking how she needed to get Tom out of her system, there was a knock at her door.

"Come in," she said, staring at the unlit fireplace as she lay in a fetal position on the sofa.

"Penny for your thoughts, princess?" said Nathan as he opened the door, stepping into the room with a tray of tea.

"I was just thinking how much I'm enjoying being here, that's all," she replied, still staring at the fireplace.

226

"Well, a cup of Earl Grey might help," said Nathan, setting the tray down on the coffee table.

Tess realized that she was in a daze and quickly pulled herself up into a cross-legged position on the sofa, taking the teapot and pouring two cups for them.

"I'm not ready to go home just yet, I suppose, and I love the new friends I've made here, including you. I'm torn."

"Am I the first black friend you've had?" asked Nathan, laughing as he said it.

"Stop it!" Tess said, throwing a pillow at him, "Of course not, but you know what I mean!"

"So don't go, change your ticket and stay a while longer."

"I can't, I don't have enough money, I need my job and I miss my parents. And anyway, I don't even have a visa for a longer stay," she replied.

"Look, Tess, California ain't going anywhere. If you need to go home, it'll still be here when you come back. If you come back, that is."

"I want to," she said.

"I want you to too, but I also realize that you've got a lot on your plate, so just deal with it one step at a time. And remember, if you do decide to return to Malibu, this gorgeous black face will be there waiting for you at the airport, so how can you not come back?"

"That's so true. Are you still taking sugar in your tea, philistine?"

"Two lumps, the brown ones, please."

"Blimey, Nathan, you really know how to ruin a cup of tea, don't you?"

227

"When they call it Earl Gay, maybe I can cut out the sugar, sugar. Maybe I'll go straight."

"Yeah, sure," Tess replied, looking out of the window, "And I think I just saw a pig fly past."

Chapter 51

"How was golf?"

"I think it might have been the best golf day I've ever had," Tom replied to Summer, her legs curled underneath her as she sat on the sofa next to him, "Scratch that, maybe the best *day* I've ever had. It was amazing."

'Might that have been due to your playing partner?" she asked, a teasing glint in her eye as she said it.

"Maybe, Mom, maybe," Tom replied, "She's a pretty special girl. And I love her accent too."

"I'll bet that's not all you love!"

"Well, I have to admit, she's pretty easy on the eye," replied Tom, "But stop teasing me, you and Dad were just the same from what you've both told me over the years."

"We were... From the moment I laid eyes on your father, I knew he was the one and I was only sixteen at the time. At least you two are at a sensible age, but what do you think she thinks about you, Tom? Do you think it's reciprocal?"

"Honestly, I really don't know, Mom. I mean, we have a great time together, she's a lot of fun and she teases me a lot... which actually I like. But I'm a bit scared to show my cards I guess, just in case I make a fool of myself and she doesn't have the same feelings toward me. I don't want to look like an idiot."

"Better be a fool in love than never in love at all," Summer replied, "And you'll only find out by stepping off the edge."

"How do you mean?" he asked.

"Well, when I was pregnant with Poppy, I thought your father would run a mile when he found out because I suppose I'd already made my own stupid assumptions. You've got to remember, he was twenty-five and I was only eighteen. So I took the easy way out and disappeared. But in retrospect, I knew that the opposite was true, Jake would have loved that I was having his baby. Although, I wouldn't change anything now, because we wouldn't have you and Lily and Casey, so sometimes things have to go the long way round to get to where you want to be. What do they say? Don't be afraid to wait, true love will always find its way."

"I see what you mean but I'm not sure it's going to be that easy. Tess goes home on Saturday so she'll never get to know me and I'll never get to really know her. It's probably a lost cause," Tom said, his features drooping at the thought of Tess leaving.

Summer looked at her stepson, his own face now filled with despair and realized how much like Jake he was. Even though they looked similar in size and features, Tom also shared his father's romantic notions, his gentleness and his emotional fragility. But what Tom didn't understand, which made him even more attractive to girls, was that these character traits were probably not lost on Tess, and from the moment they had first met that night at the dinner party, Summer had witnessed an instant attraction between the two. But Tom was right; Tess was leaving in just a couple of days so time wasn't on their side.

Chapter 52

At a little after the agreed time on Friday evening, Tess pulled up outside Tom's small but crazy cute, storybook home on Greenleaf Canyon Road in Topanga. The eight burbling cylinders of the Mustang's iconic Shelby engine seemed to reverberate through the silence of the entire canyon. Birds flew effortlessly across the void, catching the breeze and gliding down toward the canyon floor, their wings motionless as they guided their way to a sanctuary that only they knew.

The 'gingerbread' house appeared as though it was built entirely of wood construction, and her first impression was that it looked like a cuckoo clock sitting wedged into the hillside. In fact, she half expected a cuckoo to pop out of the circular window at the top of the home. She couldn't help but be entranced by the building, which was more log cabin than house.

As she closed the Mustang's door and made her way down the cottage's path, Tom suddenly appeared at the front door, smiling as he ambled toward her.

"I've been watching out for you to arrive, I didn't know if you'd find it, it's a bit off the beaten track," he said, "But welcome to Tom's tiny abode!"

"I love it," said Tess, as he embraced her and kissed her cheek, "It's like something out of Hansel and Gretel."

"Well, don't try eating the door, you'll be disappointed."

"It's just so pretty, I never expected you to live in a place like this, how on earth did you find it?"

"I know, you expected me to live in a high rise bachelor apartment in the city, right?"

"Kinda…"

"Well, I'm just not into that whole glass and concrete thing, I prefer a simple organic structure, and I love the peace and quiet out here," said Tom.

"It's beautiful, so serene too,"

"Come on in, I'll show you around, although there's not a lot to see."

They went inside the picturesque little house and Tom gave her a tour, although it didn't take too long. A simple kitchen with a wood-burning stove, two bedrooms that were furnished simply, using traditional Moorish and Mexican style furniture, accessorized with knitted pillows and throws in multiple stripes, patterns and colors. The lounge itself was vaulted, in that it was open to the second floor where the bedrooms and bathrooms were located. Tess also noted that there wasn't a television in sight, but there was an expensive looking turntable and amplifier and a set of tall loudspeakers in the corners of the room.

"So you don't watch TV but you love music?" she asked.

"In a nutshell, yes, but I'm a bit of a purist when it comes to music," he replied, "Or just old-fashioned in that I prefer vinyl over CDs. My bad."

"No, I love that, I just didn't know you could buy vinyl records these days and I've never owned a record player."

"I love buying old records," he said, "I could spend days searching in second-hand record stores just ferreting out little forgotten gems. And vinyl is making a comeback at the moment."

"What do you like to listen to?" she asked.

"Hold on, let me put something on…"

Tom plucked an album from a row of vinyl records that lined the wall above the bookcase, carefully extracted the black disc from its sleeve and put it onto the turntable. As soon as he lifted the arm and placed the needle into the groove, music immediately filled the room.

"I love this! Who is it? What's the song called?" said Tess after listening for a minute or two.

"Ah, this is the legendary Chet Baker and the song, well, appropriately I guess… "My Funny Valentine"."

"You're so sweet!" Tess squealed, "It's my song!"

You're so damned gorgeous too…

"I'd like to say that is was purely by chance that I pulled out this record, but I confess, I did kind of plan it," Tom replied, "Anyway, where would you like to go and eat tonight, there are lots of cute places here in Topanga."

Tess was entranced by the song, enthralled by Chet Baker too, having never really listened much to jazz in the past but realizing she could easily get used to it.

"Tom?" she said, "Would you mind awfully if we didn't go out? It's my last night here and I was wondering if we could maybe stay here and order something in?"

"You must have read my mind but I can do better than that, I'll make us something, how about that?"

He can cook as well, c'mon someone, wake me up…

"Let's go outside, it's a beautiful evening," he said, "And I'll get us some wine… red or white?"

"White, please, if you have some," Tess replied.

He led her out to the deck, a wooden construction of old gnarled planks and he pulled a seat out from under the teak table for her. He rushed back into the house and quickly returned with a bottle of white wine and two goblets, setting them down on the table and pouring them each a glass.

"To safe travels tomorrow," he said, offering his glass to hers.

"I'm trying not to think about that, but thank you, I appreciate it," she said, clinking her glass with his.

They sat silently, enjoying the atmosphere of Tom's back yard, comfortable in each other's company, aware that words were unnecessary.

"Okay, enough of me mellowing out here, I'm going to prepare us something to eat. Is there anything you don't like?"

"I don't much care for kale or aubergine, although I think you call it eggplant here," Tess replied, "But other than that, I'll eat pretty much anything that's put in front of me."

"I'm on it, you just sit back and chill out here and I'll put on some Miles Davis while I make us something vaguely tasty."

Chapter 53

Frank Buchanan needed a vacation. The Valentine girl was clearly out of his reach at the moment and once she was out of the picture completely, back in England, he could devote his time to finding out what Bobby Valentine had done with his money. If he actually had any, of course, which Frank now severely doubted. But at least if he took some time away, he'd come back with the impetus to figure something out and stop Mickey carping in his ear every five minutes. His whining was getting to be old.

And he also figured that he should hide the Buick he'd just acquired, for a while anyway until the dust had settled. But he did enjoy driving that thing and the Asian fella had done a great restoration on it, even down to matchless reupholstering on the leather interior. The car was probably worth north of eighty grand. Not bad for a few hours work. He chuckled to himself when he pictured the look on the fella's face when he came outside that morning and found his beloved ride gone.

Maybe I should just concentrate on stealing cars... like taking candy from a baby...

But even so, he definitely needed a vacation, just needed to get out of fucking L.A. for a few weeks, a month even. Maybe altogether. And it was a bonus that Maisie was a travel agent, she could fix something up for them in a heartbeat, Cabo maybe, or the Cayman Islands, even the Bahamas, do some gambling over at the Atlantis on Paradise Island. Yeah, that would work, sunshine and slots, Black Russians and blackjack. And he hadn't taken Maisie away for a break in a dozen years or more. Hell, she deserved it and well, he loved her. In his own way, anyway.

"Maisie!" he yelled to his wife who seemed to live in their kitchen.

"Yes, dear?" she said, coming into the room, "What's the matter?"

"Nothing's the matter, sweetheart, we're going on a vacation."

"Really?" Maisie said, astonished that her husband would take time out from his insurance work.

"Yep, pack your bags, I'm taking you to Paradise."

Chapter 54

Tom was pretty useful in the kitchen, Tess thought. No, more than useful, he was almost a trained chef. Within ten minutes of him disappearing into the kitchen, he'd returned with a plate of prosciutto-wrapped asparagus bundles, shaved parmesan already melting over them, and hot butter drizzling around the plate. He poured her more wine when he saw that her glass was empty, but Tess said she should limit it as she had to drive back to the hotel.

After they had shared the plate of asparagus, he disappeared again inside the house and she heard him change the record. This time she actually recognized the artist, the unmistakable basso of none other than Louis Armstrong.

I see trees of green, red roses too

I see them bloom, for me and for you

And I think to myself, what a wonderful world…

She was entranced by the jazz legend, and minutes seemed to tick past like seconds as the sun began to set over the distant horizon.

I could get so used to this…

And then Tom appeared again, this time returning with two plates which he set down on the table.

"Wow, what's this?"

"I thought in honor of your nationality, I'd make pan-seared Dover sole for you. Dover's in England, right? And that's a caper and lemon butter sauce. Goes really nicely with the potato gratin if you let it soak in," he said, smiling at his culinary creation.

"Tom?" she said.

"What's wrong?"

"This fish is fresh, right?"

"Er… yeah…"

"So, you were hoping we'd stay home and eat?"

"Guilty as charged," he said, holding up his hands in mock surrender, "But I only bought the fish just in case you wanted to stay in."

"Well, you're a very thoughtful man," she said, and got up from her seat and kissed his cheek, "and you're a dying breed."

~

Tess realized that she hadn't really eaten all day and was famished. She was also further amazed at Tom's ability in the kitchen when he served up Crêpes Suzette for dessert. They chatted about everything and anything, the conversation never becoming uneasy, a rhythmic flow during the entire evening which was again, something that Tess had never before experienced. She couldn't remember a conversation with Simon that had lasted more than three minutes and hadn't ended with him changing the subject to sport.

"I meant to tell you, poor Sammy, his car was stolen a couple of nights ago," said Tom, taking a final bite of his remaining crêpe.

"You're joking! He loved that car," said Tess, feeling immediately sad for the man, "Each time I've been in it with him, it's so clear to see the pride he has for it."

242

"I know, he came out yesterday morning and it was gone, right from off his driveway."

"He's a detective though, do you think he'll be able to track it down?"

"Wouldn't surprise me and honestly, I wouldn't want to mess with Sammy. He may be small but he's a black belt in Taekwondo."

"Wow!" she exclaimed, "But you and your family are pretty close to him and his wife, aren't you?"

"We are. We grew up with him always being in our lives. He's like the uncle we never had. Him and another couple of Dad's friends, two unusual men who go by the names of Talbot and Perryman. You don't know those two reprobates but I'm sure you'll meet them at some point!"

"You seem to have an amazing relationship with Summer too; if I didn't know different, I would have assumed she was your real mother," said Tess, sliding her finger around the plate to mop up the remaining powdered sugar that had fallen from the crêpes.

"I do, and so does Lily. We never knew our real mom. Her name was Tara. She died giving birth to Lily."

"Tom, I'm really sorry, your dad told me what happened," said Tess, reaching for his hand, wishing she'd never brought up the subject.

"Oh, it's fine, really, like I say, we never knew her. We've got photos of her so we know what she looks like. She was so incredibly beautiful and apparently really lovely as a person so I don't know how Dad coped when he lost her. He's talked about it but I know he holds a lot back."

"But it was a long time before Summer came into your lives, right? She didn't raise you, did she?" Tess asked.

"No, that was all my dad. He was really like a mother and a father all rolled into one for us, which I guess looking back, must have been so hard for him. And he never found anyone else to love until Summer came back into his life, which was almost twenty-five years later, I think."

"That's amazing, Tom, he should write a book about it. It's like the most incredible love story that's almost impossible to believe could even be real."

"But Summer, Mom actually, I love her like my own mother. I mean, you've met her, she's so nice, not a bad bone in her entire body. It was so natural when she came into our lives and literally overnight, our family doubled in size from three to six. It's kind of a miracle that we all get along so well, I guess."

"It's strange how sometimes these 'nuclear' families just gel so easily, maybe it's because you're not all related?"

"Yep, we're a regular twenty-first-century Brady Bunch," Tom said, laughing at the comparison.

Tess knew the old American television series, and she'd watched it with fondness back in England when she was little.

"Tell me about Bill, how well do you know him?" she asked.

"The Malibu Hobo? Not that well, really. I mean everyone knows who he is and they'd recognize him on sight but nobody really 'knows' him, if you see what I mean. He's a very insular man, pretty guarded and likes his privacy. Dad is friendly with him but not in a way that they hang out or anything, but they'd say hi if they bumped into each other."

"How about his wife, Sandy? What do you know about her? I'm guessing you never met her?" Tess asked.

"She was this beautiful hippy kind of woman. She died long before I was born but I've seen photos of her. And she was an athlete too, she was pretty much the queen of surfing in Los Angeles at the time, and she and Bill were literally made for each other," said Tom, "And the house you stayed in the other night? Well, Bill built that as a monument to Sandy so that her spirit would never be far from the ocean. He worshiped the ground she walked on."

"And she was killed in a surfing accident, it's just so tragic," said Tess, now feeling tearful at what Bill must still be going through emotionally.

"They *were* the perfect couple but the one thing we do know that Bill readily acknowledges, is that she died doing what she loved, and in some way that gives him closure."

"And they never had kids? He never remarried?"

"I'm not even sure from what Dad says that she would have ever found time for kids because she was so into her surfing but who knows, if she had had a child, it might have made her see the danger of what she was doing?" said Tom, "And no, once Sandy was gone, Bill pretty much shut up shop on the romantic front. For him, no one could replace Sandy."

They both fell silent for a minute or so, each of them contemplating what it must have felt like to have lost someone that couldn't be replaced. Eventually, Tom went inside and changed the record for a new one.

"Um... would you... I mean," stuttered Tom, "I guess what I'm trying to say is... would you like to dance?"

"I'd love to! And I love this, whatever it is you just put on, it's gorgeous," Tess replied.

Tom took her hand and led her to the center of the deck, leading her in a slow and gentle dance.

"It's pretty recent, actually, and it's on CD as it has never been released on vinyl but I love it anyway. It's Tony Bennett and Norah Jones performing a duet together, the old and the new singing a love song the way it's meant to be heard," he said, knowing that Tess was enjoying the music.

"What's the song?" she asked, stepping closer to him, feeling his heart beating as she pressed against him,"

"It's called "Speak Low"…"

Speak low when you speak, love

Our moment is swift, like ships adrift,

We're swept apart, too soon…

They danced lazily, in no hurry for anything at all, the moon now casting a bluish shimmer across the canyon. Even the birds had grown silent with the onset of the day's end. Tess felt as though they could be the only people for miles and miles, dancing on a deserted mountain, just tasting the moment and forgetting what tomorrow might bring. Tom wrapped his arms around her as he felt a small shiver run through her body and immediately Tess reciprocated, snuggling closer to him, each enjoying the other's body heat.

"I might be falling in love with you, Tess…"

She had already guessed that he might feel the same as she was already feeling, but she didn't want to ruin what was turning out to be such a perfect evening.

"You can't, Tom, I'm going back to England, and there'll be too many miles between us," she replied, "I'm sorry."

"You don't need to be sorry about anything," he said, looking deep into Tess's almond eyes, "This is more than I could ever have wished for, and I'll be waiting for you."

And without any thought about what the future might hold for them, their lips touched, their eyes closed and they kissed.

Leave slowly, Tess, come back to me quickly…

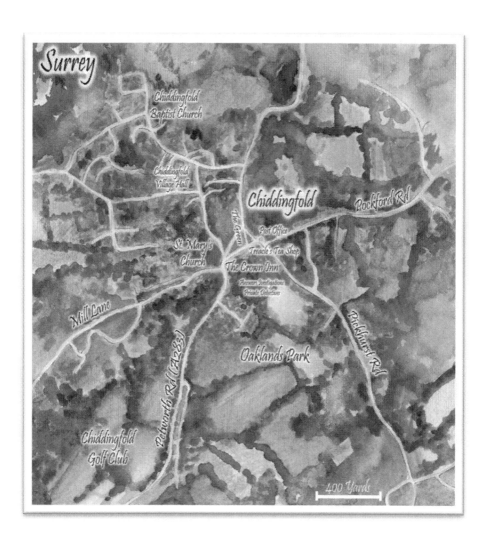

Chapter 55

Part Two

Chiddingfold, Surrey – England.

As the car rounded the curve in the road and the lighted village rose up before them, her heart warmed to the picture-postcard spectacle that appeared in the distance. Tess always found the drive home magical when she approached her little village in the evening, particularly once the nights began to draw in quickly when winter came. As the Petworth Road wound its way through Surrey, the picturesque scene that everyone saw when they came upon Chiddingfold, was like something from a Charles Dickens novel, a rich and colorful Christmas Carol.

The village was one of many tiny hamlets in this part of England and its center was the stunning church of St. Mary's, a Gothic-style building that dated back to around 1190, when the current stone edifice replaced the wooden building first erected in 978. But what Tess loved most was when darkness fell and the church lights came on, the village transforming into a Dickensian film set. She never tired of the excitement she felt each time she saw it.

And as with most hamlets that became villages, you could drive through and almost in the blink of an eye, miss the place entirely, particularly during the daylight hours. The church, along with the seven-hundred-year-old pub, The Crown Inn, formed the centerpiece of a village built around a traditional green and pond. Tess and her family were fortunate to live in one of the centuries-old flint and stone farm cottages that lay in the northeast corner of the green, just a leisurely walk from Tess's beloved Treacle's Tea Shop.

"Don't you just love it here?" she said as Franco steered his aging Jaguar left on the road that cut through the village green and onward toward their home, "I never get tired of seeing it."

"I never get tired of seeing *you*, Tess, but your mama's going to love having you back home," replied Franco, his Italian accent still quite strong, even after having lived in England for more than half of his life.

"I've missed her, I've missed you both, you *know* that!" she said, pinching his perpetually tanned and muscular arm.

As expected, Jenny Russo was waiting patiently on the doorstep of their pretty home, desperate for her daughter to arrive, and once she spotted Franco's Jaguar approaching, she rushed out to greet Tess as though she'd been gone for years.

"My baby!" she shouted, even before Tess could get out of the car, wanting to embrace her as Tess valiantly struggled out of the Jag.

"Mum! I've only been away a couple of weeks, not even!" she said, as Jenny kissed her all over her head.

It wasn't difficult to see the intense love that bound the two together and it wasn't difficult either to see that they were mother and daughter. They could almost have been sisters. Jenny was as tall as her daughter and maintained an extraordinary figure for someone closing in on sixty. She wore little make-up, her pretty face sleek and angular and she always dressed discretely, but there was no hiding her innate sex appeal. Definitely not in Franco's eyes anyway.

They hurried into the cottage, away from the cold November night's chill, and Tess was immediately comforted by the roaring fire in the drawing room as she stood with her back to it, feeling the flames' warmth spreading throughout her entire body.

"I want to hear all about your trip," said Jenny, "But not before I make you something to eat and drink. What can I get you?"

"I can't believe it, Mum, I ate like a woman possessed on the plane but I'm still hungry!' Tess replied, "And I'd love a cup of tea."

"Franco's already got the kettle on so can I make you a sandwich for the time being? I've got your favorite, chicken and coleslaw."

"Perfect, but I'm so exhausted, Mum, I think I'll have to get some sleep as soon as I've eaten and then we can chat in the morning and I can tell you everything. I'm really sorry but I didn't sleep a wink on the flight coming home, too many great movies to watch!"

"Don't worry, sweetie, we'll have all the time in the world in the morning, I'm just glad that you're home safe now. Just give me a minute and I'll have that sandwich ready for you."

"Thanks, Mum, you're the best. And you too, Franco," she said as her stepdad handed her a mug of steaming tea, wrapping a bear-like arm around his stepdaughter.

Chapter 56

Tess slept soundly. When she opened her eyes, a rare late November sun was sparkling through the curtains of her bedroom window. She turned over to look at her bedside clock, an old and traditional timepiece with alarm bells on top that she'd had for years and she wondered if it could really be that time already. It said ten fifteen so if it was right, she'd slept for almost thirteen hours. And almost immediately, she thought about Tom Delaney.

In fact, from the moment her plane had left LAX, she hadn't been able to stop thinking about Tom. She had known him for such a brief moment in time but she felt like she'd known him all her life. She was beginning to realize that she had accidentally fallen in love with the man, and just at the wrong time. It was an emotional farewell at the airport and she had promised that she would return as soon as she was able, although she couldn't see that happening in the foreseeable future.

Why does timing always have to suck?

Tom's father, Jake, had had the Mustang put into storage because he said that an eighty-thousand dollar classic shouldn't be left under a tarpaulin for any length of time. And he said that if she wanted, he would put her father's trailer home in the hands of a realtor he knew, so she could earn some revenue from it during the tourist season. But Tess didn't really want anyone else using the home before she'd had a chance to stay there herself so she had asked him to hold off on that for the time being. At least all the running costs were prepaid for more than a year ahead.

She lay listening in the silence of the Sunday morning, the church bells ringing from just a few hundred yards away, and she wondered where the creaks came from that she always heard in the house. Creaks that sounded like doors slowly opening somewhere, but creaks from doors that she knew didn't exist. And she could smell the unmistakable waft of a traditional English breakfast being cooked, winding its teasing and tempting way up the stairs and into her room.

Time to get up...

She brushed her teeth, put on a thick dressing gown and slipped down the three-hundred-year-old oak staircase to the kitchen, where her mother was conjuring a sumptuous breakfast, like a conductor corralling her orchestra.

"Morning, Mama," she said, hugging Jenny from behind, "You must have read my mind, I'm starving!"

Jenny turned around within Tess's embrace, wrapping her arms around her daughter, kissing her again on the top of her head.

"You're always hungry, baby girl, and it is Sunday so it has to be a full English this morning."

Tess loved her mother's 'full English', and it had become a staple for Sunday mornings for as long as she could remember. Fried eggs, bacon, sausages, grilled tomatoes, baked beans, black pudding, mushrooms and fried bread. And always with a couple of mugs of Twining's English Breakfast Tea.

"Where's Franco," Tess asked, "Is he not eating with us?"

"He's been up since six and he's taken the truck over to Arundel to pick up some more firewood, Jenny replied, "And he had a bacon and egg sandwich before he left. You know Franco, he always needs to get on and get things done and the fire is burning through wood at a rate of knots, now that we're officially in winter."

Tess also knew that in Franco's own unique way, he would have realized that she and her mother would have much to talk about and had obviously decided to give them the space they would need to chat. Franco was the thinking man's thinking man.

The cottage's kitchen brimmed with antiquity. Ancient beams crossed the length of the room's ceilings, exposed flint and stone walls meshed seamlessly with the newly plastered ones, and leaded-light windows fought to keep the cold of the English winter out of the cozy interior of the home. Antique leather chairs and comfortable sagging sofas were surrounded by shelves of hardcover, leather-bound books. Quaintly old-fashioned lamps and side tables, and various worn and mismatched rugs covered much of the old flagstone floor. The family's dog, a chocolate Labrador called Barney, rolled over in front of the fire to toast his tummy as the fire raged in the hearth. On Sundays, he didn't stray far from the glow of the embers unless it was for leftovers in the kitchen.

Jenny served up two enormous breakfast plates and Tess took both of them to their gnarled and ancient farmhouse table that took center stage in the open-plan kitchen. For almost a minute, there was complete silence between the two of them as Tess piled into her mother's breakfast feast, having clearly missed Jenny's home cooking.

"So come on, Tess, tell me everything about your trip, I'm on tenterhooks!"

"There's so much to tell, Mum, I don't even know where to begin. I've only been away for eleven or twelve days but so much has happened in that time and I can't believe I'll be back at work in London in the morning."

"I know, sweetie, but take your time and tell me the bare bones, I'm so looking forward to hearing about your adventures and what you discovered about your dad."

And so Tess told her mother everything. From her flight over to Los Angeles, to her swanky hotel, to all of the people she'd met there, and her father's home and car that he'd left her, and Hippy Bill, golf, Nobu and just about everything else. Although she decided to omit the part where she'd been attacked on the beach. She knew that was something that Jenny would find far too difficult to cope with, and if she did find out, she'd forever worry about Tess ever returning to America.

Jenny listened, taking in everything Tess was telling her about her trip, a melancholy feeling beginning to overflow within her own emotions, tears beginning to form in the corner of her eyes.

"What's wrong, Mum?" asked Tess, suddenly realizing her mother's distress and laying her hand gently over Jenny's.

"I've carried so much guilt for so long, Tess, I'm so sorry," said Jenny.

"Why?" asked Tess.

"Because it wasn't fair, it wasn't fair on you or Robert. Your dad loved you so much, Tess, but I wanted you all to myself. I couldn't bear the thought of sharing you, especially over such a long distance."

"I've got nothing to complain about, Mum, I suppose it's all just a bit of a shock finding out so much about him when it was too late."

"I know, and it's my fault, honey. Your dad was a beautiful boy when I met him. I loved him so much, he was like no other boy I'd ever dated. He had hopes and dreams like you'd never believe, but we were both so young. He thought that America was the Promised Land and from what you've told me now, I suppose for him it truly was. I think he was looking for somewhere... somewhere he could just call home because he'd never had one."

"So if you loved him, why didn't you go with him?" Tess asked, knowing that her mother was suffering an enormous fragility right now.

"I was scared, plain and simple. You see, your father came from a broken home, broken early in his life. His parents split after he was only a year or two old and he was placed in foster care, he was just a baby," said Jenny, "Your dad was an orphan who went from family to family, never knowing what a home really was, always hoping that the next one would be the right one. But it never was. Eventually, he decided that the only way he could make it in life was to make a life for himself, so he ran away from his final adoptive home when he was just fourteen. And he never told me how he had managed to survive in London at that age but I know it must have been so hard for him on the streets."

"Oh crumbs, Mum, I'm still learning about Dad, even now. I don't think I'll ever discover everything about him."

"But the thing is, Tess, he wasn't a complicated man at all. He just wanted to love and to be loved. He had a *joie de vivre* that he ought not to have had, considering the childhood he'd lived through. He had every reason to be angry at life, at the system, and at everyone around him but he wasn't angry at all. He just wanted to make a life for himself."

Tess went to the kitchen and grabbed a tissue from a box on the countertop, handing it to her mother and kissing her on the cheek. As she settled back into her chair, she once again took Jenny's hand and asked her the question she'd previously asked, worried that she would upset her mother.

"So why didn't you go to America, Mum?"

259

"It's a question I've asked myself a thousand times, Tess, and one that I still can't really fathom. The only thing I can tell you is that the East End in London, where I was born and where I had lived for my whole life until I was in my mid-thirties, was the only place I'd ever known. That was home to me," Jenny explained, "And then of course, I met Franco, fell in love, and we moved here as a family, but the East End, well, it's like its own little world where people rarely leave it to live elsewhere. For me, America was a far and distant, and I suppose in many ways an unreal place, that only really existed on television and in films. I was scared to death, I was so frightened by it but your dad wasn't."

"But you were pregnant! You and Dad could have been a family!" Tess said, amazed that her mother had found herself in such a difficult predicament.

"But I didn't find out I was pregnant until a month after your father had left, Tess. I didn't even know where he had gone to in America and things like email and text and the internet didn't really exist back then, so even if I had wanted to, there was no way I could have found him. And before Franco came along, I did want to, I still loved Robert, I still wanted to be with him and share our baby."

Tess was crying now, tears running down her face again, dismissing the notion that she was already all cried out. She ran back to the kitchen for a tissue but this time returned with the box. There were still many tears to shed.

"When I met Franco a year or so later, he was the knight in shining armor that came to my rescue. He was strong and he loved me and didn't even care that I had given birth to someone else's child. He was from a large Italian family where children were adored and idolized, and from the moment he met you, Tess, he adored and idolized you too. You know how he still feels about you."

"Of course I do, and I love him back in spades, he's my Dadda too, always will be. Trust me, Mum, I'm not angry at anything, I just want to find out as much as possible about Dad, and I know it hurts you to tell me but I just need to know, that's all," Tess replied, gripping Jenny's hand tightly as she spoke.

"I know, Tess. And I'll try and tell you as much as I know but you have to understand the guilt I'm feeling, that you had to find out about Robert in the way you have done over the last few weeks."

"Don't worry, I'm an East Ender, Mumma, I can handle it!" said Tess, bringing some lightness into what she knew would continue to be a difficult conversation.

"Okay... I'll try, just be patient with me."

"It's okay, Mumma, there's no hurry."

"Well, Robert was one of those people who literally had no real anger inside him, and he had every reason to be angry with me keeping you from him. But even though I wouldn't let you go and stay with him, even on a vacation, because I was scared you wouldn't come back, he never stopped supporting you financially. And I guess, he supported me and Franco too."

"How do you mean," asked Tess, sipping at her tea that she'd placed on top of the log burner to keep warm.

"You went to an outstanding school and I'm not sure you ever knew it, but it was an expensive private school and your dad paid the fees. He wanted to, and said he was doing well so he was able to fund the costs. When we moved here to Chiddingfold, Franco and I could never have afforded to buy this house on the money we made, so your dad paid for it. We don't even have a mortgage, never have had one," said Jenny, knowing how this would surprise her daughter.

"Blimey, Mum, that's huge!" said Tess, "I can't believe I didn't know that, but I can see now how he was able to afford it. From what people have told me, he was pretty wealthy by then, still should have been when he died, apparently."

261

"But you have to understand that he also thought a lot of Franco, he really liked him and not just because he'd brought you up as a surrogate father. Robert thought that Franco was a genuinely nice man and liked the effect he had on you growing up. They would even write to each other occasionally, which was interesting in itself."

"So you stayed in contact with Dad, even though you were married to Franco, and he was thousands of miles away?"

"Of course, I still wanted him to know what sort of daughter he had, and how proud he would be of you, it's just a natural emotion. He sent me money for years to help raise you. It was Robert who paid your university fees which is why you're one of the rare students who graduates without huge debts from student loans. Your dad loved the daughter he had, literally worshipped you but understood the situation. I was wrong keeping him from you, it was cruel of me and he didn't deserve it. He was a beautiful boy who became a beautiful man and if I could turn back time, I'd change everything, Tess."

"I guess you also know that he never met anyone else, Mum, he never got married either," said Tess, not fully comprehending her words as she said them. "He fell in love once and never found love again."

"I know, Tess, I know… I'm sorry, I'm so sorry…"

And then Jenny finally broke down. She could no longer hold back the pain from the guilt she'd felt for so many years, and her tears came crashing down with her sobs as Tess tried to comfort the mother she loved so much. And they sat for what seemed like hours, just holding onto each other, both of them wondering what if, but both also realizing that time would never be turned back and only the future beckoned.

Chapter 57

As Tess emerged from Piccadilly Circus Underground Station on Monday morning, into the raspingly cold November air, she pulled her woolen scarf tighter around her neck and buried her gloved hands deeper inside her coat's pockets. She still found it hard to believe that just forty-eight hours earlier, she'd been enjoying the carefree warmth and vistas of Malibu, a stark contrast to the gray skies and freezing temperature of London's Soho.

Can't do this forever...

She made her way up Shaftesbury Avenue, taking a left on Frith Street that eventually led her into Soho Square, where her firm's offices were located. As she entered the square, she thought back to the first time she'd arrived here in the summer of 2016, and of the many packed lunches she'd taken out onto the grass to eat during her lunch breaks. Memories of those priceless lunch hours, lying back in the grass, staring at a blue sky and thankful for the life she had, thankful for the job she had too.

The square itself, its full name, Soho Square Gardens, was a unique and pretty grassed area of Soho dating back to the 1670s, where the locals and employees could escape the hubbub of central London and peacefully eat their lunches, either on the grass or on the many benches that surrounded the square. At the center of the garden was an unusual mock-Tudor building, octagonal in shape, that Tess had originally assumed to be of some importance, but later found out it was only erected in 1926 to hide the utilities pipes and connections. Today it was covered in a thin layer of early season snow and looked as pretty as Tess could ever remember seeing it.

As she entered her building, she was met with many familiar faces who welcomed her back to work, some of them hugging her, some just telling her it was good to see her back at work. And she was glad to be back, she loved her job, loved where she worked and enjoyed working with the dynamic set of creatives whose world she gratefully inhabited. It was a dream job for her, an industry she had longed to join since before university. It didn't pay particularly well but she knew that if she stuck at it, the rewards would come eventually.

The company leased the five-story building and easily made use of all five floors. The ground floor was designated as Reception and client areas, with two meeting rooms for presentations. The next floor was Account Planning where all the eager and slickly groomed account executives and planners busied themselves on new and existing business, and Production occupied the floor above them. The penultimate floor was the haloed domain of the 'names above the door' along with the boardroom, and finally, the coveted top floor with its rooftop terraces was the world she loved most, the Creative Department.

Secretly, she called it the bullpen because it reminded her of an untamed and relentless hub of creativity that threatened to spark into flames at any given moment. The boys and girls who inhabited this world were some of the best that London had to offer and although she was still only a lowly junior, she felt a part of it and sucked up as much of the atmosphere as she could, desperate to succeed in the heady world of advertising.

"Morning Tess, come on, you're gonna be late, we've got a meeting on the Dacia creative brief we need to be at," said Archie, another junior creative, albeit with two more years experience than Tess.

266

"Be right there, Arch, save me a seat."

What the hell is Dacia?

~

Tess always found it mildly comical when a creative pitch brought the account execs and the creative team together in one room, a rare occurrence that harnessed together two diametrically opposed groups of people for a couple of hours. The sharp divide between the two groups was clear to see, even in the positions taken up by the combatants, the beautifully suited and booted execs on one side of the room and the t-shirt and jeans brigade on the other. Casual Friday was every day for the creatives. And it was as though they were two armies trying to win a battle, the account execs sucking up to whatever the client wanted and the creatives keen to make award-winning TV commercials to put on their showreels. Most of the time, they didn't realize they were actually on the same team.

As the account planners unveiled the latest potential client, Tess immediately discovered that Dacia was a Korean car maker, a company keen to get a shoe-in on the lucrative UK car market. But the model they were being briefed on this morning, was cataclysmically dull, something called a Duster.

Seriously? Duster?

She shot Archie a glance as he raised his eyebrows in the knowledge that there were no prestigious awards to be had from this pitch. The agency had clearly taken on the brief to target easy profit, with heavily marked-up future invoices funneling into the business. Nothing that was being planned here was going to make it onto the agency showreel. But that was how agencies were run; take on the dull stuff in order to fund the lower profit brands that would win awards, like British Airways, Budweiser and Apple. And awards meant new business… like Dacia.

"Wanna grab lunch at the Crown and Two?" whispered Archie, as Tess scribbled down notes from the briefing, "Tell me all about your trip?"

"Love to," Tess replied, "I'm gonna be starving if I have to listen to this for the next two hours."

Chapter 58

Six thousand miles away, Bill was ruminating on recent events, while seated at the outdoor dining table beyond the kitchen of his Malibu home. He sipped on a freshly brewed macchiato and watched the pelicans and gulls fighting over territorial rights on the sand below him. As was invariably the case, the pelicans were winning hands down.

A couple of years back, he'd seen a squabble between a pelican and a seagull over a fish that had jumped out of the surf and landed on the beach. It had been a titanic battle for a minute or so until the pelican, frustrated with the impudence of the smaller intruder, simply gobbled the gull up into its huge bill. Bill had watched as the gull, still alive, wriggled and flapped inside the pelican's gigantic beak but after a few seconds, the pelican stretched out its neck, made a huge and lengthy swallow and the seagull was no more. Bill had smoked a joint that day and wondered if maybe he had imagined it but having Googled it later that evening, he was astonished to find that although not a frequent occurrence, pelicans did occasionally dine on other birds.

But as he gazed out to the Pacific from his verandah, he was beginning to realize something, a fact that in truth he'd never given much thought to previously. Because he personally didn't think too much about money, even though he had enough to last three lifetimes, he suddenly understood that there was no way that Robert Valentine could be poor. Far from it, in fact. Given his partner's brilliant business mind, it made sense that Robert would probably have banked at least twice as much as Bill, simply because of the lack of care and respect which Bill afforded his own wealth. And if that was the case, Robert had secreted away an incredibly large sum of money somewhere, which made him a target for unscrupulous rogues who wanted a share of it, probably all of it.

He had been trying to think who it could be that was still alive, but because Bill had taken such little interest in where their start-up money had come from, he really didn't know any obvious candidates. Sure, there had been a number of loan sharks over the years that Robert had been forced to borrow from, but he'd repaid all of them as far as Bill knew. But he also knew that just like sharks in the ocean, if there was chum in the water, they'd be unsparingly savage and feast on it as soon as it hit the surface.

But there was one character that kept coming back into his mind, a villain by the name of Mickey Carlisle. He couldn't remember too much about him, and he was pretty sure that he was probably dead by now anyway. He'd only met the man once and that was enough, and he had to be at least twenty years older than Bill. He recalled one time when Mickey had come calling for the monthly nut and Robert hadn't quite managed to get all of the money together to pay him.

That was the night that Mickey had pulled a gun from his coat and pressed it up against Robert's temple. Bill had nearly crapped himself, because this behavior just wasn't what he was used to with the surfing crowd he hung out with most of the time. The surfer boys were usually whacked out on weed, schmoozing with hot girls, or just exchanging surf stories when he was with them. But Robert hadn't even flinched, even with the cold steel of a revolver pressing against his head. He remained completely and stoically calm and didn't miss a beat, assuring Mickey Carlisle that he would have the rest of his money by the end of the week. And it was already

270

Wednesday. But somehow, Robert had come up with the money and Mickey had been placated.

And Bill never asked Robert questions because Robert had assured him that he would take care of the business end of things. All Bill had to do was surf, look good, promote their Malibu HoBo at surfing events and just be cool. So that's exactly what Bill did.

But none of this answered Bill's questions about Bobby V's missing millions. Robert either didn't have what Bill thought he should have by now or he'd hidden it so carefully that only the dead would know where it was stashed. Which brought him back to his original statement to Tess. There was no way Robert could have committed suicide. Someone had to have shot him and staged it to make it look like he'd killed himself. Maybe Carlisle had a son, maybe a couple of boys, even. That was if Mickey Carlisle *was* behind it, and that Bill's suspicion turned out to be true.

But he owed it to Robert, and he owed it now to Tess to find out what the hell was going on and he now had an idea where to begin.

Three thousand miles due east, Frank Buchanan was enjoying his role as The Watcher. But this time, he was watching the scantily-clad girls parading their heavenly wares around the resort pool, as he sipped lazily on a drink, a Rum Punch laden with fruit and a miniature umbrella hanging off the glass. His wife, Maisie, was also enjoying the unexpected vacation, but for entirely different reasons than Frank.

He looked over at her, asleep under the parasol, a Michael Connelly novel spread open across her stomach. She was never going to be Miss World, even with a blindfold, but he still loved her. And in all honesty, she was the only person who loved him. She had been really excited about the thought of going on vacation and that had secretly tickled him, and last night, watching her win a few bucks at the roulette table in the casino was pretty sweet to see.

In fact, he could quickly get used to this lifestyle, hanging by the pool, waitresses bringing him cocktails all day and then dinner by the ocean, before he spent the rest of the evening playing poker. And he was winning, up by four thousand bucks already and they'd only been here for three days.

He carefully removed the book from his wife's tummy.

Don't want you to have a Connelly tan line, baby…

But then his cell phone rang, and when he checked the caller ID, he saw that it was Mickey.

Fuck it, you're ruining my day, asshole…

He muted the phone and went back to watching the pretty vista that played out beyond his sun lounger. Eventually, the ping came up to let him know that he had a new voicemail and he listened to it, knowing that Mickey was pissed at him for postponing the Valentine girl. But what was he going to do, follow her all the way across the Pond to Blighty and nail her there?

Fuck that…

He sent a brief text back to Carlisle, letting him know he'd got his message but he couldn't talk right now. He was so over the idea of working for the ingrate now, but he figured he might as well keep him sweet, just in case there was any mileage to be had with the girl if she ever came back to L.A. He beckoned a waitress on the other side of the pool and when she arrived at his lounger, he said,

"I'd like a Slow Comfortable Screw and my wife will have a Mojito, when you have a moment."

"I'll get that right away, sir, would you like some nibbles?" she replied, as Frank's eyes navigated her barely-covered body.

"I'll take whatever you're offering, sweetheart," he said, pressing a hundred dollar bill into her hand, "Just let me know when and where. There's plenty more where that came from."

~

Jake Delaney put his feet up on the side of his office desk, sipping a cup of Oolong tea as he contemplated the situation. He wasn't enjoying the insipid brew, but Summer had told him that it was good for him and so he complied, like he always did. It tasted pretty awful though.

His son, Tom, had told him about the attack on Tess when she had been with Hippy Bill up at Zuma Beach, or Sunset Beach as Malibu locals called it. He had been relaying the story to his close friend and longtime law partner, Edie Camarillo, who was eating her lunch on his office sofa, her usual lunchtime spot. They had also been discussing poor Sammy and the theft of the Buick Riviera, his pride and joy.

"So, do you think it's connected with Tess?" asked Edie.

Edie had been more of a friend to Jake than anyone in his life. She'd literally picked him up off the floor when he'd become suicidal many years ago. She had guided him through the time when he realized that it was up to him to raise two baby children when his first wife, Tara, had been tragically taken from his life. Even though Edie had never had children herself. And she had helped him start up the business; she'd been with him every step of the way, working her way up from paralegal to full partner once she'd passed the California bar exam.

But Edie could be as hard as nails just as easily as she could be as soft as brown sugar. She was a trim, sharp looking woman who was not attractive in the accepted sense, but her harsh and angular features and sharp wit made her attractive on another scale entirely. And there had never been any romantic notion between Jake and Edie, it was much more akin to a brother and sister relationship, an intimate friendship that each guarded and valued as highly as they did their marriage partners.

"Do I think *what* is connected with Tess?" Jake replied.

"Don't be an asshole, Jake, you know what I'm talking about."

"You mean Sammy's car being stolen?"

"For fuck's sake, what else were we talking about?"

"Oh, right… I don't think so, I think it was just opportune," said Jake.

"Opportune?" replied Edie, "What is fucking opportune about locating a classic car in an out of the way and inexpensive neighborhood, and then stealing it right off a driveway?"

"Someone might have just been passing and decided to take the opportunity," said Jake, knowing that he was already on the back foot with her. As usual.

"It's a fucking dead end street! Sammy's house is second from the end, no one just fucking passes by, Jake, except his next door neighbor! This was planned and I just can't believe that it's not connected with Tess."

"I think you have a highly active and colorful imagination, Edie. You want a game?" he asked, picking up a set of arrows from his desk and walking over to the dartboard in the corner of his office, "I think I can beat you today."

"You've got two chances…" Edie said.

"Yeah, I know… a dog's chance and no fucking chance!"

Tess and Archie found an available table in their local Soho pub, The Crown and Two Chairmen, which was pretty fortunate because in the winter months, finding any free table inside a pub was like finding gold. Tess ordered a cappuccino and Shepherd's Pie because she was so cold and Archie opted for fish and chips and a pint of shandy.

"I'm having trouble getting used to English winters again," she said, "The weather was to die for in Malibu."

"You've only been gone a couple of weeks," Archie replied, "And you've gone soft already!"

Archie, a junior copyrighter at the agency, was from Glasgow in Scotland, and he always joked about the weather there.

"I used to love summer in Scotland," he said, "The last time I was there, I think summer was on a Wednesday…"

Tess laughed, she had always been drawn to Archie. It wasn't as though he was God's gift to women in the looks department, with his shock of red hair and pure white skin that never held a tan, but his personality and humor were infectious. It was what drew women to him, although he never seemed to have a girlfriend. He'd once told her that he had an identical twin that he couldn't stand the sight of, which in itself was somewhat ironic.

"So," he said, his wide smile revealing a gap-toothed dental nightmare, "Come on, I want to know all about your trip to Hollywood!"

"Oh, it wasn't really like that, Arch, but even though I was only really there to sort out what was left of my father's estate, I admit that I had a really nice time and I did meet some lovely people too."

275

As they ate their food, Tess began to tell Archie about her trip, the pub growing more crammed-full and progressively louder as the lunch crowd packed themselves in. Eventually, she told Archie about the vague type of cryptogram puzzle that she'd discovered on her father's computer, but also that she'd drawn a blank in trying to work out what it meant.

"Do you have it with you?" he asked.

"I've got it downloaded on my phone," Tess replied.

"Show me, I'm no expert but I might be able to see something in it."

Tess retrieved her phone from her bag and pulled up the square of letters on the screen and handed it to Archie. He stared at it for two or three minutes before he looked up, shaking his head in confusion.

```
AAZHBOYMCEXIDSWWEHVEFRUE
GTTHHESHIERAJRQTKIPSLAONM
DNDNEMEOPLBPEKLQOJWRWIHS
EHRTEGTUHFEVREAWTDTXLCEY
SBNZAAKAEZSBRYOCAXMDHWIE
DVEFSUAGGTIHFSTITRHJAQTKIP
GLIOVMENTNOMYOOLUPIKLQOJ
UREIYSOHUTTGEUSFSUDEAWDD
```

"You got me, Tess, I can't see anything in this at all. Are you sure it's meant to mean something? Maybe your dad was just experimenting and he never finished it?"

"I don't know, Arch, but if you knew Dad in the same way that I am slowly beginning to understand him, you'd know that nothing he ever did in his life was without a reason. I know that there has to be something in this group of letters that is important in some way. I just don't know how I'll ever find out."

276

"Well, there is one thing I can tell you, given my weird and obsessive passion for typefaces," Archie replied.

"What's that?" asked Tess.

"The font, I'd know that typeface anywhere."

"Really? What's it called?" she asked.

"Hobo Pro," said Archie.

Jesus, Dad...

"Does that mean anything?" asked Archie.

"Yeah, it means I definitely have to work out whatever the hell this code means!"

Chapter 59

Christmas in Malibu was the polar opposite of Christmas in England. The temperature gauge rarely dipped below sixty-five degrees in December, and it was something for which Bill was eternally grateful. As a native Californian, the Pacific Ocean was about as cold as he ever wanted the temperature to be, and even that was too cold in his mind.

Navigating his Indian motorcycle north on the PCH, the bike's chrome brightwork glinting in the midday sun on the prized and world-famous stretch of Californian highway, Bill realized that he had rarely visited Robert's home. His friend and partner had given him a spare key to the place just in case he ever needed it but during the twenty years or so that Robert had owned the trailer home, Bill had been there only twice. But he still recognized the area as the turning for Old Broad Beach Ranch Road came up that took him east toward the Hope's Grotto Dude Community.

What a name…

It hadn't changed much since his last visit almost a decade previously, and in fact, Bill liked the place. It had an old-fashioned sense of original wild-west California and coming back to it once more, he was beginning to understand what Robert saw in the place. Hell, he could live here himself, Bill thought.

He parked the Indian in the carport and pulled a discarded tarpaulin he'd found over the top of it so that no one would start nosing around if they spotted the bike. He needed some time in the trailer to think and he didn't need any unnecessary interruptions from inquisitive visitors. Fortunately, Robert had never had the locks changed and the key still worked as Bill successfully opened up the trailer and snuck inside, pulling the door closed behind him.

The trailer's interior was much as Bill remembered it from previous visits years ago, with the addition of a couple more pieces of art and furniture that he'd not seen before. He sat down on what he thought was a quite stunning couch, realizing that Robert had probably paid a tidy sum for it, judging from the exquisite workmanship on the wood frame and the beautiful upholstery.

A man of taste, my friend, Robert Valentine...

As he sat there, his eyes moved around the main room, examining everything in his sightline, a place for everything and everything in its place. Typical Robert. Copper-bottomed pots and pans hung from an iron rail in the kitchen, all of them placed in a specific order of size. Cans of beans, jars of sauces and boxes of rice and pasta stood in uniform lines like soldiers, all of them with their labels facing exactly forward and symmetrically displayed. The carousel of coffee pods stood at attention in color-coded uniformity next to the Nespresso machine. Even the rows of books in the bookcase by the television were in alphabetical order by the author's name.

A little OCD, buddy...

The advantage in Robert's strict order of things was that it was far easier to locate something that wasn't in its correct order or location. For Bill, it made finding the obvious irregularity far simpler. But as he spent the next hour sifting through his partner's home, he could find no obvious hiding places, nothing of outstanding value, no wads of cash that would be worth dying for. In fact, the more he looked, the more he began to realize that the odd little cryptogram that Robert had left for Tess to find, was likely more important than any other clue. That is, if there was a clue, and they weren't just chasing something that didn't exist.

Sensing that he was probably wasting his time but glad that he had least made the effort to search, Bill saddled up once more on the Indian and made his way out of Hope's Grotto and back to the PCH, unaware that he was being followed.

~

Buchanan had enjoyed his trip to the Bahamas but the constant barrage of calls and texts from Mickey Carlisle had eventually worn him down. So once he had returned to the States, he decided that he might as well get on with the job or he'd never hear the end of it from Mickey. And Maisie had been running up shopping receipts and restaurant bills like he was made of fucking money. Well, that and the fact that in the last two days on the island, he'd managed to turn a six grand profit on the tables into a three grand loss in the casino.

As they say, the house always fucking wins…

So now, he really did need to get a move on and find out where Valentine had stashed his loot. And from what Frank had been able to find out, there was plenty of it, somewhere. All he had to do was find it. Give Mickey thirty percent and take the rest back to the Bahamas.

Maybe buy Maisie a few new frocks…

Mickey Carlisle had been so incensed that Tess was now out of the country, that he'd given Frank a grand to have someone keep an eye on her back in England. Although a grand wouldn't last long, so good luck with that. But Buchanan had called a contact over there and offered him five hundred bucks to follow the girl, see who she met up with, take a few photos, just to keep Mickey sweet. He only

281

really knew one man who would do the job for such a measly sum and that was a certain Charles William Sykes, known amongst London's East End villains as Bill Sykes, just like the fella in Oliver Twist.

But Buchanan only knew him by one name. Syko.

Wonder what they'd make of the name, Buchanan? Guess I'd be Frankie. Mad Frankie Buchanan...

And, as the asphalt flashed past him, he had a feeling that the fella on the motorcycle five hundred yards up ahead, who Frankie now knew went by the name of Bill McLaren, was maybe the key to finding something out about Valentine. Or, on the other hand, he was simply surplus to requirements. And that would be a nice little side bonus when he sent a 'deletion' invoice to Mickey.

Chapter 60

By mid-December, Jenny and Tess decided that the time to put up Christmas decorations could wait no longer. Franco was instructed to go off and find an eight-foot tree without spending more than thirty pounds while Tess climbed up into the cottage's loft space to retrieve the boxes of Christmas decorations, and Jenny waited at the foot of the ladder as Tess handed them down to her.

Each year, the joy of decorating the tree was a special moment that Jenny and Tess shared together. It was just the two of them, no one else, and they spent hours positioning baubles and trinkets on the tree, things that had been saved over the decades and stored away. Friends and family had often given unusual decorations to Jenny and Tess at Christmas, knowing how much it would mean to them, and how they would be cherished and adored and used again and again, year after year.

Franco had arrived back that Sunday morning with a giant tree and erected it in the cottage's family room, the fragrance of the Norway Spruce immediately evoking a Christmas feeling throughout the entire house. Tess hugged her stepfather, all that this colossus of a Roman needed to confirm that he had done a fine job in selecting the perfect tree for Tess and her mother. And realizing that they needed this annual moment together to decorate the tree, he went off to the kitchen to pour a cup of coffee from the percolator on the Aga stove, and then settled down in an armchair to continue reading his latest book.

Christmas in England was not always blessed with a Dickens-style snowfall, but this year, the snow had arrived and it had come early. A thin layer of snow had settled the previous morning, covering the Surrey countryside with a white glow like icing on a Christmas cake. Outside, as the girls continued with their cherished task, snow continued to fall, blanketing the gardens with a bluish-white cover, a buildup of frosty snow particles gradually creeping up the outside of the leaded-light windows.

Tess hadn't told her mother about the odd little cryptogram-style grid of letters she'd discovered on her father's computer, because she didn't think it would mean much to her. But then it suddenly occurred to her that although they had never lived life as a married couple, Jenny might know some of her father's idiosyncrasies from the time they had been together.

"Did Dad ever do crosswords or make up riddles when you were with him?" she asked her mother, who was trying to gently unravel a string of Christmas lights for the tree.

"I know he loved crosswords," Jenny replied, "He used to do the Sunday Times one every weekend. He was very good at doing it. He used to have it finished before lunchtime. Why do you ask?"

"It's just that I found something on his computer when I was in Los Angeles, and I don't know what it means or even if it means anything at all," said Tess, carefully placing a valuable Victorian decoration on the tree.

"What was it? Do you still have it?" asked Jenny, "Maybe I can help?"

Tess showed her the square of letters and the two of them stared at it, both wondering what secret Robert might have buried inside it.

"So?" said Tess, "Any thoughts?"

"Nothing about the puzzle itself, no, I can't help you there," Jenny replied, "But there is one thing I remember your father used to do."

"Come on, Mum, spill the beans, it might be important!" said Tess, impatiently.

"I doubt it, but one thing you and Robert both shared was your eidetic memory. Once he saw something or read something, it was immediately committed forever to his memory bank. It was amazing really, and well, you know you're just the same."

"But that doesn't help much, Mum!" exclaimed Tess.

"I know, but there was one other thing. Whenever he couldn't quite remember something, usually a name or a word or a place, he would go through the alphabet forward and backward until he finally remembered what it was. And the weird thing is, it always worked for him," said Jenny.

"I'm not sure how that's going to help but I'll keep it in mind," said Tess, "Maybe something else will come to you while we're doing the tree."

"I doubt it, sweetheart, it was such a long time ago and Robert Valentine was a unique individual."

"And speaking of which," said Tess, "Tom asked me something when I was having dinner with him just before I left Los Angeles, something I'd never ever thought about until he mentioned it."

"What's that?" asked Jenny.

"He asked why I had Dad's surname of Valentine and not yours."

"Well, when you were born, they asked who the father was and I told them it was Robert Valentine, for two reasons."

"Really? What were they?" asked Tess.

"Firstly, I knew categorically that Robert was your father for obvious reasons so it was only fair that he be listed as such on your birth certificate. But also, I decided that the name Valentine was a far more beautiful surname than my own."

"I just realized, I only know you as Jenny Russo, I don't think you ever told me your maiden name," said Tess, "What is it? It can't be that bad, surely?"

It is," said Jenny, " My maiden name is Scraggs."

"Oh... right," said Tess, "Good call, Mum! Haha!"

"Anyway," continued, Jenny, "Putting my awful maiden name to one side, this Tom Delaney... I sense that he's more than just a passing fling?"

"I'm not sure, Mum, I've had boyfriends before but nobody who has made me feel the way he makes me feel. And he's such a gentleman too."

"Just like your dad was, Tess, he was a complete gentleman too. So, is there any future with Tom, do you think, or is it too early to tell?"

"I honestly don't know, Mama, but I miss him like hell."

Chapter 61

Charles William Sykes hated his name. He'd always been called Bill Sykes, even by his own mother and he had grown tired of all the ribbing he got from it. "Can I have some more, please, sir?" they'd say, mimicking Oliver Twist in the film, laughing at him as they said it. It pissed him off. And he didn't much like his nickname either, Syko. Made him sound like a nutjob, some sort of violent mental case. And he wasn't that sort of fella either. Far from it, in fact.

During the late evenings, Syko spent his time working as a lookout for a couple of the prostitutes who had rooms in Soho. They weren't the high-class girls like the ones he'd met in Mayfair. No, these were the quick and rough variety that ran one-room brothels in the seedier alleys in Soho; fifteen quid, short time, no kissing. It was far from high end. It made him feel nauseous, but all he had to do between the hours of eight in the evening until two in the morning, was to keep an eye out for the coppers and occasionally pull some of the johns out of the rooms if they got a bit naughty. Nothing too taxing.

So keeping an eye on Tess Valentine during the day was child's play and it put a few more quid in his pocket. Although the four hundred nicker that Buchanan had sent him wasn't going to make him rich. But he figured that he could give him two weeks of keeping a watch on her for that kind of money. Any longer and Frankie would have to stump up some more cash. And the two weeks was almost up.

But watching Tess during the day hadn't been a difficult job. The girl didn't really do much except arrive at work, take a couple of coffee breaks and maybe an occasional lunch at the pub. And sometimes, she'd go shopping on Oxford Street but she hardly ever bought anything, so there wasn't much to keep an eye on. She didn't exactly lead an exciting life. And she seemed like a nice kid. What was he going to do, beat her up or something? And Syko wasn't like that, even if his nickname suggested otherwise. Syko was soft as a kitten, wouldn't harm a fly unless he had to, but he just didn't see his brute strength being needed on this job.

~

Mickey's patience was growing thin. He'd had enough of Frank's bullshit and his telling him to wait all the time. He needed results.

"Take the motherfucker out!" he bawled down the phone to Buchanan.

"Are you fucking crazy, Mickey?"

"Not crazy, just pissed at all the time wasting," yelled Mickey, "Just take McLaren out and he's one less we have to worry about."

"You're fucking serious, aren't you?" said Buchanan, "You think that's gonna help?"

"All I know, Frankie-boy, is that I'm the one paying the bills and I'm the boss of you, so don't you ever fucking forget it!"

"Alright Mickey, calm down, but I don't think it's a smart idea, that's all. But if you want him gone, yeah, I can do that. I need another five grand though."

"You'll get two and that's it," bellowed Mickey, "And get it done by the weekend. I don't ever want to hear the name, Bill McLaren, ever again."

Good enough, thought Frankie, it was no skin off his nose and it was two grand in his pocket. The Malibu Hobo was gonna be history soon. And then he'd need to put the frighteners on the girl too.

Chapter 62

Tom Delaney felt like his heart was going to break. He had fallen hook, line and sinker in love with Tess and every day without seeing her, was getting harder and harder to deal with. Of course, they spoke on the phone just about every day and sent each other endless text messages but the eight-hour time difference was wearing thin and he missed her so much.

He was finding it more and more difficult to concentrate at work and his partner, Matt Fenton, could see that Tom wasn't his usual self.

"You look like a lost puppy," said Matt, taking a seat on the client sofa in Tom's office, "What's up, big man?"

"I'm wondering what life is about, right now," Tom replied, "Have you ever fallen in love and not been able to do anything about it?"

"I've never fallen in love, so you're asking the wrong person," Matt replied, "I'm assuming you're talking about Tess?"

"I am, and I don't know if she's ever going to come back to L.A. so I'm in this kind of limbo. It's really difficult to concentrate too, not knowing if there's a future or not. I don't know what to do, Matt, I can't stop thinking about her. Pathetic, isn't it?"

"No, not pathetic, buddy," Matt replied, getting up from the sofa and putting an arm around his friend's shoulders, "But you're softer than most, so I understand. You're a bit of a wuss, like that, buddy.

But do you know if she feels the same way or was it one of those quick vacation flings?"

"I think so, and no, it definitely wasn't a fling. She's special, Matt, and I think… well, I hope she feels the same way about me but I just don't want to ask the question. Don't want to frighten her away. And I'm not a wuss!"

Matt sat back down again, turning his coffee cup around in his hands and pondering the situation in which Tom had found himself. The business was starting to gather momentum now and the thought of losing his partner for any length of time was unthinkable, but he also realized that Tom wasn't exactly working at his usual speed. If he didn't get a hold of himself soon, they'd need to bring in another architect to clear the backlog, even if it was only as a temporary measure. He had been dreading what he was about to suggest, and even as the words came out of his mouth, he wasn't sure about the sagacity of his idea.

"This is so not the right time to say this, but why don't you go and see her for a week or two?"

Tom looked up from his Spectrum drafting table, wondering if he had heard his partner correctly.

"Are you serious?" he asked, "With all the work we have on right now?"

"Serious as a heart attack," Matt replied, "I mean, you're not doing either of us any favors right now if you can't concentrate, are you?"

"So you noticed?"

"Everyone's noticing, Tom, even our clients."

"But I feel like I'm fifteen years old, like I'm having a first crush. I feel stupid as hell."

294

"Listen, sometimes you only have one tilt at true love, and for some people, they never find it. But if you don't find out for sure, you'll forever ask yourself "what if" and "why didn't I", said Matt, "And, I can get Duncan Hemsworth in to cover while you're away. He can even stay on for a few months to clear the backlog. Who knows, we might even need him permanently if we keep reeling in new clients?"

"Matt, you're one amazing friend to have, thank you. Let me think about it?"

"Sure, but let me have a decision this week so we can make plans if you're going to be away."

"You're amazing, I don't know what I'd do without you."

"I know, I'm truly fabulous but you need to get your interview face on, I've managed to find an intern to answer the phones for us for the next six months and she's waiting out front for us to talk to her."

Chapter 63

As Bill cruised down toward Santa Monica Pier, his fishing rods stowed against the side panniers ready for a day's fishing, he braked abruptly and made a U-turn on the highway. A thought had suddenly hit him, something that maybe everyone had missed, including the police, and he needed to head straight back to Robert's trailer to see if his hunch held any value. It was probably a long shot but he couldn't wait, and fishing could.

"Jesus!" yelled Buchanan, fuming inside his car as the Indian came hurtling past him in the opposite direction at speed.

"Fucking hippies! Learn to drive, why dontcha?" he yelled as he pulled over on the sandy verge to wait for a gap in the traffic so he could also make a U-turn.

But by the time Buchanan had found a break in the traffic to follow the bike, it was too late, the Indian was out of sight and there was no chance of catching up to it.

He had been following McLaren for a couple of days now and the man was anything but interesting in his schedule. So today, realizing that it was pretty much a wash, he decided to call it a day for now and make a plan on how he was going to eliminate the old hobo.

And right now, it had been a couple of hours since he'd eaten breakfast and his gut was beginning to ask questions of him.

Need some sustenance... seeing an In-N-Out burger in my future...

~~

Bill parked the Indian once more outside the trailer at Hope's Grotto, kicking out its stand as he jumped off the machine, and he knew exactly where he was headed. Like most of the trailer homes he'd ever seen, the trashcans were housed in a neat little cupboard at the rear of the property.

He slid the latches and unlocked the doors and from the stench that immediately swamped his nostrils, he realized that the trashcans hadn't been emptied in a long while, which is exactly what he was hoping. He ran to the door of the trailer, unlocked it, and went in search of a pair of rubber gloves in the kitchen area. Mercifully, he found a pair under the sink and slipped them on. In the drawer above, he found a Ziploc plastic bag and quickly returned to the trashcan storage cupboard.

As he began to pull the garbage out of the bins, he was sickened by the smell, almost gagging on the reek of rotting food and trash that he was piling on the ground next to him. Halfway through the second bin, he found exactly what he hoped he might find.

He knew that burglars, thieves, murderers and criminals often immediately discarded things that they'd used during a crime, usually as quickly as they could find a hiding place. How often had a knife or a gun been thrown down a drain or into the ocean just as soon as the perp could get rid of it, for fear of being found with the weapon on his or her person?

And there, just as he had suspected, right at the very scene of the crime that he now knew for certain had been committed, was a pair of latex gloves, stuffed into a Chinese takeout bag. Taking the edge of each glove, and pulling them both free, he carefully slipped them into the Ziploc bag, immediately aware of the blood splattering that was clear to see on the right-hand glove. And right there and then, his theory that Robert Valentine had not committed suicide at all, but had instead been murdered, was proven.

He was pretty certain that once the police forensics department took a look at the gloves, not only would they find gunshot residue, GSR, but they would also discover a set of fingerprints. Because there was one thing the common criminal often overlooked and that was the fact that fingerprints remained beautifully intact inside latex gloves, even when discarded. It was as good as leaving a thumbprint on a pane of glass; the killer might as well have left a calling card.

And the thought that immediately hit Bill, was that firstly, Robert was left-handed and secondly, dead men don't put things in the trash. And now, with the help of the gloves and the LAPD, he was finally going to find out who murdered his friend.

Chapter 64

Although it was snowing in Sussex, it had been raining for two days solid in London, and as the Friday work week finally came to an end, Tess found herself hurrying toward the underground at Piccadilly Circus, her high-heeled Kurt Geigers becoming ruined as the heavens continued their deluge. So, instead of following her morning route that would take her back along Frith Street to Shaftesbury Avenue, she took the shortcut as she often did in the evenings, down Carlisle Street, across Dean Street and into St. Anne's Court where she would join Wardour Street and from there, a straight shoot down to Piccadilly.

She was already halfway down the dark and crooked alley of St. Anne's Court, carefully trying to avoid the already heavy puddling that instantly appeared during London rainstorms, and she remained oblivious to the darkness that enveloped the narrow and poorly lit mews. Her face ran with the incessant rainwater, her shoes partially drenched and she was already wishing she had brought some rain boots for the journey home.

My poor shoes are already ruined...

A tall, dark shape emerged from behind one of the mews buildings and in an instant, Tess felt a pair of enormous hands grab her by her upper arms and stop her in her tracks. She screamed but no one heard, most people choosing the more populated and brightly-lit Soho streets at this time of night.

"Shhh…" came a voice from whoever was holding her in his grip.

She screamed again, struggling valiantly to escape his clutches but failing miserably. She looked up at the face of the man, a goliath of an individual, instantly realizing that he must be one of London's many homeless people. As she took in the man's terrifying face, she saw that most of his teeth were missing and his hair, long and dank, and now matted to his skin, was even more evidence of a desperate down and out. One eye stared violently back at her, the other seemingly just a badly fitting, white glass orb that protruded uncomfortably from his other socket, appearing almost like a children's oversized white marble.

"Be quiet, Tessie girl, you don't want the coppers coming," he said, in a deep but quiet and resonant whisper.

"Who… who are you?" she asked, "What do you want? I've got some money in my purse…"

"I don't want your money, that ain't what I'm 'ere for," he replied.

"P…p…please, please don't hurt me, you can have my bag, please, just take it!" she said, careful not to scream again, her mind instantly recalling the scene on the beach in Malibu.

"Tess! Calm the fuck down! I'm not 'ere to 'urt you, girl," he said, his voice rising as he spoke, "Just fuckin' listen!"

Tess fell silent, her teeth chattering in the freezing cold of December, aware that she could anger the giant if she didn't stay still and listen to what he had to say. The rain was lashing down harder and harder now, her face slapped by what felt like a hosepipe spraying down on her, water trickling down her back as she grew colder and colder in the man's steel-like grip.

"Who… are you?" she asked, so quietly that she wondered if he had even heard.

"Don't matter 'oo I am, Tess, but right now, I'm the friend you should never 'ave 'ad. I'm gonna do you a favor, although the geezer 'oo's paying me won't be too fuckin' 'appy about it," he said, as Tess stared at his mangled and partially missing left ear. She felt sick, dizzy and nauseous, wishing she was anywhere but here.

"There are some nasty geezers across the pond 'oo want me to give you a right good fright, put the fuckin' fear of God in you," he continued.

"What??" Who?" she blurted, "I haven't done anything wrong!"

"Don't matter to them Tess, but you seem like a nice kid so I'm doin' you a favor. And I ain't gonna 'urt you so stop shakin' now," he said, "The arsehole 'oo's payin' me is a wanker 'oo goes by the name, The Watcher, complete fuckin' tosser, if you ask me."

"What's his real name," asked Tess.

"Dunno. Fella never told me 'is name, I just know 'e's in America and 'e sends me a few bob 'ere and there to keep an eye on you an' 'e wants me to scare you a bit. But what he sends, ain't worth nuffin' to me. So, I'll keep an eye out, not this one of course," he said, pointing to the motionless glass orb in his left socket, chuckling at his own joke, "But no 'arm is gonna come to you, so if you see me around, which you prob'ly won't, don't worry, 'cos you won't 'ave any problems from me."

"Who are *you*?" Tess asked, now less concerned that she was in any real danger and that somehow, she seemed to have a friend in this colossal and tattered, one-eyed leviathan.

"They call me Syko, but in name only..." he replied, immediately letting go of her and quickly and silently disappearing around the corner from where he had first appeared.

Tess stood motionless, tears raking down her cheeks, mixing seamlessly with the rainwater that continued to fall on London, her

303

coat soaking wet and her ruined Kurt Geigers now destined for the garbage.

Chapter 65

Bill McLaren had a friend in the LAPD, a guy he had grown up with from when he was a teenager, often surfing together with him out at Big Sur, in Northern California. But as decent a surfer as Fletcher Kane was, he wasn't really in the same league as Bill and was therefore never deemed likely to make a living from the sport. And so, at the age of twenty-six, he had joined L.A.'s finest and graduated from the Los Angeles Police Academy at the top of his class. Which was as much of a shock to Bill as it was to Fletcher. But Fletcher had grown to love police work, thrived on it, and although he had long since passed retirement age by now, he couldn't bear the thought of not walking into the detectives' room each morning at the L.A. Police Headquarters Building.

"I'm hoping you've got good news for me, Fletch?" said Bill, as Fletcher led him through the maze of offices to the building's Latent Print Unit that was located inside the Technical Investigation's Division. The unit was housed in a separate building from the LAPD Robbery and Homicide Division, occupying real estate that lay between Chinatown and the Los Angeles River. It wasn't high on Bill's list of favorite places to visit, never would be. But having said that, this place was a hundred times nicer than the old Parker Center in downtown L.A. That place was a dump and should have been torn down years ago. But for some reason, Bill just never felt entirely comfortable in a police station, even though this was technically a laboratory. And even though as far as Bill could recall, he'd never broken the law in his entire life, these places just didn't give him a good vibe.

"We're gonna find out in a minute, just as soon as we locate Toby," Fletcher replied, "Keep your fingers crossed."

They arrived at a set of double doors, a sign warning that the general public was barred from entering the lab, and Fletcher held his magnetic card to the glass reader for access. The doors clicked open and the still tall and lanky, tousled and blond-haired Fletcher, pushed on in while Bill waited outside.

"What are you waiting for?" asked Fletcher.

"The sign… the rule," Bill replied, remaining motionless outside the entrance.

"Come on, Bill, rules are made to be broken," laughed Fletcher, as he tugged on Bill's arm and led him into the room. Fletcher immediately spotted the man they'd come to see, a diminutive lab technician looking through a microscope in the far corner of the laboratory, who looked up and smiled as soon as he saw the two larger men heading over to him.

"That's the fella we've come to see," said Fletcher, "Come on, let's interrupt whatever he's doing!"

"Toby, this is my friend Bill, Bill, this is Toby Juggs," said Fletcher by way of introduction, as they arrived at his workstation.

"Really?" said Bill, not knowing if Fletcher was pulling his leg.

Toby fucking Juggs?

"My parents had a weird sense of humor," said Toby, "But I've found that even though people often don't remember me, they always remember my name. Pleased to meet you, Bill, I've heard all about you, you're the famous Malibu Hobo, right?"

"Infamous, more like," said Bill, laughing at his apparent notoriety, "Pleasure to meet you, Toby."

Toby Juggs probably didn't hit the five-foot mark, even with shoes on, and he couldn't have weighed more than eighty-five pounds, soaking wet. The lenses in his glasses were as thick as Plexiglas and he was already balding at the age of what Bill guessed, was not even thirty years old. But the tiny man had the most infectious grin Bill had ever seen.

"So, what's the verdict, Tobes?" asked Fletcher, "Can I get a warrant for an arrest yet?"

"The prints were outstanding," replied Toby, "They were in absolutely perfect condition too. Kudos to you, Bill, excellent job."

"That's great news!" said Fletcher, although Bill remained quiet as Toby continued.

"And I can confirm we have GSR, so whoever fired the weapon, and let's assume it was the same gun as the one found at the scene," Toby continued, "It's likely GSR from the weapon used by be the person who killed your friend, Bill."

"So he *was* murdered?" asked Bill, "It really wasn't suicide at all?"

"Well, we can only assume that theory at the moment. Unfortunately, no one thought to swab Mr. Valentine's hands for GSR at the time of his death because everything at the scene indicated a suicide, but if they had swabbed and not found any on him, I think we could categorically say that the bullet wound wasn't self-inflicted. Having said that though, how does a dead man put his gloves in the trash?"

"So what do you guys think?" asked Bill to both Fletcher and Toby.

"Murder," they replied, almost in unison.

"I'll get the warrant moving, what name should I put in it for the arrest, Toby?" asked Fletcher, "I know a friendly judge who'll get this signed within the hour.

"Unfortunately, that's the problem, Fletch, we don't have a name."

"What do you mean? You said the prints were perfect, Tobes, what's the problem?"

"They are perfect, absolutely. But we ran them through AFIS, our Automated Fingerprint Identification System, and unbelievably, we didn't get a single hit. Nothing even close. We even tried it out on the other biometric systems that they use in the FBI and the CIA, but nothin' doin'. Whoever killed your friend, Bill, has either never committed a crime before in their life, or they are just extraordinarily lucky to have never been caught," explained Toby.

"So we're back at square one,' said Bill "I can't believe it."

"Not quite, Bill. The blood found on the glove was from Mr. Valentine, I've just confirmed that with my colleagues," said Toby, "And even though we have no current data on the man or woman who shot Robert, we can absolutely reopen the case now. It's no longer a suicide, Bill, now it's definitely a murder investigation."

Chapter 66

"Jesus fucking Christ," said Buchanan, almost incoherently, as he continued to munch the mouthful of bacon sandwich that Maisie had prepared for him, ketchup still drooling down his chin.

"Are they trying to make my life more friggin' difficult than it is already?" he asked himself, as he read the side column on the front page of the morning's *L.A. Times*.

"Case re-opened in death of local British businessman

– Now ruled murder, not suicide"

"Fuck me, I can't catch a break, can I?" he said again to himself.

"What's that, dear?" said Maisie, putting down a cup of coffee on the side-table next to Buchanan's armchair, "What can't you catch?"

"Nothing, sweetheart, I was just looking at the football scores. My Fantasy Team sucks this year…"

Chapter 67

It was the night before Christmas Eve, Christmas Eve's Eve, as Tess's mother Jenny liked to say, and Tess was thankful to be finally catching a train home for the holidays. She was even more grateful that her firm had decided to run a skeleton-staff throughout the festive season until they re-opened for business on the 2nd January. She also couldn't believe her luck that she hadn't been nominated for skeleton-staff duty, which meant she had a whole twelve days at home with her mom and Franco.

Someone's looking after me…

The journey home that evening had been both awful and lovely. Awful because it was freezing cold and the snow was falling thickly across the city, and the trains were packed, so inevitably, she could never get a seat. But lovely because people were so excited that it was Christmas, everyone loaded up with bags of presents, last minute shopping and bottles of wine, whiskey and champagne and other goodies from office parties. It was this type of spirit in England, regardless of the weather, that had Tess unconsciously and inadvertently smiling to herself, as she exited the train and made her way to the station car park with all the other commuters returning from London.

Chiddingfold was too small a village to have its own railway station and so Haslemere was the closest one to Tess. Haslemere itself was a *tithing* from nearby Godalming and had been around for the last seven or eight centuries. It was only about five or six miles drive from her home so generally, just fifteen minutes or so in the car. And the drive from Haslemere Station was something she always enjoyed, pretty much at any time of year, and the Christmas decorations in the town's high street always sent a tingle down her spine at this time of the year, something that never diminished no matter how often she saw them.

Twenty minutes later, she pulled her little yellow Citroën C3 into the driveway of her home and found herself smiling at the thick layer of snow that covered their cottage and the surrounding houses. All of the leaded-light, amber-lit windows in the ancient and historic properties displayed colored lights and decorations, and many of the driveways and pillared entrances were draped with Christmas lights, trees and baubles.

Christmas in Chidd, a twenty-first-century Charles Dickens Christmas scene, doesn't get any better...

She was careful not to slip on the paving stones as she navigated her way around to the other side of her car to retrieve her bags from the passenger seat. Closing and then locking the doors, she made her way up the path to the front door of the cottage, her breath escaping and evaporating from her mouth like steam in the night air, and a new layer of snow already hiding any footprints that had previously existed.

"Home, at last," she said to herself, as she put her key into the lock and opened the door, thankful for the warm burst of aromatic air that immediately emanated from the cottage's interior.

And almost as soon as she had set foot inside the cottage, her mother was there at the door, welcoming her home, taking her bags from her, tugging off her coat and hat and hugging her.

"Merry Christmas, sweetheart!" said Jenny, not wanting to leave their embrace.

"Merry Christmas to you too, Mama, it's so good to be home," Tess replied, shaking the snow from her coat and hanging it up to dry on the coat-stand in the entrance hall of the house.

"You've got a visitor!" said Jenny, "Come on through and say hello."

"A visitor?" Tess replied, "For me? Really?"

She followed her mother into the family room and saw Franco sitting in his favorite armchair, drinking a glass of whiskey, his preferred Christmas tipple, and Barney, in his usual position, rolled over in front of the roaring fire, oblivious to everything around him.

"Merry Christmas, Tess," came a familiar American voice from the kitchen.

Oh my God, I know that voice so well!

"Tom!" she replied, "What... how..."

"I missed you," Tom replied, walking over to her and kissing her delicately on the cheek, "I couldn't bear the thought of spending Christmas without you!"

"I can't believe this," Tess shrilled, still dumbfounded that Tom Delaney was standing in their kitchen, drinking a glass of Baileys with that never-get-tired-of-seeing-it smile writ large upon his face.

"Come here," she said, "A peck on the cheek isn't going to work!"

She flung her arms around the smitten young man and kissed him full on the lips, both of them impervious to the presence of Jenny and Franco, but then suddenly realizing they had an audience.

"Sorry Mum, sorry Franco," spluttered Tess, "But I've really missed this man!"

313

"Don't mind us," said Jenny, "Go on and show Tom the house, he only arrived half an hour ago and I haven't had time to give him the tour. Poor boy, we'll wear him out."

"I still can't believe you're here!" said Tess, "All the way from California to see me? Are you mad or just insane?"

"It wasn't a difficult decision, and... I even managed to sleep for most of the flight so the journey passed by in what seemed like only minutes."

"Well, I'm so glad you're here, come on, let's give you the two-minute tour!"

Tess took Tom's hand and led him through the cottage, explaining its history, but once they arrived upstairs in Tess's bedroom, she grabbed him and kissed him as though he might disappear as quickly as he'd arrived.

"Wow, that is some welcome," said Tom, "I've missed you, beautiful girl!"

"I've missed you too, Tom, I haven't stopped thinking about you since I left L.A." she replied, "But I still can't believe you're here, here in sleepy Chiddingfold!"

"I love it, it's exactly how I pictured it, pure Christmas straight off a greetings card."

"But how long are you staying? And where are you staying? Do you want to stay here? We've got room, but only just," said Tess, firing questions at Tom before he had a chance to answer. "Oh God, listen to me! I'm like a love-struck teenager and I'm not even giving you a chance to speak!"

"Don't worry! I wasn't sure if I was doing the right thing, you know... coming over, but now it seems like I made the right decision," he replied, "And I'm staying just around the corner at the Crown Inn on the village green. I got lucky because they had a very late cancelation and I managed to book their last available room at a great price."

"The Crown? That's brilliant! It's really lovely there," Tess gushed, "And I can see you all the time, and it'll be fun, sneaking out to see you. And you're going to love the olives they have there, to die for!"

"Olives? Yeah, okay… Anyway, Matt's organized it so I can stay over until the New Year if that's okay with you? But you might get bored with me being here for so long, so I could always get an earlier flight…"

"Okay? Okay??" gasped Tess, "Are you serious, Tom Delaney? You're not going anywhere so don't even think about it. You just made all my Christmases all at once! I don't need any presents this year, I already got mine and it's standing right here in front of me. Come here, I'm going to snog your face off!"

And so their kiss resumed, a kiss Tess could never tire of, and one that Tom could only have ever dreamed about. His English rose in an English winter scene at Christmas.

It doesn't get much better than this, Tess Valentine…

Chapter 68

At first, Bill didn't really acknowledge what was happening. Maybe in East L.A. but not in Malibu. The sounds seemed pretty distant and somewhat muffled and it was the blood that trickled down his arm that first caught his attention. He didn't even feel any pain, just a numb sensation that felt more like a tickle on the side of his shoulder than anything else. And that was generally what happened when people got shot. They only usually began to feel pain once they set eyes on the wound. It's the synaptic delay in our neurotransmitters that prevents an immediate electrical or chemical reaction informing the brain what has happened.

But before Bill could think about what was happening, instinct took over and he hit the ground, rolling over until he was positioned beneath the patio's teak dining table. It was only then that he glanced at the side of his left shoulder and realized that he'd been shot. He wiped the blood away from the wound and saw that it was more of a nick than a bullet hole but it was leaking blood at a rate of knots. He also knew that teak, no matter how tough it was, wasn't going to be a particularly effective shield from a hollow-point bullet.

Seriously? In Malibu?

Two more muffled sounds followed the shattering of wood above him and it became clear to Bill that he was most definitely the target and the shooter was using a suppressor to silence the gunfire. Without a thought of the immediate danger involved, he leaped from beneath the table, and ran, crawled and duck-walked into the house, where he knew he'd be out of the sniper's sightline. After quickly tying a tea towel tight around his upper arm to staunch the wound, he pulled a .357 Magnum handgun and a pair of binoculars from the drawer in his office desk and climbed the travertine staircase to a second floor window that he guessed faced in the direction of the gunman.

And high up on the sandy verge of the PCH, Bill immediately saw the location from where his would-be assassin was taking potshots at him. The sagebrush that the man was hiding behind did little to disguise the glint of the rifle's barrel that was aiming down toward the rear of Bill's house. And beyond the brush he could see the man himself lying in the dirt, waiting for Bill to make an appearance on the patio for one last shot at him.

Not this time, buddy...

He carefully and very slowly, pushed open the window, which tilted upwards to a horizontal position, until he had a clear sight of the shooter. He held the Magnum steady in both hands, safety clicked off, aiming directly at the area of the sagebrush. He knew he had little to no chance of hitting his target but at the very least, he could demonstrate to the sniper that he had some sphincter-alarming firepower coming right back at him.

Bill let rip six rounds from the monster handgun, flinching each time the Magnum bucked its recoil throughout his entire body. None of the rounds came close to the target but it was enough. Enough that the shooter quickly gathered up his rifle and clambered away toward the black Buick parked nearby, ducking inside the door as sand and gravel flew up from under the car's wheels before he'd even got the door closed.

~~~

Frank Buchanan was seething, mostly at himself for not checking the scope on the rifle. He knew he was an excellent marksman but also knew that every scope needed calibration before use, particularly when using a suppressor, but the scope had been wildly inaccurate on this occasion.

Stupid, stupid, stupid...

Mickey Carlisle wasn't going to be too pleased about his performance today so before he found out, Frank knew he needed to close the door on the hobo. Quickly and permanently.

Chapter 69

Tom had to pinch himself. He was sitting in a centuries-old English pub, a roaring fire blazing in the gigantic fireplace, and about to enjoy a candlelit dinner with a beautiful girl.

Who'd have thought?

The warmth in the Crown Inn permeated his skin and the unique aroma of beech and oak burning on the fire was something he'd never experienced before and he loved it, could never see himself getting tired of it. Something about the old-fashioned quaintness and kindness he'd been shown by the locals, ever since arriving in the village, had made a mark on him in a way he could never have imagined.

He realized he could easily settle into a life here, learning from and absorbing the gentleness and beauty of even everyday things. He'd never before seen a waitress in a traditional European black dress, black tights and white pinafore, and even the couple of occasions he'd spent at the pub bar chatting with the bartender and other hotel guests, were memorable in that he was made to feel like a local so quickly. He already loved England and its people.

"How are you enjoying England so far?' asked Tess, taking hold of Tom's hand across the table and waking him from his mellow thoughts.

"What's not to like?" Tom replied, enjoying the soft and gentle feel of Tess's palms, "Apart from having to duck my head whenever

I leave or enter a room because these beams are so low, it's more than I could ever have imagined England to be like."

"I saw you ducking even as we came in, but when these buildings were first constructed, centuries ago, people were so much shorter in those days. There weren't any gorgeous, tall and sexy Californians loping about!" said Tess, "But apart from that, is it what you expected?"

"Oh, it's so much more than I'd pictured, I'm really enjoying it, even with the cold weather and all the snow," Tom replied, "And thank you for the compliment but I feel terribly guilty, leaving Matt to cope all on his lonesome."

"You're already sounding so English, already," Tess laughed, "And you've only been here a day or so!"

"How do you mean?"

"You're using the word *terribly* to mean *very*," Tess replied, "I don't think I've ever heard an American say that. Not that I know many. Next thing you know, you'll be saying that you're *awfully* sorry!"

"I guess you must be rubbing off on me."

"Don't go there!" Tess giggled, "And anyway, Matt isn't a kid, and it's Christmas Eve, what's going to be so pressing at this time of year? You *are* entitled to take a break occasionally, you know."

"You're right," Tom agreed, looking at the restaurant's menu, "I'm on vacation and I'm with a beautiful girl, what's not to love? So… tell me what's good to eat here? I can't even understand most of this menu. The olives are fabulous by the way…"

"They're from Spain, and everything is good here! But it's funny, English food never used to be so great. Something changed maybe ten or twelve years ago and suddenly all these pubs and pub-hotels became non-smoking gastro-pubs where the food is to die for."

322

"What brought on such a change? You know that English food, along with English dental care is something we love to joke about back home," Tom replied, "Although you've got a Californian smile so your teeth aren't in question. Only your food."

"I'll take all the compliments I can get but as far as the change in food goes, it pretty much happened as soon as they banned smoking in pubs over here, suddenly pubs became food havens," said Tess, "But if you want a pointer, I'm having the grilled Haloumi followed by the chargrilled calves' liver served with caramelized onions, crispy bacon and mash."

"Yuck! Calves liver? Really? How the heck can you stomach that? Ugh! And what's grilled Houdini?"

"Stop it! It's haloumi! It's a type of cheese and it's yummy. Trust me. And if you've never had liver and bacon in England before, well you haven't lived, Tom Delaney!" Tess replied.

"I can't think of anything worse! But… when in Rome, I guess… and, as I think they say over here, in for a penny, in for a pound. So I'm gonna follow your lead and give it a try!"

~

"What did you think of Tom?" asked Jenny, pouring a glass of Pinot Noir for her husband, as Barney looked up, briefly disappointed, and then resumed his sleep again at Franco's feet, a muted grumbling coming from somewhere deep within the Labrador. Franco always found it extraordinary how dogs could wake up at the slightest noise but then instantly hit the snooze button again and be sound asleep in a second.

"Honestly?" said Franco, sipping the ruby-colored nectar as he warmed his feet in front of the fire, "I really liked him, he seems a very charming young man. I really couldn't fault him."

"Me too, although I wasn't expecting him to show up this soon after Tess arrived home. But he's the perfect gentleman and it'll be lovely for Tess to have him staying just around the corner during the Christmas period," Jenny replied, snuggling into Franco on the oversized Victorian armchair.

"If you want to know what I really think," continued Franco, in his still heavily Italian-accented English, "I think she might be in love with the boy."

"And him with her," agreed Jenny, "But I hope he's not going to take her away from us, that's my only fear."

"You mustn't worry about the future, Jennifer, it will be what it will be, trust me," said Franco, "And Tess will always love her mama, *mio amore*, you know that."

"I do, but if she moves to America, it's so far away, isn't it?"

"Oggi il mondo è un posto molto piccolo e l'amore non conosce limiti..." Franco replied in his native tongue, "But they have these things now, my love, they're called airplanes, it means people can travel far and wide these days to see their friends and families. *In verità*, all you need to do is buy a ticket, I believe..."

"You're no help!" said Jenny, gently punching Franco's huge bicep, "And I know what planes are, you idiot!"

Once Bill had finally checked the wound to his shoulder and patched it up with a bandage and lint doused with iodine, he went outside the house and climbed up the slope to the location the sniper had chosen to stage his attack. The slope was steep and the earth dry so he grabbed hold of the weeds to give him a handhold as he clambered up toward the level ground next to the highway.

324

He carefully inspected the area, noting that there were three fresh indentations in the sandy verge, all of them the size of golf ball imprints. He realized that these holes had been made by the mini-tripod that the shooter had used to support his rifle. Looking to the right of the marks, he quickly found what he had hoped had been forgotten by the would-be assassin. He pulled a Ziploc sandwich bag from his pocket, lifted away a piece of sagebrush and with a Bic pen, carefully retrieved a spent cartridge shell from beneath the brush and deposited it into the plastic bag. He found three more and added them to the one he'd already bagged.

Friggin' amateurs…

He pulled a cell phone from his pocket and dialed his friend's personal number, the connection made after only two rings.

"Fletch? I think we may have caught a break on the Robert Valentine case."

"Hey Bill, what do you have?"

"Some lunatic decided to take a few potshots at me today and I guess he ain't as smart as he thinks he is."

"Whoa! Someone shot at you? At your home?"

"Yeah, can you believe that? Nothing too bad but the guy left some identification behind."

"You got the casings, didn't you?" asked Fletcher, knowing that his friend was no fool.

"Yep. Bagged them up all ready for you, Fletch," replied Bill, "Chain of custody's intact. Come get 'em."

"I'm coming right now, don't go anywhere 'til I get there…"

Bill hung up, and looked around at the relentless traffic on the PCH, knowing that he'd got lucky today. If he'd been in clear view and the gunman had been even half as good as a trained assassin, he knew he'd be dead right now.

"You got lucky today, motherfucker, but I'm getting closer, and I'm coming for you."

~

"Have you got room for a dessert?"

"Dessert? I'm still getting over how good liver and onions tastes!" said Tom.

"Told you so, I knew you'd come round to my way of thinking," said Tess, "So, what do you think, do you want to try something sweet?"

"Are the English known for their desserts?"

"Of course, but there's a particular one on the menu that I know you're going to die for!" Tess replied, thankful that Tom was open to trying new things.

"Come on then, have at it, what are you suggesting?"

"I'm thinking... the Sticky Toffee Pudding with a glass of Baileys, you're going to thank me later," said Tess.

"For here or to go?" asked Tom.

"To go? Where?" Tess asked, inquisitively.

"Um, how about my room?"

"How quickly do you think they can make it?"

"Exactly what I was thinking," said Tom, "Shall we have it sent up?"

"Sounds like a plan!" Tess replied, "Shall we ask for the bill?"

Chapter 70

"Were you surprised that Tom upped and went across the Pond so quickly?" asked Summer, still wrapping the last of their children's presents on Christmas Eve.

"Not really, Sum, I think he's smitten, but actually in a pretty big way, if I know my son. Anyway, he works so hard, he needs a break and he'll have a great time," Jake replied, as he prepared two mochaccinos for them, standing before his prized Nuova Simonelli Aurelia II espresso machine in the Delaney kitchen.

"What if he loves it there and doesn't want to come back?" she asked, "You know what you're like and the apple doesn't fall far from the tree, that's for sure."

"Stop worrying, it'll be what it'll be. And anyway, he's hardly likely to leave Matt in the lurch. If he's nothing else, Tom's reliable and trustworthy."

"Jake! Tom's a bit more than that!"

"I know, but you know what I mean. He's bound to have a good time because he's never been to Europe before but you're fussing over him and worrying about something that hasn't even happened yet. Can't we just enjoy Christmas?"

"Okay, he of no feelings! I'm just saying that he'll be missed, that's all," Summer replied.

"I know, how do you think I feel?" asked Jake.

"Well, at least the girls will be here tomorrow and Casey's coming home for the holidays. But I miss Tom already, you know that. He's like my own son in so many ways and not just because he reminds me so much of you," said Summer, stacking the last of the wrapped gifts under the tree and sitting down next to her husband.

"And I love you for that, Summer, but we have to come to terms with the fact that at some point, kids fly the coop, they have to leave the nest and live their own lives. What do you want, all four of them living here under your feet for the rest of your life?"

"Actually, I'd like that… Oh just ignore me, Jake, I'm being silly. He'll be home before we know it."

The couple snuggled next to each other on the sofa in the family room, gazing out to the Pacific and contentedly sipping their mochaccinos, two lovers forever in love.

"It never gets old, does it, Sum?"

"What?"

"This view of the ocean. It doesn't matter what happens in the world or how upset I ever get, this view always makes me feel so calm and relaxed. How lucky am I?"

"Well, Jake Delaney, you're one very spoiled boy. And I'm one very spoiled girl."

"Not really, you deserve everything you have. Anyway, I heard from Perryman this morning," he said.

"Perryman! Really? Is he coming out here for New Year? I'm so looking forward to seeing him, I've really missed him," Summer replied.

"Well, that's the sad part, he can't come. I didn't know this, but his new girlfriend is pregnant…"

Vaughn Toulouse Perryman was a discarded child of the sixties. Discarded, in that he was born accidentally to a free-love nineteen-year-old hippy mother, who preferred her zoned-out life of searching for Lucy in the Sky with Diamonds. The joke that his mother had played on him by naming him Vaughn Toulouse was her insidious and doped-up attempt at humor in that she had already decided that her son was most definitely born to lose. So, Vaughn Toulouse, he became. It was for this reason he chose to be known solely by his last name, Perryman. And although Perryman spent his formative years growing up in foster homes, he remained constantly optimistic, a smile never far from his dazzling array of white teeth that had rarely seen an orthodontist. And after he had met Jake at school, they had become lifelong friends back in Florida.

A bronzed and chiseled Amazon of a man with the gentlest of hearts, Perryman charmed everyone he met, male or female. He was a penniless surf teacher most of his life until he 'inherited' a waterfront mansion and a sizeable bank account from an older woman. When the late Krystal Steiner had met him, she took pity on the fact that he was living and sleeping in his aging station wagon and offered to house him rent-free in the guest cottage in the grounds of her estate. She adored him much like she would have done if he had been her own son and because she had never had children, she chose Perryman as her heir.

But the irony in the way that Perryman consistently attracted women like honeybees to the proverbial pot, was that he was completely asexual. He had adopted multiple children when he had married his first love, a lesbian policewoman named Sophia, and miraculously, they had even added three more to the clan. Which wasn't bad considering they claimed that they never had sex. But Sophia eventually left to pursue her natural female longings and now lived nearby with another woman, although she and Perryman remained close friends and devoted co-parents. And then Perryman found Delilah…

"What! So hold on, with the kids they adopted plus the surprise ones that came naturally, caramba!… they'll be up to eleven kids?"

331

exclaimed Summer, amazed that their sexually ambiguous friend back in Florida was turning out kids on an Olympian level.

"Isn't he too old to be changing diapers?" she continued, "He'll be seventy by the time the kid starts high school."

"Yeah, but in Perryman's mind, he's still only eighteen himself. That's what the chicks love about him."

"Chicks? Are you serious?"

"You know what I mean, Sum, he just never gets old, never will."

"Yeah, but chicks, Jake…"

Chapter 71

The dessert now long forgotten, Tom cradled Tess's face in his hands, not wanting the magical moment to end. The coolness of her unblemished skin, the fullness of her lips and the sparkle that dazzled in her eyes, were almost too much for Tom to believe.

"Someone, pinch me," he whispered, sliding his hands delicately down to her neck, her shoulders and then to her waist.

"I feel the same way, it's hard for me to believe you're here," she replied, "Harder to think I'm not kissing your lips right now."

"I think we can take care of that," Tom replied, leaning in to Tess, gently biting her bottom lip.

Tess nuzzled back, playfully biting him in the same way until their mouths opened to feel each other's warmth, to explore each other slowly, tenderly, languorously.

Tess relished this slow dance between new lovers, something she hadn't really felt before. But Tom was so different to anyone she'd ever met, he felt so masculine, yet so feminine, so kind, so genuine, so gentle. There was no clumsiness, no rush to find the finish line, no awkwardness at all, just a melodic and entrancing dance of love.

No words were necessary, no permissions sought, as Tom lifted her cashmere sweater over her head, revealing a simple, silky white bra, stark against her still-tanned skin. He pulled down on the zipper at the back of her pencil skirt and let it very slowly drop down to reveal a matching white silk thong. Tess unbuttoned his shirt, staring into his eyes as she did so, and when the last button was freed, she pushed it away from his own tanned torso, softly raking her hands down Tom's chest to his navel. And then she unbuckled his belt, pulled open his chinos and let them drop to the floor to join their now discarded clothing. She stood on tiptoe, pulled his mouth to hers and kissed him deeply, almost harshly but she was suddenly taken by the sensuality of the moment and she felt the nascent, but growing pleasure between them.

Tom responded, wrapping his muscular arms around her, picking her up and laying her down on the four-poster bed that had previously witnessed many similar scenes over the years. He couldn't believe his eyes as they swept across her taut and lithe body, tanned from her time in Malibu, so perfect in every way. She was so crazily feminine and athletic too, as he dared to touch her bottom and run his hand down her thigh, her calf and then to her ankle. He kissed her again, not wanting to be plucked from this precious moment, scared that he might wake up and realize that the vision before him would just be a dream, taken from him as he woke.

"I've only known you for a few weeks, Tess, but I feel as though I've known you forever," he whispered.

"Oh Tom, I feel the same way too, I love that you're here, love that we have this chance," Tess replied.

He undid the clasp at the front of her bra, revealing small and quite perfect breasts, aroused as he bent to kiss them. She shuddered, holding his head, not wanting the feeling to ever end, her hands exploring his back, her fingers slipping beneath the waistband of his briefs. And as Tom slowly lay Tess back, her head finding the sumptuous goose-down pillow on the giant bed, his tongue traced a path down her chest, all the way to her navel, before pausing to explore her further. Tess moaned in sheer delight as he continued his way to the tiny white triangle of silk and she could already feel the warmth and wetness rolling over her in waves.

He tugged the small piece of material between his teeth, pulling it lower and allowed his mouth to find the spot that he'd yearned to taste as he felt her gently pull down his briefs, her fingers instinctively finding him. Tom gasped when he felt the touch of her caress, the immediate feeling only heightening his own passion, driving him to push deeply inside her to taste her lust. The two lovers, both naked now and impervious to the carnal signs of desire that they both now displayed, intertwined as Tom willingly and obediently lay back, and Tess gracefully straddled him. She took him tenderly in her hand and guided him delicately and slowly inside, their eyes still locked on each other, their simultaneous sighs of pleasure building as their bodies became one.

She swept down to kiss him, feverishly now, their tongues searching every corner of each other's mouths, neither feeling the need even to breathe. His hands held her cheeks as she rhythmically slid him in and out of her, barely able to contain himself as he looked up at the vision of beauty before him. She suddenly leaned back, driving herself down onto him, feeling him deep within her as his hands found her breasts, touching her, caressing her, moving with her as they both let out impassioned breaths, realizing that they'd found the end together, knowing that this was their moment and that they were meant for each other.

And then time seemed to stand still for both of them, their simultaneous and intensely climactic flush making them feel momentarily light-headed, dramatically and finally spent. Tess crashed down to his chest, sapped and breathless as he wrapped her in his arms, swaddling her in the sheets, never wanting to ever let her go again.

Chapter 72

As Buchanan heaved his overweight carcass off of Maisie, fuming once again that he had been unable to perform, he raged at the thought that his attempted assassination of McLaren had been as ineffective as his lovemaking. And it wasn't Maisie's fault, she was still a sexy woman in her own way. A little chunky now but he loved her anyway.

"You okay, Frank," asked his wife, sympathetic to his recent launch failures, "Don't worry about it dear, it happens to a lot of men your age. I think it's called E.D. or something."

"I'm fine, Maze, I just have a few things on my mind, that's all. Go back to sleep."

Buchanan began to get dressed, even though it was almost ten o'clock and Maisie stared at him in the darkness, wondering where the heck he was going.

Probably going out to the barn to look at his cars…

"Frank? What are you doing? It's late, come back to bed."

"I have to go out, Maze, don't worry, I've just got something to take care of on an insurance policy for a client. Don't wait up, I'll see you later."

She watched as her husband left their bedroom, amazed that his work ethic was still full-on at ten in the evening. But that was Frank, she thought. It was probably why he still had so many loyal clients at his age in a business that was populated by young people nowadays.

Once outside, Buchanan made his way across the yard to his car barn, actually looking forward to the drive tonight. It was a cloudless night because every star was showing in the inky black sky, all of them twinkling at him from millions of miles away. The still night air was heavenly in Ojai, the temperature a cool but comfortable sixty degrees, which is exactly why he chose to live there.

Looking around at the neighbors' homes, the nearest of which was a hundred yards away, he realized because of the few lighted windows, that most of them were already in bed or about to settle in for the night.

God bless you, Ojai...

He tossed the keys into the air, catching them as his other hand felt inside his jacket pocket for reassurance of what he needed for where he was going. It was good to know that this time he had a longtime companion with him.

Inside the barn, he smiled as he switched on the overhead fluorescent lighting, immediately giving life to its contents. All twelve classic cars sat gleaming in two rows, the rewards of many successful escapades during his time with Mickey Carlisle. The ultimate prize was yet to be won though, Robert Valentine's '68 Shelby Mustang GT, but that would be his, just as soon as he found out where the lawyer had hidden it.

For tonight though, there was only one car for the task, only one that would hide slinkily and stealthily under the cover of darkness, and that was his most recent acquisition, the Riviera.

He settled inside, closed the door and inserted the brand new key into the ignition barrel he'd installed over the weekend, grinning as the General Motors' V8 burbled into life. Shifting the car into drive, he eased out of his secret man-cave in sleepy Ojai and exited the barn, the door closing silently and automatically as he left.

An hour and a half later, he found himself in Koreatown, an area of Los Angeles he despised. Like many other parts of the city, it had become a melting pot for all nationalities except Americans, mostly Koreans, Chinese, Japs and Vietnamese. His blood boiled at the thought of all the wars his country had fought to keep them out of his beloved America and knew that whatever happened here eventually transgressed to the rest of the country.

Fucking gooks, fuck all of you...

Having parked the Buick on a side street, he made his way up to the apartment building, a walk he'd made many times in the past. As the elevator returned to the ground floor and the doors slid open, he stepped inside and selected the button for the seventh floor.

Standing outside apartment 706, he took a deep breath and rapped twice on the door. When there was no response, he knocked again, only this time louder.

A minute or so later, the door was eventually opened, a disheveled and sleepy looking Mickey Carlisle, resplendent in a monogrammed satin dressing gown, glaring back at Buchanan.

"What the fuck do you want, Frank? Do you realize what fucking time it is, you clown?"

"We've got things to discuss," said Buchanan, "And it's not the sort of conversation I want to have on the phone. Are you gonna let me in or what?"

"For fuck's sake, come in, then," Mickey replied, "But this had better be important."

Buchanan stepped into the apartment, a place he knew like the back of his hand. He looked around at all the furniture and knickknacks crammed inside, all completely inappropriate for Mickey's modern high-rise. Gaudy relics from the 1960s and '70s occupied most of the floor space, items that Mickey had salvaged from his long-forgotten Bel Air estate. It was like walking into a time capsule, a sad one at that.

"Sit down," said Mickey, "You wanna drink or something?"

"I'll take a scotch," Buchanan replied, "Just a small one, I'm not gonna be here long."

Who the fuck has an eighteenth-century grandfather clock in a modern apartment?

He took a seat on one of the two sofas that faced each other in the lounge, each one covered in chintzy unmatched fabrics that went out of fashion last century.

"So what's got you all messed up that you had to come over here at fucking midnight?' asked Mickey, handing Buchanan a crystal tumbler half-filled with scotch, "Is it about your abortive attempt the other day on McLaren? What, you losin' your edge or somethin', Frankie?"

Mickey sat down on the opposite sofa, taking a huge hit of scotch from his own glass and casually slipped his hand beneath the pillow next to him.

"Forget about that, Mickey, I'm just tired of the whole business now. I want out."

"What do you mean, you want out? Don't you get it? You. Work. For. Me."

"See? That's the problem. I do all the work, you do fuck nothing."

"So what's your plan, Frankie, what're you gonna do about it? Seems like I have all the cards," replied Carlisle, smirking as he took another sip from his tumbler, his hand edging further under the pillow.

340

"Well, I guess I'm handing in my resignation," said Buchanan, reaching inside his jacket.

"Fuck you, Frank, I don't need a letter of resignation, you fucking idiot, put it away."

"No letter, Mickey, just this," replied Buchanan, as he pointed a Sig Sauer at Carlisle, a suppressor mounted on its barrel, "I guess it's more a case of me forcing my resignation. Permanently."

"Don't be stupid, Frank, do you think I didn't know what you might be up to? What do you take me for? I wasn't born yesterday," yelled Mickey, pulling out his beloved Glock from beneath the pillow and pointing it at Buchanan.

"Nice try, Mickey. But it's too late," replied Buchanan, "You've been terminated."

The muffled shot that rang out was more like the sound when the cap is removed from a car radiator. A quiet hiss of escaping air but in this case, just the puff of exiting gasses from the Sig's barrel.

Buchanan couldn't help but laugh at the look of shock on Carlisle's face, his mouth wide open, his eyes staring straight at him as the dime-sized hole in the center of Mickey's forehead began to ooze a rivulet of blood.

He got up from the sofa, pleased with himself that with his old Sig, his aim was still as perfect as it had always been. But it would be the last time he would ever use the gun.

Shame to have to say goodbye to you, my trusty little friend...

He prised the Glock from Mickey's hand, carefully removing his fat finger from inside the trigger guard and pocketed the gun inside his jacket. He unscrewed the suppressor from the Sig Sauer and pocketed that also. Wiping the Sig clean of his own prints he then replaced it in Mickey's hand, but this time having set the safety on the gun and turning it so that it faced toward Mickey. He pressed the dead man's palm and chubby fingers against the grip and carefully

341

looped his thumb inside the trigger guard before finally releasing the safety once more.

Happy with his work at making the scene appear as yet another suicide, something he was getting to be somewhat expert at recently, Buchanan crouched in front of his old boss, suddenly remembering all the good times. But all good things had to end eventually, he thought.

"It was good while it lasted, Mickey, but I've got to move on now. So take this as my formal resignation. And what is it the gooks say around here? Oh yeah… Sayonara, big boy, see you in hell, you fat fuck."

Chapter 73

"Happy Christmas, baby," said Tom, placing a tray of croissants and tea in the middle of the bed as Tess slowly began to open her eyes.

"Morning, gorgeous," said Tess, "What time is it?"

"Just past nine, shall I pour?"

"Oh my God, I just realized, it's Christmas Day! My mum will be wondering where I am!"

"Don't worry," Tom replied, "I called her an hour ago and said you'd fallen asleep here so she's fine. Croissant?"

"Only if I get you too," Tess replied, "Last night was amazing by the way…"

"First time or second?"

"All of them!"

"For me too. Now, drink your tea, have something to eat and then I thought we could explore each other in the shower for an hour or so. What do you think?"

"Only an hour or so?" asked Tess, her mouth drooping comically.

"Maybe a little longer then, come here, you beautiful girl…"

Once Fletcher had been alerted to the death of Mickey Carlisle, after the gangster's cleaner had discovered him that morning with a bullet in his head, he had immediately called Bill to invite him to the crime scene.

Standing in the Koreatown apartment as the CSI team began processing the scene, Bill said to Fletcher, "That's a face I hoped I'd never see again."

"Do you remember him?" asked Fletcher, "I'm guessing he's changed a lot since you last saw him and his face hasn't been enhanced by that hole in his head."

"I barely knew who he was. Robert dealt with all the money stuff but yeah, I did come into contact with him on a couple of occasions."

"I don't think there will be any real major effort from our boys at finding out who whacked him though, because L.A. is a better place without this piece of garbage," said Fletcher, "Would just be a waste of police time, money and resources."

"I get that. But don't you think it looks like someone tried to arrange it as a suicide. Seem familiar?" asked Bill.

"That's why I brought you here, do you think it's connected?"

"I think what it tells us is that Carlisle isn't the sniper who was shooting at me."

"Why do you say that?"

"Because my guy was half the size of this bastard."

"Which means that it was someone working for Carlisle that killed Robert and now Carlisle himself, so he can take matters into his own hands?"

"Exactly. And right now, we have no clue as to who that is, so we're still no closer to finding out who killed Robert."

Christmas Day for Tom in England, was so different than back home in California. Christmas in America was usually over by lunchtime when everyone had exchanged gifts and scampered off to the stores, receipts in hand, eager to find something they actually wanted.

It's lovely, thank you... did you keep the receipt?

But in England, the day was a long one, seemingly without an ending, thought Tom, that began with a traditional cooked English breakfast followed by copious servings of finger food, wine, beer and liqueurs throughout the day, until Christmas dinner was finally served at around five in the afternoon. It felt more akin to Thanksgiving to Tom, particularly as roast turkey seemed to be the centerpiece of most Christmas dinners in England. But it was different, and he liked it.

"You know, before we have dinner, I think we should walk off breakfast," said Tess, "Are you up for a little exercise, Mr. Delaney?"

"I'm down for that," Tom replied, "Count me in."

"Perfect, let me just finish preparing the vegetables for Mum and we can go and explore."

"I can take care of that," said Jenny, shoo'ing Tess out of her kitchen, you two lovebirds go off and enjoy yourselves."

Tess blushed but quickly hugged her mother, kissing her on the cheek as she pulled off her chef's apron and took Tom's hand.

"Thanks, Mum, we won't be long, love you."

The day was a beautiful one, a rare occurrence on Christmas Day in England. The sky was a cloudless, sapphire blue, punctuated by a bright and warming yellow sun. The air was chilly but fresh, the snow a bleached white blanket for as far as the eye could see and the couple enjoyed the moment to escape momentarily from the searing heat of the cottage.

"Tess, I just wanted to say how much I'm enjoying myself here with you and your family. It's prettier than I could ever have imagined and your mom and Franco have been so sweet to me."

"Don't worry, Tom, you're not special, they're like that with all my boyfriends," she replied, teasing him.

"Really?"

"No! Of course not, you idiot, they never liked any of my boyfriends, not that I've had many, but they definitely like you, it's written all over them."

"That's good to know, and I like them too, very much," said Tom, "Speaking of parents, I spoke to mine just now."

"Blimey, that was a bit early for them, wasn't it, it must have been around six in the morning, their time?"

"It was, but they were happy to hear from me and pleased that we're enjoying being with each other."

"Oh, so you told them we are officially transatlantic lovers now?" asked Tess, not wanting to miss the opportunity to tease Tom once again.

"No! Well, yes… oh, Tess, I don't know. All I know is that now I've found you, I never want to lose you, that's all."

"So you're moving to England?"

"If I could, I would. I love it here, I love being with you here. There are a couple of problems though."

"I know," said Tess, "Your whole family is back in Malibu."

"Not just that. My business with Matt is there too and honestly? I couldn't live here without citizenship so it's a non-starter."

They walked on, following the frozen stream that ran east of the cottage, holding hands, but neither one of them realizing how tightly they were gripping each other.

"Anyway…" said Tom, after a few minutes, "Dad was telling me about his friend, Perryman – you remember? I told you about him and another guy called Talbot, we call them our uncles but they're not really, they're just old friends of Mom and Dad's from their time back in Florida."

"Yes, I remember, you told me a bizarre story about Perryman, how he went from having no luck to having all the luck in the world."

"Exactly! Well, anyway, for the past few years, Perryman has been hauling his family out to the west coast for the Christmas break but this year, he's not going."

"That's a shame, bet your parents are a bit sad about that," said Tess, not knowing where Tom was headed with the conversation.

"They are, but to be honest, all my siblings are back home anyway, so they've got a pretty full house right now."

347

"I just realized, didn't you tell me that Perryman had something like ten kids? Where the hell would he stay with a brood that large?" Tess asked.

"Well, that's the thing. Perryman got luckier and luckier. He'd inherited this big waterfront property in a nice part of Florida and his benefactor also gave him a nice fat bank account. But he didn't know what he should do with the money."

"And this was back in the 80s?" asked Tess.

"Yes and no, by the time Perryman realized he might need to make his money work for him, it was in the late 90s."

"How much did he have left by then?"

"I'm not sure but my other uncle, Talbot, gave him the best advice anybody's ever given anyone. He's a lawyer too, but specializes now in finance."

"What was the advice?" asked Tess.

"He recommended that Perryman buy some stocks in a new tech company that was being tipped for greatness."

"Which one?"

"Amazon."

"Jeez! He must have multiplied his money by a thousand times since then!" exclaimed Tess.

"Oh more than," replied Tom, "He bought a quarter million dollars of shares in '97 and now they're valued at over three hundred and fifty million bucks. He's richer than God now! Haha!"

"Oh my God! That's unbelievable, Tom! Did Talbot invest as well?"

"No, he didn't, he just didn't have the available cash but don't worry, Perryman looked after him."

"That's some story, pretty amazing actually. But how did we get on to Perryman?" asked Tess.

"Oh right, yeah, I forgot. Well, as I said, Perryman can't go to the west coast because his new girlfriend is pregnant so she won't travel," explained Tom.

"Oh my lord, it's a good job he can afford more children!"

"But you were asking where they stay when they're on the west coast?" Tom continued.

"Yes, I think they'd need half a dozen hotel rooms but I suppose cost isn't really an important factor to them now?"

"Well, that's the thing, when he began to get even richer from the Amazon stock, he bought a beach house for the family in Malibu, and that's where they all stay when they're over there."

"Nice!"

"But when I was talking to Dad this morning, he said that if you ever wanted to go back to Malibu for a vacation, Perryman said it would be fine if you wanted to stay at his house, that's all."

"Really?" said Tess, "That's so sweet."

"Well, it's standing empty most of the time and Perryman said it would be nice if it was lived in a little."

"You're trying to tempt me, aren't you, Tom Delaney?"

"I am, I guess. Guilty as charged, ma'am, lock me up!"

~~~

"Same prints as before on the other casings. And once again, no GSR on the vic."

"You don't say," Bill replied, "And once again, there's no record of the prints in any of your databases?"

"Correct. And the thing is, biometric passports haven't been around that long so if the guy travels, he may still be traveling on an old passport so until he renews it, if he ever does, we still won't match his prints," said Fletcher, "And even then, assuming he's American, US citizens aren't even required to submit fingerprints for passports. And something tells me that our man isn't the type to rush into his local TSA office and apply for Global Entry."

"Jeez, Fletch, we're chasing our tails here, aren't we?"

"I know it feels that way right now, but there is one positive from Carlisle's murder," said Fletcher.

"Hit me."

"Well, Carlisle wasn't what you call a twenty-first-century man, it would seem that he had no use for computers or maybe he simply didn't trust them."

"And…"

"So that's the thing, he had no electronic files on a laptop or a hard drive, but he did keep every paper file he'd amassed over the last forty years," said Fletcher, "We found them all in a dozen or more filing cabinets in his apartment, once the CSI crew had finished with the crime scene."

"I guess it's a start," Bill replied, "How long is it going to take to go through them though, and can I help?"

"Could take weeks, even months, and no, you're not officially allowed to look at any of it," Fletcher replied, "But unofficially, I could use your eyes, see what might ring a bell. Who knows what you may spot?"

"Got it. I'm on board so just let me know when and where, Fletch. Meanwhile, I've got some investigating of my own to do."

Chapter 74

"So what the heck is Boxing Day? Does everyone go and watch a boxing match or something?"

Tom and Tess were lying on the floor of the cottage playing Scrabble with Jenny and Franco, the four sharing a bottle of Pinot Noir. Boxing Day breakfast was over now but Tom felt as though the food train at Christmas in England was endless. And he really felt the need to visit a gym.

"Don't be silly, of course not!" said Tess, aware that the day that followed Christmas Day in England was completely unique to the UK, "It's actually a pretty sweet idea that began around fifteen hundred years ago."

"Blimey!" said Tom, "Which is a word people seem to say a lot over here."

"So rude! Anyway, for the uneducated, this is the short version," said Tess, "Dating back to the Middle Ages and starting sometime around 600AD, the village church would have an 'alms box' installed in the rear section of the church building, effectively an early version of a charity box. This box would have a slit in the top through which coins would be donated by the congregation throughout the year, up to and including Christmas Day."

"Hold on, if you did that in the States, it'd be robbed within five minutes!" said Tom, interrupting Tess's flow.

"Whatever, let me finish. So on the day after Christmas, the boxes would finally be opened up and the money distributed amongst the poorest people in the village, thereby coining the term, Boxing Day. Maybe it should have been called Unboxing Day."

"Does it still happen?" asked Tom.

"I honestly don't know, maybe, who knows? But nowadays, it's the day after Christmas when everyone recovers from how much food they ate on Christmas Day," Tess replied, "And we eat bubble & squeak too on Boxing Day, which is unforgettable."

"I'm not even gonna ask!" said Tom.

"Don't worry, you'll be eating some later on," said Tess, enjoying how Tom never took offense at being teased.

"I was thinking..." he said, "Did you ask your mom about the cryptogram?"

"She did, Tom," Jenny replied, "But to be honest, it doesn't really mean anything to me. Robert was an odd character when it came to his puzzles."

"But I was thinking," said Tom, "There seems to be two interesting things about Tess's father. Firstly, that he appeared to have an absolute distrust of banks and the whole banking system, which is understandable, but also that he had a passion for mystery."

"That's so true about the mystery part, Tom," replied Jenny, "Although I didn't know him long enough to realize that he distrusted banks. He never had any money back then so they were no real threat to him."

"I showed Mum the cryptogram, Tom," Tess interjected, "But the only thing she remembered was that he loved crosswords and whenever he couldn't remember a name or a word or whatever, he used to go back and forth with the alphabet until he found it or remembered it."

"Can you email me the letter square and let me study it then?" said Tom, "I might as well do something useful because you're all killing me at Scrabble!"

Tess stood up to retrieve her iPhone from her bag and sent Tom an email with the cryptogram attached.

"Should be in your inbox any second," said Tess, "But I'm not sure you're going to get any further with it than I have."

"Oh, that was the other thing," said Jenny, "He had this big thing about the actor, Steve McQueen. The only films he ever wanted to watch were things like *The Great Escape*, *The Getaway*, *The Magnificent Seven* and *Bullitt*. He worshipped him. That's probably why he bought that Mustang; it's identical to the car in *Bullitt*, from what I saw of the photos Tess showed me when she arrived home."

"He had impeccable taste," added the usually quiet Franco, "That car was as beautiful as the Ferrari Daytona from my country that was launched at about the same time, I think."

"Who the heck is Steve McQueen, anyway?" asked Tess, oblivious to the history of the iconic actor.

"Quite simply," replied Franco, "He was the biggest actor of his time. I suppose he was the equivalent to someone like Brad Pitt or George Clooney."

"Gotcha!" said Tess, slowly beginning to understand her father's fascination with McQueen.

"Do you think it might *actually* be the car from the movie," asked Tom, "You know, if he had such a thing about Steve McQueen, maybe he bought it at an auction?"

"Honestly?" said Jenny, "Nothing would surprise me about Robert Valentine, Tom, he was a very unusual man."

Over the next few days after the Christmas holiday, Bill spent some time back at Robert Valentine's trailer, not knowing what he was looking for, but determined to leave no stone unturned. Sadly, since Robert was not someone who kept anything that didn't have an immediate use or purpose, there was little to delve through or discover.

But finally, he got the call from Fletcher to let him know that the filing cabinets were available to trawl through, and he rode the Indian into the city to lend a hand.

"Find anything?" asked Fletcher, "In your investigation, I mean."

"Nada, Fletch, zip. The man was a conundrum. I thought I knew him pretty well but I'm beginning to think I didn't really know him at all."

"Well, we've got a shitload of stuff to go through, you sure you're up for it?"

"Yeah, I am. Let's take a filing cabinet each and just work through them, alphabetically. Something's gotta give."

Chapter 75

Tom's lodging at the Crown Inn was actually a suite, comprising of two rooms; a small lounge and a bedroom. As Tess looked around it, taking in the gothic stone fireplace, the rough and whirly lath and plaster walls and the dark and ancient wooden doors with matching wooden latches, she felt the history of the pub immerse her in thoughts of what the building had witnessed throughout the preceding centuries. The doorways were low and not quite square and even the floors were so uneven and sloped, that the wardrobe looked like it was leaning to one side. The only modern items she saw were the television and the coffee-maker but other than that, it was a truly historic and romantic setting.

And as she lay next to Tom, she realized it seemed like an eternity ago since she had boarded the British Airways flight to LAX but it was really only less than two months. And then she suddenly remembered her newly found friend, Becky, who had been working in her cabin that day and so Tess decided to make contact by sending a brief text.

Within thirty seconds or so, a new message appeared on her iPhone from Becky. Tess was amazed but also delighted that Becky had remembered her and had responded so quickly with a New Year's party invitation. She decided that Tom needed to get out of Chiddingfold for a change and see a little more of England than just her home village. If she didn't get him out and about, he would probably go stir crazy.

"So, Thomas Delaney... can you handle going out with two women?" she asked, as he lay far too comfortably on his hotel room bed, still trying to make sense of the cryptogram puzzle on his phone.

"It's hard enough handling one," he replied, "Anyway, who's the other girl?"

"Her name is Becky,"

"Not Lola from the Copa?"

"No, Tom, not Lola. I met her on the flight going over to Los Angeles, she was one of the cabin crew," Tess replied, "But she's really nice and she's asked us if we want to go to her New Year's Eve party in London."

"Do we have to?" asked Tom, stretching out and getting even more comfortable on the ancient and creaking bed, "It's a bit of a trek to go into London, isn't it? Can't we just stay here and open a bottle of champagne and get room service?"

"You're going back to L.A. soon and you've hardly left this hotel or my house! Anyway, it's not in Central London, it's in Putney, which is easy to get to. I can even drive us there because I doubt I'll drink," Tess replied, "Putney is to London what Brooklyn is to Manhattan or Brentwood is to Los Angeles. Don't be a stick in the mud, Delaney!"

"Okay, I'm in," he replied, still glued to his phone, "Do you want me to drive?"

"Ha! Seriously?" laughed Tess, "An American driving in Britain?"

"Not really, I was just being polite," he said, grinning and putting the phone on the side table, "Now, we have the whole afternoon... you wanna play?"

358

On the third day of the search, Bill found himself alone in a spare office at LAPD headquarters, having eliminated more than eighty percent of the documents in Mickey Carlisle's filing cabinets. Fletcher had been pulled away on a different case but said that Bill could continue searching if he had the inclination. The office itself was uninspiring, the walls painted in a dull beige color, the floors covered in well-used brown linoleum, with the entire room lit by a single stark overhead fluorescent light fixture. Even the coffee sucked, Bill wishing he had his Gaggia machine at hand. But at least the air conditioning system worked pretty well, even if it was irritatingly noisy.

But it was on this third day that Bill finally discovered something useful. In a file, marked 'Wells Fargo', in the penultimate cabinet, he discovered a sheath of yellowing bank statements. As he read through them, his eyes now sore from staring at so many documents for the last three days, he noticed that there were frequent and fairly regular, large-sum payments made by check to the same recipient. He had statements going back to the early 1980s right up until only a few weeks ago and the recipient was showing up on just about every monthly summary.

Mickey Carlisle, being the excellent bookkeeper he seemed to have been, was meticulous in his notation and had written the name of a company or person against every single expenditure, but this one name kept coming up, time after time. And it was only when Bill totaled the amount of all payments to this one recipient that he realized it added up to over four million dollars. Which was an awful lot of money for one person. And it certainly wasn't being paid to the housekeeper he'd met at the crime scene, or if it was, she was the best-paid cleaner in the whole of Los Angeles.

359

So who the hell is F. Buchanan?

Chapter 76

"I don't want to go home," said Tom, dancing closely with Tess, his arms wrapped around her as he whispered in her ear.

"I don't want you to go," she replied, "I love being with you, but you already know that."

Becky's New Year's Eve party was in an apartment that was one of four units converted from a four-story Victorian house in Putney, close to the River Thames. At some point in the nineteenth century, the whole house would have been a moderate and affordable middle-class family dwelling, but prices had increased so much, that to purchase a whole house now in Putney was beyond the financial ability of even the most well-to-do couples. The purchase of a single, three-bedroom apartment was beyond Becky's salary so she shared it with two other British Airways girls, like many people living in London were forced to do now.

"Becky's really nice," said Tom, "My partner, Matt, would love her."

"Maybe we should introduce them," said Tess, "She often gets to Los Angeles."

"What are we, eHarmony?"

"No," she replied, "But if we've found each other, why not pay it forward, isn't that what you say in the States?"

"You're right, of course, let's put them together and see what happens," said Tom, "But right now, as it's almost midnight on New Year's Eve, shall we escape this party and share the birth of 2018 somewhere on our own?"

"What a lovely thought, Mr. Delaney," said Tess, "Come on, I know exactly where we should go."

Becky's apartment was a stone's throw from Putney Bridge, one of the many beautiful bridges that spanned the River Thames. The capital's river snaked all the way through London, beginning in the Cotswolds at Trewsbury Mead in Gloucestershire, before dissecting the counties of Oxfordshire, Berkshire and Buckinghamshire until it finally ended in Kent, before emptying into the North Sea.

On most nights, Putney Bridge would be crawling with traffic, buses, cars and motorcycles all heading out of town for the evening but tonight, on New Year's Eve, there was barely a soul to be seen, the whole of the population of London seemingly enjoying the ringing in of the New Year at home or at parties across the capital.

Tom and Tess walked slowly along the sidewalk to the crest of the bridge, both wrapped up in coats and hats and gloves against the chill of the night air. Tess entwined her arm around Tom's, keen to soak up his body warmth, both of them marveling at the clear starlit sky on the last night of the year.

"I can't get enough of the history here, it seems like everywhere you look, there's something even more beautiful to see that's hundreds of years old," said Tom, "Even these street lights on the bridge are works of art."

Tess saw what he was looking at, ornate triple-domed lights in red enamel and gold paint that lined each side of the bridge's sidewalks, beautifully crafted pieces from another time and another century.

"I can see what you mean, Tom, but I think when you see this every day, you just become blasé about it, almost indifferent or ignorant of what's around you, just like you are with the Hollywood sign," Tess replied, "It's only when you're sitting on a bus or you're a passenger in a car that you have the time to look up and see what's around you. I must say, London is incredibly beautiful when I see it through your eyes."

"I don't think the Hollywood sign is in the same league, but I could get very used to the landscape if I lived here, but I could also get very used to you, Tess. I'm really not sure how I'm going to cope with going home."

And at that moment, as if on cue, further down the Thames towards Westminster, the unmistakable sounds of Big Ben began to ring out, bringing with them once again, a brand new year.

"I don't know how I'm going to cope either, Tom, it's too hard to think about. But right now, I want to wish you a happy New Year and hope I spend many more with you in the future."

And as the Palace of Westminster's bells continued to ring, the couple kissed as though tomorrow might never come, the warmth of their embrace a welcome addition to the crisp and chilly night air.

Sitting in the Buick, watching the pretty girls walk past in their Manolo Blahniks, Buchanan was oblivious to the fact that it was New Year's Eve. As far as he was concerned, one day in Los Angeles was like any other; the sun came up, it was warm, it rarely rained and the sun went down again. He didn't see the need to celebrate the fact that a new year was about to begin. Although he was pretty certain that Maisie would want to pop a cork or two, come midnight.

363

Women... can't live with 'em, can't live with 'em...

But what was really on his mind, as he again pondered why McLaren had been spending so much time at the LAPD office building, was what the hell the hobo was doing there in the first place. And then it suddenly hit him. Buchanan knew Mickey hoarded his files and employee histories at his apartment, and that if the cops had taken them as evidence, it was only a matter of time before they put two and two together.

The big question was how much information Mickey had stored on Buchanan himself. Frank had been ultra careful over the years with the police, avoiding being logged into their systems; he'd never been pulled over, never got caught in a crime; hell, he'd never even had a parking ticket. But it would only take one log, in one file, for Mickey to screw up Buchanan's life from the grave, in the worst way possible.

As he continued to watch the endless supply of sophisticated and beautiful women clip-clopping past his car in their too-short skirts and too-high shoes, his contempt for them grew. He wound down the window and spat on the sidewalk just as another stunning L.A. girl was walking past.

"Asshole!" she said.

"And fuck you too, lady," he said, raising a middle finger at her as she scurried away.

He lit a cigarette, deliberately blowing smoke out the window into the path of other passers-by.

Fucking L.A... you can't even shit without a permit...

The hours ticked by, Buchanan needing to change parking spots every forty minutes or so to avoid a ticket. His Buick was beginning to smell too much like the Camry, he thought, as he noticed the buildup of takeout trash in the passenger footwell.

Finally, he spotted McLaren exiting the LAPD building and watched as he made his way to the Indian that was parked another hundred yards or so further down the street. He cranked the Buick's engine and slid it into Drive and began to follow the motorcycle, but at a very safe distance. He couldn't be sure that McLaren hadn't made the Buick when he'd been taking potshots at him in Malibu and he didn't want to give the game away before it had even begun.

Better safe than sorry...

Chapter 77

Bill had known that he was in danger of wearing out his welcome at Fletcher's office. Even though his friend had cleared it with the detectives' department for Bill to be there each day, he began to feel some hard stares coming back at him now, having combed through the files for three days straight. In fairness to the cops, it wasn't so much that Bill was an intruder as much as they didn't much care if Mickey Carlisle's killer was found or not. As far as they were concerned, it was one less scumbag on the streets of Los Angeles and they weren't about to offer any help. So Bill had decided that it was time to begin looking for this F. Buchanan character back at his home office.

Taking a seat at his desk, he fired up his desktop Mac and began to search for the name, F. Buchanan, in the most obvious places first. Beginning with White Pages, he discovered that in L.A. County alone, there were forty-seven F. Buchanan listings and that didn't include places further out like Ventura County, Santa Barbara or Simi Valley.

It's gonna take me a month of Sundays to visit every single F. Buchanan in the area...

But the one thing Bill had on his side was time. So he began to eliminate candidates, one by one. Almost half of the entries listed in White Pages were women so he could ignore those. And given that Mickey Carlisle was in his eighties, he assumed that the age range he was looking at was probably forty to seventy and White Pages very kindly stated the age of each resident that had a landline, which was incredibly helpful.

He continued searching, including the immediate surrounding counties and eventually ended up with a list of eighteen potential candidates whose residences ranged from Santa Monica to Thousand Oaks, from Ojai to Carpinteria. It was still going to be a tough and drawn-out job to identify the F. Buchanan he was searching for. But for the first time in years, Bill had a feeling he once again enjoyed, a sense that he was needed and that he had a job to do.

The biggest problem was that his list of eighteen candidates spanned a pretty wide area, and so he set about formulating a plan to visit the individuals in the most expeditious manner possible. The list threw up the following males, whose ages ranged from forty-two to sixty-eight years old.

1. Floyd Buchanan – Canoga Park
2. Frank Buchanan – Pasadena
3. Farrell Buchanan – Glendale
4. Francis Buchanan – Simi Valley
5. Fred Buchanan – Santa Clarita
6. Fabricio Buchanan – Burbank
7. Felix Buchanan – Redondo Beach
8. Fielding Buchanan – Santa Monica
9. Forrest Buchanan – Studio City
10. Franklyn Buchanan – Northridge
11. Friedrich Buchanan – Ventura
12. Flynn Buchanan – Casita Springs
13. Farrington Buchanan – Long Beach
14. Farley Buchanan – Camarillo
15. Fergal Buchanan – Summerland
16. Frank Buchanan – Ojai
17. Farrington Buchanan – Long Beach

He leaned back in his office chair and swiveled around to face the rest of the vast beach home. He knew he should be grateful to be living there. But for so long it had felt completely empty since he'd lost Sandy, it was just a box, a place to eat and sleep. It hadn't felt like a home in years, which is why he chose to wander the Malibu streets as an apparent homeless man during the day, just to be away from the memories of her for a while. To escape and to be someone other than who he had become, a lost soul with a broken heart, which if he thought about for too long, made him feel even sadder.

But to even sleep in this house was hard for him because he had built it for Sandy, just for her, his only love. His life had always been about Sandy, and then he had lost her. And then suddenly, everything changed when Robert's daughter came into his life; he'd felt a sudden sense of purpose, a connection to the past and a raison d'être that had been dormant for so many years. And now, at moments like this when he looked around his home, he finally felt comfortable being here and he could feel Sandy here, watching over him as he watched over Tess, just as Robert would have done for him. And that made him smile.

Chapter 78

Saying goodbye was the hardest part. As Tess drove her Citroën to London's Heathrow Airport, barely a word was exchanged between the two of them. Tom was trying hard to keep from crying and Tess put all her thoughts into concentrating on where she was driving, so that she too didn't break down in tears. For all the love and laughs they'd shared during the previous ten days, the final ninety minutes was too painful for both of them.

"Stay in the car," said Tom, as they pulled up outside Terminal Five at Heathrow, "No sense in you getting cold."

"No, I'm not going to, Tom," Tess replied, "I don't know when I'll see you again."

She got out of the driver's side, Tom already opening the trunk to retrieve his suitcase just as an airport cop was yelling at them to move on.

Tom dropped the case as Tess fell into his arms and try as he might, he couldn't stop the tears from coming, as his barriers finally collapsed. They kissed, their faces already a wet mixture of each other's tears and Tess finally broke away as the cop approached, still yelling at them.

"Tom Delaney, this ain't over, you know that, right?"

"I do, Tess Valentine, I do, and I hope it's only just beginning."

"So, call me when you get back? Promise?"

"You know I will. I'm already dialing your number. But it's going to be so hard, sweetheart, I don't know how I'm going to cope without you in my life now," said Tom, the heartbreak of the moment immediately bringing more tears.

"I'm still in it! I'll always be in your life, you idiot!"

"I've got to go," said Tom, hugging her tightly one more time before he picked up his case and walked into the terminal, not daring to look back.

And Tess broke down then, the sobs coming quickly and easily.

"Are you alright, miss?" said the cop who had finally stopped shouting, "Can I do anything for you?"

"Not unless you can work magic," Tess replied, "But thank you anyway."

Chapter 79

The next two weeks at work seemed to drag for Tess. It always felt so bleak in January and she wondered what she had to look forward to now. It was the same feeling every year but when Tom left, it felt like her whole world had imploded. Even the snatched phone conversations with him were difficult because of the time difference between them and she still didn't have Archie to lean on, because he had taken an extended break during Christmas back home in Glasgow.

As she doodled on a pad at her desk, a familiar voice filtered through the fog of her thoughts.

"What's up, treacle?"

"Archie!" she cried, never so pleased to see the ginger mop leaning over the front of her cubicle, "I've missed you!"

"Missed you too, pickle," he replied, "Penny for your thoughts?"

"Oh… nothing. Well, nothing and everything," she said, "I've had a wonderful Christmas, that's all, and I just can't get my head back into work yet."

"Know what you mean, January's the hardest month but soon… well soon, it'll be February!" he replied, laughing.

"Yeah right, another horrid month to forget!"

"God, I'm so hungry and I only had breakfast an hour ago," said Archie.

"How about lunch, then?" Tess asked.

"Might you be suggesting Indian?"

"Deal," she replied, "Can't wait to tell you about my Christmas and for you to tell me about yours."

"Okay then, I've got to go to a meeting with the suits, shall we say, one o'clock at Gopal's?"

~~~

Gopal's in Bateman Street was a favored haunt for many Soho'ites, a family-owned Indian restaurant that had been around since the late 1980s. Tess was lucky to get a lunchtime table because the restaurant's popularity was at its height in the winter months, until the weather changed temperature in the spring, and the creative crowd suddenly felt the need to dine outside in the noise and exhaust fumes of Soho's traffic.

Tess sat down in the crowded dining area and immediately reached for the tray of relishes and stack of poppadoms, gobbling one up in a matter of seconds, the taste unique and addictive. Archie had yet to arrive so she greedily snatched another before he sat down and devoured it as he usually did, dipping it in the mint raita and chutney before she took a bite.

"Ooooh, thought you got away with that, didn't you," said Archie as he pulled out a wicker chair opposite Tess, "Don't think I didn't see you."

"Well you know your reputation precedes you, Arch, I'm just getting a taster before you snatch them all," Tess replied, "Anyway, we don't have much time, shall we order?"

"You wanna share?" suggested Archie, as a waiter silently appeared at their table, notepad in hand.

374

"Sure, how about Lamb Dhansak, Chicken Tikka Masala, Pilau rice and some Keema Naan?" asked Tess, "And a couple of pints of Cobra?"

"Go for it, I'm starving!"

This was the extraordinary thing about Archie, he was skinny as a string bean but had the appetite of a tiger. He never stopped eating, even when he was working.

"How was your Christm…" they both said at once.

"Ha! You go first, Arch, you've been away much longer than I have," said Tess.

"What can I tell you? It's always exactly the same in Glasgow, we lurch from one pub to another, from house party to house party until New Year's Eve, when we get really Scottish at Hogmanay with the haggises and the street parties and the fireworks, and that's when it all kicks off. This year, Hogmanay finished on around the fourth of January, I think, although I was so drunk most of that week, I can't really remember."

"I can't imagine you drunk, Arch, I'm not even sure I've ever seen you in that state," Tess interjected.

"Well, look at me, I weigh about a hundred and ten pounds so it doesn't take much to get me pissed as a fart," he said, laughing, "And the thing is, you go up to Scotland with all the best intentions of taking it easy on the booze, but it's like a fucking religion up there, they get upset if you don't keep up with them!"

Again, the waiter silently and mysteriously appeared, placing a hot tray between them and arranging four silver dishes on it, the aromas immediately finding Archie's nostrils.

"Oh God, I think I just died and went to heaven, I've missed this so much, Tess… it's like manna from my heaven anyway."

375

"For me too," said Tess, "Dig in, we don't have long and I'm starving."

As they ate, enjoying every bite and every mouthful as though they'd never eaten such exotic fare before, Tess told Archie about her Christmas, how perfect it had been and how Tom had surprised her and flown over to see her.

"Sound like the girl's in love, methinks," said Archie, "The boy too."

"I hate to say it, but you're right, Arch, hook, line and flippin' sinker."

For almost a minute, neither said a word, their mouths both full, enjoying a long-awaited Indian treat, until Archie finally spoke.

"I forgot to tell you…"

"What, you've got a girlfriend?"

"No! Heaven forbid! Anyway, I can't afford one on my salary."

"What's your big news then?"

"I finally worked out what your dad's puzzle was all about?"

"The cryptogram? Really? Are you serious?"

"Yeah, if you can call it a cryptogram, but really and truly, it was just a pretty simple puzzle."

"Arch! Tell me!" said Tess, "Tom and I have been trying to work it out all through Christmas and now you casually tell me that it was a cinch!"

"Well, it wasn't too difficult once I'd had a day or two sober, but the trick lay in what you told me about your dad, the way he would run backward and forward with the alphabet when he couldn't remember a name. Many people do that, and then when I looked at the grid again, I realized how straightforward it was."

376

"Our lunch hour is running down, can you tell me now or do you want to talk later? The thing is, I'm desperate to find out if it means anything at all," Tess replied.

"Well, that's the thing, I'm not sure it's going to help but I can show you right now, I made some images on my phone, hold on…"

Archie retrieved his iPhone, pulled up some graphics and showed them to Tess.

"Look at the original grid, then remove the alphabet every fourth letter, starting at the first square," said Archie, shoveling a huge mouthful of curry into his mouth.

AAZHBOYMCEXIDSWWEHVEFRUE
GTTHHESHIERAJRQTKIPSLAONM
DNDNEMEOPLBPEKLQOJWRWIHS
EHRTEGTUHFEVREAWTDTXLCEY
SBNZAAKAEZSBRYOCAXMDHWIE
DVEFSUAGGTIHFSTITRHJAQTKIP
GLIOUMENTNOMYOOLUPIKLQOJ
UREIYSOHUTTGEUSFSUDEAWDD

Tess sat staring at the grid, trying to remove each alphabetically-ascending letter from the beginning, but became exasperated when she couldn't keep the remaining letters in her notably eidetic memory.

"Having a hard time?" asked Archie.

"I just wish I could print this and then Tippex out all of the ascending letters of the alphabet, it'd be so much easier," she replied.

"Don't worry, I'm only teasing you," said Archie, "I've already done that for you and I've prepared the next grid with the ascending alphabet faded back. Hold on, let me show you."

377

He then flipped to another graphic on his phone and handed it back to Tess.

```
AZH OYM EXI SWW HVE RUE
TTH ESH ERA RQT IPS AON
DND EME PLB EKL OJW WIH
EHR EGT HFE REA TDT LCE
SBN AAK EZS RYO AXM HWI
DVE SUA GTI FST TRH AQT IP
G IOV ENT OMY OLU IKL OJ
V EIY OHU TGE SFS DEA DD
```

"I'm still sixpence none the wiser, Arch, are you seeing something I'm not?" she asked, baffled at the new sets of letter triplets.

"Stay with me, Tess, it will all become clear in a second. Okay, so now I'll fade back the alphabet from the second letter you see in each triplet, but this time the alphabet is reversed, so it's descending."

He leaned over, munching on a fresh poppadom and slid the image to the left to reveal a new square.

```
AZH OYM EXI SWW HVE RUE
TTH ESH ERA RQT IPS AON
DND EME PLB EKL OJW WIH
EHR EGT HFE REA TDT LCE
SBN AAK EZS RYO AXM HWI
DVE SUA GTI FST TRH AQT IP
G IOV ENT OMY OLU IKL OJ
V EIY OHU TGE SFS DEA DD
```

"Oh crumbs, Archie, I think I'm beginning to see it now!" said Tess, as he finally removed the alphabets altogether.

```
A H O M E I S W H E R E
T H E H E A R T I S A N
D D E E P B E L O W W H
E R E T H E R A T T L E
S N A K E S R O A M H I
D E S A G I F T T H A T I
G I V E T O Y O U I L O
V E Y O U T E S S D A D
```

"I knew you'd get to it eventually, but your old man, he was a pretty clever character, wasn't he?"

"You can say that again," Tess replied, "Now all I have to do is work out what the damn thing means in English."

```
A HOME
IS WHERE THE HEART IS
AND DEEP BELOW WHERE
THE RATTLESNAKES ROAM
HIDES A GIFT
THAT I GIVE TO YOU
I LOVE YOU TESS
DAD
```

Chapter 80

Bill had been riding his Indian door to door for three days, searching for the elusive F. Buchanan, but so far without any luck. Sixteen of the names had now been struck off the list as potential candidates and he was currently out in Ojai to assess one Frank Buchanan. He was beginning to think that maybe he was on a wild goose chase, and that the bank statement entries for this name had no relevance at all.

He pulled up in the driveway of the pretty single-story home with its well-tended front yard and made his way to the front door, pausing to take a look around before ringing the doorbell. The muted sound of Beethoven's Fifth rang through the house and after twenty or thirty seconds as Bill was about to try again, he saw a blurred figure through the door's rippled window, hurriedly approaching.

The door opened, revealing a petite and pretty, smiling and mildly overweight woman of around fifty to fifty-five years of age.

"Sorry about that, I was out back doing laundry when you rang, I can't hear a thing over the racket that the washing machine makes. Maisie Buchanan, how can I help you?"

"Good afternoon, ma'am, I have something that may interest you," said Bill, "My name is Jim Bailey from California Cable-Xtra.

"It's nice to meet you, Jim, but I'm not sure I can help you, my husband takes care of all the utilities, maybe you could come back another time when he's here?"

"Your husband, he's Frank Buchanan?" asked Bill.

"Yes, but he's at work at the moment."

"Of course, I understand, weekdays aren't the best time to catch the man of the house at home, I guess," Bill replied, "Out of curiosity, what line of business is your husband in?"

"Insurance, has been for the last thirty-something years," said Maisie, "It's a bit boring but it pays for his toys, I suppose, and we just had a lovely vacation in the Bahamas."

"We're all like that, ma'am, boys love their toys, don't they? What's his particular passion, fishing maybe, or no... I bet it's boats!"

"I wish it was," replied Maisie, "But no, Frank loves his cars, got a whole collection of them out back."

It struck Bill that the woman was extraordinarily open about everything and anything, and she really was very sweet. It seemed unlikely that a mob guy would be married to such a nice lady. But the 'car collection' comment had piqued his interest and he felt like it needed to be pursued.

"Well, it seems a shame to have wasted the afternoon coming all the way out here, but seeing as you're home and maybe if you have a few minutes, do you think I could check out back to verify if your home would be a candidate for Cable-Xtra?" said Bill, "You see, it's a very special and highly innovative method of getting television programs from across the world into your home without the need for wiring, junction boxes or dishes."

"It sounds pretty complicated."

"It's really not, Maisie... may I call you by your first name?

"Of course," she replied, blushing.

"The thing is, Maisie, your home has been chosen as a guinea pig if you like, to test the system out here in Ojai, out of all the thousands of homes in your neighborhood. And the best part of it, it's free. As a test customer, you'll never have to pay another penny for cable TV again. I'd hate to have to go next door and offer it to your neighbor, because you seem like such a nice girl."

"Free, you say? Frank would love that; he's always going on about saving money on this and that. He has this awful smelling Camry that he drives everywhere for his job when he has all those lovely cars out back," said Maisie, knowing that Frank would be proud of her, but also enjoying the fact that this handsome gentleman had just called her a 'nice girl'. She hadn't been called that in more years than she cared to remember.

"It is indeed free, Maisie, free for as long as you live here, it's the deal of a century, but only if it works on your lot," Bill replied, "But I'd need to perform a quick survey before I could confirm. Wouldn't take more than a few minutes."

"Would you like to come in for a cup of tea?" she asked, thinking that there was no reason not to let the nice man check.

"You must have read my mind, I'm parched," said Bill, "I've been on the road for a few hours now, and I would love some tea, thank you."

They went inside the house, Bill noting that it couldn't have been more ordinary if it tried. Beige walls, beige carpet, prints on the walls from HomeGoods and furniture that could realistically be straight out of a Rooms To Go store setting from the 1990s. The home was very much a beige home, albeit clean and tidy.

"English Breakfast or Earl Grey?" asked Maisie, as she headed toward the kitchen.

"English is fine with me, sweetheart," said Bill, "But while you're making it, perhaps I could go outside and do some preliminary investigations on the lot to check for antenna position?"

"Knock yourself out, Jim, I'll just put the kettle on while you're doing that," said Maisie, as she pattered off toward the kitchen, relishing the fact that the handsome gentleman had just called her 'sweetheart'.

Once outside, Bill threw down a tape measure and began pacing out the lot, wary that he might be seen from the kitchen but also keen to keep up his cover. When Maisie called out to him that the tea was ready and she would serve it in the lounge at the front of the house, he told her that he was almost done.

"I'll be right in, Maisie, just got to check a couple of measurements on the far boundary," he called out to her, "Put a tea cozy on the pot and keep it warm for me!"

He quickly made his way to the rear of the property and ducked behind the windowless car barn, gratefully finding a side door into the building. It was a common padlock and Bill easily jigged the combination until it clicked open. But once inside, he physically gasped at what he saw.

"Jesus H. Christ!" he murmured, "This ain't a weekend car collection, "This is straight out of The Pebble Beach Concours d'Elegance."

But as he walked down the rows of rare and beautiful classic cars, his mind was immediately performing a rudimentary calculation of the collection's value, and the obvious question was already forming in his mind…

"How the hell does an insurance salesman pay for a million bucks worth of vintage automobiles?"

Chapter 81

"I need to go back," said Tess.

"Back where?" asked Archie.

"Malibu, idiot!"

"Why? I've only just got you back, what can Malibu offer you, except sunshine, sand, sea, bright lights, celebrities…"

"I don't mean that, Archie. Don't you see? Dad has left me a vital clue and I'm not going to be able to rest until I find out what it means. I've got to go back."

"Well, good luck with your vacation request, Tess. I'm not sure you'll get it approved so easily unless you've got another funeral to go to."

"Bad taste, Archie, uncalled for."

"Sorry, my bad. But the thing is, you've only just had a couple of weeks vacation time and what with the Christmas holiday too, I just don't see Raúl signing off on it."

"I know what you mean, it doesn't look good, does it, whichever way you look at it?" said Tess, realizing the harsh veracity of what Archie was saying.

"Nope, it really doesn't. But there's only one way to find out. Talk to da man!"

At six-thirty, Tess noticed that Raúl Grüber, her Creative Director, was still in his office, having just spent the last two hours with a pair of creative teams. She couldn't tell what mood he was in but she decided it was now or never.

She knocked on the glass door, before pushing it open and leaning in.

"Hi Tess, what's up?" said Grüber, rummaging amongst a pile of storyboards on his desk, clearly trying to locate something he'd lost.

"Do you have a minute, Raúl? I know you're busy though."

"Sure, I'm gonna be here til midnight, so it makes no odds anyway. Come on in, take a pew. Want some pizza?"

Raúl Grüber was an interesting man. Half Colombian, half Austrian, he had taken a gap year after high school and had spent time working in and traveling around Europe. After arriving in England and exploring for a few months, he then spent the next four years studying art & design at Leeds Metropolitan University. Consequently, his accent was an odd mix of his parents' native tongues, combined with a heavily accented northern-English brogue. It was further enhanced by the fact that he'd lived for the past two decades in London's East End, thereby adding a Cockney vernacular to the mélange.

Tess sat down on the other end of the sofa that Grüber had just slumped on. His office was a colorful array of original 60s pop-art furniture and twentieth-century impressionist art, the whole room opening out onto enviable views of Soho Square. Although in truth, the most comfortable item in the room was the turquoise velveteen sofa that Tess was now sitting on.

"How is everything, Tess?" he asked, "Is it nice to be home or did you enjoy yourself too much out there?"

"It was okay, I guess…"

"I'm sorry, that was a bit dense of me. Forgive me. I know you went out there to sort out your father's estate; it must have been pretty upsetting," he interjected, Tess noticing that he didn't sound the letter 't' on his last two words.

"No, it's fine, Raúl, don't worry, I hardly knew him but I suppose it was still weird dealing with it all."

"I'm pleased that it's over for you now, it's never a situation any of us want to face," he continued, "So what can I do for you? You've got a worried look on your face."

"Well, that's just it, it isn't all over, well, not quite."

"Really?"

"Yeah… well, I guess I should explain…"

Tess spent the next fifteen minutes relating the details of her trip to Los Angeles, ending with Archie's recent discovery of the cryptogram's meaning, as Raúl sat silently listening in rapt attention.

"Christ, Tess!" he exclaimed as she finished, "It's like a Dan bloody Brown novel!"

"I know, it's been a whirlwind but I still haven't put it to bed yet and I need to do that somehow."

"So, what can I do to help? I'm no good at solving mysteries, unless you count this fucking Dacia account!"

"Raúl … I know I've only just come back to work but… do you think there's any chance I could take my whole year's vacation allowance now, all at once? I know it's a big ask and I would completely understand if you…"

"No worries, Tess. Jesus, kid, I want to see how this mystery finishes, of course, you can!"

"Really? You're serious?"

"Aye, I am. Anyway, you're kind of doing us a bit of a favor in a roundabout way."

"How do you mean?" asked Tess, still astonished that Raúl had granted her vacation request so easily.

"Here's the thing, Tess, you've got to realize that everyone wants vacation time in the summer, especially all of us with bloody kids because of the school flippin' 'olidays, so you'll be the one 'oled up here minding the place while we're all away!" he laughed, "Now go on, go and find out how the story ends, Nancy Drew!"

"Thanks, Raúl, you don't know what this means to me, I really appreciate it."

Now all I've got to do is break the news to Mum…

Chapter 82

"California Cable-Xtra? Who the hell are they? I've never heard of them."

"It was a very nice man who came to the door, he said we had been chosen as a test household for this new thing they're launching," said Maisie, completely unaware of why her husband was acting so strangely, "And anyway, you'll get to watch all your football games for free, so we'll save a fortune on cable fees."

Sometimes Buchanan couldn't believe how dim his wife could be. And there was something way too fishy to believe that his house had been chosen out of all the homes in Ojai.

"What did this fella look like?" he asked above the din, as Maisie continued to vacuum the lounge.

"Quite tall," she said, trying but failing to get the vacuum cleaner under the sofa, "A bit like the fella in that film you like about bowling, you know the one."

"The Big Lebowski," said Buchanan, mulling over this new information.

"Yes, that's the one, what's his name…"

"Sam Elliot," said Buchanan.

"I knew you'd get there in the end, yes, nice looking man, very polite too."

"I'll bet," said Buchanan, already knowing that McLaren had been inside his house.

Time just ran out…

~

When Tess finally plucked up the courage to tell her mother what her plans were, she knew she would be upset. All the way home on the journey back from London, she was trying to think how best to break the news to her. Bearing in mind how much Jenny had missed her, having only been away for twelve days or so before Christmas, Tess knew it would be a difficult task. But much as she thought she knew her mother, Tess really didn't expect the response she was about to receive.

"Mum, there's something I need to talk to you about," said Tess, pouring her mother another glass of wine as Jenny checked the chicken that was roasting in the oven, "And I don't think you're going to be too happy about it."

"Why don't you try me then, what's on your mind?" Jenny replied, removing her apron and sitting down next to her daughter.

So Tess explained what she'd found out with Archie's decoding of the cryptogram and the conversation she'd had with Raúl that evening and then waited for her mother's negative response.

"And the thing is, Mum, I still don't know enough about Dad and this may be my last chance to make the connection. I know you're already upset about the idea, aren't you?"

"Hold on!" said Jenny, "You haven't heard my thoughts on it!"

"Sorry, I'm banging on, aren't I?"

"If you really want to know, I'm as interested to find out what Robert's message is about too. It's pretty obvious to me that he wanted you to go the whole hog, so I'm not going to make you feel bad about leaving again. And I know that Tom will be taking good care of you while you're in Los Angeles which makes me feel a lot better about it, now that I've met him."

"Mum, you're as much of a conundrum as Dad was! I thought you'd go ballistic when I told you what I wanted to do!"

"Well, maybe you should have a bit more faith in us old-timers, baby girl," replied Jenny, "Anyway, Franco kindly informed me that apparently the two of us could get on a plane and come visit if you stay for any length of time. It's amazing how quickly you can travel to far-off places now, don't you think?"

"You're such a tease! But thank you, Mum, you don't know how much I appreciate this. To have your backing is really important to me, you know that."

"Well, there is something you can do right away," said Jenny.

"What's that," asked Tess.

"Get your phone out and book yourself a ticket before it's too late!"

Chapter 83

During the daylight hours, Malibu belonged to Sammy Chan, although Malibu wasn't actually his original birthplace. Originally a cop with the SFPD up in San Francisco, but pensioned off after a near-fatal shooting, he had moved south to San Luis Obispo with his wife Teresita and once there, he had become a freelance private investigator. With a near full-pay pension to financially support him as he built up his new business, and with gratefully received client referrals from the Delaney & Camarillo law firm where his wife worked, he quickly became the go-to P.I. in the San Luis Obispo County region. He had even used his skills many years ago to help bring Jake and Summer back together again, which pleased him immensely.

And Sammy and Teresita Chan had happily made San Luis Obispo their home for the better part of a decade. As far as they were concerned, they never wanted to leave. The public schools were excellent and there was a university, Cal Poly, right there in town for when Esteban graduated high school. And their standard of living was far better in San Luis Obispo than in San Francisco, now that the tech giants like Google, Adobe, Uber, Facebook and Yahoo! had taken over the city and pushed the cost of housing way beyond the reach of so many San Franciscans.

But when Jake Delaney had decided to move his business further south to Los Angeles to be closer to his kids, Sammy and Teresita had followed him, reluctantly at first, but after not too many months they were enjoying their new life there with their growing son, Esteban.

In his role as a private investigator, Sammy spent most of his waking hours trolling the PCH in his car and driving up and down every canyon boulevard that forked off it. He pretty much knew the place blindfolded. He knew every restaurant, every gas station, every plaza and he recognized a hundred people every day. And he also knew his Buick when he saw it.

Today, on a new case, he had been following the car of a cheating husband; a middle-aged sit-com producer from Brentwood who'd been spending his afternoons at the home of a teenage pop star in her newly purchased house in Bel Air. But as he was tailing the guy's cherry red Tesla on the PCH, he'd abandoned the pursuit when he had spotted his beloved Buick Riviera around six hundred yards ahead of him as he drove north, just as the Tesla took a right on Sunset Boulevard by Pacific Palisades, heading up toward Bel Air. Sammy knew it was his Buick ahead of him, even before he could see it up close. But he still had to get close enough to make absolutely certain. And lover-boy could definitely wait until tomorrow.

Dropping down a gear of the 3-speed Cruise-O-Matic automatic transmission in his recently acquired '64 Ford Galaxie, he began to thread his way through the heavy traffic that was already building up on the route out of Santa Monica, slowly gaining on the Buick. But as quickly as he closed the distance between him and the black car ahead, impatient drivers who were also heading north, eager to get home, pushed in front of him and the gap widened once more.

Sammy calmed himself. He had to pinch himself too. He couldn't believe that his car was still in L.A. but he also realized he had all the time in the world, as long as he kept the Buick in sight. And then he suddenly knew what he was going to do. The driver would have to stop eventually, and once he did, Sammy was going to snatch his car back. Fortunately for Sammy, he had just refueled and now had a full tank, and he still had the Buick's ignition key on his key ring, never having had the heart to remove it.

~~~∽

As Buchanan tailed the Indian Chief motorcycle further north on the PCH, he noticed that McLaren had begun to increase his speed, letting the bike's powerful V-Twin open up on the less populated part of the highway. Like most Los Angeleans, Buchanan knew that speeding tickets were less likely in this area because the California Highway Patrol allotted much fewer police units to the stretch of road that led up to the Ventura County line. This seemed odd to Buchanan, given the number of fatal accidents that had historically occurred amongst the Hollywood elite as they speed-tested their toys on this more deserted stretch of the PCH. Heck, even James Dean had bought the farm here, back in the 1950s in his dumbass little Porsche Speedster.

Fucking faggot...

And Buchanan was also acutely aware of the old Ford Galaxie that had been tailing him for the last six miles. It didn't take a genius to realize that it might be the Chinese fella he'd recently separated from his beloved Buick. Either that or it was just pure coincidence. But right now, he didn't think that very likely, and he wasn't about to lose sleep over it.

Might get a chance to kill two birds with one stone again...

He eased the accelerator pedal down to the point where he was doing nearly seventy in a fifty limit, keeping a distance of around six hundred yards between him and the Indian, and sure enough, the Ford stayed with him. What he didn't understand was why the guy didn't just pull up close behind and try and stop him. And then it dawned on him, the driver was looking for an opportunity to seize back the Riviera undamaged. He was clearly looking for the chance to grab it when Frank eventually stopped for gas or a bathroom break, which wasn't going to happen.

~

They had driven close to fifteen miles now, heading up toward the Ventura County line and Sammy was starting to realize that the Buick wasn't stopping anytime soon.

What Sammy didn't know was that Buchanan had stopped an hour ago and gassed the Buick so the driver had at least three hundred miles left in the tank.

He increased his speed to eighty and eased up behind the car, knowing that it was now or never.

~

Once again, Tess had found herself on a British Airways flight to Los Angeles. Her mother had been amazing, helping her to pack that same evening, generously paying for her ticket and driving her to London's Heathrow Airport the following morning. Tearful farewells and hugs on the sidewalk outside the terminal followed, with promises to update each other every evening.

This time, without the benefit of her father's generosity, Tess had experienced the pain of traveling coach, something she didn't look forward to doing again anytime soon. But on arrival at LAX, having already faced the daunting task of navigating immigration a couple of months previously, this time it had been a breeze, her carefully constructed reason for traveling to the United States wafting effortlessly over the head of the agent behind the Plexiglas.

And when she spotted Tom's grinning face, like a beacon amongst the hordes of meandering people waiting in the arrivals hall, her heart leaped. It was something she had never before experienced, certainly not with the cretinous and now completely forgotten Simon, but it was something that warmed her whole body, the sense that she was loved and cherished for who she was and not what she was.

When they embraced and kissed, Tess felt the whole world magically turning, as though she was in one of those glass globes where the snow swirls around two lovers, alone together in their own little cosmos. She had read romantic novels before but in comparison to the spark she felt with Tom, they seemed so dreary now. Feeling his lips against hers, as the world kept on spinning, Tess knew that she had found the man she had always been looking for; a man who made her laugh and who never stopped smiling.

"I could get used to this, Tom Delaney," she murmured, releasing herself from their kiss to take a breath, "You're a sight for sore eyes."

"The pleasure is really all mine, Miss Valentine, trust me. Come on, your carriage awaits you!"

~~~

Sammy was now only fifty or so yards behind the Buick, both vehicles traveling in excess of seventy-five as he slowly edged up behind the car, finally getting a glimpse of the thief in the Buick's rearview mirror. With the canyon walls whipping past in a blurred and frenzied torrent, he also saw ahead of the Buick, a motorcycle that was traveling at a similar speed. He didn't recognize the bike but realized now that the Buick was following it, possibly unaware that Sammy was behind him.

He flashed his headlights and sounded the Galaxie's horn and once again saw the driver's eyes in his mirror as he checked behind him. The car sped up even more but Sammy stayed with him, this time attempting to pull up alongside the Buick, his speedometer now edging past eighty miles per hour.

The shock of his beloved Buick swerving toward the Galaxie and the sound of metal on metal, caught Sammy unaware and he braked harshly, his car fishtailing across the center line with Sammy working hard on the car's oversized steering wheel to keep the Galaxie on the asphalt, while the Buick began to quickly disappear again into the distance.

There was no time to stop and inspect the damage so Sammy floored the accelerator and began to gain once more on the Buick. After only a couple of minutes, he was within ten yards of the black car and now the driver was brake-checking Sammy, but this time he was ready for it.

Rage stirred in Sammy's gut, the thought of someone else enjoying his ride was almost too much to stomach and now the bastard had damaged the Galaxie too. But there was no way this thief was keeping his old and cherished Buick and so he made a decision.

If I can't have it, no one else can…

Sammy mirrored every brake-check with his own, simultaneously braking as the wild eighty-mile-per-hour chase on the winding cliff-side road became a test to see who blinked first. And finally, Sammy caught the guy off guard, the thief still way too intent on his own quarry up ahead. So Sammy took his opportunity.

This time, he didn't pull alongside the Buick, already knowing how the driver would react. After dodging two approaching vehicles,

400

he pulled out sharply and put the nose of the Galaxie a foot or so ahead of the Buick's right fender. The Galaxie's engine was screaming from the punishment it was taking and Sammy wondered how long he could keep it up.

Holding steady, matching the Buick's speed and seeing the driver check his passenger-side mirror, Sammy whipped the steering wheel to the left, lightly nudging the tail of the Buick on its right side fender. Which was all it needed to start a chain of events that Sammy couldn't ever have predicted.

It all seemed to happen in what felt like minutes but in reality, the whole thing could only have taken a few seconds. The Buick spun, smoke pouring out from beneath the tires, its front wheels colliding with the center median, the rims buckling inwards as the vehicle continued its graceful pirouette. Sparks shot up from the road as the car careered on its relentless and spiraling journey, fishtailing on a broken axle and chassis, the front fenders crushing and crumpling under the now unsupported and colossal weight of the car.

And as the aging Buick meandered, rudderless, toward the dirt and rocks that lined the highway, separating the asphalt from the cliff edge, it looked as though the steel Armco guard rail would do its job and put a halt to the car's momentum. But strangely, all the safety barrier did was to provide a permanent and immovable barrier that caused the car's now lowered nose to bury deep into the earth beneath it and flip the Buick as though it had just hit an invisible trip wire.

Sammy skidded to a halt just as the Buick was completely airborne, and he scrambled to get out of the Galaxie. This had not been his intention and a sudden veil of guilt engulfed him as he realized that the driver faced certain death over the irrelevant fate of a fifty-year-old motor car.

Running to the Armco barrier, Sammy arrived just in time to see the car complete a final somersault before landing at the very bottom of the cliff, glass shattering and metal crunching as it found its final resting place. He retrieved his phone from his jacket pocket and dialed 911, knowing that there was a chance that the driver may have survived the wreck. Because he knew, that unlike in the movies, cars generally didn't explode into a raging fireball when they went over the side of a cliff and there was a good chance that the driver could be airlifted out.

"911, what's your emergency?" said a voice on the other end of the line.

And then, just to prove him wrong, the biggest explosion Sammy had ever seen or heard in his life, drove a jet black mushroom cloud into the air, reaching almost to the ledge where Sammy stood.

"Hello? 911, what's your emergency?" the voice said again, waking Sammy from his reverie.

"I'm sss...sorry, no emergency, it was a false alarm. I apologize."

Too late...

As Sammy stood fixed to the spot, staring down at the burning wreck, he heard the sound of a motorcycle approaching. The rider kicked out the bike's stand and dismounted, making a beeline toward Sammy.

"Sammy?" the man said, as Bill began to remove his crash helmet, vaguely recognizing the diminutive man standing next to the Armco.

"Bill? Bill McLaren? Is that you under there?"

Sammy had only met Bill on a couple of occasions, but the man was pretty hard to miss in a crowd, not least because of his size.

"Hey Sammy, what the fuck happened, man?" asked Bill, "I'm pretty sure that car down there has been following me all the way out from Santa Monica."

"I think he was following you too, from what I saw anyway. And I was following him."

"Why?" asked Bill, staring down at the blazing wreck below where they were standing.

"Because that used to be my car."

Chapter 84

"It's a bloody mansion!" said Tess, as she eyed the house that dwarfed every other abode along the beach side of the highway in Malibu.

"Right?" replied Tom, pulling the Bronco into the driveway in front of the four-car garage block, "That's what happens when you bet on black and it comes up black."

"And I can stay here? Are you friggin' serious, Tom?"

"That's what Dad said. Uncle Vaughan won't be coming back until the summertime, so it's just standing empty."

Tess could barely believe her luck as they got out of the Bronco and Tom retrieved the keys that unlocked the entrance door to the house.

"And voila!" he said, opening one of the enormous doors and beckoning Tess inside.

"Jeez..." said Tess, marveling at the home's sumptuous interior and simultaneously eying the enviable Pacific view from the lounge further inside the home.

"I think I need to pinch myself," she continued, "This is all like a dream to me."

"Well, it's yours for as long as you need it," Tom replied, "At least until Uncle Vaughan and his brood return, that is."

Tess immediately made a beeline for the outdoor area, sliding the doors back so that the entire rear end of the lounge was open to the ocean breeze. While Tom went off to the kitchen to rustle up some cold drinks for them, Tess leaned forward on the verandah railings and gulped in the salt air, her jetlag already beginning to wear off.

"You must be thirsty," said Tom, ambling outside carrying a tray replete with drinks and snacks.

"What have you conjured up in there?" Tess asked.

"I made us a couple of very weak Mojitos because I know you're going to need to sleep soon and I don't want you to drift off too quickly."

"I already feel like I could sleep for ten hours but I don't want you to go just yet. I've missed you, Tom."

"Not as much as I've missed you but we have plenty of time. In fact, I have to get back to work for a few hours after we've toasted your arrival but tomorrow's the weekend, and I can spend it with you if you like?"

"I want to spend some time with you back in your house, I really like where you live. I mean, this place is amazing but your home is so cute. And private."

"And give up these amazing views?"

"I'd give up these views in a heartbeat to be with you."

"Music to my ears," Tom replied, raising his glass to hers, "So here's to your second Malibu vacation."

~

After Tom had left, with the promise that he'd be coming by the following morning to take her for breakfast, Tess wandered the halls of the labyrinthine home, marveling at the quality of the furnishings and art, wondering if she should leave a *Hansel & Gretel* style trail to find her way back to the family room. She had lost count of how many bedrooms there were, but she thought that she had numbered at least eight bathrooms so far on her stroll through the property.

Finally, she found what must have been the master bedroom suite because it wasn't just the biggest of the bedrooms, it was simply vast, with staggering views out across the ocean and down toward Santa Monica Pier. She lay down on the oversized king bed, and it was so soft and so comfortable that she began to feel her eyes closing almost as soon as her head hit the pillow.

And in many ways, it wasn't the *Hansel & Gretel* fairytale that came to mind as she slowly slipped into a deep and welcoming sleep, but actually the story of *Goldilocks and the Three Bears*. And she hoped the bears wouldn't come back too soon to wake her from her dreams.

Chapter 85

Bill was beginning to put the pieces together now. He thought he had pretty much summed up in his own mind what the events of the last few months had been about. He knew that Robert had been financially sound with the money side of things when they had been in business together, so Bill couldn't believe that he had ever let a debt go unpaid. Robert Valentine was just not that kind of man.

But people like Mickey Carlisle would never let go of what they perceived to be the goose that laid the golden egg. And his hitman, who he guessed had perished over the side of the cliff, was likely no longer a threat. But with both Carlisle and Buchanan now out of the picture, he realized that Tess was probably finally safe. What he had yet to ascertain, was whether or not it had been Frank Buchanan from Ojai who had been in the car that had died in the wreck or someone else entirely, and that still bothered him.

The chirping of his iPhone awoke him from his thoughts as he sat in his home office, contemplating the situation. His phone rarely rang because deliberately, very few people had his number, so he could almost guess who was calling, which was confirmed when he looked at the caller-id on the screen.

"Hey brother, what have you got for me?" Bill asked wearily as he connected the call.

"You sound like a bear with a sore head," replied Fletcher,

"I'm sorry, buddy, I'm just in a bit of a quandary on what happened up the coast with the car wreck, that's all," Bill replied, "Did you find out anything more on the victim?"

"Your theory on this individual, Frank Buchanan, hasn't shown up anything yet, but I'm still working on it."

"Okay, but what about the fact that when I visited his home last week and found his stash of antique vehicles in the garage and that I'm pretty certain that the car that went over the cliff was one of them? Surely that has to mean something?"

"Right now, it's just supposition and having visited with his wife yesterday to check on the whereabouts of her husband, she says that although he's not been home for a few days, it's apparently nothing new in his line of work."

"Come on, Fletch, it's gotta be Buchanan! What about ownership records from the wreck?"

"I'm on your side, Bill, and I agree with you, it's almost a certainty that your Frank Buchanan was the victim. It makes so much sense. But, as you well know, the location where the car ended up wasn't exactly the easiest place to get to. The paramedics and rescue teams didn't even get to the crash site until well over four hours after the accident occurred, and you saw what happened, there must have been forty gallons of gas in that thing when it went up."

"So what are you saying?"

"I'm saying that the car was pretty much molten metal and rubber by the time they could see if anyone had survived. It took a chopper to douse it with a thousand gallons of water before they could even get close," said Fletcher, realizing his friend's frustration, "But we're still working on it."

"Well, what about dental records? Surely that could tell you something?" asked Bill, now clutching at straws.

410

"Ha! That's a friggin' joke. I didn't see the explosion, you did, but from the impact it must've had, whatever remained of the victim would have been scattered out across a thousand yards of hillside scrub, including his teeth."

"But when you do find them, surely you can get a match?"

"*If* they find them," said Fletcher, "And if and when they do, who knows how long it would take to get a match?"

"So what are you saying?"

"What I'm saying, Bill, and you know I hate to disappoint you, but right now, we have no absolute proof of what the vehicle is, we have no VIN number or tag, and we don't even have a corpse, let alone teeth."

"I'm pretty sure it was a '73 Buick Riviera Boattail," Bill replied hopefully, "Sammy was absolutely certain that it was his car."

"And that's the problem, Bill, it's just hearsay, not proof and we need stone cold evidence. And it doesn't help much, I'm afraid, because if it was stolen, then it was probably on false plates and there are likely no records to attach it to the thief," said Fletch, "And we don't even know if it was stolen. Do you realize how many '73 Rivieras there are out there, still being driven on American highways today? They must have made a hundred thousand of them in the early seventies alone."

"I get it. I'm chasing my tail, aren't I?"

"Not necessarily, but right now, the Malibu PD is still working the case with a lot more resources than you have to hand. And, I've kept Sammy's name out of it like you asked, because right now, he's pretty lucky he's not being charged with vehicular homicide," replied Fletcher, "If I were you, I would think a better use of your time would be making sure your girl was protected if she ever comes back to California."

"I understand, although I'm not sure she is ever coming back so I think she's pretty safe anyway, back in England."

"And if you want my own take on it, buddy, I think you're right, I think this character Buchanan is probably your hitman fella, so I don't think Tess is in any danger, when and if she ever does come back. As far as I can see, it's pretty much an open and shut case and Tess is safe."

"I hope you're right, Fletch," Bill replied, "And thanks, man, I really appreciate the heads-up."

Chapter 86

Later that evening, Tess called Bill but she didn't go into too much detail because she was looking forward to seeing him again in person.

"Hello stranger," said Bill, immediately happy to hear from Tess, "It's wonderful to hear from you again, but where are you exactly? I was just talking about you today, are you still in England?"

"No! I'm here in Malibu! In fact, I'm not too far from you, maybe only six or seven hundred yards away," Tess replied, "I'm staying at the Perryman house. I say 'house', it's more like a bloody mansion!"

"Really?!! That's fantastic," Bill replied, his immediate joy tinged with fear over her immediate safety, "I know the property, they knocked over two homes and built the one mega-house on the combined lot, although it was the developer that did that before Mr. Perryman bought it. It's a little overkill for the area, but each to their own, I guess."

"I'm rattling around like a pea in a drum, but it's really sweet of the owners to let me stay for a little while," said Tess, eager to catch up with Bill once again.

"Well, now you're back, when am I going to see you?" he said, careful to avoid discussion about the auto wreck from the previous week.

"I'm easy, Bill, no plans except to try and find out the mystery of my Father's puzzle. We've gained some ground on it since I last saw you."

"In that case, come over tomorrow for dinner," said Bill, now excited at the thought of seeing Robert Valentine's daughter once again.

"Can I bring a friend?"

"Of course, who's the lucky man?"

"It's Jake Delaney's son, Tom, you'll really like him."

"Oh, I've met Tom a couple of times over the years, he was a really sweet kid."

"Well he's all grown up now, but he's still really sweet. So what time tomorrow?"

"Well, let's start early, I'll barbecue on the patio… say, six?"

"Done deal, we'll see you then, and I can tell you all that's been going on back in England."

"Okay, Tess, see you tomorrow," Bill replied, disconnecting the call.

But as soon as Bill had ended the call, his stomach began to roil, a wave of nausea enveloping him as he sat down in his office chair. On the one hand, he was delighted to be seeing Tess again so soon, but on the other, he was still worried about her immediate safety.

Chapter 87

Saturday morning arrived and Tom collected Tess from the Perryman home in his Bronco. For both of them, it felt as though they had never been apart and Tom, in particular, wondered how you could know someone for such a brief period of time and almost immediately feel like a couple, hand in glove. He had had girlfriends before, of course, but no one had ever entered his life and become so much a part of him, and so quickly. He felt so incredibly connected to her, physically, mentally and emotionally, and in many ways, it scared him. He was frightened that he might wake up one morning only to find that it had all been a dream. And he didn't know if it was because Tess was English, or more simply, that she wasn't a typical California girl, but he truly felt as though they had somehow been inexplicably drawn to each other in an ethereal and mystical way.

And it all feels so damned natural...

Tess herself, was experiencing very similar emotions, albeit tinged with the fact that she was six thousand miles away from her mom and Franco. But even when she had mentioned to Tom that they'd been invited for a barbecue at Bill's home, he had been completely unfazed, actually excited about the thought of it. Again, for Tess, it was something she had never before experienced with Simon, or for that matter with any other boys she had dated. It was clear to both of them that they no longer wanted to hold back on anything, or to be 'cool' about their flourishing relationship, And so when they finally sat down at a table across from each other at the Marmalade Café in Malibu Village on that pretty and warm Saturday morning, Tom couldn't hold back his feelings for her any longer.

"Ummm... so... are we officially an item?" he enquired uneasily, sipping at the tall glass of steaming cappuccino that Tess had ordered for him, "And by the way, I don't know what you ordered here, but it's incredible."

"It's something Bill introduced me to; it's pretty special, isn't it?" Tess replied, nibbling on a biscotti.

"It is, it's yummy, but you didn't answer the question."

"You mean, are we serious, like a boyfriend and girlfriend kinda thing?" she replied in a humorous attempt at a west coast accent, "Sounds kinda soppy to me."

"You know what I'm trying to say, Tess!" Tom sputtered, aware that the cappuccino was far hotter than he had imagined, "I just don't want to think I might lose you, that's all."

"Cards on the table, then," she replied, realizing that Tom was becoming acutely embarrassed, "I'm going to be straight up and honest with you, Tom. From the moment I first laid eyes on you at your parents' house, I fell in love with you. It hit me like a flippin' steam train! I have never met anyone who is not only beautifully mannered and fun to be around, but who's also immaculately dressed and stupidly good-looking too. You also have that fabulous accent. What's not to love?"

"Phew!" said Tom, "I'm not sure I can ever live up to all those amazing compliments, but I'll try. And putting my own cards face up too, I fell for you when I first saw you, like an oak tree being felled by a lumberjack. You simply took my breath away, and you still do, every moment of every day. I don't need to tell you that you're beautiful and sweet and delightful because people probably always tell you that all the time. In fact, you probably get bored with

418

it. But you're funny too, and with that great British accent, it doesn't get any better."

"Yeah, I left the 'funny' part of *you* out of the equation but we can work on that…"

"See, there you go again!"

"Tom, that's not humor, that's a statement of fact," she replied, grinning as she said it.

Tom was blushing now, he knew she'd caught him again in one of her teases but he didn't care, she could do it all day long and he'd love her even more.

"Oh, and one thing, the accent," Tess interjected, "It's not British, it's English. There are some British accents that even I can't understand."

"I get it, like the difference between the east coast and the west coast over here."

"No, like the difference between Malibu and Los Angeles… but going back to your original question," Tess replied, all traces of humor now gone, "I want us to be official, if that's what you want too. I truly love being with you and I don't want it to ever end."

"You've made my day, Tess, I can't even begin to explain how much sleep I've lost thinking about us and wondering if we could really be together. I know we have to address the distance between here and England and your parents and everything," Tom replied, reaching for her hand across the table, "But my stomach has been doing flips for weeks, and now I'm so very happy, you make me happy."

"Good. So now you've got all the gooey stuff out of the way, can we please order some lunch? I'm bloody starving!"

They spent most of the afternoon at Tom's parents' house, as Jake and Summer were both desperate to see Tess again. She was grilled with endless questions about England and the Christmas holiday Tom had spent there with her, and by the time they had finally buckled up in the Bronco to go to Bill's house, Tess was exhausted. After a brief stop at Tess's temporary abode to shower and change, the couple walked the short distance to Bill's house so that if either wanted to drink, they didn't need to worry about driving anywhere afterward.

Tom rang the doorbell as Tess looked around, remembering the last time she had been at Bill's house. She was still amazed that the 'homeless' man she had befriended in the Village was the polar opposite of the man she now knew. Bill McLaren man was a complete conundrum. Just like her father.

Within a few seconds, they could hear footsteps approaching and the bolts being slid from within.

"Tess!" said Bill as he opened the door, picking her up in his embrace as though she was a doll. The sight of you makes a grown man cry!"

"It's good to see you too, Bill, really good!" she replied, astonished at the man's strength.

After putting her back down, he stretched out a hand, "And you must be Tom? Man, you've grown, but I guess I haven't seen you in years."

"Yes sir, thank you, sir, it's a pleasure to see you again. Thank you for inviting me."

"Come on in, the pair of you, and it's Bill, not sir, Tom. I've got some food grilling out back, so go on through to the patio. You want some wine?"

They followed Bill through the house, Tom marveling at the simplicity of the design and the minimalist feel of the home, his architectural mind already working overtime. Bill invited them to sit down while he fetched a bottle of wine from the kitchen, quickly returning and pouring each of them a glass, with Tom noticing that he poured himself a tumbler of Pepsi and ice.

"So fill me in," said Bill, "It's been what, two months or so since you left to go back home?"

"It feels like forever, but it's so good to be back," Tess replied.

She began to tell a summarized version of events while Bill continued to cook steaks and lobster tails on the grill, coming back to the table every so often to refresh himself with another sip of Pepsi. She told Bill about the man who called himself Syko and how she had been accosted by him in a London alley one night, which was news to Tom, who sat dumbfounded as she related the encounter.

"I can't believe you didn't tell me about this Syko fella," said Tom, exasperated that Tess had kept it from him, "Who knows how much danger you might have been in?"

"I know and I'm sorry, Tom, but although he initially seemed a pretty scary character, I don't truly believe he meant any real harm. I think he was taking someone's money to scare me and that was the end of it."

"Yeah, but still…"

"But Bill," said Tess, wanting to change the subject, "Have you any idea who this man, The Watcher, might be? It's kind of scary coming back to L.A. knowing that someone is here who still wants to do me harm."

421

"I think the man that your 'friend' Syko was talking about is a gangster called Frank Buchanan, but without wishing to go into too much detail, I'm pretty sure you don't need to be worrying about him in the future," said Bill, "As far as I can tell, he's out of the picture. Permanently."

"Okay, I'll take your word for it as I can see you don't want to elaborate," Tess replied, "Anyway…"

After five or six minutes, Tess had brought Bill up to date, including Archie's discovery of the meaning of her father's puzzle.

"So, you're sure your friend Archie knows what he's doing? How can you be certain?" asked Bill.

"Well I'm sold on it," said Tom, "I think if you saw what he had worked out, you would be too."

"It's easier if I show you," Tess replied, "Here, take a look at these images on my phone."

She handed Bill her iPhone, and wiping his hands on a tea towel, he sat down at the table to study the images, astonished at what he saw.

"By God," he exclaimed, "This is extraordinary, but what can your father mean with this? It still seems a little out there to me. Although Robert was pretty out there too."

"We were hoping you might have a clue," said Tess, "You probably knew him best."

"I knew him well, loved him too. A unique character, your dad, with odd proclivities and passions for things I never quite understood."

"How do you mean," asked Tom, "Maybe whatever they were might shed a light on the puzzle?"

"Well, the biggest thing about Robert was that he hated banks, which I think you already know by now. He despised them actually,

422

and never trusted them. He always thought that they were institutions that took absolutely no risks whatsoever, but they still came out ahead. And he's right, they're all scumbags."

"Yeah, Mum said that too," agreed Tess.

"And he never spent money on anything irrelevant, and I mean absolutely nothing that didn't have a purpose or that was inconsequential, although he loved his art and had a passion for unique and curious design."

"I could see evidence of that back at the trailer," said Tess, "He wasn't what you would call over-cluttered."

"Right. And then finally, he just had this thing about Steve McQueen. I never quite understood it, but I think he secretly worshipped the man, wanted to be him."

"In what way, Bill?" asked Tom, tucking into the filet and lobster tail that Bill had just placed in front of him."

"Hold on, let me grab a fresh bottle of wine, I'll be right back," said Bill, as he made his way into the kitchen.

"I love him," Tom whispered to Tess, "He's such a cool guy. I've seen him down in the Village before in his hobo guise, and you wouldn't know that it was the same person. He reminds me of someone too, an actor…"

"Sam Elliott," said Tess.

"That's him!" said Tom, he's the spitting image."

"He is, but don't tell him because I'm not sure he's keen on being compared to him. He likes to be himself, either Bill McLaren or the Malibu Hobo, but mainly the latter."

Bill came back outside to the patio, a bottle of Rombauer in his hand, and poured generously into Tess and Tom's now empty wine glasses.

"You see, Robert loved cars as much as he loved McQueen," Bill continued, "As you can probably work out from the Mustang he left for you, Tess."

"I know, I can see that," she replied, "It's stunning."

"Hold on a minute, are you saying that his car might be the actual car from the *Bullitt* movie?" asked Tom.

"If you want my honest opinion, I have little to no doubt that it's the *Bullitt* car," Bill replied, "What better way to spend your money and keep it out of the banking system?"

"But that would mean... well, that would mean that Tess is sitting on a million dollar car!" said Tom.

"What?!!" cried Tess, "You must be joking?"

"Correction, Tom. More like five million," said Bill, "That car is one of the most valuable movie cars in the world. It's the most famous one anyway, except for maybe the Aston Martin DB5 from the early Bond movies. From memory, I think the Aston sold at auction a few years ago, for around five million dollars."

"Are you serious?" gasped Tess, "You mean I've been hacking around L.A. in a car that's worth five million dollars?

"I think it *might* be the car and it would be pretty easy to check too, just by looking at the frame and engine serial numbers. If they *are* matching numbers and they tally with the official database, then yeah, you're driving one of the most valuable cars in California."

"Blimey, if that's true, I'm glad Jake had it locked safely away for me while I've been gone," replied Tess, "And I am never going to drive it again, I'd be petrified of wrecking it!"

"I can check with my buddy, Fletcher, in the morning but in the meantime, going back to Robert's passions, he also loved McQueen's movies. He could watch them over and over again, all of the well known ones, of course, but also including an epic car-racing movie called *Le Mans*. He even tried to buy the Porsche 917 from that film at an auction."

"Did he succeed?" asked Tom.

"I know the answer to that one, because I was with him when he was bidding and the answer is no, Tom, it was way beyond his checkbook at that time, the car eventually selling for fourteen million bucks as we stood there in shock."

"Jeepers!" said Tess, "Men and their cars!"

"Crazy, right?" said Bill, "But getting back to the cryptogram message again, I'm not sure any of this really helps."

Tess was still numb from the idea that she might now be the owner of the *Bullitt* Mustang. If it was true, it might change her whole life, everything about it, which in a way, scared her. She had never known real wealth before, but realizing the car's potential value, she made a mental note to check with Jake that the Mustang was still safely hidden away.

"I agree with you Bill, but there must be some connection?" she asked.

"Hand me your phone again," said Bill, "Maybe there is."

They once again stared at Tess's phone screen, all of them silently questioning the meaning of the revealed clue.

> A HOME
> IS WHERE THE HEART IS
> AND DEEP BELOW WHERE
> THE RATTLESNAKES ROAM
> HIDES A GIFT
> THAT I GIVE TO YOU
> I LOVE YOU TESS
> DAD

"There is one thing…" said Bill, staring fixedly at the screen.

"What's that?" asked Tess.

"Well, it's a long shot," he said, retrieving his own phone and pulling up a photo he'd taken on a recent visit to Hope's Grotto, "But do you remember when you went out to your dad's place, do you recall seeing this when we first arrived?"

"I'm not sure what you're getting at," said Tess, "Apart from recalling that that was the sign at the entrance to Dad's trailer park. What are *you* seeing?"

"Hold on, let me enlarge the image…"

"Oh my God, I see it!" Tess exclaimed, as she spotted the mosaic heart in place of the apostrophe, "Home is where the *heart* is!"

"Exactly," said Bill, "And on Monday morning, we'll take a trip out there and see what we can find. But for now, who likes Key Lime Pie?"

427

Chapter 88

Tom couldn't help but gaze at Tess's face as she lay sleeping next to him in the giant bed, unconsciously smiling as he peered silently at her flawless and make-up free skin. He marveled at her refined nose, her petite and exquisite ears and eyelashes that although free from mascara, were richly thick and long. Her dark chestnut hair cascaded across her pillow, glimpses of subtle but rich red tones highlighted by the sun that was now beginning to shine into their room.

He wanted to wrap her up, keep her safe from everything, and never let her leave his arms. In light of what she had revealed the previous evening at Bill's house, he was shocked that anyone could ever want to harm her but he was determined to protect her nonetheless.

He lightly drew his finger down her slim, tanned and toned arm, traveling slowly all the way to her palm, where he wrapped his fingers around hers.

"I am awake, you know," she murmured, "But you can carry on, I could so get used to being woken up like this each morning."

"I thought you were sound asleep," he said, bending to kiss her tenderly on her cheek.

"I was, but I'm awake now," she replied, "Come here, sexy man," she said, reaching for him and wrapping her hands around his shoulders.

"But I haven't brushed my teeth yet and I've brought breakfast up for you," said Tom, forever finicky about his personal hygiene.

"Okay, the kiss can wait, dog-breath, because I'm starving!"

"You're always hungry and you never put on any weight," said Tom, "What's the secret?"

"No idea. Good genes? Who knows?" Tess replied, biting into a Danish pastry, "No coffee?"

"It's downstairs in the kitchen, I couldn't fit it all on one tray, hold on ma'am and I'll go fetch it."

Tess couldn't take her eyes off Tom as he left the room, tall and with an immaculately fat-free physique, seemingly permanently tanned and a youthful appearance surrounding a very masculine and manly body.

Think I'll make him walk around in pajama bottoms the whole day today…

When Tom returned minutes later, he set the tray down on the bed next to Tess, and began to pour from the cafetière.

"I've got regular milk or coconut milk," he said, picking up two small jugs and offering her the choice.

"Coconut," she replied, "I need to drink less milk, I like it way too much and too much is not good for you."

Tom poured the coffee into a pair of bone china mugs he'd found in the kitchen and they sat up against the bed's mauve, velvet headboard, sipping their coffees and gazing out to the now sparkling blue ocean, watching as the gulls began their morning feeding frenzy.

So, what would you like to do today, baby?" asked Tom, "We have the whole day to ourselves and nothing in our way."

430

"What I'd really like, is to go out to the storage facility where your dad hid the Mustang and find out one way or another whether it is the *Bullitt* car," Tess replied, "Aren't you curious, just a little bit?"

"I'm more than curious, Tess, I'm desperate to find out."

"So let's go take a visit this morning. And then if it is the *Bullitt* car, or even if it isn't, I'd like to come back here, snuggle with you on the sofa and watch a whole bunch of Steve McQueen movies."

"We have a plan," said Tom, "Snuggling's my forte."

Later that morning, Tom and Tess arrived at Malibu Horizons Auto Storage further north on the PCH, and Tom parked the Bronco in front of the white electronic gate. Spotting the rental office to the right of the gate, he said to Tess, "Come on, let's go and see about gaining access."

They locked the Bronco and made their way over to the office, where a young Hispanic man stood behind the counter, his badge revealing his name as Alejandro.

"Good morning, Alejandro, we need to get into unit number 104, do you think you can help us?" Tom asked.

"Yes sir, I just need to see some identification, please."

Tess rummaged in her purse and found her passport and offered it to Alejandro.

"Thank you, Miss... Valentine? Let me see... ah, yes, it was rented by a Mr. Delaney in your name, let me get you the key and combination."

"Is the unit air-conditioned?" asked Tom.

"Yes sir, all of our units are climate-controlled. There are some people in Malibu who store very expensive items here so they need 24-hour protection," Alejandro replied, handing the key and combination code to Tess.

"That's good to know," said Tom, "And thanks, we'll be right back."

"De nada," said Alejandro with a smile.

After locating the correct unit in the pretty group of white stucco and red-tiled buildings, Tom keyed in the combination from the slip Tess had been given, and then turned the key in the lock before raising the shuttered door of the unit.

As the shutter began to rise, Tess had a moment of angst as she suddenly wondered if the car was still there, or whether someone knew about the car and had stolen it. But her fears were assuaged when the back end of the gleaming green Mustang was revealed, even before the roller door was fully open.

"She *is* beautiful," Tess said, "I can understand why Dad loved this car so much."

"She is that," said Tom, "Now, let's get some lights on and find the serial numbers, there should be one under the hood on the driver's side fender and then a second matching one inside the driver's side door jamb. Can you open the door and take a look? You might need to use the flashlight on your phone to find it."

Tom pulled up the hood as Tess opened the driver's door and knelt down by the door jamb.

"Okay," he said, "I've got *8...R...0...2...S...*

"*...1...2...5...5...5...7*" said Tess.

"It's a match!" said Tom, excitedly.

"Does that mean that this is the car?"

"Not yet, unfortunately," said Tom, "But it's good to know that those two numbers match. It proves that it is an original '68 Mustang and not a couple of wrecks welded together. I just need to check the engine block to see if there's a date-of-manufacture stamped on its side."

"Why?" asked Tess.

"It's all about authenticity regarding the value," Tom replied, "If it has the same engine that it left the factory with then the value is much greater. But if it had a replacement engine that was built after the car was built, then the car is still really desirable, but not quite as desirable and the value is significantly reduced."

"How do you know all that?"

"Remember, I told you about how I had rebuilt the Bronco? Well, along the way, I just picked up knowledge and information. The whole history of cars fascinates me."

"I never knew you were such a car man," said Tess.

"Well, here's a thing that you'll like, which is kinda cute. American cars were originally built as right-hand-drive in the late nineteenth century, just like you have in England. But then the manufacturers realized that the passenger, who would often have been a lady, would have to exit the car on the left, out into the danger of oncoming traffic. So they changed all future production to left-hand-drive, which also made it easier to see when it was safe to pass other cars."

"Fascinating, and actually really sweet and noble!" said Tess, once again enjoying and admiring Tom's sensibilities.

"Told you it was cute," he said, "Now let's see if we can find that other number…"

Keen not to waste too much time at the unit, Tom used the light function on his own iPhone to navigate his way down to the side of the engine block and used his fingers to wipe away some dirt where he could see a vague imprint of the engine number.

"I think I've got it, hold on… *8…C…1…0*"

Tess wrote the number down on the slip of paper Alejandro had given her, so she wouldn't forget.

"What does that even mean?" she asked, as Tom carefully closed the Mustang's hood.

Pretty simple really, the *8* is the year of manufacture and because the 60s was the first decade it was built, it didn't need to have a *6* in front of it so it's definitely a '68 engine," Tom explained, "And the *C* represents the month, March, and the *10* is the month build date, so this engine was made on March 10th, 1968."

"But when was the *Bullitt* Mustang made?" Tess asked.

"1968!" said Tom, smiling.

"So it's the *Bullitt* car?"

"I don't know yet," Tom replied, wishing he had the answers for her, "We need to check the serial number on Bill's friend's database. Apparently, he's a detective so he has easy access."

"So we need to wait?"

"We do, it's Sunday, but I have a website on my phone that lets you check the VIN number we just found on the door jamb and fender, so at least we'll find out if it's the correct model."

"I wrote that down too, shall I read it out to you?"

"Okay, here we are," said Tom, navigating to a historic Mustang website where he could easily decipher the serial number, "Read it out one digit at a time."

"Okay… *8*"

"That's the year of manufacture so that's good, 1968."

"*R*"

"That means it was built in San Jose, California, so that's really good."

"Then a zero followed by a two, *02*?"

"That means it's a fastback as the *Bullitt* car was also."

"*S*"

"That means it had the 390ci V8 motor which is exactly what the *Bullitt* car used," said Tom.

"And then I've just got six numbers remaining, *125557*."

"They're the sequential build numbers so that will be down to Bill's friend to check but... *557*... I seem to remember something about those three numbers, but I'm not sure and I don't want to guess."

"When your dad and I first discovered the car, he said that it was pretty valuable, maybe a hundred grand or so," said Tess, "But the thought of it being worth so much more money has the hair standing up on the back of my neck. I almost don't want it to be the *Bullitt* car."

"I know, it's a bit surreal, isn't it?" Tom replied, "But don't think about it for now, let's go home and watch some movies. I'll see what I can do about the hair on the back of your neck too."

Having spent the rest of the afternoon watching McQueen movies on Netflix, Tess had become more than acquainted with the superstar actor and she could absolutely now understand her father's fascination him. Steve McQueen was Brad Pitt, Channing Tatum and

Ryan Gosling all rolled up into one. Definitely a man's man but also terribly sexy.

By ten o'clock that night, having watched four of McQueen's films and having also prepared and eaten a meal of steak and salad, along with a bottle of Pinot Noir, Tom and Tess finally succumbed to travel and exhaustion and fell asleep in each other's arms, eager for the next day to arrive.

Chapter 89

At nine the next morning, there was a knock at the door of the Perryman house and Tess got up from the table on the deck to go and see who was calling so early. Tom quickly followed her to the entrance foyer to make sure it wasn't a stranger at the door.

"Good morning, Bill," said Tess, opening the door and immediately hugging the big man, something Bill appreciated more than Tess could ever know.

"And good morning to you, sweetie," said Bill, "But I come with good news and bad news, I'm afraid."

"Oh," said Tess, slightly disappointed.

"She's not Eleanor," he announced, "She's not your *Bullitt* Mustang."

"Eleanor?" asked Tess, wondering what he meant.

"Oh, that was the name they gave her in the *Bullitt* movie, and Eleanor is who she will always be, I guess."

"That's a shame," Tess replied, "Never mind."

"But the good news," he continued, as Tom stood silently listening to what Bill had to say, "Fletch did some quick research on it early this morning and it turns out that your car is still highly desirable and extremely valuable."

"I would have to agree with that," chipped in Tom, "She's a numbers-matching car and when I checked the odometer yesterday, I realized that she's only covered 28,000 miles which is crazy for a fifty-year-old car!"

"Precisely. And he found out that in the *Bullitt* movie, the film crew actually used two cars, with serial numbers ending 558 and 559. The 558 car was used for all the car chases where it was beaten up pretty badly, and 559... Eleanor, was the one they used to shoot the beauty shots where McQueen was driving around San Francisco."

"And Tess's car is number 557, which means it was the exact car that came out of the factory just before 558 and 559," said Tom, "So that's pretty amazing in itself."

"Well, Fletcher also uncovered some extra information that most people aren't aware of. Apparently, the production company that shot the movie, actually bought three identical Highland Green cars, just because they didn't know if the 'action' Mustang would hold up in the chase scenes in San Francisco. You've got to remember that the city is full of hilly roads where the car made a lot of jumps."

"You're saying that this is the third one in the triumvirate?" asked Tom.

"Exactly," said Bill, "Which means that according to Fletcher, and notwithstanding the fact that Tess's car was never actually used in the movie, she still has a value north of $250,000 and there's only one way the value is heading, and that's up."

"Well, if I'm honest, I'm not really disappointed," said Tess, "Because if it had been Eleanor and worth five million dollars, I don't think I'd ever want to drive her. I'd be too scared of damaging her."

"You and me both," said Tom, almost relieved that Tess's car was not the *Bullitt* Mustang, but still amazed that it had a minor link to the film's history.

"I think your dad was pretty smart buying the one he found though," said Bill, "Because I'm not too sure that even he would have been comfortable driving Eleanor around, with that kind of crazy value."

"But knowing what I know now, I think I'm just going to keep her forever and drive her occasionally, you know, when it's a perfect day," Tess replied, "And I think it's exactly what Dad would have wanted. And... I'm going to call her Jacqueline, after the English actress, Jacqueline Bisset, who played McQueen's girlfriend in the film."

"Perfect! And I couldn't agree more, Tess," said Bill, "Robert bought that car for a reason and that reason is you."

"And after yesterday, I now know all there is to know about Steve McQueen, so Dad would have been proud."

"Exactly. Now, do you kids want to take a ride out to Hope's Grotto and see what we can find?"

Chapter 90

As the road opened up before them, winding its way past Pepperdine University and leaving central Malibu behind, Tess could only stare in wonder at the beauty of nature's creation in God's own playground. It was a far cry from her own little village back in England and she had to pinch herself as she gulped in the ocean air and felt her hair blowing in the wind. She was also aware that Bill wasn't appropriately sized to be crammed into the Bronco's rear seat so she had offered him the passenger seat up front, for which he had been grateful.

She could also feel her nerves jangling at the thought of what they might discover once they arrived at her father's home, and as she glanced down, she saw that there were goosebumps on her arms, even though the weather was wonderfully sunny and warm.

On arrival at Hope's Grotto, they stopped briefly and looked at the community's entrance sign, the 'apostrophe heart' easy to see this time.

A home is where the heart is…

Tom guided the Bronco to the far end of the community and parked up in the space where the Mustang had been previously secreted. Once inside the trailer, Tess immediately opened up all of the windows to let some air in, as the place smelled a little musty from having been closed up for so long. She smiled to herself, chuckling at her father's odd and bare minimalist style of living, everything in its place and everything with a purpose. But her enjoyment of her father's idiosyncrasies was quickly replaced by the thought that she would never get to witness them firsthand. And as that thought embraced her, she suddenly felt the sadness of knowing that she would never get to meet the man again, and soon her eyes were filling with tears.

Almost immediately, Tom realized what Tess was feeling, now that they were standing in her father's home, and he wrapped his arms around her, kissing the top of her head.

"I know, baby, I know," he said, pulling her tighter to him.

Bill had been foraging outside, checking for any other clues that Robert had left but came back into the trailer, his face etched with a frown.

"Nothing out there," he said, as Tess and Tom broke from their embrace, "It's got to be something inside."

Tom thought about the cryptogram message once more, and offered up an idea.

"Do you think the message was literal?" he asked.

"How do you mean?" asked Tess.

"All I'm saying is that rather than it being a key that we need to somehow work out, maybe your dad meant for us to take his message at face value."

"Help me out, son, I'm not with you," said Bill, confused over what Tom was saying.

"Well, where do rattlesnakes go when they're sleeping or hiding out?"

"They look for shade," Bill replied, "Keeps their skins moist."

"Exactly!" said Tom, excitedly now.

"And in someone's home, they'd go to the basement. That's where a lot of rattlers set up their own homes," Bill confirmed.

"But there's no basement here," said Tess, "It's a trailer."

"But," replied Tom, "There is shade underneath the trailer, and it keeps really cool too, especially in the summer months out here."

"Let's take a look outside again," said Bill, turning to Tess, "Maybe Tom's got a point."

Once outside, the three of them examined the perimeter of the trailer but saw no obvious places where snakes might make a home. In fact, the unique course of cement foundation blocks that circumnavigated the trailer, three feet in from each side and end, suggested that it had been designed by Robert to keep all varmints away from the underside of his home. It was rational and logical thinking personified. There was just nowhere underneath the home to hide anything, or anywhere for creatures to nest.

Disheartened, they went back inside the trailer once more to think about where to look next, but none of them had any new ideas. Tom felt particularly downcast because he thought that he had solved the riddle, and he flopped down on the sofa opposite Tess as Bill went to the kitchen to brew some coffee.

"There's no milk here, so I hope you're good with black coffee," he said from the kitchen.

"It's fine, Bill, I don't mind," Tess replied, bending down to smooth the rug where a corner had flipped up just as Tom had sat down, "At least Dad had the good sense to buy a Nespresso machine."

But as she bent down to smooth the rug, she noticed something odd.

"Tom," she said, taking a closer look at the floor beneath the rug, "Take a look at this."

Tom joined her on the floor and ran his finger along an almost invisible cut in the wood.

"What the hell?" he said, pulling the rug back to reveal a perfect razor-thin rectangle cut into the trailer's wide plank floorboards.

Chapter 91

"It looks like a trapdoor," added Tess, "But there's no catch or ring-pull."

Tom continued inspecting the cutout at close range, following the line to the far end of the rectangle from where they had been sitting.

"What have you found?" asked Bill, bringing a tray of coffee mugs to the lounge area.

"We think it's a trapdoor of some kind but there doesn't seem to be any way of opening it," Tom replied, "Here, take a look."

Bill set the tray down on the side table and knelt down to examine what they had been looking at. He ran the palm of his hand around the inside of the rectangle, searching for any peculiarities or discrepancies in the wood.

Finally, he stopped, his finger circling a knot in one of the planks.

"There's something not quite right here," he said, "Look at this, Tess."

She bent down to where he was kneeling, seeing the small quarter-sized knot that Bill was pointing to. She pressed on it and the knot slipped down with a click as the rectangular cutout in the floor slowly inched up a couple of inches.

"I'll be damned!" said Bill, "That crazy father of yours painted the release button to look like a knot!"

Tom came over to help, the three of them lifting the trapdoor fully open to reveal a metal staircase below. Tess was stunned into silence that they had happened upon this secret door just because the rug had been tripped over when Tom had flopped down on the sofa.

And deep below where the rattlesnakes roam...

"I guess we should take a look," said Bill, "I'll go first, just in case there *are* any rattlesnakes down there."

Tess shivered as Bill made his way down the ladder.

"All clear, I think," he yelled up to them, "I just need to see if there's a light down here, hold on..."

Tom and Tess looked at each other, neither of them thrilled at the prospect of going down into what appeared to be an eight-foot-deep chasm beneath the earth.

Bill must have found a switch, because suddenly a light went on, revealing a concrete floor below.

"Jesus, Mary, mother of God!"

Chapter 92

"What is it, Bill! What's down there," Tess yelled.

"You'd better both come down and see. Jesus, you're not gonna believe this, Robert built his own version of the tunnel in *The Great Escape!*"

They climbed down the ladder, Tom going first so that he could help Tess at the bottom of the steps.

"Shit!" said Tom, as he turned around from the ladder, "You really aren't gonna believe this, Tess, it's incredible!"

When Tess landed on the chasm's floor, she was as shocked as the other two. It wasn't a hole at all; it was a vault, almost a bank vault. Aluminum racks lined each side of the room, the entire space measuring around twenty feet by ten. But it wasn't the sheer size of the room that shocked them; it was what was stored on the racks that literally took their respective breaths away.

On one six-foot rack alone, there were trays and trays of gold Krugerrands. On another, there were glass cases containing diamond necklaces, ruby and sapphire rings and emerald earrings, so much jewelry that Tess couldn't take in everything behind the glass.

"My word," exclaimed Bill, "Where to even begin?"

"I know your father didn't like banks, but..." said Tom.

"He disliked them so much, he built his own!" laughed Bill, amazed at his old friend's logic, "And he was the only customer!"

"I don't know what to say," said Tess, "I'm really too overwhelmed right now. I think I need to sit down."

Lies a gift that I give to you…

Tom quickly pulled out a metal box that was lying beneath the racks so that Tess could sit for a moment. As Bill continued to itemize the contents of the vault, Tess noticed some *Superman* and *Batman* comics, each housed in their own individual Perspex containers.

"I know this is going to sound weird, given everything else that's down here, but why would Dad keep old comics in a vault?"

Tom picked up one of the containers and looked at it. He noted the price marked on it, ten cents, and also a date of publication, June 1938.

"This isn't a *Superman* comic, Tess, it's an Action Comic, although I think Action Comics introduced *Superman* to the world. It's eighty years old, and it's the very first Action Comic. I think I know why your father collected comics. This one alone could be worth over a million bucks."

"Stop it, Tom!" Tess replied, "How can that thing be worth money?"

"I'm not saying it is worth that much, it's just that perfect-condition examples are incredibly sought after these days. And looking at this, and I'm no expert but it looks in absolutely mint condition."

"So it really could be worth that much money?"

"Yes, but it may be worth a whole lot more, Tess."

"I think I've just hit the mother lode," said Bill, "Take a look at this."

Tess got up from the metal box she'd been sitting on, and went to join Bill, Tom following behind.

"Is that for real?" she asked, "Is it really what I'm thinking it is?"

"Bill put his hand into the box and pulled one of the bars out, handing it to Tess.

"Oh my God, it is!" Tess exclaimed, shocked at the weight in her hands, "This must weigh twenty-five pounds! It's gold, isn't it?"

"Sure looks that way and from a quick visual count, it looks like there are eleven more from where that came from," said Bill.

"What's a bar of gold worth, Bill?" asked Tom, taking the shiny gold bullion from Tess's wilting hands, "A hundred grand?"

"Try six hundred grand apiece, maybe more," said Bill, still in awe of what Robert had constructed and stored beneath his simple home.

"Tess, you know what that means, don't you?" said Tom.

"I'm rich?"

"Richer than your wildest dreams! It's just incredible, I still can't believe your dad would risk you never discovering all of this if you had never solved the puzzle."

"I know and I'm sorry if I don't seem like I'm one happy girl but it's all too much to take in," she replied, tears beginning to form once again in her eyes, "I'd forego all of this just to have Dad back in my life."

"You and me both," Bill added, "The world is a sadder place without him."

"I guess we should go through everything while we're here and catalog it," said Tom, "At least we'll know what he left for you."

"I suppose so," Tess replied, reaching for an old *Jetsons* metal lunchbox on one of the racks at the far end of the vault.

449

"I hate to say it," said Tom as Tess opened the tin lid, "But that thing is probably worth a couple of grand too. Man, your dad had a keen eye!"

When Tess finally had the box fully open, there was nothing inside of monetary value as she had first expected, but instead, a pile of aging photos. She pulled out another hefty box from beneath the rack and sat down, carefully examining each photo as she removed them from the lunchbox, now almost oblivious to what Tom and Bill were doing. They were all photos of her, photos that her mother must have sent her father over the years.

As she looked at each photograph, she realized that it was a complete timeline of Tess's childhood, as a baby, then as a toddler, through primary school and high school and eventually through university. And right at the bottom of the tin, she pulled out a final photo that she had never before seen, maybe the only one that had ever been taken. Just a faded Polaroid of her father holding her when she was maybe four or five years old. And on the thick white border below the photo, Robert Valentine had written a final message...

I love you, Tess. Dad xx

Chapter 93

Three months later...

The couple was just like any other pair of lovers on that crisp and sunny spring morning. As they cruised leisurely down PCH in Tom's old Ford Bronco, both of them salivated at the thought of pastries and cappuccinos at their favorite breakfast place, the irresistible Malibu Farm Pier Café on the Malibu Pier.

They didn't even notice the beige-colored Toyota Camry that had crossed the central reservation; they were too caught up in a moment of pure and unadulterated happiness.

Why would they? How could they have known?

The last anyone had seen of Buchanan was the moment Sammy's beloved Buick crossed the emergency lane months earlier, plummeting over the side of the cliff, and a minute later bursting into flames as a black and fiery ball exploded from the rocks below. And it wasn't a report that Bill or Sammy was ever about to file with the CHPD, preferring to let sleeping dogs lie.

But Buchanan hadn't died, his survival instincts immediately kicking into overdrive as he dragged himself through the shattered window of the upturned vehicle on that fateful afternoon, desperately clawing his way to safety before the Buick exploded into a million pieces.

And nothing fuelled the need for revenge more than the repeal of a death sentence in an auto wreck that had been caused by someone else.

No one fucks with The Watcher...

He glanced down at the tracker screen, a small green light pulsing and beeping as the Bronco approached, getting closer and closer on the other side of the highway. And that was the moment Buchanan yanked the Camry's steering wheel and crossed the median, aiming his Glock through the side window at the Bronco, dispensing a torrent of shells in a three-second spate of hatred.

Neither Tom nor Tess heard the sound of the bullets that came from somewhere ahead of them. Two star-crossed lovers in an immaterial world...

And even as the sound of metal crunching on metal and the explosion of glass invaded their private universe, they weren't ever aware that their own world was about to be shattered.

It was only when they felt the Bronco lifting up as the Camry's nose burrowed underneath it, flipping it over and over as a feeling of weightlessness launched their stomachs toward their throats, that reality suddenly began to set in.

And after what seemed like minutes but what was only a couple of seconds in time, the old Ford came crashing down onto the beach's esplanade, parts flying off it as the Bronco found its final resting ground, its occupants seemingly no longer part of the living world.

But while the couple lay motionless, the Bronco's wheels still spinning in the air, the Camry bucked and spun wildly out of control, Buchanan grappling frantically with the steering wheel to try and gain control of the car. Frank was mercifully unaware of what would happen in the next few seconds as the Mack truck's brakes screeched and its tires smoked black plumes in an effort to stop in time. But it didn't. It couldn't. Thirty yards wasn't quite enough for a forty-five-ton chunk of metal to stop in time.

The Watcher's eyes met the Mack driver's eyes for only a split second before the Camry was metaphorically beheaded as the truck ate the defenseless little Japanese car.

And Buchanan, The Watcher, the man of mystery, had one last thought, just before he literally lost his own head.

Fucking Japs...

Epilogue

Eleven months later…

Thursday, February 14th, 2019

Remarkably, Tess hadn't been hurt badly at all in the accident although she'd suffered a concussion and a broken arm. And Tom had luckily only sustained glass lacerations, three broken fingers and a gash to his head when the windscreen had partially folded in. In fact, they were incredibly fortunate, the police had said. Buchanan wasn't so lucky. His body was found fifty yards away. And his head was eventually found under the Mack truck, wedged in a cross-member of its chassis.

At the Los Angeles Coroner's Office, Frank's wife, Maisie, was unable to identify her husband from the remains of his mangled and unrecognizable head, but as soon as she saw the tiny penis on the bloated body, she immediately recognized it as that of her husband.

Bill finally dispensed with his daily 'hobo' routine, having discovered that life could go on without Sandy, even though he still missed her terribly. But he had met someone new, which had astonished everyone close to him. He had begun to mix with the current surfing crowd again and he had been immediately treated like surfing royalty. When he met forty-nine-year old ex-pro surfer, Melanie Kincaid one night at a barbecue on the beach, the mutual attraction was instant. The two haven't spent a day apart since.

Oddly, Sammy was still pissed at Buchanan for stealing his Buick, even after having replaced it with the restored 1964 Ford Galaxie with the insurance payout. Although secretly, he liked the new car better, but he wasn't about to let on.

Summer and Jake didn't much care about either the Buick or the Bronco, they were just happy that Tess and Tom were alive, and had by now completely recovered from the wreck. And after Jake had finalized the total monetary value of her father's hidden assets, he had the enormous pleasure to inform Tess that she would never have to worry about money again. There was more than enough; she could go where she wanted, whenever she wanted.

But Tess already knew where she wanted to be, she'd tasted the ocean now and it was the only place she ever wanted to live. And because of her father, a man she barely knew, she was able to do that now. It was like he had subtly told her all along that he knew what she would want and had taken extraordinary steps to look after and provide for her. But it was all still so surreal for Tess, something that she realized that she would never fully grasp.

When she had finally absorbed the enormity and value of her inheritance, she had made a plan and enlisted Tom's mom to help her put it into action. So Summer had helped Tess find a piece of undeveloped, residentially-zoned land, less than two thousand yards from where she and Jake lived, and Jake had negotiated a deal for Tess to purchase it so she could build the home of her dreams.

But Tess hadn't opted for the modernist cubes that seemed to be springing up everywhere along the California coast, instead choosing to build something similar to Jake and Summer's home, a house that she'd immediately fallen in love with on her very first visit almost two years ago. And there was only one person she knew who could design the dream that nestled inside her head and deep within her heart.

"It's like a dream come true," Tess said to herself, "How could I have been this lucky?"

Tom had found her in the empty and smell-of-new-paint bedroom, the master suite still lacking any furnishings, and he paused at the doorway to watch as his girlfriend gazed out at a blue, blue ocean.

"I know you're there," she said.

"I swear you've got eyes in the back of your head," Tom replied.

"I'm so glad that Mum and Franco are going to spend the winters here. It'll be so good for them and I get to have the best of both worlds."

During the design process, Tess had asked Tom to include a casita to be constructed further down the lot toward the ocean for her mother and Franco, big enough and homely enough that she thought they might eventually call it home.

"I think they're going to love it, seriously, who wouldn't?" Tom replied, as he walked toward the girl with whom he hoped to spend the rest of his life.

Tess pinched herself as she stood in her little piece of ocean paradise, barely able to believe that this beautiful beachside cottage was really hers. She could already imagine tiny feet pattering across the bleached oak floors, shrieks of laughter from children she was just beginning to dream about.

But she hadn't felt at all well recently, well really only in the last couple of weeks or so, but particularly in the mornings. A trip to Walgreen's and the purchase of a test kit confirmed her suspicions.

I wonder if he'll be a wonderful father too?

"Tom," she said, "There's something I want to ask you, something that's been on my mind recently."

"What's up, sweetie, you seem perplexed," he replied, kissing the back of her neck and wrapping his arms around her as she continued gazing out at the Pacific.

She turned herself to him, keeping his arms wrapped around her.

"Do you think, I mean… you can think about it, of course, but… well… will you marry me?"

Tom's face lit up, breaking into a grin, now wishing he'd asked the question first. His dream girl had become a reality and he was giddy as he replied.

"A proposal like that, from the original Valentine girl? And on Valentine's Day? How could I possibly say no?" he said, "I love you Tess Valentine, and I'd marry you in a heartbeat!"

Tess didn't really think he'd say no and she loved the idea of proposing on this particular day but when he had said 'yes', she felt that her life had become complete.

"I've got one more surprise…" she said, "How do you like the idea of being a father yourself?"

"You're serious?" asked Tom, a look of astonishment on his face, "We're having a baby?"

"Well, technically, it's me who's having the baby, but you'd better start practicing your diaper skills, Mr. Delaney!"

The couple embraced and kissed, long and deep, each of them wanting it to be never-ending, until Tess finally broke away and leaned her chin on her husband-to-be's shoulder. She suddenly realized at that very moment, that she had found the place her father wanted to show her, and she had met the man of her dreams. As her father would probably have told her, this is about as good as it gets.

Tess looked up through the glass skylight of the bedroom, warm and comfortable in Tom's embrace, and sent a final whisper to her father.

Thank you, Daddy, I love you so very much, and I hope you know that I always will...

Author's Note

The people I admire most in this world, are the builders. They create things that never existed previously. They lay the foundations, they build the walls and they put the roof over our heads. They are remarkable and under-appreciated. I'm not a builder, but I think I can build stories that hopefully, people will enjoy for many years to come. *Malibu HoBo* is my latest story for you.

I am English, but I write for a predominately American audience, and because of the subtle differences in the two languages, I am often prone to making critical writing errors, be it *cinema* instead of *movie theater, afterwards* instead of *afterward* or just when using English words and expressions that don't exist in the American vernacular. And there are plenty of them, trust me. Even an English word like *aluminium* in the UK, that becomes *aluminum* in the US, means that you have to look pretty closely to see where the subtle differences lie. In this book, the protagonist is an English girl, and so of course, there are further complications when simultaneously dealing with narrative and dialogue. For example, Tess would naturally say *Mum*, as the word is spelled in the UK, but of course, for American readers, it might look odd, the spelling in the US being *Mom*. It's not easy. I am therefore deeply indebted to my American friends for keeping the car safely on the road by alerting me to these mistakes.

In my former working life, I was privileged to work with an extraordinary team of people in the UK film industry in London. The list is too long to mention here, but the usual suspects know who they are, because most of them are still making films around the world. But everything about my career in that field was based on teamwork, a collaboration of unique and wonderful talents coming together to work as one. If you've ever been to a film shoot or a production meeting or even attended the post-production process, you'll understand exactly what I mean. An invisible web that harnesses multiple talents and passions as a team to perform like a well-oiled machine. It's a joy to behold.

Unfortunately, writing is the polar opposite. It requires silence, peace, harmony, tranquility and above all, selfishness. It can also be an incredibly lonely existence. Most days, I get up, shave, shower and make tea, with the hope that the day will be a positively creative one. But there are many days when you simply find yourself at a dead end or your mind doesn't function in the way you need it to, and it's frustrating. The flipside of this is that when you have a positive day and your thoughts are flowing and suddenly you've managed to write ten pages, it's more rewarding than anything in the world. It's the joy of those days that keeps the fire burning. But without the support and encouragement from close friends and family, *Malibu Hobo* would never have been completed and for that, I remain eternally grateful.

I am indebted to two people in my immediate family, **Jayne** and **Lucy Robson,** for their love and support and for believing in me that I could actually write stories that readers would enjoy. Jayne admits that she's not an avid novel reader, so I truly appreciate her love of what I write and her keenness to read my meager scribblings. I also thank her for being an incredible mother to our baby girl and for bringing Lucy into this world. And although I came to love my central character, Tess Valentine, almost as a daughter the more I wrote the story, no father could be more fortunate in life than to have a lovelier, kinder, more beautiful and inspirational daughter than my own. Lucy is, and will always be, my perfect and precious angel and I wrote this book entirely for her, after we had found ourselves spending time together in Malibu in 2018. If she gives this novel the nod of approval, I'll consider my time well spent.

I am also eternally grateful to **Jodi Whitby**, my friend, my creative buddy and my soundboard, an exceptionally talented girl and a joy to work with on all the projects we share. Jodi has once again made invaluable artistic and editorial contributions to this story, never afraid to tell it how it is. Jodi has also been a life teacher to me in the art of listening, thinking, and observing everything that surrounds us, an unconventional free spirit in a predominately conventional world. Please don't ever change, Jodi.

I also have a lovely friend in Sweden, **Cornelia Södergren**, herself a fabulous award-winning author with a beautiful mind. Notwithstanding the fact that English is not her primary language, her end-of-term reports have been equally vital to making *Malibu Hobo* a better book. Namaste, Cornelia.

My mother, **Avril Robson**, taught me how to cook, to be well-mannered and courteous, to treat the female race as the superior one, and above all, to wear good shoes. These lessons have served me well. I'll always be grateful, my feet forever comfortable.

Paul Grubb, a man I've known since his Aston Martin days at the best advertising agency ever seen in London, the wonderful institution that was GGT. I had to include you in the story, Paul, and I thank you for your encouragement and plaudits. You learned your trade from the master himself, **Mr. Dave Trott**. Less is more.

I am also thankful to my sweet friend, **Lisa Holland**, who made time in her busy schedule to scrutinize the story as I drip-fed chapters to her, always returning with helpful thoughts and suggestions to make Hobo a better book. I know it's an unpaid task that I ask her to perform each time, but her suggestions and thoughts always make a difference.

A huge thank you goes to my wonderful friend, **Glenn Greenspan**, who has precious little time on his hands at the moment, but still finds the time for me. He has also cast his fabulously sharp eye on the draft manuscript for critical errors and attention to detail, and he found so many of them. What I like about Glenn is that he cuts right to the chase when he spots glaring errors and he is exactly what I need in order to achieve the correct American parlance and vernacular.

I want to thank my inimitable American friend, **Craig Dallas**, for his support and encouragement during the writing of *Malibu HoBo*. He is a real-life Superman who shrugs off everything life throws at him but always remains endlessly optimistic, and is the kindest and gentlest man to have as a buddy. If I had ten percent of his stamina and lust for life, I'd be more than happy. And the truth is, if Craig doesn't put a smile on your face, then there's no smile to be had.

Peter McGlasham, a multi-talented, charming and brilliant man I had the pleasure to work with for many years in Soho's film industry during the 1990s, but a man who also thinks so much outside of us mere mortals' box. He's a revelation for me. He has his own business to run, so my requests are a burden on his valuable time, but his thought process on creating a synopsis is as unique as his lyrical philosophy on life itself. Sherry trifles, Pete.

They say that the English and the Scots don't mix too well, but I can slay that myth right now. My Scottish friend of almost forty years, **Matt Forrest**, a man I love for so many reasons, is a rare breed, a priceless Glasgow diamond, and his enduring friendship is something I value immensely. It began with a chance meeting all those years ago in Soho, two eager young men trying to make a name for themselves in the film business. A friendship was immediately carved in stone one evening, but one that will endure forever. Matt's enthusiasm and moral support for everything I do is also priceless, as are his talents as a film director, animator, designer, storyteller, plumber and chef…

So, to all of the people mentioned above, to everyone I have forgotten to mention, and to all the readers who spend their hard-earned money on my books, I thank you all, truly, from the bottom of my heart.

William Sykes

In this latest story, I decided to include an interesting new character, Bill Sykes. Most people will recognize a similarly named character as the murderous criminal in the Charles Dickens story, Oliver Twist. Coincidentally, I have a number of ancestral grandfathers, all named Bill Sykes, and I decided to use the name of one in particular, my great, great, great, great grandfather, William Sykes, who was born in Yorkshire, England in 1827.

He worked initially as a miner in a coal pit and later as a *puddler* on a pig-iron manufacturing furnace. But on the 10th October, 1865, William Sykes made a life-changing mistake when he decided to join a group of six other men for a few hours of late-night poaching. On this fateful night, the men were challenged by a group of gamekeepers, and in attempting escape, Sykes and a number of other men assaulted one of the gamekeepers. Sadly, the man died from his injuries, and a reward or pardon was offered for information about the attack.

One man from the gang, Robert Woodhouse, seeing his chance of freedom via a pardon, decided to give evidence against the other six. Once given, four of the men, including Sykes, were tried and found guilty of manslaughter, each receiving life sentences. William Sykes served the first nine months of his sentence in solitary confinement at Wakefield prison in England, before being transferred to Portsmouth prison.

But on 2nd April 1867, he was deported with a number of other prisoners and sent by ship to Western Australia to serve the remainder of his sentence in an Australian prison. And because of a bad decision he made that ended in a man's death, William Sykes was transferred to the other side of the world, leaving behind in England, a wife and four children he would never see again. Remarkably, on the voyage to Australia, Sykes wrote a diary that still exists to this day.

By 1877, at the age of fifty, William Sykes received his *ticket to leave* and so after being freed prison, he began working as a servant and later as a general laborer in Toodyay, a town fifty miles north-east of Perth. He spent his final years working on the railway line at Clackline, but his health eventually began to fail him and on New Year's Eve in 1890, he was found lying in his railway hut in a desperate state. Five days later, on the 4th January, 1891, William Sykes died from chronic hepatitis.

He was buried in a mass grave in Toodyay Cemetery. His few belongings that were found in the railway hut where he had effectively been living, included his dog and an old gun. Both were sold to recoup the £2 and 15 shillings that it cost the government to provide the coffin for his burial.

But my great, great, great, great grandfather, William Sykes, may have disappeared without trace, had it not been for the discovery in 1931 of a collection of letters written to him by his wife, Myra, during the twenty-five years before his death. The letters were found in a crevice during the demolition of an old police building in Toodyay.

Many years later, the social historian and author, Alexandra Hasluck rediscovered the letters and she decided to research William Sykes. The results of her research were published in her 1959 book, *Unwilling Emigrants*.

In 2006, a second book was written by the author, Graham Seal, and published by ABC Books; *These Few Lines - A Convict Story: The Lost Lives of Myra and William Sykes.*

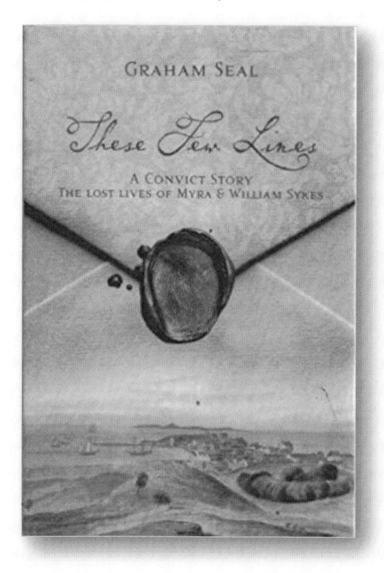

Printed in Great Britain
by Amazon